THE RETURNED

Seth Patrick was born in Northern Ireland.
An Oxford mathematics graduate, he spent thirteen
years working as a games programmer on the award-
winning Total War series before becoming a full-time
author. He lives in England with his wife and two
children. *The Returned* is his second novel.

You can follow him on Twitter
@SethPatrickUK

By Seth Patrick

THE REVIVER

THE RETURNED

THE RETURNED

SETH PATRICK

PAN BOOKS

First published 2014 by Pan Books
an imprint of Pan Macmillan, a division of Macmillan Publishers Limited
Pan Macmillan, 20 New Wharf Road, London N1 9RR
Basingstoke and Oxford
Associated companies throughout the world
www.panmacmillan.com

ISBN 978-1-4472-6723-2

1 3 5 7 9 8 6 4 2

A CIP catalogue record for this book is available from the British Library.

Printed and bound by CPI Group (UK) Ltd, Croydon, CR0 4YY

THE RETURNED

1

The girl paused on her way across the top of the dam and looked out over the town far below.

The sun was setting, she noted, dipping behind the mountains; lights blazed in the distant windows of the town, car headlights weaving through its streets. How was it so late? The last thing she could recall was sitting in a coach heading out on a school trip, bright morning sun outside as she watched the pines fly past her window. She'd been listening to music, trying to drown out the lecturing voice of her teacher.

How many hours ago had that been? And how had she got here, now? She tried to remember, tried to bring it back. All that came was a sense of panic. Panic, then darkness. And then nothing.

Something had happened.

She continued walking hurriedly over the dam, the temperature falling as night came. She should have felt cold, she knew. Her cardigan was thin – she'd been dressed for the heat of a midsummer's day, not the bitter chill of night air. But somehow she didn't feel cold, not even slightly. Instead, she felt scared. And she felt *hungry*.

She picked up her pace, her breathing tight and fast. She thought of her parents. Her mother would be out of her mind with worry, her father angry. She thought of her sister. And she thought of Frédéric.

They'd be waiting for her. They'd help her find out what

had happened, help her fill in those missing hours. She felt such a longing then – so fierce in her chest that it stole her breath away.

Home, she thought.

It was time to go home.

2

Anton Chabou stood on the dam and watched the still water. The first time he'd seen the lake, eleven months before, low cloud had flowed slowly down the valley to cover the water's surface. It had rolled onward, over the top of the dam like the ghost of a waterfall, heading for the town below.

Now, an hour after the sun had gone down, the air was clear. The lake's surface was like black glass. Behind him, occasional cars drove by. The dam acted as a bridge for all but the heaviest vehicles, the fastest route out of town for those heading north and prepared to make the climb up the steep valley-side roads. He'd even seen a young woman crossing on foot earlier, shortly before he'd left the control room. It was a rare sight. Most people who wanted to savour the view came by car.

His phone was in his hand. He didn't want to make the call, but he knew it had to be done, even if he was the new guy. Eric, his partner for the shift, had been in the job for ten years, and Eric had shaken his head, muttering, wanting nothing to do with it.

'Wait until the shift change,' Eric had said. 'Act like we just noticed it, and let *them* make the call.' Then Eric had sat in the control room, storm-faced, refusing to discuss it further.

Anton had already made the preliminary checks required of him, before raising it with Eric. A remote visual examination of the abutments showed no sign of seepage, and the flow measurements seemed correct. Getting a better idea of the current water intake would be necessary, but even if every source of water into the reservoir had done the impossible and conspired to stop, they simply weren't taking enough water out to result in the fall he'd seen since coming to work that morning.

The lake was emptying, and he had no idea how.

As the senior engineer on the shift, Eric's advice to wait almost amounted to a command, but it was advice Anton knew he would have to ignore. He had spent the next hour satisfying himself that nothing obvious was wrong. That meant taking the central maintenance shaft down to the upper and lower inspection galleries.

'Gallery', he'd always thought, was an odd word for what was really just a cramped grey circular tunnel running through the structure of the dam, sickly lighting strung along one side, and barely enough room to stand. He had to keep his head down to avoid constantly scraping his hard hat on the cold concrete above.

By the time he'd walked the upper gallery, his neck was aching and his mood was sour. But he'd bitten his lip and gone down, down, to the lower gallery. In theory, the lower was indistinguishable from the upper. The same restricted space, the same weak lighting. The same cold grey. But every time he went down there, it made him claustrophobic in a way the upper gallery never did. He was vividly conscious of the weight of water above him, somehow; reaching the end of the tunnel and turning back again, he always had the same image flash in his mind of dark water rushing towards him, icy and vengeful.

4

His impromptu inspection revealed no problems. The next stage would be to log the measurements on each of the ninety expansion strips throughout the galleries and compare them with the last recorded values, normally a weekly chore that took up most of the shift of whoever drew the short straw. He would go down again and make a start on it, once he'd had a break from the confinement and a little fresh air.

Once he'd made the call.

And so he was back at the top of the dam, phone in hand. He hunted for the number he'd been given almost a year before, when he'd first taken the job. The breeze picked up, suddenly bitter, but he preferred the dry sharpness to the damp chill of the tunnels below, a chill that got deep into your bones and was hard to get rid of.

He dialled.

'Yes?' said a man's voice.

'This is Anton Chabou, sir. The water level is dropping. We can't account for it.'

For a moment, the voice stayed silent. Then: 'You're sure?'

Anton was about to give a typical engineer's response: explain the possibilities that remained, explain the procedures they would follow to fully assess the integrity of the dam. But the voice knew all of that; all he wanted from Anton was a single word. Yes or no.

'Yes,' Anton said.

'I'll be there within two hours.'

'There's a chance it could just be . . .' Anton started, but the man had already hung up.

Anton put his phone in his pocket, readying himself to

go back down to the galleries and begin taking measurements. Feeling cold, he stamped his feet and moved around, trying to rid himself of the chill in his bones. It made little difference.

He stared out across the lake and thought about what lay underneath. He thought about what he'd been told officially when he took the job, and about what he'd heard in the months since – rumours, inconsistent, conflicting. He thought about what he *believed*.

Shivering, he started to descend.

3

Jérôme Séguret sat in his car outside the Lake Pub and wondered what the hell he'd done to deserve it all.

Disappointed and confused, he'd just left Lucy Clarsen in the room above the pub.

'Sorry,' she'd said. 'It can't work every time.'

He'd given her the usual money, even though things hadn't gone to plan. When he asked if he could see her again next week she shrugged and said something non-committal, completely at ease with a situation that he found painfully awkward. He avoided eye contact and wondered how he could kid himself that there was anything good about their sessions. On his way out to the car, he saw his daughter Léna by the bar with her friends. He was too slow; she spotted him, and spotted who he'd been with. The look in her eye was a blend of irritation and disgust. He'd slunk outside to his car, angry with himself.

He flipped down the sun visor, slid back the cover of the mirror, and glared. It wasn't that long ago, he thought, since everything had felt right, had felt *normal*. The family finances had been solid, he'd had a wife he adored and two daughters who made him proud, even as they were entering the hard teens. He'd had a smile, back then.

Now the haunted eyes staring at him in the mirror were those of a different man. He was forty-four, by rights. Four years ago, he'd felt younger than his age, and had looked it. Now? Hell, he could be taken as a decade older, maybe more. His hairline was decimated, his skin mottled, and his eyes . . .

'Christ,' he muttered, and flipped the visor back up. He couldn't meet anyone's gaze any more. Especially not his own. Shame and guilt, in equal parts. That was all his eyes held now. Hope, like his smile, was long gone. Extinguished on the day they'd lost Camille.

His daughter had died in a coach accident that ended the lives of the driver, one teacher, and thirty-eight children from the town's largest school, all in the same year group. There had been two children booked on the biology field trip who had happened to miss it. One, David Follin, had shattered his ankle two days before while trying to take on the town's highest set of steps with his skateboard, his best friend Martin filming it on his phone. Martin had put the footage on YouTube the night before he himself had died in the crash.

The other child to miss the trip had been Léna, Camille's twin sister. She'd claimed illness that morning; Jérôme's wife, Claire, had suspected Léna was feigning it but had given her the benefit of the doubt. He still didn't know the truth of it, and it wasn't a topic he ever wanted to raise. It had been Claire who had attended the counselling sessions with Léna; Claire who had held the girl for the long nights that followed Camille's death. Jérôme had seen the distance growing between him and his daughter, and between him and his wife, but consumed by his own grief he'd felt powerless to do anything about it.

He and David Follin's father, Vincent, had been friends before the accident, and found themselves becoming drinking partners in the aftermath.

'David can't cope with it,' Vincent had said. 'Whenever he sees a parent, a friend, a sibling of one of those who died, he believes they're thinking: "Why you? Why did you live?" He wants to get away from it. The boy can't even breathe without feeling guilty.' Within a year David and his family had moved back to Vincent's home town of Cholet.

Jérôme had missed the company on those nights when he couldn't bear being sober. For over two years following the accident, that had been most nights.

Now, he drank less, and in his own living room. It was cheaper, and he preferred the solitude: he lived in a shitty apartment in town, not in the house on the outskirts where Claire and Léna still lived. He needed to be careful with money, and not just because of the rent he was paying; he'd been seeing Lucy Clarsen more often than he could really afford.

Everything had been right in his life, four years before. Then a coach had veered off a mountain road and taken his life down with it.

It was a ten-minute drive to the Helping Hand, a shelter co-funded by the church and the town hall. Jérôme had managed to bury his frustration a little by the time he got there for the regular parents' support meeting.

The parents. Well, those who were left.

He'd added it up one night. He'd actually gone to the trouble of enumerating the grief.

Thirty-eight children, thirty-eight families: seventy-six parents, and twenty-nine siblings. The coach driver had a wife, and two sons in their early twenties. The teacher was married but childless.

One hundred and nine immediate relatives, and he'd stopped counting. So much for arithmetic.

Like David Follin's family, many had moved away. Too many memories. Of those parents who had stayed, most had other children still at the school and had decided against dragging a grieving child away from their friends, from all that was familiar and comforting to them.

For almost all of those parents with no other children, staying had been impossible. Jérôme had often wondered what would have happened to him and Claire if Léna had gone on the trip that morning. He found it hard to imagine feeling emptier than he already did, but he was certain that if both girls had died, Claire would have been another fatality of the accident.

Léna. Jesus Christ, Léna. So cold towards her parents now. So closed off and untouchable. She and Camille hadn't just been twins, they'd been *identical* twins. When she walked around town after the crash, people looked at her with a wariness greater than Jérôme had ever felt himself. Greater, surely, than David Follin had experienced.

When people saw her, they also saw Camille. Their whole lives, the girls had played on the confusion, each pretending to be the other when it suited them, amused that people couldn't tell them apart even when (they insisted) it was so *obvious*. Once Camille was dead, it was as if that confusion was still present, as if people couldn't remember which of the two had been on the coach. Some found themselves meeting Léna and calling her Camille, silenced by the horror of their mistake and the distress on the face of the young girl. Léna had become a ghost. A walking, talking reminder of everything they'd lost.

I'm not dead. That had been Léna's cry to her parents, whenever their frustration with her increasingly wild behaviour had boiled over into a shouting match. *I'm not dead. Maybe if it had been me who'd died, you'd be happy.*

And while Claire had attended the support groups for a time, she'd stopped when her relationship with Pierre, who ran the Helping Hand, had started to evolve into something closer.

Jérôme had been oblivious at first. He'd taken her at her word, that she'd simply grown tired of the group and knew Jérôme got more out of it than she did. It was only when she'd finally told Jérôme about her and Pierre that it really made sense.

The ensuing row had led to him packing his bags. There had been no question of who would go, of course. Léna needed her mother more than she needed him.

Jérôme paused outside the entrance to the Helping Hand. The shelter consisted of a main building and several outbuildings, sited high on the valley slope overlooking the town. It was a peaceful place; out of the way, but with the town laid out in front of you it never felt isolated. Perfect for mending broken souls, Jérôme supposed.

He wished he'd given himself time for a cigarette. The view was one he liked after nightfall – the town never looked more alive, and life was something he missed. He was already a little late, though, so he went inside. There were the usual number, twenty or so. Most of the parents took turns with their partner. He noted that Sandrine and her husband were both present, but they were the exception – Sandrine volunteered much of her spare time to help out at the shelter, and she never missed the support group meetings.

Jérôme grabbed a chair from the side and brought it over to the gap next to Sandrine, trying not to clench his fist when he realized Pierre was talking. He'd never punched anyone in his life, but with Pierre it would be a pleasure.

Pierre ran the Helping Hand, and he took most of the support groups himself. Alcohol, depression, drugs, divorce (God, the irony); whatever your problem, Pierre was there to grant sanctimonious advice that might leave you no better off but would, guaranteed, allow him to feel self-satisfied. Pierre was a religious man; born again, with the zealotry which came from that. He was also surely the biggest prick Jérôme had ever met.

Claire had brought the topic of divorce up more than once in the eighteen months since Jérôme had moved out, and she'd probably done so at Pierre's suggestion. Jérôme had no idea if they'd even slept together yet; given Pierre's religious commitment he suspected not, and Jérôme certainly wasn't going to agree to a divorce. He knew Claire still felt something for him; not as much as he felt for her, but it was a spark he believed could save their marriage. Time was running out, though. It wouldn't be long before his desire to have his wife back counted for nothing in the courts, and then the way would be open for her to marry Pierre.

Jérôme kept coming to the support group, even so. It helped him. Why it helped, he wasn't sure, but it did. Perhaps it was because he liked imagining his fist shutting that mouth; perhaps it was just that, with Pierre in the same room, Jérôme knew the man wasn't with Claire. With his *wife*.

'. . . and you can all have your say in a few minutes,' Pierre was droning. Jérôme felt his fist ball up, and had to concentrate hard to relax it again. 'But first,' Pierre said, 'I believe Sandrine has something to tell us?'

Sandrine smiled, not something Jérôme saw much of in this group, except for Pierre's gracious leer. Everyone else, after all, had had the same kind of immunization against smiling as Jérôme. 'Yes,' she said. 'Yan and I wanted to let you all know that we're having a baby.'

More smiles broke out across the group. Jérôme tried, but nothing happened.

Sandrine went on, hesitant, sounding almost apologetic. 'It wasn't easy, but still, we wanted to tell you . . . and to thank you all. Especially Pierre. These meetings really helped us after the accident. Because of you we've been able to carry on, move forward. And now we have this. Life prevails. It's such a beautiful gift.'

'That's your gift to us, Sandrine,' gushed Pierre. 'You too, Yan.'

The group started to clap. Jérôme kept his hands by his side.

'Now,' said Pierre, 'you all remember Charlotte, the mayor's assistant?' He gestured to the woman sitting to his left; she smiled and nodded, and the group did likewise.

Not Jérôme, of course. He knew she was there to talk about the commemorative monument again, and he remembered the last time too clearly. He would try and keep his cynicism reined in, but God . . . People made that hard sometimes.

Soon after Charlotte began, the overhead lights stuttered and failed, and darkness took over. A ripple of groans and uneasy laughter passed around the circle, before phones were brought out to give some light.

Jérôme stood and went to a window. 'Looks like the whole town is out,' he said.

'It should be back soon enough,' said Pierre from his seat. Jérôme found a bitter smile creep onto his face. Pierre's tone had been almost scolding. There was simply no room for pessimism with the man.

Small talk ensued, bathed in the pale phone light. Jérôme stayed by the window to avoid the empty chatter. After a few minutes, the lights in town came back on. He returned to his seat as the strip lights above him flickered into life.

'Good,' smiled Pierre. He looked to Charlotte. 'Let's continue.'

Charlotte stood, holding up a folder with drawings of the planned monument for the group to see. 'So, as I was saying . . . The monument is in the form of a circle. It comes out of the foundry on Monday, and it'll be installed by the end of the month ready for the ceremony. There are thirty-eight holes, one for each student.' She handed out two copies of the drawing for people to take a closer look.

Wonderful, Jérôme thought. *Another empty space for Camille.* And he would have to look at the damn thing every day.

'Does anyone have any questions?' asked Pierre.

Jérôme's hand went up.

'Jérôme?'

'Was that thing expensive?' Beside him, Sandrine and Yan looked up from the drawing they were holding, wary.

'Because it's quite ugly, to be honest with you.' Silent, the group exchanged uneasy looks. 'You think it's nice? You like it?' He was doing it again, he knew; being honest when silence was the right option. 'OK,' he said. 'If everyone else likes it, I'll keep quiet.'

Pierre shook his head, dismayed. 'You made your thoughts clear when we first discussed this. We listened to you, we voted. Can't we move on now?'

'No,' said Jérôme. 'Back then I said it was pointless. Now I'm saying it's ugly. There's a difference.'

'OK,' sighed Pierre, looking away.

'Jérôme,' said Sandrine, 'I think we've all had enough of your sarcasm. If these meetings seem so ridiculous, then don't come.'

'Sarcasm? It's not . . .' He stopped, feeling tears at the edges of his eyes – he absolutely was not going to give Pierre that satisfaction. He took a breath. 'I come because it does me good. Believe it or not, it does me the *world* of good, just like you. Without this, all I would have is despair. Maybe life will bring *me* beautiful gifts, one day.'

Sandrine's eyes showed a mixture of pity and hostility. Jérôme looked to the floor, silent as the meeting progressed and the arrangements for the ceremony were discussed. He heard a phone vibrate nearby, and saw the awkward look on Pierre's face as the man reached into his pocket to reject the call. A few seconds later his own phone rang. Claire, the screen said. He stood and went to the door, stepping outside to take the call from his wife.

'Jérôme?' said Claire. 'I need you to come over.'

'What's wrong? Is it Léna?'

'No,' she said. 'It's Camille.'

'What about her?'

'Please.'

There was a desperation in her voice that scared him. She sounded lost.

'I'm coming,' he said.

4

Claire had been in the shrine when the power had cut out across the town.

Shrine. Jérôme had called it that whenever his patience had worn thin. Camille's bedroom, kept almost exactly as it had been the day she died.

Before the age of ten, Léna and Camille had shared a room. Then the approach of adolescence had given them a need for their own space, marked by increasing squabbles over the smallest of things. As soon as they each had their own bedroom, the fighting stopped. It had fascinated Claire, to see how the girls were careful to keep their rooms distinct; marking out their differences allowed them to remain as inseparable as ever.

Claire had been in the process of tidying Camille's room when the news of the accident had first come through. When she'd started tidying, she'd known what reaction to expect from Camille, and had almost been able to hear the girl's outraged voice in her head: *Mum, why did you touch my stuff?*

Then Jérôme had rushed into the room, distressed, unable to speak at first, Claire becoming more and more anxious until at last he'd managed just one trembling word: *Camille.*

And she'd known. In that second the fear that nests in the heart of every parent had become a horrifying reality.

She'd been living with that fear in the background for

fifteen years, living with the realization of what parental love really meant: a need to protect that was so overwhelming, it was almost *debilitating*. Every time one of them was ill or still out even a few minutes longer than agreed, the worst-case scenarios had played out in her mind. Every news story about children in peril had left her feeling a terrible guilty relief that it hadn't been her daughters – that it had happened to someone else. But now it had happened to her. Camille was gone.

Being a parent was not easy. Losing a child was impossible.

She didn't remember much of the immediate aftermath. It was like drowning in dark water – muted sounds filtering through, Jérôme desperately trying to hold her. She just pushed him away and stared at the pristine floor of her daughter's bedroom, feeling as though she'd been caught in an act of sacrilege. That maybe if she hadn't touched anything, Camille would still be here.

So Camille's room had remained untouched since, and became a shrine. Candles lit, photographs on the chest of drawers. Claire would sit on the bed and watch the candles reflected on the glass frame with her dead daughter's face, and convince herself that the sharp pain might one day start to dull. At first, she restricted her time in there to whenever she was alone in the house. She wanted to spare her husband and Léna. Spare them from the extent of her grief.

But they'd known. Jérôme's initial careful remarks had grown increasingly concerned, and then angry, especially as she'd been drawn more and more to Pierre and to what Pierre told her.

God answers prayer, God has the power to heal.

'I want her *back*,' she'd told Pierre. 'Can God do that?'

Pierre had given her a typically elusive answer: 'Through God, you will find Camille again,' he'd said. 'She will come back to you.'

But it wasn't enough. She wanted Camille home, she wanted their life *back*. She wanted to wake and find that the last four years had been an error, a bad dream, somehow, and in the shrine she prayed every day for God to make things right again.

When the power cut came, it took her a moment to realize it wasn't just a blown bulb in the lamp in the corner of Camille's room, the only electric light that she had on. In the glow from the candles she went to the window and saw that the street lighting was also off.

She waited for the power to return. She thought of Léna, out with her friends; probably at the Lake Pub, if the girl's word still counted for anything. And back when? 'When I'm back,' was all the assurance Claire had managed to extract before Léna had gone. Still, any kind of assurance was better than none, better than her sneaking out of her bedroom and climbing down the trellis at the front of the house with no hint of what her plans were.

She checked the time. She didn't expect Léna back for a while yet, unless she'd had another argument with Frédéric.

Claire went into Léna's bedroom, a riot of mess. The bedroom of a nineteen-year-old girl, who Claire would still think of as a girl when, God willing, Léna hit her thirties and beyond; even when Léna had children of her own, and discovered how such a gift from God carries a crippling price.

She bent to the floor, grabbing clothes she would throw

in the wash, just the smallest concession to tidying – exposing enough floor to actually walk on.

But nothing that Léna would notice. Never that. Never again.

Claire heard the front door shut. 'Léna?' Had to be a problem with Frédéric, Claire thought, readying herself for a long night of comforting. The irony of motherhood, that you feel least useful when your child is happy, and most useful when she's in turmoil.

She went down the stairs, and stopped. The fridge door was open, a girl's hand on it. Claire's view was obscured as the girl raided the fridge's contents, plastic tubs of leftovers being taken out and put on the breakfast bar; flashes of tied-back red hair.

'Léna?' said Claire.

The fridge door swung closed. A young girl stood there. Long red hair, and a face Claire knew better than her own.

Claire stared. She was dreaming. She had to be.

There, opening the tubs and taking what she wanted, acting as though everything was completely normal, was Camille.

The girl saw her. 'I know it's late. You must have been worried. But it's not my fault. Something really weird happened.'

Claire stood there in breathless silence, not daring to speak. Saying something would break it, she thought, make the moment fracture and crash down around her. Reveal it for the hallucination it was. All she could do was stare.

'Don't look at me like that!' said Camille, making herself a sandwich. 'It sounds funny, but I woke up in the mountains, above the dam. It took me ages to get home. Honest.

I'm not making it up.' She topped her sandwich and started to eat. 'I'm *so* hungry.'

Claire managed to take a step towards her, silent. She had to keep everything slow, or risk panic.

'Are you OK, Mum?'

'Yes,' said Claire, on autopilot. 'I'm OK.' And the terrible fear in her heart was joined by something else: a terrible hope, just as sharp. She wanted to reach out and touch whatever it was that stood before her. Reach out and grab *hold*, and never let go.

'Is Léna home?'

'No,' said Claire. The shock of seeing Camille was overpowering; every word she spoke took considerable effort. 'She's . . . at a friend's house.'

'Is she better then?' asked Camille.

Claire had no idea what she meant. 'Better?'

'She was sick, wasn't she?'

'Yes,' said Claire. *As if it's the same day*, she thought. 'Yes, she was. She's better now.'

Camille reached over the tubs and picked up a frosted glass Claire had bought the year before. She considered it. 'Wow, this is ugly,' said Camille, before setting it down and heading for the stairs. 'I'll clean up later.'

Claire stood where she was as Camille went out of sight. In the silence, she could hear her rapid pulse loud in her own ears. Surely she was alone in the house. *None of that happened*, she thought. *None of it is real. No matter how much I want it to be.*

And then she heard water running in the bathroom, and bounded up the stairs, down the corridor, her hand moving towards the handle on the bathroom door.

The door opened wide, startling her. Camille stood there, a towel wrapped around her, the bathwater running. 'Can you get me my dressing gown, please?' she said.

Claire nodded; Camille closed the door again.

Claire turned, hardly able to breathe, then rushed to Camille's room. She blew out the candles, and took them and the photographs, everything that didn't belong there, and bundled it all into the top of a wardrobe. In the chest of drawers were the things that had been there before, the day of the accident; Claire put them all back in their original places.

Everything had to go back. She thought of Camille's dislike of the frosted glass, and she mentally tallied the changes that had happened in the house over the last four years. Everything had to go back to how it had been.

She gathered Camille's dressing gown, then composed herself. She knocked on the bathroom door, holding it out.

'Thanks,' said Camille carelessly, taking the dressing gown and shutting the door again.

Claire walked down the stairs, every movement slow and considered, as if she was walking on glass. She paused, then took her phone and dialled the number of the man who would know what to do. It rang through to voicemail.

'Hello, this is Pierre. Please leave a message.'

'Pierre, it's Claire. Could you come over, please?'

She hung up.

She thought for a moment, then called Jérôme.

5

The rain was coming down hard by the time Jérôme got home – and 'home' was still how he thought of it. The house where he and Claire had brought up the girls, where they'd experienced so much joy and sorrow – not the bare apartment in town he slept in now.

Claire opened the door, dazed and red-eyed, and Jérôme braced himself for some kind of impact. She looked just as lost as she'd sounded on the phone.

'Come in,' said Claire. The words came out as if they were escaping from her.

In the year after Camille's death, he'd watched Claire come apart piece by piece as he'd withdrawn into the solace of alcohol. He'd ignored every sign, perfecting his denial until Léna had stepped in and brought him to some kind of sense, and he had truly seen the look in Claire's eyes. A look that had been growing in plain view but which he'd managed not to notice.

The same look was there again. Raw, fragile, close to breaking. *Oh Jesus*, he thought, and felt an almost physical pain at the sight. He loved her, and she was suffering.

'Why did you ask me here?' He was almost scared to find out.

'You should come inside,' she said. Jérôme hesitated. Claire dropped her voice, secretive and fierce: 'Camille is here.'

'Claire . . .' he said, despairing. This was how it had been on the worst days. Claire would see Camille in town, walking around a corner; she would see Camille in the shot of a crowd on television. And on the worst days of all, Claire would call Léna by her dead sister's name, and insist Léna was playing games with her if she denied it. It wouldn't last; disoriented, panicked, Claire would finally go to sleep and when she woke she would have recovered her bearings, and sob.

The passing of four years had brought just enough change in Léna's face, altered it from precise match to close resemblance, enough for that confusion to subside. It was a relief to Jérôme, too, not to see the face of Camille every day on her living sister, because he'd suffered from the same kind of momentary error more than once; certain, just for an instant, that it was the other twin standing there.

He'd often wondered if Léna had experienced the same thing, catching her own reflection and finding Camille's name dying in her throat.

Claire took a breath; her words tumbled out. 'She's in the bathroom. Do you want to see her?' She was nodding on his behalf, agitated: *of course you want to.*

He said nothing and came inside the house, following her up the stairs, walking as quietly as possible. He could hear someone in the bathroom. Léna, of course. He hoped Claire hadn't given Léna any indication of her state of mind. Then he could manage this, he could deal with it. Spare Léna the trauma somehow.

Claire guided him to the door. 'Listen,' she said, looking like a bemused child.

He took a breath. 'Léna?' he called. She would answer,

and he would lead Claire back downstairs and they would sit and talk and . . .

'No, it's me,' said Camille's voice. Jérôme turned and looked at Claire. She looked back at him with a desperate smile, and Jérôme opened the bathroom door.

She was there in the bath. Camille, arms suddenly across her chest, angry and embarrassed. 'What are you doing?' she said.

Jérôme paused.

'Get out!' said Camille.

Jérôme shut the door. The look that he'd seen on his wife's face, a mixture of fear and hope, suddenly made sense to him, because he could feel it on his own face now.

He headed straight outside to the patio, and couldn't get his shaking hands to light his cigarette fast enough.

'She doesn't remember the accident,' said Claire, her voice clipped. There was a hint of madness in her eyes that Jérôme empathized with. 'Only that she was on a school trip this morning.'

'No,' he said. 'This isn't possible.' He shook his head, feeling as if he was trying to shake the sight of his dead daughter out. *We buried her*, he wanted to say. *She's in the town graveyard, deep and cold and silent.*

'I know it's not possible,' said Claire. 'But she's here.'

'There has to be an explanation,' he said, and took a long drag on his cigarette.

'Like what? I'm going mad? That means you're mad, too.'

Jérôme didn't answer. He knew that the possibility of some kind of breakdown was exactly what had been going through Claire's mind when he'd arrived at the door. The relief that he'd shared in her vision was making her almost giddy.

'You saw her,' she said. 'Didn't you?'

His back was to the house; Claire's eyes caught something behind him.

'Look,' she said. 'Look at her.'

He couldn't turn. Insanity was the only explanation he could think of, and he wanted nothing of it. Then the door behind him slid open.

'Is something wrong?' asked Camille. 'What are you doing?'

He turned around. His dead daughter was standing there in her dressing gown. Her hair wet. Completely normal. Completely alive.

Her eyes went to his hand. 'Dad, are you smoking?'

His hand dropped by his side. He couldn't stop staring at her. Camille carried on talking, oblivious to the behaviour of her parents. 'Did Mum tell you? Weird, isn't it? I must have had a blackout or something, right? Shouldn't I see a doctor?'

Jérôme wondered exactly how *that* would play out. 'Do you feel OK now?'

'Yeah . . . but I'm a little freaked out. So where's Léna?'

'I told you,' said Claire, sounding uneasy. 'At a friend's.'

'Which friend?'

'I don't remember.'

Camille shrugged and went back inside, heading for the kitchen phone. Claire and Jérôme followed, exchanging looks.

'Who are you calling?' asked Claire.

'Frédéric,' said Camille. She dialled.

Claire shot a look of panic at Jérôme. 'It's late,' she said. 'You'll wake him.' They watched, fearful, just able to hear the sound of the phone ringing, ringing, expecting it to be picked up at any second.

Then Camille hung up. 'Not answering,' she muttered. 'Well, I'm exhausted. I'm off to bed. Maybe tomorrow will be a little less weird.'

Claire and Jérôme wished her goodnight and watched her go; watched her all the way up the stairs, step by step. Only when they heard her bedroom door shut did they realize they'd both been holding their breaths. They looked at each other apprehensively.

Maybe tomorrow will be a little less weird.

Jérôme didn't think the chances were good.

6

Julie Meyer sat on her sofa with her legs curled under her, working through the huge amounts of paperwork that came with the job. Three metres away, people were being torn to pieces.

Somebody screamed. She looked up at the television, unable to remember what the film was or how long it had been on. The faces on screen contorted in pain as undead teeth sank into skin. Julie glanced casually at the horror in front of her, feeling nothing.

She got back to the paperwork. It had been a long day, her busiest of the week. Seven clients visited, two of them borderline dementia; one whose daughter was there to supervise, suspicious that the work wasn't being done well. Julie had been suspicious, too; she wasn't the usual nurse for the patient, and she wondered if her employers had somehow caught wind of the daughter's suspicions and sent her to avoid trouble. Julie had done her job; the daughter had been satisfied.

'I'm sorry I doubted,' the daughter had told her as she left.

'I'm not her usual nurse,' Julie had said. 'Keep doubting.'

It depressed her, sometimes, the things that people tried to get away with when nobody was watching – especially with those who had no way of defending themselves.

At last, she came to the end of her write-ups and set her folder down. Tired, she wondered if she should eat something. She wasn't hungry, but she couldn't remember having eaten much all day. She sat and watched the people die on screen, bored of it but immobile. Eat or not, it didn't seem to matter to her. Watch a film or not, she didn't seem to care. Get to bed, then? Maybe. Or maybe she would just fall asleep where she sat, and wake in the night and wonder why she was continuing to live at all.

It wasn't a *life* she was living. Everyone had the drudgery of work, the tedium of all the regular hoops you had to jump through just to survive, a long series of the same things over and over like breath or pulse. That was what food had become to her, and sleep; something that just had to be done, and no end in sight.

But everyone else had the moments between the drudgery: the moments that counted, the moments that made it worthwhile.

That was what life was, she thought. The moments between.

And she had none. She was paralysed by the inertia of it all. Sometimes she wondered if she'd died in that tunnel seven years ago, because *this* was not life.

The phone rang. She switched the television off.

'Hello? Monsieur Costa, calm down . . .' The man was agitated. She liked Michel Costa: he was old but still sharp, a teacher at the local school until he'd been pushed into late retirement. On every heart medication known to science, it sometimes seemed, but his mind was still bright. 'OK, I'm listening.'

Chest pain; palpitations. Not unusual for him. She questioned him long enough to be sure it wasn't more serious, but she promised she would get out to him as soon as she could manage.

'It's urgent,' he said.

'I can only go so fast, Monsieur Costa. I'll be as quick as I can. Meanwhile, you should lie down. Try and stay calm, OK?'

'I'll be waiting, Julie.'

'I'll see you soon, and don't worry, you'll be fine.'

There was a pause. 'Julie? I wanted to . . .' He trailed off.

'Yes?' She waited; it was five or six seconds before he replied.

'I'll see you soon,' he said, then hung up. The curious distraction that had been in his voice wasn't encouraging. Julie looked at the phone for a moment, wondering if the light of Michel Costa's mind was finally starting to fade.

She left her apartment and went downstairs. As she approached the exit to the apartment building, she saw a man outside angrily keying into the security pad. Tall, young, a great mop of unruly black hair; she didn't recognize him, but then she didn't pay much attention to the other residents. As she opened the door, he gave her a look of relief.

'Evening,' she said, passing him.

'Has the code changed?' he asked.

'No.'

He opened his mouth to say more, but Julie didn't slow. 'Goodnight,' he called after her. She kept walking.

She was lucky with the bus across town, getting to the stop just before it came around the end of the street. Then it was a ten-minute trudge up steep roads to Michel Costa's house.

When he answered the door, he seemed less than eager for her to come in.

'Julie, I, uh, I called again to tell you I was fine, but you must have already left. No need to come out, I'm afraid, I'm much better now. Much better.'

She gave him a small smile, but inside she was thinking about his state of mind. The man had nobody left to look after him. His wife had died decades ago, and the couple had no children. Chest pains and disorientation – it could be much more serious than the usual little twinges she treated him for. 'Well, I'm here,' she said. 'Let me take a look at you and make sure, yes?'

He just stood in the doorway. Julie raised her eyebrows and smiled again. 'Can I come in?'

He blinked. 'Yes, of course, Julie, of course.'

She sat him down in his living room, keeping a close eye on his behaviour; his eyes were darting to the corridor, agitated, almost frightened.

She checked him over. Everything was reasonably normal, despite his heart rate being slightly elevated – certainly no sign of a stroke or anything more serious. She put his heart rate down to anxiety and gave him what she could to calm it, but after the injection there was little else for her to do here.

'You seem very distressed, Monsieur Costa. Will you be OK?'

He looked at her. She thought for a moment that he was going to tell her something, confide in her, but then he looked away. 'I'll be fine,' he said.

She stood and packed up. As she was about to leave, she

heard a sound from elsewhere in the house, like the clatter of plates. 'You're not alone?' she said, moving for the door.

He stood and intercepted her with a burst of speed that left him breathless. 'Yes, I am. It's just . . .' Again, that look of almost confiding came and went. 'It's no one.'

Was there someone here? She leaned close to him and whispered: 'If you need me to call the police, just nod.'

He shook his head. Slow, steady. Sad, almost.

She looked at him, wondering if she should push further, but his privacy had to be respected. 'I don't want to pry, but I'm here if you need to talk, OK? Call me, any time.'

'Yes.'

'You're sure you're all right?'

'I'm sure,' he said. 'And thanks, Julie. See you next week.'

When she left, it was raining. It mirrored her mood. Whatever had happened with Michel Costa, she hoped it was temporary. The man had always shone, an example to her that old age held more than indignity and decrepitude.

That was the problem with dealing with so many of the older patients in town, those without support from relatives, those near the end of their days and susceptible to the ravages of dementia. She saw it too often, the accelerating decline to the inevitable. One by one, the key parts of their lives – those moments between – would fail them, and vanish, mourned like lost children.

Perhaps that was the advantage to being the way she was. There was little to warrant mourning.

7

After Camille had gone to bed, Jérôme and Claire stood in restless silence in the kitchen. A few minutes later, Jérôme caught movement outside the window. Someone was approaching the house: Pierre.

'What's he doing here?' he asked, knowing he sounded bitter even as the words left his mouth. Claire threw him a look that left him in no doubt that she'd called him. Jérôme followed her to the corridor, but stood back almost out of sight as Claire opened the door. Pierre smiled at her and put his hand on her arm, saying nothing.

'Camille has come back,' said Claire eagerly, grasping his hand and pulling him through the door. Jérôme was almost amused at the way Pierre's expression changed at once, extreme wariness and a failed attempt to mask it. *She hadn't told him why he was invited*, Jérôme thought.

'Just like you said,' Claire continued. 'You said He would listen to my prayers.' Pierre looked dazed. 'Do you want to see her? She's in her room.'

'Yes,' Pierre managed.

'She's so beautiful,' said Claire, with a manic edge. 'I'm so happy.'

Pierre gave Jérôme a quick look of surprise as he walked past. *Hadn't thought the husband would be home, huh, Pierre?* Not the kind of visit the man had expected, Jérôme thought. Not at all.

Jérôme let them go upstairs. When they were out of

earshot, he took his mobile and called Lucy Clarsen. She didn't pick up, so he left a message: 'Lucy, it's me. Jérôme. I need to talk to you. Call me. *Please.*'

Claire thought Pierre was the one with the answers, but Lucy was the only person Jérôme knew who had ever claimed to speak to the dead – the only person he'd thought might be telling the truth, at any rate. *And it didn't work tonight*, he thought. Because how can you contact the dead, if the dead have already come back?

Standing outside the bedroom door, Claire could hear movement from within. She'd expected Camille to be sleeping, expected to just sneak the door open so that Pierre could see the miracle before him. She knocked instead. 'Camille? Can we come in?'

Camille wrenched the door open, angry. 'Have you been tidying? Mum, why have you moved all my stuff?'

Claire took a deep breath. 'Yes, I tidied. I'm sorry.' She smiled, even so. She'd waited a long time to hear Camille complain about that. 'This is Dr Tissier,' she said; Pierre was no doctor, but the white lie Pierre had suggested on the way upstairs would help him reassure the girl.

'Hello, Camille,' said Pierre. There was hardly a flicker in his eyes when he saw her, Claire noted; he was considerably calmer than she had been when confronted with her resurrected daughter. It was why she'd called him. He seemed unsurprised by almost everything.

Camille frowned, immediately suspicious. 'Why isn't Dr Delouvrier here?'

'He's on holiday,' said Pierre, improvising. 'I'm filling in.

Your mum told me what happened, but I'd like you to tell me, in your own words. Do you mind?'

'There's nothing to tell. I was on the coach, and I woke up in the mountains. That's all I remember. I think I had some kind of blackout. Maybe it's amnesia . . .' Camille's eyes widened. 'Perhaps it's a brain tumour?'

Pierre smiled to calm her. 'No, I don't think so. Where did you get that idea?'

'Will you examine me?'

Pierre hesitated. 'Yes, of course.' He indicated for Camille to sit on the bed, while he took the chair. Camille offered her wrist. Pierre took it in his hand, pretending to take her pulse, looking at Camille with a degree of wonder. Claire stood in the doorway still trying to come to terms with the sight in front of her. But now three people had seen – it was no shared delusion. Camille was *real*.

After a moment Camille pulled her wrist away, her eyes narrowing. 'You're no doctor. You don't even have any equipment with you. What are you, a psychiatrist?' She looked at her mother, but Claire said nothing. As far as Claire was concerned, her daughter was with exactly the right person.

'No, I'm not a psychiatrist. Do you think you need one?'

'I'm not mad.'

'Camille, what do you think madness is? Shall I tell you? Madness is denying reality. We all do it at some point in our lives. Sometimes it seems it's the only option. A coping mechanism. When reality is too hard to accept, we would rather deny it, or pretend to, just to avoid facing the simple truths around us.'

He glanced up at Claire. She realized that Pierre was speaking to her, just as much as to her daughter.

Pierre looked back at Camille. 'And I don't think you're one of those people. Whatever this is, Camille, promise me. Promise me you won't run from it.'

Camille sighed, bemused and a little wary. 'I'm too tired for this.'

'You need to rest,' said Claire.

'I already tried to. I'm so tired, but I just can't get to sleep.'

'We'll give you something to help,' said Pierre, still in his doctor's role. He looked to Claire, who nodded. She'd had more than her share of sleepless nights, and her medicine cupboard was well stocked.

Jérôme was waiting for them when they came back downstairs. He'd been straining to hear what they'd been talking about, trying to make out the muffled words coming down through the floor. Some, he'd caught; most had been unintelligible, and the thought of Pierre having this privileged role rankled with him.

There was another source of his anger, though. Irritation with Pierre hadn't been the only reason he'd not gone up to Camille's room. While he'd been waiting, it had occurred to him that his wariness of Camille was perhaps a little more than just caution. He thought he might even be scared of her.

'So, *doctor* . . .' he said to Pierre, belligerent. 'What's the diagnosis? Spontaneous *resurrection*?'

'Please don't be so disrespectful,' said Pierre.

'Come on then,' said Jérôme. 'Out with it.' Pierre looked

at him, still as infuriatingly calm as he always was; if this didn't shake the man, what the hell would? 'For Christ's sake, Pierre,' said Jérôme, his voice low. 'My daughter's risen from the *dead*. What do we do?'

Pierre thought for a few seconds, then shook his head. 'I don't know,' he said. 'It's never happened before. Well, once, obviously . . . but I imagine you're not interested.'

'You're right, I'm not. Save it for Claire.' Jérôme found his patience at an end. Frustrated, he could feel his aggression towards Pierre growing. 'Now answer the question – what the hell do we *do*?'

Claire stepped towards Jérôme, holding out her hands to try to calm him. 'Why take it out on us?'

'Because after years of praying for this, I thought you would at least know how to *welcome* her. That's why. I'm disappointed you're not more prepared. I may not know what to say or do, but at least I didn't pray for this to happen.'

Pierre, maddeningly, was still unfazed by Jérôme's outburst. 'Claire prayed for her daughter to be returned to her,' he said. 'But it was God's grace that saw fit to answer her prayer this way.'

'It must be good to be so sure it was *God's* grace.' Jérôme felt the tears sting. He turned away and walked to the other side of the room. Claire followed, put her arm around him. Held him. He gave way to it, to the grief and the fear and the confusion, sobbing.

Pierre cleared his throat. 'When she finds out the truth, it won't be easy. She must be told what happened, and that so many of those she knew died. She must be told that she shouldn't be afraid. What she's going through is terrifying but also wonderful, and that must be what she focuses on. She has to understand that we'll be here for her.'

Jérôme looked at him. 'If you think you can tell her that . . .'

'No, you're going to tell her,' said Pierre. 'You and Claire. You belong here, Jérôme. With your daughter.'

Jérôme glared at the man, so impossibly reasonable, so intolerably *understanding*. He clenched both hands, Pierre's throat becoming too tempting a target, and spoke through gritted teeth: 'Then why are you still here?'

'Stop it,' said Claire, close to tears herself. 'Pierre is here to help us. All of us. Our *family*.' She looked up to the ceiling, to Camille's room.

Drained, Jérôme said nothing. His eyes drifted up to where Claire was looking, and he found himself saying a prayer of his own. Praying that what had come to the house today was exactly how it seemed; praying that it really was his daughter lying upstairs in that bedroom.

8

After leaving Michel Costa's home, Julie had waited twenty minutes at the bus stop under the shelter, the rain still coming down and the sky rumbling. The bus was empty when she got on, but as she sat she was surprised to see a small boy of about nine climb on board and stand by the driver. She'd thought nobody but her had been at the stop.

She watched the boy. There was something about his clothes that struck her as curiously outdated, but wasn't that how clothing went? In cycles, where styles from thirty years before could just resurface unannounced?

The boy didn't pay – he just stood looking at the driver, standing perfectly still. The driver said nothing, but after a moment closed the doors and set off. The boy went to the back of the bus and sat in silence.

As the bus drove on, Julie's worries about Monsieur Costa distracted her. By the time she reached her destination and got off, the boy had slipped entirely from her thoughts.

The rain had thankfully stopped, but the night air was chilly. Back in her apartment she took off her damp coat, then went over to the window to get her patient logbook. She wouldn't mention anything strange in her paperwork for the visit to Monsieur Costa, she decided. Keep an eye on him, sure, but hope that the disorientation had been a one-off.

Outside at the rear of the apartment block, far back on the grass four floors below, stood the same boy she had seen on the bus. Hands by his side, standing in the patch of illumination from the apartment block's security lights, just as still as he'd been when she'd seen him earlier.

Her first thought was concern for the child. On the bus, she'd presumed the driver knew him, that he might even be a relative. She hadn't noticed him get off the bus at her stop, but there he was, alone. Looking at the building.

Julie frowned and couldn't shake the feeling that he was looking at *her*.

She watched him. He didn't move. She shook her head. *Not my problem*, she thought. She took her logbook over to the sofa, but it was only a matter of seconds before her nature got the better of her and she went back to the window.

The boy was gone.

Her doorbell rang. It made her jump slightly, and she swore. She hadn't realized she was so on edge. She went to the door. When she opened it to find the boy standing there, somehow she wasn't surprised.

She should have been, she knew. The distance the boy had covered in so short a time; the entry key code for the building. It wasn't *possible*, but it was real.

'Are you lost?' she said. The boy just looked at her, calm and still. 'Can't you get home?' Nothing. His face showed almost no emotion, but Julie saw one thing there: a need. He needed help. 'What's your name?'

The door across the corridor opened. Julie's neighbour, Nathalie Payet – one of the few people in the building Julie ever spoke to, and then it was hardly by choice. A car-crash of a woman, she was the kind who was pushing fifty and still in denial that she'd ever hit thirty, dismayed if anyone should refer to her as 'madame'. Horribly overfamiliar, she was chronically unable to keep her nose out of other people's business. Julie made a conscious effort not to look to the heavens, but a bolt of lightning would always be welcome at times like this.

'Is everything OK?' said the woman, then she made a show of 'noticing' Julie's uninvited guest. 'What a handsome little boy!' she cooed, crouching down to him. 'Hello there!'

Julie felt the boy's hand slip into her own and tighten.

Nathalie Payet stood. 'Does he live with you? He's a shy one. What's his name?'

Julie looked at the boy, caught by his gaze. She wanted to get rid of her neighbour – just to answer quickly, shut the door and then try to get to the truth of her unannounced visitor. Time to improvise. 'Victor,' she said.

The woman's eyes narrowed. 'Mmm,' she said, in a way that Julie didn't like the sound of. 'Anyway,' she continued, affecting girl-to-girl camaraderie. She lowered her voice, all smiles, none kind. 'A young man rang at your door earlier. Quite handsome, actually. Dark and curly, the kind of hair you can really *grip*.' She leered. Julie felt the boy's hand leave hers, as he moved into the apartment. She shot a glance after him before forcing her attention back to the woman in front of her. Her unwelcome neighbour took this as a cue to get even more suggestive. 'Called himself Simon. He was looking for Adèle Werther.' The leer widened. 'Is that your dating name? Don't be shy, we've all done it. Playing away.'

'Not at all,' said Julie, as stonily as she could manage. 'She lived here before me. Whoever he was, he obviously didn't know she's moved.'

Her neighbour's face dropped with disappointment. No sauce for her here, as always. 'Ah. OK.'

'Goodnight, Mademoiselle Payet.' Julie stepped back, forcing a polite smile. She started to close the door.

'Goodnight, Julie,' her neighbour managed, just before it shut in her face.

Julie found the boy in the kitchen, calmly eating from a packet of biscuits as though he belonged there. 'Make yourself at home,' said Julie, but her sarcasm was lost on him. He looked at her, and gave her the slightest of smiles. 'You're hungry?' she said. He nodded. 'I'll cook you something, if you talk to me. Something nice. Just tell me where you live, so I can get you home safe.' She had had enough experience of kids to know bribery was usually the fastest way to get results. He said nothing, however. Julie shook her head. So much for that. 'Then you'll get what you get,' she said.

For all she knew the boy could be allergic to everything, but she had some frozen rice in the freezer and reckoned she was safe enough with that. He watched her as the rice heated in the microwave; she watched back, staying silent too in a game she felt she was destined to lose.

She put the plate of rice in front of him, and he ate without a pause. As he ate, Julie wondered about the young man her neighbour had mentioned – presumably, the man she had passed on her way out to see Monsieur Costa earlier. He'd come looking for Adèle. Thoughts of Adèle led, inevitably, to thoughts of Laure; Adèle was an acquaintance of Laure, and that was how Julie had learned this apartment was available when she'd first taken it, eight years before. A different time. A different life.

The apartment had been a bright place, a happy place, for a while. She and Laure had even started making plans; Laure's job as a police officer had been going well enough for her to hope for a promotion. Then things changed, and everything Julie had was ripped away . . . Ever since that night in the tunnel, her apartment had been more like a tomb.

She looked at the boy. Whatever the circumstances, she was glad of the company, but the circumstances were likely to catch up with them both before long.

'OK,' she said. 'I've waited long enough. Talk.' Nothing. 'You understand me, yes?' He nodded. 'And you have the ability to speak?' Nod. 'So if you won't tell me, I'll call the police. They'll come for you, and your parents won't be happy. Shall I call them?'

There was no reaction. He just kept eating, watching her with that same flat expression. She went to get the phone, to show she meant it. 'OK, I'm calling. Here I go.'

She dialled. When they answered, she said nothing. The boy was watching her, that need in his face, and she couldn't do it. She tried, but she just couldn't. If he was running from something, she couldn't just send him back to it. At least not until she knew what it was.

She hung up. 'Just for tonight, then. Tomorrow I'm taking you to the police, you hear me?'

He ignored her, just continued eating until he'd finished his rice.

'Was that enough?' she asked.

He nodded. Julie took his plate to the sink. When she turned, the boy had gone. She went through to the living room. He'd switched on the television, still on the horror channel she'd been watching earlier. Screams filled the room; she hurried over to switch it off.

'Uh-uh. Not for you.' A clock caught her eye, and she realized how tired she was. 'Isn't it time you went to sleep?'

The boy said nothing.

'At least tell me your name.'

He looked up at her with that same need in his eye. 'Victor,' he said, and he smiled.

For a moment she was taken aback that he'd spoken at all; then, she was annoyed at his response. But her annoyance vanished as the boy's eyes locked onto hers; Julie found herself smiling in return. 'Victor it is, then. For now. Maybe one day you'll tell me what your real name is, huh? Come on, shoes off. Sleep.'

He lay back on the sofa; she fetched a blanket and put it over him. He closed his eyes. She had to resist the urge to put her hand on his head, stroke his hair before she went, but she managed.

Julie left the room and put out the light. She didn't notice the boy's eyes open again, as he watched her go.

9

Léna had spent the evening the way she usually did: in the Lake Pub with Frédéric and Lucho. Away from the house, away from those fretful eyes her mum had worn for as long as she could remember. Well, ever since Camille died, and her mother's overprotection started to go through its destructive loop – growing until Léna couldn't breathe and she pushed against it hard, and her mum stepped back and sank into whatever state it was she'd found herself in. Depression, anxiety, grief, loneliness. All that and more, round and round in a vicious cycle.

Her mum close and in her face, shouting and crying and angry and scared, or her mum distant and mute. Whatever state her mother was in, the best option for Léna was always the same: to be out of the house.

The night had started pleasantly enough, but then it had soured a little.

'Hey, Léna,' Lucho had said. 'Your dad's seeing Lucy again?' He'd pointed over to the far end of the pub, where her dad was talking to Lucy, offering her a cigarette. 'That's the third time this week.'

As Léna looked, her father's eyes met hers for an instant. He looked away, a kid caught in the act.

'*Awkward*,' said Lucho.

Frédéric sighed and cuffed the back of Lucho's head. 'You're such a prick.'

Léna ignored all of it and drank her beer. Lucy saw

plenty of men. She worked behind the bar, but given the reputation she'd developed Léna had no idea why Toni Guillard, the man who ran the Lake Pub, kept her on.

The obvious answer – that Toni was sleeping with her too, perhaps in lieu of rent – was one she didn't buy; Toni was as straight-laced as they came, a hulking great man who looked ashamed of himself if he even *swore*. The thing was, Léna didn't mind Lucy, and so far that was how the rest of the pub's clientele seemed to feel too. She was a strange one, a woman who came across as confident and outgoing, but never actually talked about herself, about where she came from.

Lucho found it all very amusing, though.

The night had got back on track soon enough. Pool, beer, more pool. People turned up and she chatted and mixed, but it always ended up with her, Lucho and Frédéric. It had been that way for a long time. They were both in the year below Léna, but she'd known Frédéric since forever. He was only three months younger than her, on the wrong side of the school intake cusp.

The pair had, Léna thought, saved her life after Camille's death. Almost every friend she had, and of course the closest of all, had died that day. Lucho, meanwhile, had been seeing Léna's classmate Mathilde for a couple of months at the time of the crash, all cloyingly sweet first-love stuff. Mathilde had also been on the coach; her death had hit Lucho deep and hard.

And Frédéric . . . the less said about that, the better.

But with all three of them in free fall together, they'd managed to take care of each other. Tonight, that meant doing shots until they couldn't walk. She'd already lost count when Frédéric held his mobile towards her. 'Léna, it's your mum. Shall I get it?'

Léna scowled. She wasn't late, not yet. Sure, she'd turned off her mobile, but really . . . trying to get hold of her by calling Frédéric? Her mum could fuck off. 'No, she's a pain in the arse.' Frédéric nodded and put his phone away.

Lucho gave her a gentle punch in the arm and pointed to the drink in front of her. 'Léna, it's your turn.'

She nodded, but she needed a moment. The call from her mum had left her out of sorts. She stood.

'Giving up?' said Frédéric with a sly smile.

'Not on your life.' She took the last shot from the table and downed it, feeling more unsteady on her feet than she'd expected.

'Your round,' she said to Lucho. 'I'm going to the toilet. Won't be long.'

Frédéric put his hand on her shoulder, concerned. 'Are you OK?'

'Yeah.'

'No throwing up!' called Lucho, grinning.

'Come on,' she laughed. 'Who do you think I am?'

In the toilets, she splashed her face and then ran cold water over her hands until they ached, looking at herself in the mirror. It had been a long time after the crash before mirrors had held anything for her but ghosts.

As she walked back past the bar, a good-looking guy she'd not seen before entered and looked around, then headed over. For a moment Léna thought he was coming specifically to her; she allowed herself a little smile. His dark curly hair was untidy and he looked as if he'd dressed himself in a suit from a charity shop, but she could forgive that.

Then he veered away and Léna's smile faded. It wasn't her he'd been heading for.

'Excuse me?' the young man said to Lucy, behind the bar. Léna paid close attention, while trying to look as uninterested as possible.

Lucy nodded.

'Is Adèle around?'

Lucy shook her head. 'Adèle? I don't know her.'

'She works here.'

Lucy looked distracted as another customer demanded a drink. 'If an Adèle worked here, I would know. Sorry.' She turned away to serve the person waiting.

Léna smiled again and sat down next to the guy. 'I know an Adèle,' she said. 'There can't be many of them.' He looked sceptical, but Léna wasn't going to give up there. 'Tall brunette, pretty, green eyes? Works at the library?'

'She doesn't work at the library,' he said. 'But the rest sounds like her. Adèle Werther.'

'I don't know her last name, but she lives near here. Buy me a drink and I'll take you.' She held out her hand. 'Léna.'

He took it, his grip cold and strong. 'Simon,' he said. 'So, what are you having?'

A voice came from beside her. 'Haven't you had enough?'

She turned to Frédéric with a glare. 'Who are you, my mother?'

'Come on, Léna,' Frédéric tried. 'Let's go.'

'I'm fine where I am,' she said, giving him a run-along gesture with her hand. Frédéric shook his head and slunk off.

She and Simon had a half-pint each; he necked his almost without a pause. Léna shrugged and did the same. As they got outside she looked around, suddenly regretting leaving the warmth. The ground was wet, and the sky looked as if it could rain again any minute.

Still, she'd had the beer, and the price was a few minutes' walking with a cute guy, even if he was almost completely distracted. After that, she'd just head on home and let Frédéric suffer.

'That way,' she said, and pointed. The guy set off. 'Can't you slow down?' she said. Simon was walking as fast as he'd been drinking. He slowed a fraction, and Léna kept pace. 'I've never seen you at the Lake Pub before,' she said.

'I've never seen you, either.'

'Really?' said Léna. 'I practically live there. Not much else to do in this town. Have you lived here long?'

'I was born here.'

'Right,' said Léna. 'I wondered why you were so cheer-ful.'

'How do you know Adèle?'

'She tutored me last year,' she said, then frowned. 'It was a complete waste of time. Not her fault, though. I was failing to give even the slightest shit about anything much. And you? Did she tutor you?'

He stopped walking and looked at her, bemused by something. 'No.'

Léna laughed. 'You're pretty mysterious.' She pointed to a row of houses ahead. 'OK, beer payment. See the first house, there? That's her place.'

He was already walking again before she'd finished, faster than ever and without looking back.

'You're welcome, dickhead,' Léna called after him.

It was another ten minutes before she reached home, climbing up the trellis and into her room rather than using the front door. She was still annoyed with her mum for ringing Frédéric. Let her worry.

As she took off her jacket in her bedroom, she heard a sound. Two knocks on the wall. A pause. Another knock.

She froze. It came again.

The code she and Camille had used. A request. *Can I come in?*

Léna went to the wall that separated her room from Camille's. She put one hand on it, and tapped out an answer with the other. *Yes, you can come in.* She was dreaming, she knew. Drunk and overtired and dreaming on her feet.

Then she heard a door open: Camille's door.

She took a step back away from her own door, watching as the handle began to move. Slowly, the door opened.

A mirror, four years into the past: Camille, looking at her with confusion on her face, as if she didn't recognize her. Camille took a step nearer; Léna started to panic, tried to scream but didn't have the breath in her lungs. She backed away, away, reaching the bed and climbing over it, getting it between herself and . . .

'Who are you . . .?' said Camille. Then her eyes widened in horror. 'Léna?' she said. '*Léna?*'

And as one, they both started to scream.

10

Lucy Clarsen left the Lake Pub twenty minutes after the last customer had gone, Toni sending her on her way before the clear-up was completed.

'I'll finish it,' he told her, and she thanked him. When she'd arrived in town one year before, she'd lived in the room above the pub for a few weeks, the one she still used for clients. Now, she had a small apartment in the centre of town, but she'd learned from prior experience to keep home and business life separate. Especially with the kind of business she had. People thought she was a prostitute, of course, but it was easier that way. The reality was much more complicated. Much less likely to be accepted.

As she walked home, she checked her mobile. A dozen messages had built up over the day; she would wait until she was in her apartment before she sorted through them, but they were almost certainly requests for new appointments, or changes to those already made. Business, in other words, and she was off the clock now.

The late-night streets were quiet as she approached the main road and started down the long stairway to the underpass. There was nobody else around. As usual, the tunnel smelt slightly of stale piss and damp earth, but it was well lit. After the rain earlier in the night the banks along the road were still draining off, and a long thin stream ran along the centre of the tunnel. She stayed to one side, keeping her shoes dry.

At the other end of the tunnel she saw a man enter, walking towards her. She glanced quickly: hooded top, hands in pockets and head down. She had a knack for spotting trouble, she thought, and she didn't reckon this guy was anything to be worried about. Even so, as the echo of their footsteps mingled in the harsh fluorescent lighting, she kept an eye on him. She could take care of herself. She'd been in enough bad situations over the years to have taken every self-defence course she could.

As she and the man passed each other, Lucy tensed, just in case.

The man lunged from behind.

She'd been so sure he wasn't a threat that the surprise nearly did for her, but she moved quickly enough to grip the hand holding the knife, grip and twist, the way she'd learned, wrenching it up, biting until the knife fell, then . . .

Then she saw his face.

She couldn't place it, couldn't work out the feeling, but there was something about the man that startled her, like a splash of cold water. They looked at each other for a few seconds, and for Lucy the pause was catastrophic.

The man pulled his hand free and retrieved his knife from the ground, then grabbed hold of her. Lucy saw the knife come up and she slapped it away, feeling the deep cuts in her hand as the blade bit into her flesh. She didn't feel the pain, though, only sensed the damage, but dread was building inside her. She knew where the advantage lay now. She managed to fend off another blow but the next found its way through: the knife plunged into her stomach.

The shock of it was absolute, an intense burning agony that stole away what hope she had left.

She opened her mouth ready to plead with him to let her go, but she saw his eyes, eager, ecstatic. No mercy in them at all. The words wouldn't come.

He stabbed again. Again. He was sighing, breathless.

Lucy felt tears drop from her eyes. She started to convulse, and realized she was sobbing.

'There, there,' he said, wiping the tears away with his left hand, the fingertips lingering on her skin. 'No need for tears. It's OK.'

There was suddenly no strength in her limbs. Her back was against the wall of the tunnel and she started to slide down. He took her weight, slowing the fall, lowering her gently to the ground. She could feel the legs of her trousers grow wet in the stream of cold dirty rainwater on the tunnel floor; around her midriff, it was her own blood that was soaking through her clothing.

He stabbed again, five more times. Each was slow, deliberate. Even over the terror, the pain was everything in her mind. *Almost* everything: there was also despair.

'It's over,' he whispered in her ear, as if he thought he was being tender. 'It's over.' He let her fall to the side now, slowly. Holding her, caressing.

She felt him pull up her shirt. He unbuttoned her jeans, then splayed the top of the material, but made no attempt to lower the zip more than a few centimetres. He placed his hand on her bared stomach, blood pouring from her. He took his hand away and brought his lips down to her bloody skin, breathing like a consumptive, ragged and sickly.

He kissed her once. She felt his tongue enter a wound, and she prayed for dark, prayed not to be there any more.

He sat up. 'Yes,' he said. '*Yes.*'

He still had his knife. And he wasn't finished yet.

11

Michel Costa was walking. He'd been walking for hours now, without really knowing what his intention was. The sun was rising; maybe that was it, he thought. Maybe he'd been waiting for the daylight to come back. Maybe it would show him his path.

He'd burned her. What else could he have done? His wife, thirty years dead, back at the door. Hungry. Dismissive, as she'd always been. The shock of seeing her face had nearly killed him. She'd seemed so *young* to him, looking exactly how she'd looked when she died. She'd been forty-five, and even then had regularly bemoaned the loss of her youth, but now after all that time . . .

She'd seemed so young.

He'd almost told Julie about her when she came to help. Almost. But as he'd waited for Julie to arrive, he'd made his decision. He would handle it in his own way.

His wife had let him tie her up in the kitchen. She hadn't struggled. She'd looked at him with something halfway between amusement and derision, and she'd kept talking, talking. He hadn't listened. He didn't want to know.

He'd spent his life as a teacher, devoted to the children he taught, passionate about sharing with them the joy to be found in knowledge, in comprehending the workings of the world.

He was a man of reason, a man of science. Not a man of God, not by any means. Not for a long time. If he had any god at all, now, it was gravity, it was light, it was the idea that things could be understood, and superstition could be banished. For all the good it had done him.

He had burned it all. His life, and everything in it, putting a flame to the pile of photographs and documents he'd assembled in his living room. A lifetime of certificates, of deeds, of bills.

There are always costs, he thought. Always payments to be made.

The flames had spread; too late, he'd realized that the fire was out of control. He'd run from the house, his wife calling for him to untie her. He didn't stop. She didn't stand a chance, he knew, but he just kept walking as the fire raged behind him. He wondered if that hadn't been his intention all along.

He'd felt so tired; so glad it would soon all be over with.

It was the sight of the water that snapped him from his thoughts, as he realized where his walking had taken him. He was halfway across the dam. Of course, he thought. Given everything that had happened all those years ago, where better?

Michel Costa climbed the low wall at the edge of the road that formed the top of the dam, looking out over the town that was waking after a long night. He moved his gaze to the hard ground far below him. He looked to both sides, taking in the sweep of the arch that was holding so much back, standing guard over the people in the valley ahead. Such a graceful structure, he thought.

But always payments to be made.

He leaned forward until gravity claimed him.

12

Adèle Werther lay on her bed and tried to think of nothing, because whatever she thought of, it brought her back to *him*. To Simon.

She'd not told Thomas about what had happened the night before, not yet – if she ever would. She had managed to ease the fears of her daughter, Chloé; ease them enough for Chloé to promise not to mention it to Thomas either.

But she saw Simon whenever she closed her eyes, saw him the way she'd seen him last night: standing outside the house, looking in through the living-room window, his hand on the glass.

Thomas had been out working, the downside of him being made police captain. He was justly proud of what he'd achieved, and she was proud of him too: 'Captain Thomas Pellerin' had a ring to it, and in a fortnight they would be married. But it was a small town, and Thomas was diligent at his job. Any significant police incident meant he would be gone.

Chloé had been upstairs in her room at the time. If she'd been with Adèle in the living room, Adèle could have asked her to look.

Do you see anyone there, Chloé? No? Nothing. It's nothing. All in your head.

But Chloé hadn't been with her. Adèle had closed her eyes, and when she'd opened them again Simon had gone from the window. Two seconds of relief was all she'd had before the knocking on the door had paralysed her.

Then: 'Adèle, it's me.'

His voice. Ten years since Simon's death, and in all the times she'd imagined seeing him since, she'd not once heard his voice.

'Open up!' he shouted. 'Open the door!'

No, she thought. *Not again. I can't start this again.*

'Adèle, I know you're in there. What's going on?'

The knocking became more violent: hard, repeated thumps, Simon losing his patience suddenly, something she remembered so well no matter how hard she tried to forget. Adèle found herself beating the wall beside her in time with the knocking.

'I know you're there,' he said. 'Open the fucking door.'

'Leave me alone!' she yelled. The knocking stopped. She heard Chloé's door, heard her footsteps coming down the stairs.

'Mum?'

She looked at her daughter. Nearly ten years old, and Adèle could see much of Simon in her face. Not in her temperament, thank God.

She could feel the tingle in her hands from hitting the wall, and she looked at them, wondering if it had been her own fists making all the noise. If it had all been her.

Of course it had.

'It's over, Mum,' said Chloé, holding her tight. 'It's OK.'

She'd got Chloé to bed again, then had gone to bed herself. Checking the security locks on every door, closing all the curtains, crying and trembling in her bed.

Thomas had come home soon after midnight and Adèle

had pretended to be asleep. Her eyes were closed, and all she could see was Simon's face.

The last night she and Simon had spent together, she'd been working a shift in the Lake Pub while Simon's band played. Every chance she could, she caught his eye, smiling, knowing what she knew and wanting to tell him.

After the set had finished, she'd gone to him, hugged him. A little red-headed girl, one of the Séguret twins, had sat in the band's drum kit and started to mess around. The girl's father had told her off, but Simon had gone over and shown her what to do.

Adèle had borrowed a camera, and caught the moment on film.

The girl had probably been the same age as Chloé was now. Adèle imagined the picture, imagined Chloé in place of the twin, sitting at the drums and smiling. The closest thing Adèle would ever have to seeing Simon as a father.

She'd stuck the Polaroid on the pub's photo wall ten years ago, and she'd not been back in that building since. Not once.

They had spent the night in her apartment, and the night was long and good. They were twenty-three, and in a matter of hours they would be getting married. She was happy.

In the morning, they woke much later than they'd intended. Time was pressing.

'Shit!' she said. 'We've hardly slept.'

'We can sleep when we're dead,' said Simon, kissing her until she pushed him off, laughing.

'Stop it! I need to get ready.'

'Go on then,' he said.

She shook her head. 'It's bad luck if you see me in my

dress.' They'd talked about this already, Simon finding the superstition amusing, but he was willing to indulge her.

'OK, OK,' he said. 'I'm going.' He moved to get up, but saw it in her face: her sudden need to tell him something. 'What is it?'

'Nothing,' she said. Her smile said otherwise.

'Come on, out with it . . .'

She hesitated. Tempting as it was, it didn't seem like the right moment. 'I'll tell you tonight.'

'Come on,' he said. 'What is it?'

'No, tonight.'

'What? Are you pregnant?' He'd been kidding, of course, but he'd got it. She raised her eyebrows in answer. 'Really?' he said. 'You're really pregnant?'

She nodded, suddenly unsure how he would take it. 'Are you glad?' she said. He hugged her close, and she realized he was crying.

The good kind of tears, he'd told her, and by the time he left to go to his own apartment and get ready, she'd believed him. Three hours later she was standing in the church, and he was late. She was already becoming angry with him when she saw the priest's eyes move to the church entrance behind her. She saw something in those eyes. The smallest hint of panic.

And she turned. When she saw the police, the bouquet fell from her hands. She'd looked down at it, and had left it on the floor. She'd known she didn't need it any more.

Adèle was alone in her bedroom; Thomas and Chloé had both been up and around for a couple of hours. Thomas had left the bedroom door open so the sounds of activity and the smell of breakfast would come up to her. Gentle nagging that she should get out of bed; Thomas always on guard, always there to make sure she didn't slip back into her old ways.

But not pushing. She was glad of that. At work, she knew, Thomas had a reputation for accepting nothing less than total commitment, but at home he was all kid gloves.

Even when, like this morning, they had an appointment to keep.

At last she dressed and went downstairs. She paused outside the kitchen when she heard Chloé's voice from inside.

'What's Mum doing?'

'She's having trouble getting up,' said Thomas.

'Like last time?'

Adèle felt her stomach twist, hearing Chloé say that; so much anxiety in the girl's voice. *Last time*, which had only been a few months back; Adèle had hardly left her bed for a week, the depression sudden and severe.

'No,' said Thomas. 'She's just tired. Eat your breakfast.'

Adèle took a breath and went in. Thomas saw her and beamed. 'You OK?'

'I'm sorry,' she said. She walked over and hugged him.

'It's OK, you're up now. Should I go to the church on my own?'

'No, I'll come,' she said. 'Just give me five minutes.'

He lowered his voice so Chloé wouldn't hear. 'I can call Dr Boisseau.'

'No, I'll be fine. Please, I'm OK.'

Thomas watched her closely, appraising her. After a few seconds he nodded, satisfied that she was being honest.

Thomas understood. He'd been there that day, one of the police to give her the terrible news; and after, he'd helped her pick up the pieces that her life had become.

'Sorry I was asleep when you came in,' she said. 'How was your night?'

He grimaced. 'There was a fire. You remember Michel Costa?'

'The teacher? Of course.'

'His house was destroyed. Arson.'

Her face fell. 'Was he . . .?'

'There was nobody inside,' said Thomas. 'And he was nowhere to be found. But not long after I got up this morning, there was a call. He'd –' he paused, just for a moment – 'fallen from the dam.' Thomas looked to the floor. 'We, uh, don't think anyone else was involved.'

Jumped. She knew that was what he'd meant to say. But there would be no talk of such things, not in this house. He was always looking out for her.

When they got to the empty church, Father Jean-François was as warm as ever. They talked through their options for the ceremony, Chloé sitting a few pews back playing video games with the sound turned down.

Thomas did all the talking; Adèle found it difficult to pay full attention. She kept thinking about that day ten years ago, when she'd been left waiting in this very church. She kept looking at where she'd stood; she could even remember exactly where the flowers had fallen.

'If you decide by Thursday,' said Father Jean-François, 'we can include the texts.'

'Thursday is fine,' said Thomas. He turned to Adèle. 'You'll have time to think it over.'

'I'm sorry,' she said. 'I don't really like any of them.' She could see Thomas and the priest share a concerned look.

'It's OK,' said Thomas, giving her hand a squeeze. 'We can work something out.' His phone rang. He took it out and glanced at it. 'Work,' he said. 'Sorry.'

He left the church to take the call.

'Mum,' said Chloé. 'I need the toilet.'

'There are loos through there,' said Father Jean-François, as Thomas rushed back in.

'I have to go,' said Thomas. 'Emergency. Will you be OK without me?'

Adèle saw the look on his face – she could tell this was something serious. She stood and put her hand on his arm. 'Go on,' she said. 'I'll fill you in on everything later.' He nodded, apologizing again as he hurried away.

She looked at Father Jean-François. 'It's been a busy day for him,' she said. 'There was a fire last night, and then this morning . . . Did you hear about Monsieur Costa?'

'Yes,' said Father Jean-François, grim. 'I heard. And whatever has called Thomas away, I'm sure I'll be told promptly if it's serious enough. Sometimes it seems that to be a priest is to be a conduit for bad news.' He caught himself, and gave her an awkward smile that was part-wince. 'Back to business. Were there any of the texts that appealed more than others? I'm sure I could find some you'd like.'

'I don't know. Nothing stood out.'

'Well, in that case maybe we could sing more hymns?'

She shrugged, finding it difficult to raise any enthusiasm.

'That might be better.' He looked at her, smiling kindly, saying nothing. 'What?' she said.

'I get the sense you don't trust me any more.'

'Why do you say that?'

'I know you, Adèle,' he said. 'Something's wrong and you won't tell me.'

She nodded, and he waited for her to get her thoughts in order. 'Last night,' she said. 'I thought Simon came back.' There was no judgement in the priest's eyes, only concern. 'It felt so real. He talked to me. Shouted, even. It hadn't happened to me in years. I thought it would never happen again. I thought I was cured, but . . .' She stopped, and shook her head.

'You know, Adèle, yesterday a parishioner came to see me. She was devastated because she'd spoken to her husband who'd been dead for twenty years. She told me that it was as if he'd reappeared in the flesh. As if he had come back.'

'You think that's possible?'

He shook his head, smiling. 'The people we have loved carry on living within us. It's common for us to see them again, to imagine them talking to us. And it can feel just as real as you and I talking now, because we miss them so much. We want them to be here. It's normal for Simon to be on your mind, so close to your wedding day. But you mustn't worry. Marrying Thomas won't stop you thinking about Simon, but that's OK. Once you accept that, you'll find peace. It's very important to be at peace with our ghosts. Contrary to what people think, they mean us no harm.'

Adèle nodded, trying to absorb what he was telling her. She hoped he was right. 'And if I see him again?'

'Don't turn him away,' he said. 'Talk to him.'

There was a sudden deep thump from the structure of the church, followed by a long watery rumble. Father Jean-François looked up with a resigned expression. 'The plumbing's been acting up all morning,' he said.

Then Adèle heard Chloé shout for her, fear in the girl's voice. They ran through to the toilets to find Chloé standing in front of a row of sinks. She looked towards her mother with terrified eyes. Adèle went to her and took her in her arms, staring at the sinks.

In each, dirty water was rising slowly from the open plughole, as the room filled with the smell of decay.

13

Alain Hubert hadn't liked the look of the guy from the moment he came in.

The diner Alain ran was as brightly cheesy as the food it served, fifties-America themed with the building mocked up to look like an aluminium railway car, albeit about three times as wide as the real thing. It was on the edge of town, the last eatery on the road south, and most mornings the place was quiet enough to let him run it alone, extra staff starting shortly before the lunchtime rush.

This morning the diner's only customer was the strange woman who'd been waiting at the door when he'd opened up; she'd then muttered endlessly about the prices, accusing him of trying to mug his customers before finally ordering a big plate of food.

The comment about mugging stung him, although the woman couldn't have known about his less-than-savoury past. It had been a long time since Alain had given up that kind of thing.

'You're not homeless?' he said, noting the old clothes she was wearing and her sour demeanour.

She gave him a curious look, then sighed and disdainfully handed him a fifty-euro note. 'Toy money,' she said, shaking her head. 'What was wrong with the franc?'

It was the kind of comment he expected from older customers, but she looked to be in her mid-forties. Homeless or not, there was something about her he just didn't like, but she seemed clean enough and she had cash. Alain settled on *eccentric*. He hoped she didn't plan on becoming a regular customer.

Saturday was normally deserted until eleven, giving him time to get his head around the weekly stock reorder, but so far he'd hardly even got started on it. It meant he would probably have to stay late to get it done, so by the time the ruffled guy in the suit came in Alain was already in a bad mood.

The man came over. 'Hello.'

Alain looked him up and down. Young guy, unruly black hair, good-looking and confident. It made Alain dislike him even more.

'Yes?'

'What will this get me?' He held out some loose change.

Alain doubted there was more than forty cents there. He sneered. 'Get lost.'

'Just a piece of bread? I'm starving.'

Something about the man bothered him. Smug, sure, but that wasn't all. He smelt of trouble, and Alain wanted him out. 'I said, get lost.' They locked eyes for a moment, but the man shrugged. He didn't look pleased, of course, but Alain was happy he'd got the message.

As the guy turned and took a step towards the door, Alain went behind the counter, turning his back on him as he did so.

Big mistake.

Alain felt the glass hit the back of his head. He fell to the floor, and the next thing he felt was the bastard's fists impacting his face. Two, three times, the guy's eyes on fire, lost in his rage.

'Please,' Alain managed, and his attacker stared, as if realizing what he was doing. There was an instant of shame on his face before he stood and backed off, then made for the door. Alain got up slow, just catching sight of the guy sauntering off down the road as though nothing had happened.

He looked over to the woman, who was still sitting, eating. 'You saw that?' he said. She shrugged, completely uninterested. He called an ambulance. By the time they came, the woman had gone.

The police got there a few minutes after the ambulance, long enough for Alain to work out what had made him so uneasy when the guy who'd attacked him had first come through the door.

There had been something feral in those eyes. The anger was already there, just waiting for an excuse to explode. Alain had known more than his fair share of people like that in the past. Hell, the desire to get away from that kind of company was why he'd finally got his act together.

A guy like that was always bad news. There was no telling what he was capable of.

14

Léna woke. It had been a long night, and she hadn't fallen asleep until close to dawn.

A *long* night.

Her parents had run upstairs the moment they'd heard the screaming, hers and Camille's. Her mum had held Camille and offered her hand out to Léna, and all of them had cried and cried, until Léna had insisted on explanations. Camille had woken in the mountain, she was told. Camille had walked home. Camille was back, and prayers had been answered.

Léna listened, and found herself growing colder with every word, colder and more frightened.

Camille's distressed eyes were trained on her the whole time. 'What happened to Léna?' Camille asked, and it took Léna a moment to realize she was talking about how old she looked. *She doesn't know*, Léna thought. *She thinks it's still four years ago. She doesn't know what happened to the coach.*

Léna could see it in her father's face too, and in her mother's. The news had to be broken to her. They went to her mum's room, to a drawer where all the photo albums were kept. Alongside them was another book of memories – morbid, Léna had always thought, to keep what amounted to a scrapbook of the accident, of the memorial service, but her mother's mental state had hardly been *even*, at the time. Or since.

She watched Camille hear how most of their friends had died; how *she* had died. Léna watched the terror grow on her dead sister's face.

And she felt nothing. Only unease. Watching, and wondering what it was that sat in tears a few metres away.

Léna had excused herself, run to her room, gone to bed fully clothed and unable to stop shivering. Sleep had come eventually, and when she had woken the urge to stay in her room was overwhelming.

But she couldn't stay there forever. At last, Léna got up and ventured out to the landing. She opened the bathroom door and managed not to jump when she saw Camille standing in front of the mirror, staring at her own reflection.

'Sorry,' Léna said, backing out.

'Wait,' said Camille. 'Do I scare you?'

She lied. 'No.'

'I scare myself,' said Camille. She took a step towards Léna. 'What happened to me?' Another step. Camille went to embrace her, to put her head on Léna's shoulder. It was too much. Léna moved back and closed the door, breathing hard. She went to her room and sat, restless, on her bed for over an hour, until she couldn't sit any more. Then she went downstairs to find that her parents and Camille were having breakfast around the table.

'Anyone want a yoghurt?' asked her mum, overly bright, fussing. 'Want some tea, Camille?'

'Yes, thanks.'

Léna watched, frustration growing. Her mum saw the look in her eye and gave her a forced smile.

'Léna . . . Do you want some coffee, maybe?'

Léna shook her head and took out a cigarette, enjoying

the disapproving look her dad gave her. Disapproving, but silent. *Let them shout at me*, she thought, *and I'll damn well shout back.* 'So is this your plan?' she said.

Her mum looked wary. 'What do you mean?'

'Pretend everything is normal?'

'No,' said her dad wearily. 'Nothing is normal. But *this . . .*' He gestured towards her. 'This isn't helping.'

Léna could feel everything bubble up inside her. 'You're both crazy,' she said. 'How do we even know it's her? She might be an impostor.'

'Stop it, Léna,' said her mum, suddenly looking on the verge of tears.

'What? It happens. People pose as someone else.'

Camille stood, and shouted back: 'Who else would I be?'

Léna scowled at her. 'You're someone who read about the accident and realized you look like her. So you came here to see what you could get.'

'You're being ridiculous,' said her mum.

'*I'm* being ridiculous? I tell you who she *can't* be, Mum. She can't be Camille. *That's* ridiculous.'

'How do you think I feel?' said Camille. 'Put yourself in my place.'

'I don't care how you feel,' said Léna. 'You're a fucking liar.'

Her dad stood and yelled, glaring at her. 'That's enough!'

She glared back for a moment, then walked out, making sure to slam the door hard. She stood in the driveway, fuming. After a few seconds her father came out too.

'Why are you taking it out on her?' he said.

'My God! Doesn't anyone realize what's going on here? Camille can't just come back like this. It's not possible.' She looked at her dad, loading her voice with as much sarcasm as she could muster. 'Is it like *baby Jesus*? She died, and was resurrected?'

'Please, Léna.' He looked around at the neighbouring houses. 'People will hear.'

'What? You think you can hide her?' The look of near-shame on his face told her that was exactly what he'd been thinking. 'If you think it's so fucking *great*, why not shout about it?' she said, flinging her arms around and raising her voice. 'We should throw a big party to celebrate.'

Her dad took hold of her. 'I said that's *enough*!'

'Or what? Will you hit me?'

It was a low blow; her dad's face fell. He took a long breath before looking up at her, almost despairing. 'I don't know how this has happened, but your sister needs you.'

'My *sister* died,' said Léna. 'Do you understand? She's dead. And while *that thing* is in the house . . . I won't be.'

She started walking.

Claire was in the kitchen alone when Jérôme came back in.

'Where's Camille?' he asked.

'She's gone to her room. She wants to be left on her own. Maybe she can get some sleep. Where's Léna?'

'She's gone out,' he said, resigned. 'She needs some time. Please try not to worry – she'll come home later. I think I'll go back to my apartment and change, if you'll be OK? I'll be back soon.'

She nodded, then thought of something. 'Jérôme? What if you brought some of your things here? For Camille's sake?'

Jérôme raised an eyebrow. 'What would Pierre think?'

She shook her head, scolding: *There was no need for that.*
'I'm sorry,' he said. 'You're right. I'll see you later. And
really, don't worry about Léna.'

'I'll try,' she said. She saw his eyes flick upwards to
Camille's room, but she stopped herself commenting on it.
He was still clearly uneasy in Camille's presence, but he had
to get past his concerns, for all their sakes. She didn't even
think he'd held his daughter since her return; he might not
even have touched her. How could Léna accept Camille, if
Jérôme didn't?

It would happen, though, Claire knew. She could tell
they had no doubts about who Camille was, not really;
Jérôme's wariness and Léna's denial were symptoms of their
unwillingness to accept the miracle they'd been given, this
second chance. Soon, they would see it for what it was: a gift
from God.

She called Pierre and asked him to come round. She hugged
him when he arrived but there was a formality to it, a
symbol of how their relationship had to be, at least for the
time being. They sat and she told him of the unease in the
house, and of Léna going off somewhere.

'I called her several times,' she said. 'She won't pick up.'

Pierre smiled at her. 'Doesn't she often do that? There's
no need to worry about her, or Jérôme. They'll accept her,
Claire. Soon enough. Has Camille said much? Has she . . .'
He paused, as if he was having trouble finding the right
words. 'Has she any memory of the time between the crash
and now?'

'No,' said Claire. Pierre looked disappointed. 'She
remembers everything before the accident. Her life, all her

friends . . .' Claire looked away, thinking of Camille's face when she'd learned that most of those friends were dead. 'Have you happened to speak with any of the other parents?'

He nodded. 'Some. Of course, I've not said anything about Camille, but I thought, perhaps . . .'

'That maybe others had come back? So did I.' She looked at him, expectant.

He shook his head. 'It seems not,' he said.

A voice came from the stairs, a combative edge to it. 'Hello, doctor. Still no bag?' It was Camille, looking at Pierre with suspicion.

'Did you manage to sleep?' asked Claire.

'No, not for a second.' She turned to Pierre. 'What's your explanation for that?'

'Everything has an explanation,' he said.

Camille sighed. 'Great.' She went to the front door and grabbed a coat.

Claire stood, immediately tense. 'Where are you going?'

'Out. I'm suffocating here.'

Claire looked to Pierre for support. He stood and went over to Camille. 'That isn't a good idea,' he said, putting a hand on her shoulder.

She brushed the hand away. 'What do you know? Who are you anyway?'

'Pierre is a good friend,' said Claire. 'He's here to help. You can trust him.'

Camille didn't look at all convinced. 'So tell me, *Pierre*. Am I some kind of zombie?'

He shook his head slowly, smiling. 'No, you're not some kind of zombie.'

'That's not what Léna thinks,' said Camille. 'She said I

was an impostor, but she doesn't think that, not for a second. She knows who I am, and it scares her.'

'Léna missed you so much,' said Claire. 'It's difficult for her to accept that this is real.'

'So if I'm not a zombie, what am I?'

Pierre smiled. 'You're a miracle.'

'I don't believe in miracles,' said Camille, her voice flat.

'It's the truth,' said Pierre. 'I went to your funeral. I saw you in your coffin. And here you are. You've been granted a new life, a new existence.'

'But why me? There were forty people on the coach. Why was I saved?'

Pierre shook his head. 'I don't know,' he said. 'We don't have all the answers, but there's no need for you to be afraid. What's happening to you is miraculous, however you choose to believe it's come to be. Someone is watching over you.'

She looked at Claire, lost. 'I just want a normal life, like before.'

My little girl, Claire thought. How could Léna and Jérôme not see that? How could they deny her? She wrapped her daughter in her arms and renewed her vow to keep her safe. Whatever happened.

Soon after Pierre left, Camille went to her room again to try and get some sleep. Claire made a start on preparing dinner, and as she did she realized she was smiling: making dinner for Camille. Her worries about Léna were still with her, yes; but those were everyday worries, and miracles always won out over the mundane.

She went upstairs to freshen up, but as she reached the

doorway to her own bedroom she stood dumbfounded, staring. The drawer with the photo albums was open; the album they had shown Camille had been torn into pieces and strewn across the bed, alongside another one that contained pictures of Léna.

Cuttings and photographs alike had been torn up; Léna at every age between the time of the crash and now. Everything Camille had missed.

Claire stared at the destruction for a long time, appalled that Camille would do such a thing. Resentment was inevitable, she thought, but even so. This was unacceptable.

She went to Camille's door and opened it carefully in case she was asleep. Her daughter was sitting on her bed staring at the wall, her expression blank.

'Camille?' There was no movement, no answer. '*Camille?*'

Then her daughter's eyes seemed to focus. She looked around herself, disoriented, before turning to face her mother. After a few seconds, she smiled. 'What?'

'Sorry, were you trying to sleep?'

'Yes, but no luck. What is it?'

'Did you . . . did you go into my bedroom?'

'No,' said Camille.

'Please,' said Claire. 'You can be honest. Tell me if you . . . touched anything.' She recalled the blank look on Camille's face as she'd entered the bedroom, and thought of sleepwalkers. 'Maybe you don't remember?'

'I swear, Mum, I haven't been out of the room. I promise. Why are you asking?'

Claire looked at her daughter for a long moment before shaking her head. She was telling the truth, Claire decided.

The truth, as far as Camille was aware of it. 'No reason,' said Claire.

There was no need to tell her, Claire thought to herself; no need to tell anyone.

She fetched a bin bag and returned to her bedroom to tidy the mess. As she collected the ripped pieces, she stopped when she realized the covers of the albums had also been torn in two. One was thick vinyl-covered card; the other was leather. Torn, just as easily as the paper of the photographs.

She put it all in the bin bag out of her sight, not wanting to think about it.

Because there was no need to worry. No need to worry at all.

15

Hell of a day, Inspector Laure Valère thought. The night before had been interesting, with the Costa man vanishing after setting his home on fire and almost taking his neighbour's house along for the ride. Then this morning, the old man had been found. A phone call came in from the technicians at the dam, and Laure, as the senior officer on duty, had packed Alcide and Bruno off to handle the scene. She'd called Captain Pellerin at home to let him know – Thomas liked to be kept up to date on anything significant, even when, as this morning, he'd been off duty.

Laure had been living in the town for nine years now, and Michel Costa had only been the second suicide at the dam in all that time. That struck her as odd. Perfect location for the suicidal, offering great views and melodrama for those wanting to make a statement on their way out.

And certainty of death, of course. A little messy, from the sound of Alcide's voice when he'd called in.

The mess had kept coming, though.

The attack at the diner was more run-of-the-mill. The perpetrator had done a bit of a number on the manager, who had, frankly, been lucky to get away without needing stitches on the back of his head where the glass had hit. Bruno had known more about the manager than Laure did; Alain Hubert had been in trouble with the law many a time, when he was a younger man. With the only witness leaving the scene before the police got there, there was more than a little suspicion that Hubert had been paid a visit by some old associate. For all the man's protestations about having left criminal behaviour behind him long ago, it wouldn't be a surprise if debt – unofficial and unpaid – had been behind the assault.

Still, they had CCTV footage, and the town's security camera system was being used to keep an eye out in case the assailant made an appearance, but surely he was long gone.

Yet that hadn't been the end of the mess. The worst of all was still to come.

A man had been walking his dog through the underpass by the town hall when he came across what he thought was a woman's corpse hidden in the bushes at the tunnel exit. As second in command, Laure had gone to the scene, only learning on her arrival that the victim was still alive.

She had been stabbed repeatedly in the abdomen at least a dozen times, but it was even more disturbing than that: a ragged fragment of human tissue sitting on the skin of the woman's belly had been tentatively identified by one of the paramedics. *From the woman's liver,* he'd said, giving her the information in a whisper away from other ears, because that paramedic knew about the older cases, seven years before.

Laure felt herself grow cold. She thought of Julie, then: of that New Year's night when they had gone their separate ways, Laure heading back to the party, Julie back to her apartment. It had been the next afternoon before Laure had surfaced, hungover, to the terrible news.

From the scene of the present stabbing, she called the captain at home once more to inform him of this new discovery, and he told her he would come to the station immediately. Seven years before, there had been two killings, one survivor, and half a dozen suspects. None of the suspects panned out, but the man who'd been police captain at the time, hounded by the mayor, had done his own piece of hounding – he and a group of like-minded officers had focused on one of the suspects and had pushed hard. They managed to scrabble together a sloppy case from hearsay and coincidence, and ran with it until the case fell apart in a mess of litigation. Too close to the victim at the time, Laure had watched it all happen from the sidelines.

The fallout had been the end of the old captain's career. The mayor, just as culpable in the eyes of some, had tried to save his position by funding the state-of-the-art CCTV system which the town had ended up with. Ultimately, though, the only thing that saved him was the fact that the attacks stopped.

Stopped, and no one was ever brought to book. A bigshot forensic psychologist had come down from Paris and pronounced that the killer had either left the area or was dead, since if he'd still been around, the killings would have just kept going. The investigation petered out, and the files were left open.

Back at the station now, Thomas summoned her and Bruno to his office to discuss the attack. She dug out the files from the previous cases, and brought along the photographs of the new victim. As they laid them all out together, old pictures and new, it was impossible to deny the similarities in the injuries.

'Christ,' said Thomas. Bruno was just staring.

'Her name is Lucy Clarsen,' said Laure. 'She's been a barmaid at the Lake Pub for the past year.'

'Shit, yes,' said Bruno. 'I know who you mean. Alcide's taken a shine to her.'

'As far as we know,' said Laure, 'she has no family in the area, but we're keeping the identity quiet until we've been able to track down relatives. And of course, we're keeping the details of the attack from the press.'

'Bruno,' said Thomas, 'once we're done here can you have a word with Alcide? Let him know about Lucy Clarsen, and make sure he understands that he can't discuss the case with anyone.'

Bruno nodded, then started to look through the older case notes.

'So what do we have?' asked Thomas.

'She's still critical,' said Laure. 'She'd probably been lying there for at least four hours. Last I spoke to the doctor treating her, he said it was a miracle she was alive. The blood loss was severe.'

'And the diner attack?' said Thomas. 'Could that be linked?'

'Possible,' she said. 'The manager hadn't seen the guy around before, and the assault was vicious.'

'CCTV of the tunnel?'

'Indistinct, but it shows a guy in a hooded top, no image of his face, no way to rule the diner assailant in or out at the moment.'

'OK.' Thomas took a long breath. 'Thoughts?'

Bruno stepped in. 'The manager didn't recognize his assailant, so if it is the same man maybe he hasn't been around for a long time and he's come back. It would explain the hiatus in the attacks.'

Laure's turn. 'There was one key suspect before, sir, and he has a link to the victim. We should bring him in. Now.'

Thomas raised an eyebrow. 'He was cleared, Laure.'

'Captain Onesto didn't think so.'

'Onesto was under too much pressure to get a result. The evidence wasn't there, and nobody who knew the suspect thought it was plausible.' Laure started to interrupt; Thomas held up a hand. '*But* . . . we have to talk to him anyway. Bruno, bring the pub manager in for interview. Don't tell him anything.'

Bruno looked surprised. 'You mean Toni Guillard? He was the suspect?' Bruno had only transferred to the town three years ago.

Thomas nodded and sent him on his way. Once the office door closed, he turned to her. 'Laure?'

She understood what he was asking. 'I'm fine, sir.'

'I need to know you can handle this. If it's too personal . . .'

'As I said, sir. I'm fine.' After all, it hadn't been personal for a long time.

She reviewed the old cases as she waited for the pub manager to be brought in. The details had been kept from the press back then, of course. Stabbings, they were called; the ferocity of the attacks and the grim mutilations were not revealed. Julie's identity had been protected; Laure had always feared it would become common knowledge, but mercifully it never did, even after the inevitable rumours of the severity of the assaults emerged.

Among the police, the attacker immediately earned the nickname of the Cannibal. Each of the three attacks had been in a different part of town. The last had been in the same underpass where Lucy Clarsen had been assaulted; it would make sense to keep a careful eye on the other two locations, in case the killer was reliving old memories.

The pub manager was a huge man, physically imposing from sheer height and bulk, and a little overweight. He was no athlete, that was certain, but he was easily capable of overpowering someone. When Bruno led him in Laure found herself looking at him, picturing him with a knife in his hand. It didn't take much imagination.

'Have a seat,' said Thomas. The man sat. Laure watched his face carefully; his expression was wary. 'Do you know what happened to Lucy Clarsen?'

'No,' said Toni Guillard. He didn't exude confidence by any means, but if anything he was bemused rather than frightened.

'Was she working with you last night?'

'Yes.' Matter of fact.

'At what time did she leave work?'

'I don't know exactly. About two a.m.?'

'What were you doing when she left?'

'Closing up.'

'Alone?'

'Yes.'

'Then what did you do?'

'I went home.'

The captain paused for a moment. 'Can someone confirm that?'

'Why all these questions?'

Laure couldn't hold back any longer. It was time to push him. 'Seven years ago you were suspected of murder and attempted murder.'

'It wasn't me,' said the man, fear showing in his eyes for the first time. 'I was innocent.'

She thrust a photograph of Lucy Clarsen's injuries in front of him, feeling her anger grow. 'Look at your barmaid. It's a miracle she's still alive.' The man just stared at the image, horror in his eyes. 'You're the one who put her in that state. And the others, too. But if that wasn't sick enough, you started to *eat* them.'

'That's enough,' said Thomas, glaring at her. She knew she'd overstepped the mark. 'You can go, Inspector. I'll take it from here.'

She looked down at the floor, angry with herself. 'Yes, sir.'

Then Toni looked up from the photograph, dazed. Gawping at both of them. 'I don't believe it,' he said. 'It isn't possible . . .'

She and Thomas shared a look. The man's reaction was genuine.

He was as shocked as they were. He wasn't their killer.

16

After Léna had walked away from her father, she had ended up where she always did. Even for the afternoon, the Lake Pub was quiet. Frédéric was there as usual, playing pool with a few others. He looked over at her from time to time but at the moment she just wanted to sit alone with a beer and unpick what she was feeling.

She didn't know how to deal with what was happening, but the idea that her mum was right – that Camille really had come back, that a miracle *had* happened – was difficult for her to accept. She *wanted* that version to be true, wanted it badly. That was why she was so cautious, she thought. And there was something else about Camille, now, that fed into her unease. She'd always known what her sister was thinking, always. Sometimes even when they were apart, she'd known. But last night and this morning? Nothing. Her sister, if that was what she really was, had been unreadable.

Then Simon, the dark-haired guy from the night before, came in, looking around. He saw her and came straight over, a cagey look about him. She watched him with a little suspicion. He was wearing the same clothes as last night, his suit a little crumpled. She wondered if he'd slept in it.

'Well, if it isn't our mysterious regular,' she said. 'How are things? Feeling any less vague these days?'

'Where did you say Adèle works?' he asked.

She wondered if the guy even *had* a sense of humour. 'Ah. Straight to business. She works at the library.'

'Near the church?'

'No,' she said. She tried to think how long ago the new library had opened. Six years, at least. 'Next to the town hall. I thought you said you lived around here?'

'I've been away.'

'Right.' She peered at him; he looked back at her, clearly uncomfortable. 'So why do I feel like I know you?' she said.

He shrugged. 'Just that kind of face.' Then he thanked her and went on his way.

'What did he want?' It was Frédéric, showing up conveniently to check on her.

'To sleep with me.' She grinned. Frédéric said nothing, just looked hurt – a little more hurt than she'd intended. 'But he's not my type.'

He held up the pool cue he had in his hand. 'You want a game?'

She shrugged. Why not? She could do with the distraction. She beat him with ease, relishing the discomfort he felt in defeat – something he always found hard to mask. He could be very competitive, could Frédéric, however much he claimed otherwise.

'Another game?' he asked.

'If you can stand it,' she smirked. 'Back in a minute.'

She headed for the toilets, and on her return two police officers came in through the front door and walked towards the bar. She hung around to see what the excitement was. They asked for Toni, had a quiet word with him, then left the pub with the bemused manager in tow.

She turned to the barman, Samuel. 'Any idea what that was about?'

'Not a clue,' said Samuel.

'Did Toni leave you in charge?' she said, a coy smile on her lips.

Samuel scowled. 'No freebies, Léna.' She gave him a worth-a-shot shrug before he turned to serve a customer.

Léna drifted over to the windows at the front and watched Toni get inside the police car. After they'd gone, she was about to head back to Frédéric when something stopped her. The wall beside her was covered in photos, old and new; full of the regulars of the Lake Pub. One of the pictures was very familiar. It had her in it, nine years old, sitting and pretending to play the drums. Beside her was the guitarist from the band that had played that night. She moved closer, suddenly feeling cold.

Dark, curly hair. Looking the same. Looking *exactly* the same. Simon. She wondered what he wanted with Adèle Werther.

She went back to Frédéric, dazed. He could see something was up. 'You want to go?' he asked.

'Can people come back from the dead?' she said.

'Yeah, sure,' he said. 'In *films*. Not in real life. Just as well, or we'd all be fucked.'

She glared at him. 'Forget it.' She started to walk away.

'Wait,' Frédéric said. 'I'm sorry. Léna, what is it?'

She ignored him and kept on walking, leaving the pub. Frédéric took the hint and let her go. This wasn't something anyone else could help with. The only person who might have the answers was Camille, and she either didn't know or wasn't letting on.

She took the long route home, liking the solitude. When she got there, her parents were both at the door before she'd even closed it behind her.

'Why was your phone off?' her mum asked, her voice sharp, something usually reserved for when Léna came in at two in the morning.

Léna looked to her dad for an explanation.

'Camille,' he said. He looked exhausted. 'She slipped out. She's been gone for an hour, at least.'

'Why did you let her do that?' said Léna.

'I thought she was sleeping,' snapped her mum. 'She'll come back, won't she?' Her face went pale. 'What if she doesn't? What if that was all the time we were allowed? If you two rejected her, and now she's gone away?'

'She'll come back any minute, Claire,' said her dad.

'I couldn't bear to lose her. Not *again*.'

Léna offered to go out to try and find her, but her mum gave her a fiery look: 'Don't even think about leaving this house,' she said.

The three of them sat in the living room, in complete silence. Half an hour later the front door opened, and they all hurried over.

Claire grabbed Camille in a hug, palpably relieved. 'Sweetheart, where were you?' she said. 'You mustn't leave like that. I was so worried.'

Camille looked as if she'd been crying. 'What could even happen?' she said, sounding wretched. 'I'm already dead.'

'Where were you?' asked her father.

'The Lake Pub. I wanted to see Frédéric.'

Too quickly, Léna asked: 'And did you?'

The more she spoke, the closer Camille came to tears. 'I

watched through a window. I saw him and Lucho playing pool. Marc was there too. I wanted to talk to Frédéric, but I didn't know what would happen. Then Marc came outside. He spoke to me.'

Her dad's face darkened. 'He recognized you?' Léna felt it, too: the fear of discovery, the complications it would bring. She felt nauseous at the thought.

'No,' said Camille miserably. 'He didn't. He looked at me for a moment and I thought he'd recognized me, but then he asked if I was new in town. So I ran.' She started to cry. 'How could he not know who I *was*?' Her mum stepped forwards and comforted her.

Léna turned to her dad, whispering: 'Why wouldn't he recognize her?' Marc hadn't really known them well before the crash, but surely . . .

'I don't know,' said her dad.

'But if it's really her,' said Léna, 'I can't see how—'

Her mother interrupted. '*If* it's really her? You expect someone to recognize Camille, when you and your father both deny it?'

'Claire, I—' said her dad, but her mum cut in.

'Look at her. *Look* at her. Whatever you choose to believe, at least believe your *eyes*.'

Camille was watching both of them, and Léna knew she could see their lingering doubt. Camille ran up the stairs, sobbing. Claire gave them both a disapproving look before going after her.

Léna looked at her dad and shook her head. 'Do other people even see what we see?'

Jérôme sighed. 'The moment I saw her, every part of my mind was telling me it was impossible, that it couldn't be her. Perhaps that's all it is – people see someone who looks very like Camille, but their minds don't allow them to consider that it *is* her.'

'But it *can't* be her,' said Léna, her voice almost a whisper.

'Léna, your mother's right. I don't understand what it means, or what the future holds. You say it can't be her. But tell me, and tell me honestly – seeing Camille run from us just now, didn't you feel ashamed?'

He watched for her reaction. She looked away. Yes, she'd felt ashamed; because however impossible the situation was, seeing Camille in tears had caused her real pain. Her denial was rooted in desperation, not in what she truly felt. When she looked back at him, he had a weary smile. 'You too?' she said.

'Yes,' he replied.

Léna nodded. 'It's not going to be easy.'

'Of course it's not,' he said.

Léna slowly went up to Camille's room and pushed the door ajar. Camille was sitting on her bed, her mum beside her, holding her. They both looked up at Léna.

'Can I have a minute?' said Léna. 'Alone?'

'Who with?' asked her mum, defensive.

'With my sister.'

Claire's tired face broke into a cautious smile. She stood from the bed and gave Léna a brief hug before she left.

Camille looked at Léna warily. 'I'm your sister now?'

Léna sighed and sat down beside her. 'I'm trying. It's not easy for any of us. But I'm sorry. I let you down.'

Camille sniffed and wiped her eyes. 'I guess that's a start.'

Léna looked at her, uncertain whether she should tell

Camille what she'd seen at the pub. But if it could help her sister, she supposed she had no choice. 'There was something else,' she said.

'Yes?'

'At the Lake Pub, I saw someone. I think he's like you.'

'Like me, how?' said Camille.

'Dead,' said Léna. 'I think he's dead.'

17

Adèle was tidying part of the children's section in the library when she had another vision of Simon. The area was quiet, deserted; she had a window of opportunity to clear up before another group of children was due to arrive. There was only the young man wearing his crumpled wedding suit, looking, turning, seeing her. She watched him for a while before walking towards him, mindful of what Father Jean-François had said.

Make peace with your ghosts.

God, he looked so real. So *solid*. In the years since his death, whenever she'd thought she'd seen him it had been fleeting, or late and in the darkness of her bedroom. Never so much detail, not before. He looked exactly as he had the last time she'd seen him alive. Her vision blurred as the tears came.

'You were always so handsome,' she said gently. 'Just because I'm marrying Thomas, it doesn't mean I'll forget you. I won't. You're part of my life, then and always.' He was watching her with the half-smile she had loved. She hadn't always known what he was thinking, what mood he was in. Hadn't always been sure which Simon she was with. But that smile, like a shy little boy's, was a sign.

She was with the Simon who loved her unconditionally. Not the dark, angry man he sometimes became.

'I won't forget you,' she said. 'For a time, I tried. I was falling apart, and I had no choice. I wanted it to be like I'd never met you. But I couldn't do it.' Her eyes roamed over his face and she smiled, joyful at how rich her memories must still be to conjure such a vision. 'I know you're a ghost. I know you don't really exist. It doesn't scare me to see you. Not any more. I won't ask you to leave again. It's wonderful for you to be back.' She reached up with her hand, up to his face, his hair, her mind allowing her to feel the touch of him. She closed her eyes, and smiled. 'Even if it's only in my head.'

A group of kids charged in through the far stairwell, the noise startling her. Her hand was suddenly just touching air. She opened her eyes.

Simon was gone.

Laure came through to the captain's office, knowing she wasn't bringing the news he would have wanted.

'The assailant from the diner has turned up, sir,' she told him. 'CCTV spotted him leaving the library building. A patrol was sent and he was apprehended a few minutes ago.'

Thomas's face lit up with expectation. 'And? Anything linking him to the Clarsen assault?'

She shook her head. 'Nothing. He's a little dishevelled, looks like he spent all night in what he's wearing. They're checking his jacket at the moment, but I don't get the feeling he's our man.'

'Don't discount him so quickly, Inspector,' said Thomas. 'Any idea who he is?'

'Well, there's the thing. He didn't tell us, but we checked his fingerprints. Those prints are on our files from an affray charge a dozen years back, but for a man who died ten years ago. The dead man's name is Simon Delaître.'

For a moment Thomas stared at her, his face turning pale under the fluorescent lighting. 'Simon Delaître?'

'Yes,' said Laure. 'You know the name?' The captain said nothing, just kept staring. 'Have you seen anything like this before?'

Thomas seemed to focus again. 'Anything like what?'

'He must have given a false name,' said Laure. 'But tricking the system shouldn't be that easy. Someone must have slipped up.'

Thomas stood. 'Come with me,' he said. 'We'll talk to him.'

They both entered the room where the man sat in handcuffs. He looked up, his expression one every police officer knew well: surly indifference. Affray, twelve years back; the diner assault this morning. Laure would be surprised if there hadn't been a string of other offences, convicted or otherwise.

She caught the look in her captain's eye when he first saw the man sitting there. Extremely wary, shocked almost; then he snapped out of it and nodded to Laure to throw the first question.

'We have a small problem,' said Laure. 'According to our files, you're dead. How do you explain that?'

'That's your job,' said the man.

'Your name is Simon Delaître. Is that right?' He nodded. Laure held up a print from the diner's CCTV footage, the man clearly identifiable. 'Do you deny that this is you?' The man shook his head.

Before she could ask her next question, Thomas cut in: 'Do you know Adèle Werther?'

'Yes,' said the man. 'Why do you ask that?'

'That means you must have known Simon Delaître. They used to live together.' Thomas looked at Laure; she knew the surprise was written across her face. Laure's house was next door to Thomas's. She knew Adèle a little, knew that her fiancé had died a decade ago. She hadn't known the details, nor the man's name, but it explained her captain's earlier reaction.

'So,' said Thomas, 'you must know Simon Delaître is dead.'

The man's expression of indifference didn't change.

'Simon Delaître is *dead*,' said Thomas. 'What happened? Did you pretend to be him when you had to give your fingerprints?'

The man glared at Thomas, ignoring the question. 'Who is Adèle to *you*?'

The captain stood, tired of it. 'Put him back in a cell, Inspector. We're keeping him in custody until we work out who the hell he is.'

18

Julie went to the police station that afternoon, reluctant and wary. The nagging certainty that the boy's parents would be going through hell made her do it, but she was cautious. She left Victor alone in her apartment – she wanted to find out what she could, not simply hand him over, and bringing him along would have risked that decision being taken out of her hands. Especially if Laure saw her with him.

But even without the boy, she didn't want to bump into Laure.

Old wounds.

When she arrived, she felt conspicuous. The lights in the station were overly bright, as if they wanted to illuminate any dark recesses in the minds of those who came through the doors. Julie always preferred to stay in the background, out of sight, but there was nowhere here that allowed that comfort. She felt eyes watching her.

She scoured the noticeboards in the reception area, just in case it was that simple; surely if Victor was a local child, something might be there. She found a missing-persons poster: there were no children on it, but as she looked at the poster, at the array of lost faces, she felt a kind of kinship. It was why she felt such a connection with Victor, she supposed. They were both lost.

'Hello, can I help you?'

She turned to the police officer, caught off guard. 'I, uh, just wanted to know if you had a missing-persons report, for a young boy, brown eyes, brown hair, about nine, maybe younger.'

'Why?'

Julie thought quickly, stumbling over her words. 'Well, because as I, uh, was going home yesterday, I saw a little boy. It was late, he looked lost . . . I just wondered.'

'Didn't you ask him if he was lost?'

'No, not really.'

'Not really?'

She paused, suddenly aware of what she was saying, scared of giving herself away. 'No, because I was on a bus. He was by the side of the road. So all I did was see him as we passed. Look, it doesn't matter.' This had been a mistake, she thought. Time to go.

'Wait. You saw his eye colour from the bus?'

She nodded, hoping she sounded more convincing than she felt. 'Yes.'

'You could have reported it sooner,' said the officer, with a sigh. 'Come with me. I'll take your statement.'

'I have to give a statement?'

'Of course.'

He led her off to a small room. It didn't really take long, but it felt much longer; sitting there answering questions, trying to avoid too much detail that might contradict itself. She kept it vague, but by the end she knew what she needed to know. They had no reports of a missing child locally; nationally, none fitted the description. It made her more certain that her fear for Victor was justified, that he was running from something too difficult for him to talk about. What else could prevent parents from reporting a lost child?

A nagging voice was telling her that she should hand

Victor over to the police anyway, and let them deal with it
– that she'd done her part, and it was time for him to move
on. But the police failed people all the time, and until she
knew Victor's story, she wasn't going to let that happen.

She made one detour before she went home, to buy
something for Victor.

Outside her door, she hunted in her bag for the keys.
Her heart sank as she heard the sound of her neighbour's
door opening.

'Hello, Julie!' said Nathalie Payet. The woman's voice
was like fingernails on a chalkboard.

Julie sighed inwardly and kept looking for her keys; she
found them, and made a mental note always to have them in
her hand in future by the time she reached her door. 'Hello,
Mademoiselle Payet.'

The woman made a show of looking around. 'Your
young friend went back home?'

If she thought she could have got away with it, Julie
would have lied. 'No,' she said. 'He's inside.'

Her neighbour looked scandalized. 'Really? But you
went out. Isn't he a little young to be at home by himself?'

'He's a good boy,' said Julie. 'I had, um, an urgent
appointment. I wasn't long.'

'Mmm. OK. So, is he family?'

Julie looked her steadily in the eye. 'Yes.'

The woman raised an eyebrow but dropped the topic. A
sudden gleeful eagerness spread across her face. 'Have you
heard about Michel Costa, the old teacher?'

'No.' Julie tensed.

'You haven't? This morning, he . . .' She made a slitting

motion across her throat, and Julie felt the floor shift under her.

'What?'

'He jumped from the top of the dam.' The woman smiled, as if it was some crass titillation she was passing on, not the death of an old man. 'Without a bungee rope!' She let her words settle for a moment, watching Julie's reaction, then her smile suddenly vanished and she feigned sympathy. 'You knew him, didn't you?'

'Not really,' said Julie. 'A little.' She felt sick. She could have been the last person to see the man alive. Worse, she might be partly to blame. She'd spotted something wrong. Nothing urgent, nothing that would have indicated any-thing like *this*, but still. She knew that she had let the old man down.

She wondered if she should talk to the police about it; it was certainly possible that they would discover she was one of the last people to have seen him, and come to question her. *Well*, she thought, *if that happens, so be it*. But if not, she wanted nothing more to do with the police.

'Poor Monsieur Costa,' said her neighbour, turning on an air of melancholy. 'He burned his house down before he did it, you know. He was nearly seventy-five, wasn't he? He didn't have long to wait. Must have been desperate to end it all like that. He's to be buried in the old chapel graveyard, by his wife's grave. The funeral will be tomorrow, I heard.'

'So soon?' said Julie.

The woman lowered her voice and looked around, as if she was imparting a great secret. 'Isn't it. I suppose there are no relatives to summon, and they'll certainly not want an open coffin . . .' She pulled a face. 'But they obviously want it out of the way as quickly as possible. I imagine burying a suicide victim in consecrated ground might stir up some resentment, if they let it fester.'

'Don't people know what century we live in?' said Julie, genuinely angry that anyone might take it on themselves to object.

The woman simply shrugged. 'It's the worst of sins, don't they say?'

Julie felt her stomach clench and gave her neighbour a withering look. *Oh, I can think of worse*, she thought.

'*Goodbye*, Mademoiselle Payet,' she said, and went into her apartment.

Victor was in the kitchen, in what seemed to be his usual state: silent and eating. He gave her a gentle smile as she walked in.

Julie sighed. She needed answers from him. 'Victor? You have to talk to me now. I went to the police station. No one is looking for you. You have to tell me where you got lost, or why you ran away. Was it a different town?' Victor took another bite of a biscuit and watched her, smiling. He always looked as though he knew something she didn't, and it unnerved her.

'I can't keep you,' she said. 'Even if I wanted to, I can't. And . . . I don't have any toys. Nothing for children. You'll be bored here.' Not even a flicker. *Shit*. It still felt like a staring contest, and the boy wasn't going to blink any time soon.

A few more days then, she thought. *But no more*. She would have to find a way to make some discreet enquiries, and in the meantime hope he would open up to her. Otherwise she would have no choice: hand him over to the police and throw him to the mercy of fate. Even the *thought* of doing that made her feel ill. She had experience with how merciful fate could be.

He sat there looking at her, seemingly straight into her heart. Still silent, still smiling. Julie shook her head, exasperated. 'Come here, then. I want you to try something on.'

A coat. She'd thought of it after leaving the police station. If nobody was looking for him, there was little need to keep him cooped up indoors all the time. And if he was going to go outside she needed to dress him better, keep him warm. His hands were always a little cold, she reckoned.

And she would have to get him some toys. Some paper and crayons. Something to do while she was out working, when there was no choice but to leave him in the apartment.

Victor got down from the table. The coat was a good fit. She snipped the price tag off and hung the coat beside her own, liking how the two looked together. She thought about how odd it was, that she should be so taken by Victor and feel such a bond in so short a time.

When she turned back to him, she gasped. The living-room window was wide open, and Victor was calmly sitting on the windowsill. The apartment was four floors up. He smiled at her, then fell through the open window, out of sight.

Horrified, she cried out and ran to the window. She looked down. Nothing was there.

She ran down the stairs and out, breathless, still fully expecting to see a small crumpled form lying on the ground before her. But there was nothing. It wasn't possible. She looked up to the window of her apartment above and saw him there, watching, smiling. He waved. She stared at him, wondering if she was losing her mind. She waved back cautiously.

Had she even seen him fall? Had she imagined it, while Victor had been inside the whole time?

Confusion swamped her, suddenly one thought foremost. Was Victor even real? Nobody had interacted with him, perhaps he was . . .

Then she thought of Nathalie Payet, and for the only time in her life she was glad her neighbour existed. *She* had seen him. She was the proof. The boy was real, and Julie's mind was sound.

More or less.

Thinking of her neighbour reminded her of Monsieur Costa, and of the woman's comment. *The worst of sins.* Maybe that was all that the vision of Victor falling from the window had been: suicide on her mind. If she was honest, it had been on her mind for seven years, as an option to consider. And now she'd projected it out of herself, onto someone she'd started to feel strongly for.

Feel. It had crept up on her. She'd started to feel strongly for another person. It was something she hadn't allowed herself since that night in the underpass, when her life and everything in it had gone to hell.

That evening she and Victor sat watching TV, eating dinner. She talked for both of them; asking questions and then providing the answers as he watched her with adoring eyes. Despite the strangeness of the situation it was the most normal she'd felt in a long, long time. It was good to have someone there. It was good to stop feeling so alone. So dead to the world around her.

Come nightfall, with Victor tucked in on the sofa, Julie went to have a shower. She undressed, then looked at herself in the mirror, deliberately examining the patchwork of scars; the ghosts of the slashes and stabs and incisions she'd suffered that New Year's Eve, seven years before.

She started to cry. But it wasn't despair she felt. It was something much rarer, something she almost didn't recognize. Something that had come to her the moment she'd begun to think the boy might stay, just for a while.

Hope.

19

When the police came to the Lake Pub for Toni, he thought it was the wolf that had brought them.

He had been out at dawn, hunting deer in the woods surrounding the lake, when he'd seen it: a dark shape at the far edge of a large clearing. He thought it was a dog at first. For all the whispered talk of wolves coming back to the area, he'd never seen one himself. It had probably been eighty years since the animals had had any real presence in this valley.

It had a dark pelt – almost black – and he struggled to make out the shape as it slunk out of the shadows of the trees. It was the striking white flash on the top of the head that had first caught his attention, but when he noted the length of the legs, he realized what he was looking at. Not a dog; a *wolf*.

Fascinated, he had to get closer. A big man, Toni found it hard to move in silence. His brother Serge had always been the natural hunter, quiet, quick and deadly. Now, though, Toni had no choice. If he wanted to see the animal better, he had to move. He cursed gently to himself as he made his awkward way, worried that every rustle of clothing or leaves would send the animal scurrying off, but each time he stopped and looked to where the wolf had been he had a surprise.

The animal was still there.

It was watching him.

It doesn't see me as a threat, Toni thought. And he wasn't really. Hunting a wolf was illegal, whatever the price he could get for the pelt, or the mounted head. Or even a full animal.

The idea had appeal, of course: taxidermy was something he was good at, a hobby he enjoyed. He'd worked on plenty of foxes in his time, but a wolf would be a challenge. As he got closer, in his mind he rehearsed how he would go about it.

It stayed where it was, watching him fearlessly, almost aggressively. That wasn't what he expected at all, and he found it unnerving to have such an animal stand its ground like the beast of legend.

He'd been brought up on the old superstitions surrounding the area. They were in his blood, put there by his mother and father; mainly by his mother, though. He'd only been four when his father had died. His brother Serge, three years older, had spent much more time in the man's company. Which, perhaps, explained how things had turned out.

Those natural fears were bubbling up within him now, as the wolf watched him; but despite his cautiousness, Toni's feet were bringing him closer, closer. It was a fascinating creature, and a beautiful one.

And then he knew he'd come too far.

Twenty metres away, the wolf curled its lip. The growl that came from it was deep and slow. Full of intent, and unlike the growl of any dog he'd ever heard. He could feel his bowels rumble at the noise. Instinct screamed at him to run, yet his blood seemed to chill and thicken in his legs because he found himself unable to move.

The wolf had no such problem. It came for him.

For an instant he was paralysed with fear, seeing the bared teeth and imagining them ripping at his throat. With shaking arms he raised his gun. Then the long years of hunting took over, the years of Serge's patient teaching, and he heard his dead brother's voice in his mind: *Steady, Toni. Steady.*

He shot it as it ran, bringing it down in one. It had covered half the distance between them by the time he pulled the trigger, tumbling in a spray of leaves as its momentum carried it almost to his feet. When it breathed its last, Toni let out a cry of both victory and relief, then suddenly thought of the trouble he could find himself in.

He took the carcass back to the old stone cottage, the house where he had grown up. For four years after Serge's death he and his mother had continued to live there together, Toni suffering his mother's acrimony. When she'd died he'd moved to the town, keeping the old house mainly as a hunting base, high above the lake and surrounded by pristine wilderness. The home where his mother had died, where his brother had breathed his last. Rather than be buried in the town's cemetery beside her husband, she'd wanted to be buried beside her beloved son. Beside Serge, with a view of the valley.

By the time Toni got to the Lake Pub to open up he'd already called a few contacts, enquiring how easy it would be to find black-market buyers for a wolf. Not hard, it turned out. Within two hours he had a firm offer for the pelt and another for the head, mounted. Satisfied with his morning, he had a cheerful day.

Right up until the police walked in.

His first thought was that the buyers had really been part

of a police operation, and he'd walked straight into it. But the police would tell him nothing. A few questions down at the station they said, that was all.

When they got there, Toni was put in a room where he sat and waited, hoping the worst they could do was slap him with a fine. He could explain that it was self-defence, of course, given that the wolf had been about to attack him; but there was a risk they would see it as a cynical lie, making them even less sympathetic.

Then the interview began, and he realized he'd got it all completely wrong. It was nothing to do with the wolf. It was much, much worse.

The initial questions about Lucy made him think she was the one the police were targeting. He knew what people said about her, and about the men she brought up to the room above the Lake Pub. He'd always turned a blind eye to it, but perhaps it was inevitable the police would take an interest sooner or later.

Then they'd mentioned the charges of murder and attempted murder they'd thrown at him seven years before, and followed it up with the photographs of Lucy's horrifying injuries. All he could do was stare. Lucy, attacked in exactly the same way the women had been back then.

It wasn't *possible*.

Because Toni knew who had killed those two women, and who had attacked the third. It was knowledge that he'd buried deep up on the mountain, something the police had come close to unearthing when they'd put Toni's life under a microscope seven years ago.

It had been Serge. And Serge was dead.

After seeing the photographs he didn't hear much of

what the female officer shouted at him. He was lost in a world of memories, of blood and death. The police left him for a few minutes, the captain and a different officer returning to complete the questioning. Toni gave a dazed account of the night before.

Soon enough he was taken back to the Lake Pub. He wasn't sure if they believed him or simply had their hands tied without evidence. He fervently hoped it was the former. The last time, people eventually seemed to accept that he'd had nothing to do with it and moved on, but he couldn't go through all that again.

And now a copycat killer had taken a liking for Serge's old hobby.

Toni found he couldn't concentrate at the pub, though. He left early, putting Samuel in charge for the rest of the day. He tried to put Lucy's attack out of his mind as much as he could. He had the wolf to deal with, and it would distract him.

He prayed for Lucy to live. It was partly a selfish prayer, he knew, because although he liked the girl and hoped she would pull through for her own sake, if she *did* survive she would identify the attacker. The previous attacks would be blamed on whoever it was too, Toni's name truly cleared at last. And there would be no chance of his life going under the microscope again, no risk of old secrets being dug up at last.

He drove back to the cottage. As he approached the door, he could feel that something was wrong. Then he saw that the door was slightly ajar. He was sure he'd locked it when he left. He took the hatchet from the woodpile, brandishing it as he went inside.

For a moment he wondered if the police had come here while he was in custody, taking the opportunity to poke around while he was out of the way. There was a spare key hidden around the back of the house, not that hard to find. The thought enraged him: a violation of his privacy, and the knowledge that if they found the wolf *now*, they would come down on him as hard as they damn well could.

But he didn't think the police would have been able to carry out a search without much stronger justification; and they certainly wouldn't have released him so soon. If not the police, though, then who?

The idea of vagrants came to him, and his grip on the hatchet tightened. His mother had always had an obsession with the idea of people living rough in the forest and turning up at the house, something that – as far as Toni knew – had never happened, but it had been burned into his mind all his life.

'There are crazy people who live deep in the woods,' she told him more than once. 'Crazy people with crazy ideas. Kill you, soon as look at you.' It was the kind of paranoia that had bred a distrust of everyone outside the immediate family; and which, perhaps, had bred a far greater darkness in the heart of his brother.

Cautiously, Toni went through to the back of the house where he kept his hunting trophies. Two dozen stuffed animals glared his way with glassy eyes. Some were his favourites, and he liked them too much to part with. The others were a little ropey, early efforts that he wouldn't ever try to sell. Too much sentimental value, anyway; he could look at each one and remember exactly the circumstances of the hunt, remember the laughter he and Serge had shared.

And he remembered the love, too: brothers finding adventure among the trees, looking out for each other.

Yes, thought Toni. *It's possible to love monsters.*

Everything in the room seemed untouched. The wolf was still hanging from the wooden beams, trussed, a hook through the rope that bound its feet. This room was always cold, so he would have plenty of time over the rest of the day to do what needed doing before there was any risk of the carcass starting to spoil. First, though, he had to check all over the house and see if anything had been disturbed or stolen by whoever had broken in.

He went up into the attic. There were still boxes and boxes of his mother's possessions packed away carefully up there. He had kept everything, unable to part with any of her belongings when she'd died, or any of Serge's – but he had wanted it out of his sight. Not in the house as a constant reminder of what he'd done, that terrible betrayal. His mother's bedroom was the one exception. That, he'd left untouched.

He went down from the attic and made a room-by-room check until he was in the kitchen. And there it was, the only other sign of activity besides the unlocked door.

A bird, decapitated and roughly butchered, still raw. He recognized it as a black grouse; its unplucked skin had been pulled back from the breast to give access to the meat, ragged pieces of which still lay around the carcass, looking torn rather than cut. Its head and guts lay strewn across the table.

'Jesus Christ,' said Toni, immediately ashamed for his blasphemy, another thing his mother had drilled into him.

Clean it up, he told himself. Whoever had been here was

gone. Some other hunter, presumably. Maybe they saw the dead wolf and fled, wanting no involvement.

Leaving such a mess.

He took a bin bag and gathered the pieces of flesh from around the bulk of the grouse carcass. Then he took hold of the legs and started to lift it.

He cried out suddenly and dropped it, then stared, horrified and bemused. *I just imagined it*, he said to himself. But the feeling had been so real: the flesh had twitched as he held it. *Just nerves firing*, he told himself. *It can happen.*

He waited until his own nerves settled before cleaning it all up and scrubbing the blood off the table.

The wolf was waiting for him, the challenge of the taxidermy promising to take his mind off everything. He went through and lifted the animal down from the hook, then cut the binding rope. The carcass was almost too big for his work area, a large, shallow steel basin over a metre across, but he had handled deer before so he knew he just had to take care. The sink was on a pedestal close to the middle of the room, giving access all around.

First, he cut around the top of the animal's shoulders, enough to let him start to skin it. He took the pelt carefully a little way back from the nape, then stopped to look. The fur was glorious, deep black and flawless. He wondered if – maybe – he would forgo the sale of the pelt and keep it for himself. It was good money, though.

Before he really got on with the skinning he wanted to work out the extent of the mount, to make sure he retained enough of the fur beneath the head to make something magnificent. He sized it up and cut around, peeling the fur back, taking some of the flesh away and exposing the bones of the shoulder.

He paused. He would have to think this through for a minute or so before he did anything else. Making a mistake with something like this would be unforgivable. He set down the blade and stepped back to mull it over. And as he thought, he was glad of it. Glad that his mind could be taken up with something less miserable than a woman who was half-dead and all the memories that her attack had brought back to him. And a family who, for all their faults, he had still loved.

Decision made, he reached for the knife again.

And he froze.

A growl had broken the silence. At first Toni thought the sound had come from outside, surely the only place it could have originated. But as he stared in horror, the half-flayed carcass before him moved, the rear legs shifting slowly. *Just nerves firing*, he told himself as he had with the grouse, feeling his sanity start to fracture.

The growling became a whimper; the legs began to shunt rapidly, scrabbling on the metal surface. It lifted its head, and howled.

Toni felt the knife fall from his hand. Trembling, he backed away; he stumbled and fell. The animal began to writhe, then it fell over the back of the basin, hitting the floor with a wet slap.

It was out of sight, now. Toni remembered to breathe, his mind telling him that none of what he'd seen had really happened. Staying on the floor, he backed away until he had retreated through the door frame.

The growl started again, deep, loud and full of intent.

Toni stood and put his hand up above the doorway to where his shotgun was kept, relieved when his hand found it, equally relieved when he scrabbled desperately through the drawer in the hall and found that the cartridge box wasn't empty. He loaded and took a step forward into the room, gun raised, moving in a slow arc, as far from the sink area as he could get, tensing as the angle brought the creature into view.

The wolf stood there, whole, complete. No sign of injury. It took a second for the shock of the sight to hit home. It was like a replay of the encounter they'd already shared: Toni with his raised gun, the wolf baring its teeth.

Then Toni fired. The wolf went down. He stepped closer and fired again, wanting the damn thing utterly destroyed. Its head came apart.

He reloaded and stood over the animal for ten minutes, watching. Just in case.

Shaking, he wrapped it in plastic and dragged the thing outside. He wanted it buried with a huge rock on top. He fetched a shovel and started to dig. Then he looked across the field, to beside the fence thirty metres away where a simple wooden cross marked his mother's grave. Beside it, a large round stone marked the grave of his brother. Tears started to come. His brother had been another predator he'd buried under a rock.

When the hole was a metre deep, he heard a voice from right behind him. A voice he'd never expected to hear again.

'What did the poor creature ever do to you?' it said.

Toni stood up and turned, shovel in hand. He stared.

Serge. Standing right there, thirty metres from his own grave.

Toni looked at his brother. He looked at his own hands. Then he swung the flat of the shovel hard at his brother's head.

Serge went down, groaning. Toni dropped the shovel and wandered away, confused. A nightmare, he knew, and he just wanted to wake up. As he headed to the house he turned to look back, and caught movement. Serge was up again, up and running towards him, rage in his face.

Toni made it inside and closed the door just as Serge reached it and kicked it hard, again and again, yelling. He realized he'd left the key on the kitchen table, and had no way to lock it.

'Why did you hit me? Are you fucking insane? Open up!'

Toni began to mutter as he put his considerable weight against the door. *Hail Mary, full of grace, the Lord is with thee; blessed art thou amongst women . . .*

Serge kicked harder, but Toni's sheer bulk was enough to keep the door shut.

'It's me, Toni,' yelled Serge. 'Jesus Christ, open the door!'

. . . and blessed is the fruit of thy womb, Jesus. Holy Mary, Mother of God, pray for us sinners . . .

Serge was screaming now, screaming and pushing harder than ever. And even though as an adult Toni dwarfed his big brother, Serge's strength was considerably greater than it had ever been – almost too much for Toni to withstand. It was only the adrenaline of fear that gave Toni enough reserves to hold the door closed, as if his life depended upon it.

. . . now and at the hour of our death. Amen.

It all stopped: all the screaming, and the pushing. Silence. Toni drew breath and stood his ground until the passing minutes brought with them a hope that this trial, whatever its cause, had come to an end. That Serge's vengeful ghost had returned to the grave. That Toni had been punished enough.

He waited fifteen more minutes before he opened the door and stepped outside. He went down cold when the shovel hit him from behind.

It was dusk when he finally came to. Serge stood over him, shotgun in hand. Toni looked at his brother properly now; he was wearing precisely the clothes he'd worn when he died. *The clothes I buried him in*, Toni thought.

'What's going on?' Serge asked. He looked distressed. 'Why was the house locked? Where's Mum? Did something happen to her?'

'She's dead,' said Toni. He sat up carefully, watching his brother. Serge seemed real enough, and surely a vengeful ghost would remember why it had come back from the grave. Serge didn't seem to remember anything. Not even *dying*.

'What happened? What did you do?'

'I didn't do anything,' said Toni, looking to the ground. It wasn't quite the truth. His mother hadn't cared much about living, once Serge had gone. Once Toni had dealt with him.

'When did she die?'

'Three years ago.'

Serge was shouting now, crying: 'What are you talking about? Why don't I remember it?'

'Because you weren't here,' Toni said, his voice quiet.
'Where was I?'

Toni pointed over at the wooden cross marking her grave. 'You were with her,' he said. 'In the ground.'

Serge lowered the gun, and fell to his knees.

My big brother, thought Toni. And look at him now. So young. So lost.

Serge started to sob. Toni stood and went over to him, and held him, comforting him with the words their mum had always used whenever they cried.

'There, there,' said Toni. 'No need for tears.' Serge had come back, and this time Toni would be a better brother. He wouldn't fail him. Not again. 'It's OK,' he said. 'It's over.'

20

For Anton Chabou, work had become a strain. Having made the original call about the decrease in water level, he had earned the suspicion of most of the other engineers. Eric had been the only one to defend him openly, perhaps because Eric had known how close he had come to being in the same position.

'Ignore them,' Eric had said. 'They don't know what's really going on, any more than the rest of us. All they have is rumour.'

Yes, thought Anton. Rumour, and the extra money in their salary every month. Everyone at the dam was paid at least 30 per cent more than they could get for the same role elsewhere. Discretion was always emphasized, and being indiscreet had led – in the past at least – to pay reduction or dismissal. To Anton's knowledge it had been years since any of the staff had been punished this way, because they knew what was expected of them.

The man Anton had contacted had given his name as Dreyfus when he'd arrived. By then it had been time for a shift change, but Anton and Eric had both been asked to stay for a few hours more. Dreyfus requested a permanent volunteer to assist him while he was there; naturally, Anton found himself nominated by the others.

'Has this happened before?' he asked Dreyfus, getting nothing but a glare in reply.

Anton had gone home to an uneasy sleep, and had come

back the next morning to an old man's ragged corpse being scraped from the base of the dam.

'Old Monsieur Costa,' Eric told him.

'You knew the man?'

'I knew *of* him. He was a teacher, well respected. His older brother used to be mayor.'

Then Dreyfus had taken him to one side and given him a list of tests to oversee. Small submersible drones were on their way, and would let them examine the upstream face of the dam. The staff accompanying the drones were outsiders, and Dreyfus wanted everything to be played down. Made to seem routine.

But this was anything but routine. The water level kept dropping, yet the water wasn't seeping through and appearing anywhere else. Despite Dreyfus's insistence that speculation should be avoided, Anton couldn't help it. A fissure, perhaps? Should they get divers in to check the lake bed?

Dreyfus looked pale at the thought. 'First things first,' he said.

And the rumours continued.

When he and Eric finished their shift at dusk and walked to their cars, Eric stopped and looked out over the water. 'You know,' Eric said, 'there had been a settlement on the site of the old village since the Bronze Age. Maybe longer. When the old dam failed, they found small voids in the rock near the abutments. Caves, two or three metres across at the widest. Not noted by the original surveys. And in one of those caves, they found the skeleton of a large boar. They brought someone in, someone local who they trusted. The earliest inhabitants would have been precursors of the Celts, animal worshippers. The boar would have been one of their most sacred animals. There were marks on the boar's vertebrae that, they said, could be sacrificial wounds.'

Anton felt the cold wind pick up. He looked out over the lake, to the far side where the old dam had been. After the dam had failed three decades ago, what remained of it had been demolished, and the vegetation on the valley side hid the scars. A tragedy hidden in plain sight, invisible unless you knew what you were looking at.

And now there was a new lake, and a new dam, built with curious haste. When the site for the original dam had been chosen, two possibilities had been available. One was simpler and cheaper, but it would have required the flooding of the old village and meant everyone had to move down to the town; the other option was higher upstream, but construction would be considerably more expensive, and more complicated. The villagers had mounted a campaign to protect their homes; the townspeople had joined them, and together the more expensive plan was chosen.

Then the dam had failed, flooding the village after all, with the loss of more than a hundred lives. The dam was unsalvageable, but the time-consuming planning and surveying work on the alternative site had already been completed, so they built another one there. The rush to rebuild was a crass way to distract from the tragedy and call it progress. Disrespectful, at the very least; at worst, it bordered on desecration.

'They took the bones from the cave,' Eric continued, 'and had them dated. They expected them to be ancient, maybe a find of historical importance. When the results came back, they were disappointed. The remains had been dated to the time of the dam's construction.'

Anton looked at him, surprised. Eric seemed to read this as scepticism.

'Seriously,' Eric said. 'You ask around enough, you can find all that out for yourself. But there's one thing nobody will tell you.' He lowered his voice. 'They found a child's skull in that cave.'

21

Thomas sat at his desk and watched the streams from the hidden cameras that were set up around his own home. He went through each of them again and again: living room, bedrooms, bathroom. All empty, of course; Chloé was at school, and Adèle was at the library. Checking the live images was habit more than anything else.

The cameras were a secret. He'd installed them himself two years ago, after Adèle's close call. Neither Adèle nor Chloé knew they existed, but it was the way it had to be. Whenever he was worried, he could watch, and be sure that no harm had come to his family. From outside, or from within.

His nerves were on edge, his temper short. The night before, he had gone up to the attic while Adèle slept, and had hunted through the box where she kept everything from her old life – her life with Simon Delaître.

Even as he opened the box he knew he was being a fool, that the man in custody must have been an old acquaintance of Delaître. Yet the first time he'd seen the guy the feeling of recognition had shocked him. He'd only ever seen Delaître alive in photographs; photographs he'd never looked at closely, only glimpsed. He'd seen the body at the time, of course, but nobody could have recognized the living man from that shattered face. It had to be his mind playing tricks on him. Surely.

And then he'd found Adèle's photographs, and had seen.

It was him. It was no failure of Thomas's memory.

It made no sense. All Thomas could do was keep him in custody as long as possible, and keep all of it away from Adèle. There were only two weeks until the wedding and . . .

Perhaps that was it. After all, Delaître had died on the morning of his wedding to Adèle. To come back when she was about to marry someone else did make a *kind* of sense. Thomas had enough belief in the paranormal to accept the idea of ghosts, but he was also a supremely practical man. Whatever kind of ghost Delaître was, and whatever his intentions, Thomas wasn't going to give in to fear. There had to be things that could be done. There always were.

After all, Delaître was safely in the cells now, wasn't he?

There was a knock on his office door. 'Enter,' he said, closing the images from his home cameras.

Laure and Alcide came in.

'Update on the Clarsen case, sir,' said Laure. Thomas nodded for her to go ahead. 'We've been questioning every-one who lives near the tunnel. We have nothing new to add to the CCTV footage. No one saw a thing. It's deserted at night.'

'And Pascal?' asked Thomas. Pascal was the officer he had tasked with attempting to track where the attacker had gone after leaving the tunnel. Twenty-four hours of footage from thirty cameras spread across the town was a tough job for one officer, but Pascal had a knack for it. And besides, they weren't exactly overstaffed.

'He's certain the offender didn't reappear within the sight of any of the nearby cameras,' said Laure. 'It limits the routes he could have taken, but it's not that helpful. And so far he's found no sign of him reappearing elsewhere.'

Thomas nodded.

'Sir?' said Alcide. 'We could question that woman, Julie Meyer. Our file says she was attacked in the same place seven years ago. She may have remembered something since then.'

Thomas saw Laure stiffen. 'I know the case,' he said, reining in his sarcasm. Alcide, keen as a puppy, and only on the force for two years.

'I can question her,' said Laure. 'If you like.'

'We need to talk to her anyway,' said Thomas. 'To let her know what's happened, and assess her personal security. But there's no need for you to do it, Laure.' It was always important to keep private life and the job separate, Thomas thought, before remembering Delaître in the cells downstairs.

'I want to, sir.'

'Fine, then. Take Alcide with you.'

'It's OK,' said Laure. 'I'll go alone.' She looked at Alcide. 'You find out more about Lucy Clarsen.'

Alcide nodded. 'Yes, ma'am.' His voice was uneven, Thomas noted, the young officer still affected by his fondness for the woman.

'Close the door on your way out,' said Thomas. And once it was closed, he opened the camera feeds again, and watched. He had a nose for trouble. He could smell it now, but he'd be damned if it was going to ruin his wedding.

Thomas wondered how long you could keep a ghost in jail.

22

Pierre made sure he was at Michel Costa's funeral early. It was held in the old chapel graveyard, high on the valley slope looking down on the town. If the Helping Hand was to achieve the goals he envisaged, he needed the community to support it. As such, he made it his business to know all that he could about the townspeople, to forge links, and to keep as high a profile as he could.

He took in the view of the town. It seemed subtly changed to him, he realized, knowing what had happened with Camille, but he was by no means sure that his suspicions about her return were correct; that it was the beginning of something that would change the lives of everyone out there. Of everyone in the *world*.

All he could do was pray for guidance, and see what happened next. See if there would be others like Camille.

Slowly, people started to arrive. So many had known Michel Costa; so many had been taught by him. But there were fewer attendees than might have been expected. There was the manner of his death to consider, thought Pierre. Suicide carried a considerable stigma, especially in a town so bogged down in traditions. So unwilling to accept new truths.

Pierre had been on the phone to various people that morning, asking if they would be coming to the funeral. Most had told him they would have come, if only the man hadn't died in such disgrace. A few had expressed surprise that the burial was being allowed at all, their outrage barely concealed.

Pierre saw the police captain and approached, greeting him. The police were always useful allies, of course. He moved on, spotting the captain's wife-to-be.

'Hello, Adèle,' Pierre said. 'I heard about your wedding. Congratulations.'

'Thank you, Pierre,' she said. And she looked happy. Happier than all the times she had come to him for bereavement counselling over the last decade.

When he saw Claire arrive with Léna – Jérôme absent, of course, because someone had to stay at home with Camille – he waited until they had finished speaking to others in the graveyard before going over to them.

'And how is Camille doing?' he asked quietly.

'She's going stir crazy,' said Claire. She was glancing left and right as she spoke, wary of people nearby, her voice muted. 'We only allow her to go outside if she stays in the back garden. It's secluded enough that nobody would see her.'

'She must be patient,' he said. 'It's vital that she keeps out of sight.'

Claire suddenly gripped his arm. 'Pierre, do you think there might be others? I know none of the other parents have said anything, but . . .'

It felt to Pierre as if the air had become charged, loaded with some kind of *potential*. He tried to keep his voice calm. 'Why do you ask?'

'Léna thinks she met one.'

Pierre turned to Léna, keeping his eagerness masked. 'Where?'

'The Lake Pub,' said Léna, almost reluctantly. 'But I'm probably wrong about him.' She was looking at Pierre with genuine dislike. He'd not had much contact with Léna; while the Helping Hand had arranged the counselling of parents after the coach crash, it had been the school that had provided direct support for the affected children. Given his relationship with Claire it was reasonable that she should show such distrust. As long as it didn't tip over into disrespect, it didn't really bother him.

'What if there are more?' said Claire. 'What if Camille isn't the only one? She wouldn't need to hide. It would destroy her to have to hide forever.'

'I understand how difficult it must be,' he said.

'A fat lot of use that is . . .' snapped Léna.

Pierre bit his tongue. It wasn't his place to instil discipline in Claire's children. 'If there are others,' he said, 'then she would be able to come out of hiding eventually. But she should still lie low for now. The consequences of her situation becoming known would be unpredictable, Claire. The biggest news story the world has ever seen. And the authorities . . . They would fear her, and anyone like her. She *must* be careful. But let's not get ahead of ourselves. She may still be the only one.' He turned to Léna, ignoring the hostility in her eyes. 'So,' he said, 'What do you know about this person you saw?'

'He's called Simon,' said Léna. 'He was behaving weirdly, and I just thought he was odd, but then I realized I remembered his face from somewhere. I saw a photo of him, from ten years ago. He looks exactly the same. I think he knows Adèle Werther.' Her eyes darted over to where Adèle stood at the far side of the graveyard.

Simon, thought Pierre. Could it really be Adèle's Simon? The charge of potential in the air seemed to coalesce around him, filling him with an excitement that he found hard to disguise. 'Leave it to me,' he said. 'I'll see what I can find out.'

It was when he got the call from the police station later that morning that Pierre knew everything he hoped for might truly be coming to pass.

Once Michel Costa was in the ground, Pierre had returned to the Helping Hand to arrange some of the more specialist supplies he thought might be needed.

In case.

In case what Claire and Léna had said was true, and there were others.

The hope was almost painful for him, but it had been there since the moment he had seen Camille, back from the dead. He had been praying for a sign ever since.

With his jobs done, he sat in his office seeking the wisdom of the scriptures, his Bible open at the first chapter of Revelation. He was formulating a plan of action, wondering how to go about looking for the man Léna had spoken of. He had so little to go on; speaking with Léna in more detail seemed unavoidable.

Then the phone rang. It was Bruno, a policeman he knew, calling from the station. Bruno told him they had a lost sheep for the Helping Hand, someone right up Pierre's street; a man with nowhere to stay, forbidden to leave town. A mystery man, who wouldn't even give his real name.

'Could you pick him up from here?' said Bruno. 'He calls himself Simon Delaître.'

Pierre froze, just for a moment: it *was* Adèle's Simon, and Pierre wouldn't even need to look for him now.

'He was arrested for assault,' said Bruno. 'If that's a problem.'

'It won't be,' said Pierre. He told Bruno he would be there as soon as possible, then hung up. He looked again at the passage from Revelation, and read it aloud.

'*Fear not,*' he said. '*I am the first and the last, and the living one. I died, and behold I am alive forevermore, and I have the keys of Death and Hell.*'

He had been praying for a sign; this was much more. This was like a *commandment*.

At the station, Pierre waited impatiently, eager to see this man. He knew Simon Delaître's face, knew it from the photographs Adèle had brought to the early counselling sessions, and when the guy was brought out Pierre found himself unable to breathe. The awe he felt was palpable, staggering.

It was *him*. There was no doubt.

Pierre couldn't stop himself smiling at him, making the man nervous.

'It's Simon, yes?' said Pierre.

Simon Delaître nodded.

'That's what he says,' said Bruno. 'If you can talk him round into telling us who he really is, it'd save a lot of trouble. For him, too.'

Pierre looked at Simon. 'If he wants to, he'll tell me,' he said, wondering if Simon could detect that Pierre was only playing along, that he *knew*.

He led Simon to the car and drove, unable to stop glancing at the man in the passenger seat. 'We can get some food at the Helping Hand,' said Pierre. 'You can rest there. We have a dorm for visitors. Nothing terribly swish, but it's warm and comfortable. We can give you money, too.'

'Who are you?' said Simon, almost sneering. 'Father Christmas?'

'I try to help people who have, let's say, gone astray.'

'You think I've gone astray?'

'I don't know,' said Pierre. He didn't want to come right out with it, not yet, but he was interested to know how much Simon had remembered, and how much he had worked out. 'I've met many people who were lost, and I've helped them find their way again. Only this morning, I saw a woman I helped. Adèle Werther.'

'You know Adèle?'

'Yes, a little,' said Pierre, casually observing Simon's wary reaction. 'A tragedy like that is hard to forget.'

Simon's face grew pale. 'What tragedy?'

'Her fiancé died. On their wedding day.'

Simon looked at Pierre, desperation in his eyes. 'Do you know what happened?'

Pierre nodded. 'He was hit by a car.'

Simon was silent, stunned.

He doesn't remember, Pierre thought. *Just like Camille.* 'I don't think I've seen you before,' he said. 'Have you lived here long?' He wondered what Simon thought had happened, and if he knew how many years had gone by.

'Yeah. But I . . . I had to leave.'

'And you were gone for a long time. Am I right?' He looked at Simon, and saw the sudden increase in the man's wariness. 'Do you mind if I ask why?'

Too much, Pierre realized; Simon's expression went from

wariness to outright hostility. 'You can drop me here,' he said.

'Don't, Simon,' said Pierre, angry that his curiosity had spoiled things. 'There's no need for you to go.'

'*Drop me here*,' Simon shouted.

Pierre pulled the car over. The sudden anger on Simon's face was intimidating. He thought of the assault charge Bruno had mentioned, knowing that he had naively hoped the reborn Simon would be the model of benevolence. 'Simon, please. I can help you.'

'I don't think so.' Simon opened the door and started to walk away.

Pierre leaned over, raising his voice so Simon could hear. 'Come to the Helping Hand if you change your mind. You're not alone, Simon. Do you understand? You're not alone.'

Simon gave no sign that he'd heard. They'd stopped by the town's only industrial estate, a mishmash of faceless concrete buildings half of which were no longer occupied, now abandoned and vandalized. This town had always had aspirations of success that had overreached themselves; *exactly what I just did*, Pierre thought. With success close, his lack of caution had put it at risk.

But self-recrimination was not appropriate. What had happened had to be God's will, of course. It was all God's will, and so this must have been the path Simon needed to follow.

As Pierre watched Simon walk into the distance, he thought back to the scriptures. From memory, he recited another verse from Revelation: '*Death and Hades gave up the dead who were in them, and they were judged, each one of them, according to what they had done.'*

Pierre smiled. There were two things he was absolutely sure of.

He would see Simon again, soon.

And the end was coming.

23

While Claire and Léna went to Michel Costa's funeral, Jérôme stayed at home with Camille. She sulked in her room, eager to go somewhere, *anywhere*, having tried and failed to get her dad just to take her for a drive, to give her something to *do* that didn't involve being trapped in the house or garden.

Jérôme had refused point blank. He wondered if it was because he still felt the same unease around his dead daughter, but he didn't think that was it. It was fear *for* her, now, not *of* her. The thought of discovery appalled him, because he had no idea what it would mean. At the very least, their lives would no longer be their own. Press hysteria, *public* hysteria, and Camille . . . He didn't want to think about what would happen to Camille.

The only place for her was out of sight, safe and monitored.

He was having another cigarette in the back garden when Camille came down. She gave him a nervous half-smile, and he gave her an apologetic shrug. When he'd refused her request to get her out of the house he'd kept his specific fears to himself, hoping to spare her. It had made her all the more difficult to convince.

'If you give me a cigarette,' she said, 'I'll forgive you.'

Jérôme raised an eyebrow.

'What?' said Camille. 'You're worried I'll get cancer?'

Jérôme found himself smiling – Camille had always had

132

a sharper sense of humour than Léna. Besides, she was right, and here was a chance to earn some trust. He offered her one. 'Don't tell your mother.' She lit it with a practised ease that left Jérôme in no doubt she'd done it many times before.

'Are you and Mum separated?' Camille asked, casually blowing out a lungful of smoke.

'No,' he said. Claire wanted them to keep it from her, for as long as they could. 'Why do you say that?'

'You're being nice to her. It's weird.'

He laughed. It was the first time he'd laughed like that since Camille's return, he thought. Then he corrected himself. It was the first time since Camille had *died*.

'And you're sleeping in the spare room,' Camille said. 'Don't tell me it's because you snore.'

'I thought I was being careful, going to bed after you were asleep.'

'I don't sleep.'

'Still?'

Camille shrugged. 'I get tired, and I lie down. After a while I'm not so tired.' She seemed very matter of fact about it. 'But don't change the subject. You and Mum?'

'Let's just say that we've been taking some time off. Things were complicated after the accident. I was selfish and your mum had had enough of me. I have a little apartment in town now.'

She put her arms around him and gave him a hug. 'It can't have been easy.' He hugged her back, suddenly emotional; it was the first time he'd touched his daughter since she'd come back to them. Flesh and blood, the reality of her impossible to deny.

'God, no,' he said. 'It was especially hard on your sister.'

Camille pulled out of the hug and nodded. 'I know. I've lost a sister, too.'

Jérôme put his hand on her shoulder. 'Hungry?'

'Always.'

When Claire and Léna came back from the funeral, Léna went off to change for college, Camille following her upstairs.

'Things seem a little better between them,' said Jérôme.

'And what about with you?' asked Claire.

He nodded. 'Yes,' he said, with confidence. 'Things are much better. And I was thinking. Camille can't stay bottled up inside forever. We have to consider moving.'

'To go where?'

'I don't know yet. A place where no one knows who she is. Camille could live normally, without running any risks. We could breathe.'

'I'm not sure,' said Claire, looking anxious. 'With so much upheaval already, Jérôme, we can't do anything hasty.'

'It would change everything, Claire. We could have a normal life again, go back to being a family. Nobody would know us, or what had happened to us.' He saw the reluctance in her face. It was as if she didn't even want to consider it, and he realized what her problem was. Moving away was, it seemed to him, the only way to bring their marriage back from the brink, and Claire clearly wasn't sure if she wanted that. Jérôme thought of Pierre, and it took real effort not to let anger show in his face. 'It would be good for Camille. Think it over, OK? I have some things to sort out at my apartment, but I'll be back later. We can talk then.'

His relationship with Claire wasn't the only one that needed rebuilding. Léna had certainly never forgiven him for letting her mother down so badly after Camille's death – and for letting Léna down, too, not least by allowing the family to disintegrate the way it had, giving up on it almost without a fight. He had failed them all.

When Léna came down, Jérôme insisted he give her a lift to college. She was, as always, frosty with him, but she accepted. He'd hoped they could talk, but instead they spent the journey in silence. Just as she was about to get out of the car he stopped her.

'Léna,' he said. 'Have you mentioned Camille to anyone?'

She scowled. 'Yeah, loads of people. I thought I'd put it on Facebook.'

He waited for her sarcasm to settle. 'Please, this is serious.'

'Don't worry. I'm not going to say anything. Besides, who would believe me?'

'Your mother and I think it's best for Camille if we move. Things are too complicated for her here.'

Léna's eyes widened. 'What about me? It's not complicated for me? I have friends here. My *life* is here. I've already had to rebuild it once before. I don't plan on doing it again.'

'Come on!' he shouted. 'You know it's harder for Camille.' Léna was looking at him coldly. He took a long breath, then shook his head. 'It would be for the best, for all of us.'

'So we move, and it'll all be perfect?'

'It would be a damn sight better than it is now. This can't work, not long term. I'm sorry, but that's how it is.'

Léna said nothing more. She just got out of the car and walked away.

Camille's death had torn the family apart; by rights her return should bring them closer together, and let Jérôme be the husband and father he'd once been. So far, though, he felt as if he was failing all over again.

When Jérôme and Léna had left, Claire spent half an hour tidying the kitchen. The moment she'd come back from the funeral, she had quietly noted the mess it had been left in. Jérôme and Camille making sandwiches, jars open, crumbs everywhere. Léna's bedroom might always be chaotic, but at least in the kitchen she took some care to clear up after herself.

The mess didn't annoy Claire, though; quite the opposite. She smiled as she tidied, imagining her husband and daughter interacting in such a simple, innocent way. He was getting his head around the situation, getting better at seeing Camille for who she was, and here was the physical evidence.

Finished, she took the full rubbish bag from the cupboard under the sink and took it out to the bins at the back of the house. She opened the lid, ready to toss the bag in, and gasped when a cloud of blowflies buzzed out and circled her before settling back inside.

It took her a moment to work out what it was, sitting on the few bags already in the bin. All she saw at first was the blood, and the innards. A rabbit, she realized. Torn open; ripped into pieces and discarded here, and whoever had . . .

She stopped the thought that came into her head, stopped it dead in its tracks. She guessed that the rabbit would have been put in there overnight, but how it got there wasn't something she wanted to think too much about. *A fox*, she told herself. *A fox must have got it and someone put it in there afterwards rather than just leaving it lying around. Jérôme, maybe.*

Yet she knew she wouldn't raise it with Jérôme. All she could picture was the torn photo albums, and the blank expression Camille had had on her face.

Wanting the rabbit gone, she fetched a large refuse sack and tipped the contents of the bin out into it, tying it again and again, the flies still buzzing inside the black plastic.

She washed her hands and went upstairs.

Camille was in the bathroom. Claire felt suddenly uneasy. Camille saw her and smiled.

'Did you sleep last night?' said Claire.

Camille shook her head.

'And did you go outside at all?'

'Of course not,' said Camille. 'I tried to read for a while, then I ended up listening to music.'

Claire nodded, trying to tell herself not to think so much, not to worry so much. She washed the thoughts from her mind, just as she'd washed her hands.

'So how do I look?' said Camille.

'Is that Léna's shirt?'

'Yeah. Does it suit me?'

Claire saw how desperately Camille wanted her to say yes. She nodded. 'It's a little big, though. Why don't I go out and buy you one in your size?'

'Can I come, too? Please? We won't stay long, and we won't see anyone. I promise.'

Claire paused. She knew what Jérôme would say, but it

was distressing to see her daughter shut in like this. Who knew what effect it was having on her?

She nodded, telling herself it was for the best, to give Camille some relief from her imprisonment. She also made a mental note to be sure to lock the doors at night.

Claire took them to one of the quieter clothes shops in town, one with a car park at the back. It wasn't busy, she was glad to see; empty, almost. And while Camille went through the racks at the rear of the store, deciding what she would try on, Claire tensed, keeping one eye on the few other customers drifting in and out of the front entrance. She didn't recognize anyone.

'How about these?' said Camille, holding some tops and jeans. 'This one's nice, isn't it?'

'Very pretty.'

'How many can I have?'

Claire smiled. Why not be generous? She had four years to catch up on. 'Today, you can have all you want.'

The look of simple joy on Camille's face made Claire's heart swell. Camille went into the changing room with her selection while Claire waited, marvelling at how fate had given her this chance to spoil her daughter. And she would: she would do everything in her power to spoil the girl, and make up for lost time.

'Excuse me, can I . . .?'

Claire managed not to jump as the other customer spoke, trying to reach past her. 'Yes, sorry,' she said, stepping aside.

'Claire?' said the woman. 'How are you?'

Claire looked. For a long moment she couldn't place her, and then she felt ice on her neck. Sandrine. Another of the parents from the coach crash that had taken Camille. Claire looked quickly at the changing-room curtain, then back. She made herself smile.

'Sandrine, how are you?'

'I'm fine. Did you hear about me and Yan?'

'No.' The curtain twitched. Claire's pulse was getting faster every moment. It would only take Sandrine to see Camille now, and everything would change.

'We're expecting a baby,' said Sandrine.

'That's wonderful,' she said, trying to sound enthusiastic while willing her daughter to just stay in the changing room just a little longer . . . 'Congratulations.'

Sandrine looked at her with concern. 'Are you OK? You don't seem well.'

'Yes, I'm fine.' *Just a little distracted*, she thought, so tense that she felt as if she would pass out if this went on much longer.

'Claire, it's been so long since I've seen you. Why don't you come to the meetings? Is it because of Jérôme?'

'No, not at all,' said Claire. 'Jérôme always got more out of them than I did.'

Sandrine lowered her voice, and put a sympathetic hand on Claire's arm. 'Have you separated?'

Claire said nothing, stealing glances at the curtain, lost for any way out of the inevitable unless Sandrine went, and went now.

'Everyone knows,' said Sandrine gently. 'It's a small town. And we know how he was with you and Léna.'

She had a sudden urge to defend Jérôme, but it wasn't the time. 'Thank you, Sandrine,' she said, trying to sound as final as she could. 'It's very kind.'

Then the changing-room curtain swept back, and out walked Camille proudly sporting her new outfit. Suddenly nauseous, Claire looked at Sandrine and saw the dawning shock. Sandrine looked at Claire, mouth open, then back at the girl.

But there was no hesitation from Camille. She walked forward and held her hand out to Sandrine. 'Hello,' she said. 'I'm Alice. Léna's cousin.'

Sandrine didn't seem able to raise her own hand in response. Claire sympathized. It took a few seconds for the woman's expression to settle back, although the shock didn't quite leave her eyes. 'I . . . I thought there was a . . . family resemblance,' said Sandrine, looking at Camille with deep unease. 'Right, well . . . I'll get going. Call me, Claire?'

Claire looked at her; Sandrine seemed to have accepted the lie, although Jérôme would be furious with them. 'Yes,' said Claire. 'See you soon.'

'Goodbye, Alice.'

'Goodbye,' said Camille, looking pleased with herself.

Sandrine made her way out of the shop, stealing one nervous glance back at them. Claire closed her eyes and let out a breath.

Camille smiled at her. 'Quick thinking, huh?'

Claire felt exhausted. 'Let's go home,' she said.

They got back shortly before Jérôme returned from his apartment. Claire told Camille to say nothing about the trip. The chances of Jérôme noticing the new clothes were minimal, but Léna would. In that case, better that everyone thought Claire had gone alone, and left Camille at home by herself.

Camille calling herself Alice, though, had given Claire some hope. If Sandrine had believed it, surely everyone could. Surely it was a viable plan.

If Sandrine had really believed it.

With Camille in her room, Claire went to the bathroom to freshen up. There was a knock; she looked towards the door to see Jérôme.

'Sorry,' he said. 'I don't want to disturb you.'

'You're not.' She smiled at him tentatively, realizing she was genuinely glad to have him around again.

'So, have you thought it over?' he said. 'Moving away?'

'I'm not sure it's a good idea,' said Claire. 'I don't know if taking Camille somewhere else would help. This is her home.' There would be a time, soon, to tell him what she was really thinking – that they'd found a way for Camille to stay without anyone knowing who she really was.

'You think? It's all so different for her now. She's lost all her bearings . . . and so have we.' He came over to her, and put his arms around her. He kissed her forehead. 'You smell good.'

Claire didn't know how she felt. The distance that had grown between them was still there, for her. Too much had happened for it to be easy. The wounds were deep.

Jérôme kissed her neck. 'I love you, Claire.'

She held him, wishing for her old feelings to return. Knowing that if she could find that love again then the clock truly would have been turned back, just as she'd spent so long praying for.

Then in the bathroom sink she saw a cockroach emerge from the plughole. Startled, she gasped and pulled back from Jérôme, seeing the hurt and disappointment in his eyes.

'Sorry,' she said, flustered. 'I'm sorry. It's too soon.'

'It's OK,' said Jérôme. 'My fault.'

He left her alone. She looked in the sink. There was nothing there.

24

Adèle was reorganizing a shelf in the philosophy section of the library when she felt him. She didn't need to turn – she knew Simon was there.

'I was thinking about you,' she said. In truth she'd been thinking about him all morning, hoping for another visitation, or vision. Whatever it was. She wondered whether Thomas had noticed anything different about her – he'd seemed a little distant when they woke, but it was probably her own distraction that had made it seem that way. He had a lot on his mind, with work and the wedding.

'That's the idea,' said Simon, gently teasing. 'You think of me and I appear.'

She smiled. 'That's handy.'

'It might not last.'

'Why not?' she said. She turned now, still startled by the fact of him, of his youth.

'Shouldn't I leave?' he said. 'You don't need me. You have Thomas. Do you love him?'

'Yes.' He looked hurt by the word, but she wouldn't lie to him. 'I love you, too.'

'I'm dead, Adèle.'

'You came back to tell me to forget you?' She smiled. 'It's not a great plan.'

'I'm sorry. I should go.' He turned, ready to leave her again. Perhaps for the last time, she thought. And while that might be for the best, there was something she wanted to do first. Whether Simon was a real spirit or an imagined one, there was one thing she had always wanted: for him to see Chloé, just once.

'Before you go,' she said, 'I want you to meet someone.'

She walked through the town with him, and took him to the town hall. There, rehearsals were underway for the commemoration of the coach accident. Chloé was taking part; each child wore a T-shirt with the face of one of the children who had died, and they took it in turns to take a microphone and speak the dead child's name. Lucas. Honorin. Alexandre. Audrey. Sacha. Maiena.

Then Chloé's turn came: 'Camille,' she said.

'That's her,' said Adèle. 'Her name is Chloé. Beautiful, isn't she?' Simon said nothing. Adèle watched him as he looked at his daughter, his expression one of yearning and pride. She found herself wishing for something that could never be.

They kept watching. When Chloé saw her mother, she waved. Adèle waved back, then glanced to her side. Simon had gone.

When Adèle and Chloé got back home, a young woman was waiting on the doorstep for her. It took Adèle a moment to place her as Léna Séguret.

'Hello, Léna,' she said. 'What brings you here? I don't tutor any more.' She unlocked the door to let Chloé go in, eager to do some drawing.

'I know,' said Léna. 'I need to talk to someone who was looking for you. He's called Simon. Dark hair, curly. He asked me where you lived the other night.'

Adèle's grip on her bag tightened. She wondered if Léna was playing some kind of cruel joke, but surely not.

'Do you know who I mean?' said Léna. 'The last time I saw him was at the Lake Pub yesterday. He wanted to know where you worked. I'd assumed he would go to the library to find you. Did you talk to him?'

Adèle felt the blood drain from her face. 'You . . . you saw him? You spoke to him?'

Léna looked puzzled, and a little concerned. 'Obviously,' she said. 'Look, it's probably nothing, but I need to talk to him. Do you know where he lives?'

Adèle shook her head. 'I don't think I know him,' she said, her insides churning. She shut the door behind her, trembling. Whatever kind of ghost Simon was, he wasn't just in her head.

25

Julie started her day at Michel Costa's funeral. She'd left Victor at home, of course – armed with several packets of those biscuits he couldn't get enough of, and orders to keep the door locked whatever happened.

She had been at the graveyard for ten minutes when she saw Laure arrive, she and her captain there as police representatives – Monsieur Costa had been a respected man. Julie skulked at the back, hoping that Laure wouldn't notice her.

Nathalie Payet, however, did.

'Hello, Julie,' came the unwelcome voice. 'Didn't the little boy come?'

'No,' she said. 'Funerals aren't really for children.' She watched the woman with suspicion. 'I didn't know you knew Monsieur Costa?'

'Oh, a little,' said her neighbour, clearly lying.

'Right,' said Julie. She didn't know if the woman was keeping tabs on her, or was just there for the thrill of tragedy and the opportunity for gossip. All of the above, probably.

'Have you heard about Lucy Clarsen?' said the woman.

Julie shook her head. 'Who?'

'A girl who worked in the Lake Pub. Anyway, she was walking home, and she was attacked by a man in an underpass. Brutal, I heard. The whole town is talking about it.' There was genuine glee on her face as she spoke. 'They were trying to keep it quiet, but I heard a rumour that he . . . *ate* part of her. It's happening again, like seven years

146

ago. Remember the rumours back then, too? The night-mares I had . . .'

Julie felt her legs start to give way. She reached out, found herself leaning on Nathalie Payet for support. She pushed herself away quickly, feeling a sudden revulsion at the idea of getting anything from that woman. Even if it meant collapsing in a heap at her feet.

'What's wrong?' said Mademoiselle Payet.

Julie took a breath and started to walk. She sensed Laure's eyes on her from across the graveyard, but all she wanted was to get out of there before she threw up.

She walked home in the cold air. Her neighbour hadn't known what had happened to her, seven years ago; her iden-tity had been protected, the police suggesting that the victim had been from out of town. She thought of the expression on her neighbour's face, one of lurid joy. That was all Julie had been to her, and to the town. A gruesome tale to tell, and then think no more about. To the police, she'd just been a useless witness who could remember almost nothing about her assailant. She wanted to get home to Victor, to someone who cared about *her*, for who she was.

Nobody seemed to. Not even Laure.

Home from Monsieur Costa's funeral, she hugged Victor tightly. Then she cooked some lunch. He ate everything and said nothing, as usual.

'I'm working later,' she told him as they ate. 'Are you OK if I leave you again?' She saw a flicker of panic in his eyes. She smiled to reassure him. 'Not for long, Victor. Never for long.'

Later that afternoon she left him curled up on the sofa

watching the TV while she treated herself to a bath. She lit some candles and put her headphones on, submersing herself in music as well as in water. Before Victor, she couldn't have done that: eyes closed, unable to hear anyone approach. She wouldn't have felt safe, especially now, if what Nathalie Payet had said was actually true. But the boy's presence gave her a strength she'd thought had deserted her for good.

As she relaxed, Laure's face came to her, and she wondered what Laure had thought as Julie had fled the graveyard. What Laure had *felt*. Laure's feelings had been a mystery to her, then and now. They'd spoken very little after she'd been attacked, but it had always felt as though Julie was with a police officer first, and Laure second. As Julie had retreated, shutting the world out, Laure had been her last link; but whatever they'd had, it wasn't strong enough to survive the aftermath of New Year's Eve, seven years before.

They'd both come as superheroes; Laure was Batman, Julie was Catwoman, her costume uncomfortably tight. It had been fun for a while, but it wasn't long before she'd had enough. She went outside for some air and to get away from the overloud music.

'That's me finished,' she told Laure. 'I'm off home. I'm supposed to start work at five a.m.'

'Don't be stupid. You go now and you'll get, what, three hours in bed? Why don't you stay up all night?' Laure grinned. 'I'll keep you awake.'

Julie shook her head. 'I need to get some sleep, Batman. I've been on call three nights this week.'

'But the party's just getting going. And the fireworks are in ten minutes!'

'You go ahead, Laure. I won't stop you. I saw Snow White eyeing you up.'

Laure put her arms around her. 'I love it when you're jealous. Come on. Stay. I'll show you my superpowers.'

Julie shook her head and laughed. 'Batman doesn't have any superpowers. He's just rich enough to have loads of gadgets. I'll see you tomorrow.'

She pulled away and walked on.

'Come on, Julie . . .' called Laure. Then she gave up. 'You have let me down, Catwoman! But we will meet again!'

By the time Julie reached the top of the stairway down to the underpass, the fireworks had started. She turned and watched for a moment, half-wishing she was with Laure. But she really needed the sleep.

In the underpass, the deep thump of the fireworks was amplified. All she could think of was a hot bath and bed. She hardly even noticed the man coming the other way.

He grabbed her as he passed, covering her mouth. She felt the knife go in; she screamed under his hand, the fireworks drowning it out. He kept stabbing, and all the while he was making soothing noises.

'There, there,' he said. 'It's OK. No need for tears.'

The knife, again and again. It was an eternity.

'It's OK,' the man said. 'It's over. It's over.'

He was lying.

Julie knew she was close to death. Every part of her had gone past the stage of feeling cold. She thought of the hot bath she would never have, and of the bed she would never reach. Even as the man started to eat, she felt herself slip in and out of consciousness.

I'm tired, Laure, she thought. She didn't want to wake from this, not any more.

Then she felt herself lifted; felt herself in a vehicle, staring at the black sky.

When she had woken in hospital, she'd felt more tired and more alone than she had ever been; and that was how she had remained, in all the years since.

She opened her eyes now and took off her headphones. Here she was, in the bath she'd thought she would never have, and in the next room was someone who cared. She felt suddenly protective of Victor, with a force that took her by surprise.

The doorbell rang. She ignored it, but it kept on ringing. Eventually she got out of the bath, wrapping a towel around her before she went to the door.

She looked through the spyhole and was shaken to see that it was Laure. Her very presence seemed like an intrusion, as if she'd known about Julie's innermost thoughts. Julie wanted her gone. She made sure Victor was keeping out of sight and then snatched open the door. 'What do you want?' she said.

'It's been a while,' said Laure, looking deeply uncomfortable.

The hostility in Julie's voice was clear. 'Yeah.'

'I saw you earlier,' said Laure. 'At the funeral. Can I come in? Just for a moment.'

Julie shook her head. 'It's not a good time. Just tell me what you want and go.'

Laure paused, soaking up the punches Julie was throwing. 'Have you heard about the woman who was attacked?'

'Yes, I heard. What about it?'

'I want to make sure you're safe. That you know to be careful.'

'You really think it's the same guy, after all this time?'

'It's possible it was a copycat, but the similarities are compelling. A copycat attacker would need to have more details of the case than were made public.'

'Everyone knew the rumours.'

Laure nodded. Another police failure; it had to rankle with her. 'Promise me you'll be careful.'

'The building's secure, Laure. And I have enough locks on my door to keep out the devil himself. Besides, I'm damaged goods now. Isn't that what the police psychologist said?'

Laure winced. It had been a detail of the case Julie knew Laure regretted telling her – the reason they considered that a follow-up attack was unlikely. 'I . . . I just wanted to make sure you would be OK. And . . . Julie, we wanted to know if there was anything else you'd remembered. Anything you can tell us.'

Christ, she thought. *Still the same old Laure.* 'Always a police officer first, huh?' she sneered.

'I never stopped caring about you, Julie . . .'

'So why did you stop coming to see me in the hospital? And when I got out, *you never came*. Not once in seven years.'

Laure flinched. Julie knew she was being unfair, but she would do whatever she could to get this woman away from her door. For good. That was the past, and the past was dead. 'But you didn't want me to come,' said Laure, meeting Julie's gaze. Julie could see the pain in her eyes. 'You made it pretty damn clear.'

And Julie had, my *God* she had. Hurtful, spiteful things, all with the purpose of pushing Laure away. Laure's great crime, in Julie's eyes, was simple: she'd done as Julie had wanted. Julie had wanted to cut herself off so completely that she would never feel anything again, and she'd only succeeded because Laure had allowed what was between them to die. Laure had been the only person who could have stopped Julie from amputating her emotions, and she'd failed.

'I have nothing to say.' Julie closed the door. She got back into the bath, where the tears would be only so much extra bathwater.

An hour later, she and Victor were sitting watching television when the doorbell rang again. Whoever it was, they were impatient: a knock, a ring, another knock. Julie wondered if Laure had come back. Part of her hoped she had, but she silenced the thought at once.

'Julie,' called a voice. 'It's Mademoiselle Payet.'

Shit.

'I know you're at home, Julie.'

The woman's voice had an element of taunting that worried her. She nodded Victor towards the kitchen, and waited until he was out of sight before opening the door. 'Yes?'

Her neighbour didn't even bother with niceties. 'Why were the police here earlier?'

'It's none of your business,' said Julie. She went to close the door again. Her neighbour stopped it with her hand.

'He's illegal, I'm guessing?' Her expression had the same kind of glee that had been there earlier, when she'd told Julie of the stabbing. The woman only ever seemed happy when she could revel in other people's misery.

'What?' Julie felt goose pimples rise on her arms; she realized the woman was a little drunk.

'You adopted the boy illegally, didn't you? I saw a report on TV. Don't try to deny it.'

'You watch too much television,' Julie said, scared now. The woman seemed hell-bent on causing trouble. 'He's family.'

'Prove it. I know you're lying. You're breaking the law. And I'm sorry, but I have to report you. For the child's sake, and your own.'

Julie had had enough. 'Get out!' she said, pushing hard on the door, her neighbour resisting. At last she got the door closed. She was trembling.

'If he's here tomorrow,' Mademoiselle Payet shouted, 'I'm calling the police!'

'What's your problem?' shouted Julie. 'You old *witch*. Why don't you just drop dead? It'd be better for everyone.'

Julie looked up to see Victor watching, fear in his eyes. She crouched down, and he ran over to her. She hugged him tight. 'Don't let her get to you, Victor. She's all talk.' And there was a good chance she was, of course – that she'd just been fishing to see if there was anything more serious. The police wouldn't pay attention to someone like her, would they?

The thought came to Julie of packing a bag, ready, just in

case they needed to leave in a hurry. Then she realized how ridiculous that seemed. She stood and looked at the boy, wary of him. Why did she feel this way? He wouldn't even speak to her, but she was willing to do anything for him.

He looked back at her, need and love in his smile, and she understood that whatever the reasons underlying it were, one thing was undeniable.

She couldn't lose him. Not now.

When it was time to go to work, Julie was more reluctant than ever to leave Victor by himself. 'I'm going now,' she told him. 'Lock the door. Don't answer for anyone, you hear me?'

Victor nodded and smiled. Julie hugged him and went on her way. She glanced at her neighbour's door, hoping that her neighbour would find some other source of gossip, some other distraction to focus on. Anything, as long as the woman left her and Victor alone.

Nathalie Payet watched through the spyhole as Julie Meyer left her apartment. God, she was itching to get the police back again. At the very least, to stir up a good dose of havoc for her stuck-up neighbour. The way that woman spoke to her! Sometimes, it was borderline criminal.

She was about to feed her five cats when the doorbell rang. She almost exploded with delight when she saw who it was. The little boy.

'Hello, young man,' she grinned. 'Is something wrong?'

The boy said nothing, just looked at her with eager eyes. Dear Lord, had the Meyer woman abandoned him again?

'Has she gone?' she said. The boy nodded. 'Are you hungry?' He nodded again. 'I'll make you something,' she said, relishing the prospect. She would get the boy to tell her everything, and then she could get the police here. She would be a hero. Maybe even be in the newspapers! She hadn't felt so excited for months. 'Come in!' she said. 'What would you like to eat?'

The boy looked at her, smiling. Then he came inside.

26

The briefing on the CCTV footage had been disappointing. It wasn't Pascal's fault, Thomas knew; the task was huge. He, Pascal and Bruno were in the CCTV observation room, two dozen monitors on the wall showing live feeds from the town's thirty-camera network, as well as the station's own internal cameras.

'No one followed her from the pub as far as I can tell,' Pascal said, playing the key footage back on his own monitor. 'We can track her much of the way, until she goes into the tunnel. Then, five minutes later . . .'

The attacker emerged, shadowed, in a hooded top.

'This is still the best image we have. I've tried everything to follow where he came from, where he went, but I've got nothing. There are some blind spots, of course, but the moment he goes down there . . .' The footage showed the man step off the pavement into a dark alley. 'There are a few places he could have gone, but I haven't been able to locate him on any of the cameras that cover those areas. It's like he just vanished.'

'Get an extra pair of hands on the case,' Thomas told him. 'Keep looking. There has to be something.'

'Yes, sir.'

That was when Thomas noticed the feed from the cells in the station.

The *empty* cells.

'Where is he?' asked Thomas.

Bruno blinked. 'Who?'

'The suspect from the diner.' Thomas could feel his anger grow.

'The investigation was over,' Bruno said. 'It's procedure.'

'Fuck the procedure!' Thomas shouted. Bruno flinched, and Pascal looked away, keeping out of it. 'You freed our only suspect in this stabbing!'

'There was nothing linking him to it, sir,' said Bruno, almost pleading. 'We had no legal right to hold him.'

'A woman is on her deathbed,' Thomas hissed, 'and you didn't think to ask for an extension?'

'Sir, I told him to stay in town. He was picked up by Pierre from the Helping Hand.'

Thomas scowled at Bruno and left, saying nothing. Bruno was normally a good officer, but this was sloppy; Thomas wouldn't allow him to forget it.

He drove to the Helping Hand himself, trying to contain the anger he was feeling. The 'ghost' had escaped, and it had been nothing more mysterious than sheer incompetence that had done it. Everything felt much more dangerous with Delaître on the loose, but he would be in custody again soon enough. And Thomas would make sure he stayed there this time.

Pierre Tissier greeted him at the door of the Helping Hand. Thomas wasn't sure about Pierre. The man always came across as a real creep. Since becoming police captain, Thomas had got used to that kind of obsequious behaviour from others, but with Pierre it made his skin crawl. 'Can I help?' asked Pierre.

'The man you collected from the station earlier,' said Thomas. 'I need to talk to him. Now.'

'Simon?'

'Yes,' said Thomas, his eyes scanning the interior. 'Where is he?'

'Well, I suggested he came here, but . . .'

Thomas swore under his breath. 'He's not here?'

'He had business elsewhere,' said Pierre. 'I dropped him off in the centre of town.'

'What kind of business?'

Pierre shook his head. 'No idea, I didn't ask. But I doubt he would have answered – he wasn't very talkative. Can I ask why you're interested in him?' Pierre smiled, but Thomas could see it in his eyes: for whatever reason, Pierre was enjoying this.

'If you see him, let me know.'

'I have a certain amount of confidentiality to protect, Captain.'

Thomas leaned close. 'Let me know *immediately*.'

'Otherwise, I'm an accessory?'

'Precisely.'

Damn, thought Thomas. He needed to get Delaître back under his control and off the streets, before the guy went looking for Adèle. He didn't want to think about what kind of shock it would be for Adèle to see Simon.

He had business elsewhere, Tissier had said.

Thomas went back to the station, frustrated and desperate. He would have to rely on the cameras in his house and monitor Adèle closely, but it didn't seem enough. Then he had an idea. He went to see Pascal.

'I want to do all I can to help you in the case,' said Thomas. 'Is there any way I can get access to the town's CCTV footage?'

Pascal smiled warily. Of course, Pascal was trained, experienced; it was arguably unprofessional to step on his toes this way, to suggest that he could do a better job of it. He could understand the man's discomfort. But he didn't care.

'Of course, sir.'

'Can I access it from my own desk?'

'I'm sure you already have the access rights. It shouldn't take long for me to show you the ropes.'

Thomas nodded, satisfied. He already had his own home monitored. This way, he could keep watch on the whole town. Wherever Adèle was, he could keep her safe.

And if he should spot Delaître before anyone else did? Then maybe he could take care of things himself.

27

The main thing that stayed with Léna after the funeral that morning was her impression of Pierre. Her mother had mentioned him often enough, and she'd seen him around, but that was the first time she'd really paid much attention to the man.

Her opinion of him had formed pretty quickly: creepy.

Back home, she went to her bedroom to get ready for college when someone knocked on her door. It was Camille. Léna had promised to make the effort, but despite her best intentions, an *effort* was exactly how it felt. She was still uneasy around her sister.

'You're so pretty,' Camille said. 'I bet the boys like you.'

Léna's unease increased. She wondered where this was going. She'd noticed Camille looking at her, jealousy in her eyes. She could remember how she'd felt at that age, before the crash; when being older seemed like the best thing in the world.

'Have you slept with Frédéric?' asked Camille.

Shit, she thought. Well, it had only been a matter of time. 'What? We aren't together.' She felt flustered, her guilty conscience flaring up.

'Why not? You used to like him, and he liked you.'

'But we agreed, didn't we?' said Léna. 'You liked him more, so you had first say.'

'Exactly,' said Camille. 'So after the accident you were free.'

THE RETURNED

'Nothing happened.' She couldn't meet Camille's gaze; the old Camille would almost certainly have known she was lying.

'You're still friends, though? You still hang out?'

'Sure. Us, Lucho, and a bunch of others.' Léna was desperate to change the subject. 'Look,' she said, 'once I'm done I'll go to the pub to find that guy I mentioned. The manager might have seen him around.' She started to change clothes.

'OK,' said Camille. 'If he really is dead, maybe me and him can start a club.' She smiled.

'I'll let you know if I find out anything,' said Léna. She took off her shirt, and looked pointedly at Camille. 'Haven't you got anything else to do but gawp at me while I change?'

Camille shrugged. 'I don't mind.'

Léna sighed, and turned her back to her sister. 'Whatever,' she said.

'What's that on your back?' said Camille. 'Is it a scar?'

Léna twisted her head to get a look in the mirror on her wall. There was a small red patch in the middle of her back, just on her spine. She'd felt it that morning: an itch, and one she'd had a good scratch at. She'd assumed it was an insect bite or something. It looked pretty angry now. She'd scratched too hard, that was all. 'It's nothing,' she said. 'Can I get changed now? In peace?'

Her dad offered her a lift to college. Normally she wouldn't have bothered but he looked as though he needed to feel useful. With the way things were, she actually felt as if they were both in the same boat concerning Camille, trying to make the best of things and still very cautious, while her mum was so positive about everything it was almost scary. She thought that for the first time in years she and her dad might actually agree on something. Instead, he'd brought up the idea of moving away from town, and they'd already started bickering before she got out.

The irony was, moving away might be good for her, too. Frédéric had been standing on the college steps, waiting for her and watching; the first person she saw as she got out of the car. Her best friend, in theory. Saying goodbye to him could well be a good thing for both of them.

'Hi,' said Frédéric. 'Talking to your dad again?'

'If you can call that talking,' Léna said. 'You got much this afternoon?'

'No, I'm all done. I'll see you later.'

In the pub, of course. Went without saying.

She only had basketball and one class for the afternoon, but in basketball her back started to play up. She could feel it whenever she stretched the skin. She bowed out early, and had a look. The flesh looked much angrier than before, raised and red. She thought it might be infected.

She had a shower, washed it carefully and vowed not to scratch at it again, although now that it was getting painful she didn't think that would be a problem. With luck it would settle.

Afterwards she headed for the Lake Pub to see if she could get any information on the man she'd seen, Simon. She wondered what it would mean if she *did* find him. When she'd asked Frédéric before about the idea of the dead coming back, he'd laughed it off: *Just as well, or we'd all be fucked*, he'd said. Since she'd told Camille about Simon, Léna had wondered if she'd been reading too much into their encounters. The more she thought about it, the more she thought it might be better if she was wrong about him.

The pub wasn't open yet, but the front door was unlocked so she walked in. There was a guy she hadn't seen before sitting at the bar.

'Excuse me,' she said. 'Is Toni here?'

The man jumped. 'I don't know,' he said.

He looked in his mid-twenties. A little rough around the edges, but in a good way. She threw him a smile. 'Sorry. I didn't mean to scare you.'

'No, it's fine,' he said, smiling back, but his smile was awkward. Shy, Léna thought. Shy, but cute. 'I'm his brother. Serge.'

'I didn't know he had a brother. You don't look alike.' By which she meant: *You're not two metres tall and built like an overweight tank.* But she liked Toni enough not to voice that.

There was a yell from the back of the pub. Toni's voice. 'Shit. *Shit.*'

'He sounds happy,' said Léna. She nodded farewell to Serge and headed to the source of the voice: the toilets.

'It stinks in here,' she said. All the sinks were blocked, filled with murky water. On cue, one bubbled.

Toni was on the floor in one of the cubicles. The toilet bowl, like the sinks, was full, and Toni was mopping up the overspill. He looked up at her. 'Hey, Léna,' he said, sounding defeated. 'Don't get too close. I don't know what's wrong. The plumber can't come until tomorrow, says there are problems all over the place. Maybe the sewers are blocked, but I hope not.'

'Whoa, Toni. Don't tell me you're not going to open up?'

'We'll open on time,' he said. 'Fingers crossed. We have the disabled toilet working still, somehow. For now. At least it'll not be a busy night, huh? There'd be one hell of a queue.'

Léna nodded. 'Yeah, good luck,' she said, then moved things on to the reason she'd come. 'Toni, remember that strange guy who came in yesterday? Dark hair. I was talking to him.'

He shrugged. 'Vaguely.'

'Do you know him? Had you seen him before?'

'I don't think so.'

'You sure? Any idea where he lives?'

The toilet bowl bubbled, effluent sloshing onto the floor with a stench that made Léna retch.

'Shit shit *shit*,' yelled Toni, and Léna wondered if he was swearing or just describing what was bubbling up around him. He looked at her with eyes that had just had *enough*. 'I don't know, OK?' he snapped.

'Calm down. Just tell me if he comes back?'

'Yeah.'

'Oh, and Toni,' she said, smiling. 'You never said you had a brother.' She winked. For whatever reason, Toni looked horrified.

With no luck at the pub, Léna went round to Adèle Werther's house and waited a while. The pub wasn't due to open for another hour – plumbing disasters aside – and with the only option being to head back home she was in no hurry. She sat and thought about Frédéric and Camille. About the promise she'd made to her sister. The promise she'd broken.

Adèle turned out to be a dead end too. She didn't seem to know who Léna was talking about, and she'd acted a little odd. Other stuff on her mind, Léna supposed.

Léna thought about heading over to Frédéric's house, then decided against it. By the time she got back to the Lake Pub, it had been open for half an hour. Toni had pulled off a miracle, it seemed; there was no hint of the stink, although every door and window was wide open and the air was full of a mixture of harsh artificial scents.

'Your brother not around, Toni?' she asked.

Toni gave her a strange look before he answered. 'Other things to do,' he said. He sounded odd too, just like Adèle.

Everyone was fucking odd today, Léna thought. 'Toilets good to go then?'

At least that got a wry smile from him. 'No, but they've stopped backing up. I got the ladies' cleaned, but the gents' is a disaster area. I've sealed it off.'

'Like a crime scene,' joked Léna, but what little sense of humour Toni had seemed to desert him. His smile vanished.

'I've put an out-of-order sign on them both until the plumber finally gets a look,' he said. 'We still have one working toilet, so we'll play it safe. But like I told you, expect queues.'

She sat and drank slow beers, fending off friends, especially Frédéric. Right now she just wanted some time to try and sort out her head. Frédéric, for all his good points, was a distraction she didn't need.

'Coming out for a smoke?' he asked.

'I don't want company,' she said. 'Just leave me in peace, OK?'

'What's up? Is it because of your dad?'

'Leave me alone for a bit, huh?' she said. 'I'm just not in the mood.'

He got the message and left her to it, going outside alone for his cigarette. Five minutes later, Léna's blood froze. Frédéric was coming back in, and who was trailing behind him?

Camille. In new clothes, made-up with lips the colour of blood, and a knowing grin on her face.

'So you were hiding your cousin?' said Frédéric, teasing.

She shot Camille a look. *What the fuck?*

'Hi, Léna,' said Camille, acting oblivious. 'You were right about this place. It's great!'

Camille leaned close enough to whisper in Léna's ear: 'I'm Alice. Your cousin. Simple, huh?'

It deserved another harsh look, and Léna gave it. Fuck, it wasn't just that Camille was out in public, a huge risk for them all. It was that she was *here*, the one place that Léna could call her own. Somewhere to get a little space, a little peace, and now *she* swanned in as if everything was completely normal . . .

'What would you like?' asked Frédéric.

'Same as you,' said Camille.

'You two look so similar,' he said, gazing at Camille intently. 'You know, when I first saw Alice, I thought, well, Christ . . .'

'Tell me,' said Léna, unable to keep the anger from her voice. '*What* did you think?'

Frédéric shrugged.

Léna turned to Camille. 'Do my parents know you're here, *Alice*?' she said.

'Yes, of course.'

'Like hell. They wouldn't let you out. You're only fifteen.'

'You're fifteen?' said Frédéric.

Léna wondered if the disappointment she heard in his voice was really there, or if she was just thinking the worst of him. 'I think you should go home, Alice,' she said. Camille was staring daggers at her.

'Or what?' she asked.

'Or I'll call and tell them to come and get you.'

'Come on, Léna,' said Frédéric, trying to diffuse the situation. 'Give her a break.'

'You stay out of this, OK?' said Léna. She gave him a look that immediately shut him up.

'You want me to go?' said Camille. 'Want me to leave you and the *boys* in peace?'

'Exactly.'

They tried to stare each other down, but it was Camille who finally backed off. She stormed out. Léna saw the upset on Camille's face, and she couldn't help but feel guilty. But fuck her, really, she thought – it had been Camille's stupid idea to come here, so she had nobody to blame but herself.

Frédéric looked at Léna, exasperated. 'What's your problem with her?'

Léna couldn't talk to him. Where the hell would she even begin? She stood and went to the ladies' loos, ignoring the out-of-order sign. It was empty and clean, that was all she wanted. She looked at herself in the mirror.

Frédéric trailed in behind her, unwilling to let it go. 'What's going on?' he said. 'Why won't you tell me what's wrong?'

She burst into tears: sudden, brief – she didn't know

whether it was rage or misery that caused them. Then she put her hands on Frédéric's neck and pulled him close, kissing him hard. She pushed him away again and they looked at each other, a deep need in their eyes. Then they were kissing, kissing, and she was pulling at his shirt, hunting for the buckle on his belt, undoing it, wanting him with a desperation that bordered on pain. Anything, anything to make her feel normal again, just for a while.

Frédéric was equally frantic. He unbuttoned her shirt and pulled it off. He lifted her onto the sink unit; then, suddenly, he stopped.

'What?' said Léna.

'What's that?' he said, looking at the reflection of her back in the mirror behind her. She turned to see. The wound on her back had grown. Reddened, weeping, it was at least ten centimetres long, running down her spine.

She pushed him away. Before he could touch her again, she did up her clothes and ran, leaving a confused Frédéric staring after her.

28

Pierre was arranging additional supplies for the basement storeroom; *specialist* supplies, of the type that could arouse the interest of the police if he wasn't careful. It was necessary, but he felt uneasy about dealing with the kind of people who arranged these things. The medical supplies had been relatively easy, but defence was a different matter – and the Helping Hand needed to be able to defend itself, if it became the refuge Pierre thought it might.

He looked up and saw Simon through the window, walking up the road to the Helping Hand. He smiled to himself. He hadn't been certain that the young man would turn up, but he realized that he should have had faith. He vowed that his faith would be total from now on. He went out to meet him. 'You found us OK?' he said, smiling. Simon still had that expression of distrust, but Pierre hoped there was a hint that it was thawing.

'Yeah,' said Simon. 'I decided I might stay for a few days after all. I'm sorry if I seemed ungrateful before.'

'That's fine,' said Pierre. 'I'm sure you had your reasons to go, but I won't pry.'

Simon looked thoughtful for a moment. 'I had some things to think about,' he said. 'Some things to come to terms with.'

'But you're here now,' said Pierre. He took Simon's hand, shook it firmly, and gestured towards the main building. Pierre was proud of it, even if the paint was starting to peel here and there. It had been his persistence that had led to the church and the town hall funding its construction, fifteen years ago. The outbuildings nearby were older, and had been left as they were. They sufficed, and had meant that the budget for the work could be spent on some of the more unusual elements Pierre had insisted on. The sturdy metal window shutters that could be deployed as protection, for example. 'Welcome to our little refuge!' he said. 'Follow me. I'll show you where you'll be sleeping.'

As they walked towards the entrance, Pierre was certain the skin of his fingers was tingling where he'd touched Simon. Some kind of harbinger, Pierre knew. Some kind of *herald*. Simon and Camille must be the messengers of God's will, and he didn't think God would mind the pride he was feeling, now – that Pierre Tissier, of all people, should be chosen to help them. He thought of the captain's warning for him to contact the police if Simon should reappear. A laughable idea.

They went inside. The dormitory was low-ceilinged but long, with sixteen simple beds. 'Here we are,' said Pierre. 'Any bed you like. They may not look that comfortable, but appearances are often deceptive. You'll sleep well.'

'It looks fine,' said Simon. His eyes drifted up to look above the door, to the carved crucifix that had once hung in the vestry of the old village church, the church that had been drowned when the dam collapsed. Pierre had been there in the aftermath. It had changed him, of course. He had started that year on a precipice, involved with evil men for whom crime was a calling. Pierre had little to offer the world, and had thought such a life might be his calling, too. And then one Sunday morning, the dam had failed.

The mournful wail of the sirens had filled the town, and fear gripped everyone as they heard the sound of distant collapse, the roar as the lake broke free. Panic, people running to high ground, thinking first of themselves as the weak struggled.

Pierre's first instinct, too, had been to protect himself; the urge to help slowly crept up on him as he saw the need others had.

By the time the water reached the town it was a spent force, a slow river carrying with it debris that told of horrors elsewhere. As one, the people around him looked towards the old dam far upstream, wreathed in impenetrable mist, and their thoughts were the same: *the village.*

It took twelve hours before any kind of outside help was to reach the area; until then it was the volunteers from the town who braved their way up treacherous roads, Pierre foremost among them. They waded through deep, cold mud that threatened to suck them down with every step. Pierre saw two men lose their lives that day, trying to help others. He had been the first to enter the ruined church; he came out in tears, with a fierce grip on that crucifix. Forty had died in the church alone, trapped and drowned in the building that was now a tomb.

The dead were everywhere.

They found fifteen villagers alive. Ten of those died from their injuries before they could be taken to safety. Five survivors, in all. Five who would have perished, if the volunteers had not come.

Many would lose their faith because of such appalling loss, but Pierre emerged with a determination. He had been a part of the darkness in the world for so long, and now he would *fight* the darkness.

Yet the worst was still to come. Driven by his new determination, he had been involved in committing a sin that overshadowed all that came before, a sin that took him to the brink of total despair. His greatest misstep of all, a terrible crime born of the disaster itself. Born of the anger that followed it.

But God's plan, weaving and complex, was always at work.

For while the collapse of the dam had shown him it was time to become a better man, it was only once he had fallen completely that he could start to rise. To let the old Pierre die, and the new be born.

'Rebirth,' he found himself saying.

Simon looked at him, puzzled.

Pierre looked back up at the crucifix. 'Do you believe in God?'

'Not really, no.'

Pierre smiled knowingly. 'But you believe in resurrection, don't you? I know I do.'

Simon looked at Pierre with narrowed eyes. *He understands*, thought Pierre. *He understands that I know.*

Then the distrust seemed to slip away, replaced with a deep melancholy. Simon nodded. 'I went to the town graveyard today,' he said. 'I saw my own grave. I suppose I have to believe.'

'And? You think it can just happen to anyone?'

'Maybe for Him . . .' said Simon, looking at the crucifix. 'But I'm nobody.'

'Don't be so sure. Perhaps you're not just anyone.'

Pierre stepped forward and put his hand on Simon's shoulder – on the *herald's* shoulder. 'Don't worry,' he said. 'I'm sure it will all become clear soon. I won't leave you on your own. I won't abandon you. There is a reason you're here. It is the reason we are *all* here.'

'Tell me,' said Simon. 'Tell me the reason.'

Pierre smiled. 'I will,' he said. 'In time.' *When it is all ready*, he thought. *When the end approaches.* And in that, he had total faith.

29

Julie hoped she hadn't been too distracted to do a good job. Whatever else was happening, she owed it to her patients to try her best and leave her life outside their door. Normally that was easy, as her life consisted of little more than surviving.

Today, though, it had seemed to take forever for time to roll around. Her thoughts were mainly with Victor. Was he OK, alone in the apartment? Why had he run away in the first place – or had he been abandoned? Why wouldn't he talk to her? She'd bought him some paper and colouring pencils before getting the bus home, but she'd been unable to pick any toys for him. She had no idea what he would like, not yet.

It was good that she had him to think about, though. Without him, she would have been thinking of nothing but the attack on the barmaid and the thought that *he* might still be out there. The man who had tried to kill her.

Through the bus window, she saw a man walking past. Just a guy, but with a hooded top, his face obscured. Adrenaline hit before she'd had a chance to reason with herself. It was just another random man, nothing to fear, but her heartbeat grew rapid and her breathing became panicked. She was on the verge of hyperventilating. Her first few months out of hospital had been exactly like this, she remembered. It was a bad sign. But she'd learned ways to deal with her anxiety, techniques that she brought into use now. Gradually her breathing slowed and she managed to settle her nerves.

When she got back to her apartment the door lay open.

Victor.

She stared at the door in shock for a few seconds, the self-recrimination hitting hard. How could she have left him by himself? Anything could have happened! She went inside, hurriedly checking the rooms. Victor wasn't there. Had he gone? she thought. Gone, just as mysteriously as he'd turned up?

She went to shut the front door and heard a noise from the hallway. A curious sound, one she couldn't work out. A regular thud. She went back inside her apartment and grabbed a pair of scissors from her desk, then went out into the hall. She listened.

'Victor?' she said, hopeful.

The noise came again.

Slowly, she went down the stairs, scissors in hand, her grip on them tightening with each step.

With two flights to go before the ground floor, the noise stopped. She continued, treading as quietly as she could, until she reached the bottom of the stairs. She looked around.

Nobody. The area was deserted.

Without warning the lights flickered and died. Only the dregs of the street lamps outside reached in here. She stood motionless, hoping for the lights to come back, waiting for her eyes to adjust.

She sensed something: a presence behind her in the gloom. As she turned, the lights flickered on, and off, unable to lock in, but she could see him standing there.

The man who'd attacked her, seven years before. Back then, she'd somehow blocked all memory of his face, unable to give the police any useful description, but she had no doubt who it was standing a few metres away from her.

He was back. Seven years ago he'd all but killed her; her life since then had been an oversight, a technicality that he'd come to correct.

He came at her, his speed and strength astonishing. One hand gripped her wrist, trying to wrestle the scissors off her, as his other hand covered her mouth.

'It's OK,' he said. 'No need for tears. Shh. Shh.'

She felt him wrench the scissors from her grasp, saw him turn the point towards her, bringing the tip closer, closer to her stomach.

'It's over,' he said. 'It's over.'

Closer.

She closed her eyes, powerless.

Then suddenly the man's grip on her vanished and she felt instead a small cold hand wrap around her own. She heard a voice, one she'd heard just once before. Victor.

'Put it down,' said Victor gently. 'You're safe now.'

She opened her eyes. He was holding her hands, with a strength far beyond that of a child. She looked down to where he held them stationary, preventing them from moving any further. Her own hands: with the scissors still in them, turned towards her stomach.

She stared at the scissors for a moment before dropping them. Her attacker had never even been there, she realized. It had all been in her mind. Victor had saved her from herself.

'You're safe now,' said Victor again. He stroked Julie's hair. She wrapped her arms around him, sobbing in dry heaves, and knew that he was right.

30

Thirty-five years ago, a small boy sat under the sheets of his bed while his brother told him of all the monsters he knew.

Outside the sheets the room was in darkness. Dressed in their pyjamas, they both held torches, casting their shadows against the white coverings. His brother was nearly eleven, two full years older than him, and his list of monsters seemed endless.

'Have you heard of Damien, the Devil's son?' his brother said. The boy shook his head, midway between terrified and thrilled. 'He steals children. Steals them from their homes and buries them in boxes in his garden.'

The boy wrote it down in his notebook. 'He plants them? Do they grow?'

'He doesn't plant them, idiot. He keeps them there and trims off pieces when he's hungry. He'll cut off their toes and fingers and boil them for a snack. He'll take their eyes as dumplings for a stew.'

'Don't they scream in the boxes?' asked the boy. 'Don't they scream for help?'

'No,' said his brother, grinning. 'Because the first thing he does is cut out their tongues.'

The door to the bedroom opened suddenly, and both boys jumped.

'OK, you two,' said his mother. She walked over and pulled the sheet away. 'Time for bed.' She saw the nervous expression on his face, and frowned at the older boy. 'You haven't been scaring him again?'

'He asked me to!' said his brother, looking at him to confirm it.

His mother looked at him too. He nodded.

'Just because he asks, doesn't mean you should do it. Now, come on. Get to your own room. I'll check on you in a minute.'

His brother went, complaining; when he'd gone, the small boy's mother looked at him and smiled. 'Are you OK?'

He nodded. She took his notebook and glanced through it, shaking her head. He had taken down the details of six monsters already, and drawn little sketches. He had titled it 'MONSTERS AND HOW TO AVOID THEM'. So far he had gleaned only one piece of advice from his brother on the avoiding part: be silent.

'You know,' said his mother, 'I'm sure you can think of better ways to spend your nights than worrying about monsters.'

He looked at her, and thought how lucky he was to have the most beautiful mother in the world, the most loving. And the bravest.

'What if the monsters come?' asked the boy. 'I need to know how to fight them.'

'Well, you don't need to worry,' she said, smiling. 'We have an agreement. Monsters just aren't allowed here. Now, lie down.'

He reached across to the little bookshelf next to his bed and pulled out his favourite: *The Fairy of the Woods*. It had been his mother's when she was his age; that was why he loved it so much. He offered the book to her. 'Read to me? I'm worried I'll have nightmares.'

Gently, she shook her head. 'It's too late for a story,' she said. 'And I'll just be in my room next door.' She took the book from him, and held it up for him to see. The Fairy of the Woods smiled out at him from the cover, a promise of safety. 'And whenever I'm not here, you'll always have the fairy.'

'Does she really exist?'

'Of course,' she said, putting the book back in its place. 'If ever I'm gone, she'll look after you until I come back.'

'But how will I know it's her?'

She smiled. 'You'll see her, and you'll just know. Now, it's time to sleep.' She kissed his forehead, then left him with the night light on in the corner; slowly rotating, it projected jungle animals across the ceiling and walls. He didn't think he would sleep easily, but he drifted off soon enough.

Then he woke suddenly. The sound that had woken him had been brief, deep and loud. He sat up. The sound came again, quickly followed by his brother's worried voice.

'Mum!'

He heard his brother's door open, heard feet run on wood. Then he heard his brother scream in fear: '*Mum!*'

His brother screamed again but it was cut off by that same deep sound he'd heard before, and he suddenly understood what it was.

Gunfire.

The monsters had come.

Be silent, he thought. He stood and walked towards the wardrobe, his breathing rapid. He stepped inside.

One of them came into his room. The boy gasped when

he saw the figure, thin and dark, a man wearing a balaclava. He felt the urine flow down his leg, stream down and out under the base of the wardrobe door.

The man heard his gasp and saw the liquid. He turned his gaze to the wardrobe and stepped towards the boy's hiding place. 'Don't let him see you,' the man whispered. 'Stay where you are, whatever happens. I'll come for you later. You'll be safe.'

A different voice, a *darker* voice, came from outside the room: 'Where are you?'

The boy felt his panic rise. He thought of his mother and brother. He started to sob.

'Calm down,' whispered the man in the room desperately. The boy knew his sobs were loud, that they would give him away, but he couldn't stifle them. 'You know what to do when you're scared? Imagine yourself somewhere else, somewhere you've been happy. Imagine yourself there, and sing your favourite song. Sing it in your head.'

Be silent, the small boy thought, and he tried to do what the man had told him. He thought of the beach at Toulon, his mother's birthplace, where they'd had their last holiday as a family. His father had taught him a song, then – an old one, with nonsense words but a tune that he'd thought he must always have known, it was so simple. He sang the song to himself. He concentrated on the words, how the music should sound, the tenor of his father's voice; it was enough to calm his sobbing and let him stay quiet.

Then the other monster came into the room, huge and fat, cold eyes visible beneath the balaclava.

'What are you doing?' the monster said to the thin man. 'Who were you talking to?'

The thin man didn't reply, but the fat one sensed something and turned his head to the wardrobe. He started to raise his arm, and on the end of that arm the monster wore a gun.

'He's just a child,' said the thin man. 'He's just a *child*.'

The small boy watched as the monster's gun fired its bullet. He felt it strike his chest; felt the warm blood trickle down him, then pour.

Then the boy felt nothing, for a long, long time.

Julie had woken early, lying on the sofa with her head on Victor's lap and his hand on her hair. She sat up to find him asleep, the first time she'd ever seen him like that. He was still sitting upright, propped against the arm of the sofa; carefully, she moved him across and laid him down, then covered him with a blanket. She watched for a few moments, but he didn't stir. She went to the kitchen to make breakfast.

When she heard Victor's cry ten minutes later, she hurried to him.

'What's wrong?' she said. 'Was it a nightmare?'

He didn't speak. He just put his arms around Julie and held her tightly, trembling.

'You're safe,' she said. 'I'm here.' Under his breath Victor seemed to be humming. Julie could make out a simple tune. She wondered if she'd heard it before, but she couldn't place it.

There was a sudden scream from the hallway. Victor let go of her and looked fearfully at the apartment door, then back to Julie.

With trepidation she stood and went out to the hall. Nathalie Payet's door was open. Inside the apartment stood a woman with her hands clamped to her face, staring further in; the woman turned and looked at Julie, terrified, then looked back inside.

Julie stepped slowly across the hall and into the apartment. She looked to where the woman's gaze was directed. Nathalie Payet lay on the rug in her living room. She was motionless, surrounded by a wide red pool. Julie could see the vicious wounds to her stomach.

The wounds where, even now, her five cats lapped at the blood.

Julie retreated back into the hall, breathing fast, back into the safety of her own apartment. Then she turned every lock on the door and ran to Victor. She held him close.

Together, they were safe, Julie knew. They would protect each other from the monsters in the world.

31

Claire had woken before dawn that morning. For the first time in two years she had looked at the empty space in her bed and wondered if she could – maybe – take her husband back. In some ways it would simplify the situation, and dear Lord it needed simplifying. Jérôme's suggestion that they move had sounded like the right thing to do, but she'd been suspicious that his motives weren't all about what was best for Camille.

When she caught herself looking at the bed and thinking of Jérôme beside her again, she realized that she was rationalizing the decision she had already made. She wanted to move. Yes, it would be better for Camille. Better and safer. Yes, Léna would be angry, but she would come to understand. And Jérôme?

That would take longer. But after everything they'd been through over the last four years, he would just have to accept that.

In the meantime, her relationship with Pierre had completely stalled. From the moment Camille had returned, he had backed off; honourable, yes, but it left her disappointed. Tellingly, though, she had let him do it: her prayers had always been for her old life to return, and surely that included Jérôme.

She got up and made coffee. When Jérôme emerged half an hour later from the spare room in the basement she poured him a cup. He looked terrible. She was glad to have had the benefit of an hour up and about. 'Still not sleeping?' she said.

He shook his head. 'Not much.'

'I think you're right,' she said. 'About moving. It's only a matter of time before she draws too much attention for us to fend off.'

He smiled at her, and put his hand on hers.

'I'm doing it for Camille,' she said, perhaps a little too quickly. 'I don't know about the rest. You didn't make it easy for me, Jérôme. I can't promise we could ever . . .' She trailed off.

'I've made mistakes,' he said. 'But I've changed. *Everything* has changed. We have another chance, and we have a responsibility to our daughters. I really will make this work, I promise.'

She smiled. She could see the hope in Jérôme's eyes and she knew some of that hope was within her, too.

Then the doorbell rang. Jérôme went to answer it.

'Hello, Monsieur Séguret,' said a voice. Curious, Claire joined her husband. Two police officers stood there. Her first thought was of her daughters, and she immediately did a mental check: Camille was in her room, she was sure, and she had heard Léna stumble in from the pub in the early hours. 'We have a few questions to ask you,' said one officer. 'Can you come to the station with us?'

Jérôme looked at Claire, baffled. 'What's it about?' he asked.

'It's about Lucy Clarsen.'

Claire looked back at Jérôme, but the bafflement in his expression had gone. Instead, there was a weary recognition. Claire felt weary too: she'd heard the name several times

185

before in the last year, and knew the woman's reputation. 'You know her?' said Claire, not bothering to disguise the hostility in her voice.

'Don't worry,' he said. 'It's nothing. I'll explain later.' He took her hand and squeezed it, but she let it sit there, limp, her eyes cold. She shut the door once he'd gone.

'What was that about?' said Camille.

Startled, Claire turned. Camille was on the stairs, already dressed.

'You made me jump,' said Claire. 'I didn't hear you come down.'

Camille shrugged. 'I don't always stomp around like an elephant, whatever Dad says. Is he in trouble?'

Claire looked towards the door. She didn't want Camille to see the anger and worry on her face. 'Nothing serious,' she said, thinking: *Like hell it's not.* 'Sleep OK?'

'No, but . . .'

Claire recognized what words were coming next, and joined in. 'I'm hungry,' they said in unison. Camille laughed.

'I'll make you something,' said Claire. As she cooked she talked the conversation around to the decision to move. Whatever Claire's feelings for Jérôme, she knew it was the right choice. She hoped Léna would see that too, eventually, but she hadn't expected any resistance from Camille. She'd been wrong.

'Where would we go?' said Camille, and Claire could tell at once that she didn't like the idea.

'We haven't got that far, not yet,' said Claire. 'It'll be better for you. You can see that, can't you? You won't have to hide. You can live a normal life.'

'I already don't need to hide.'

'It's not that simple, Camille.'

'Alice,' she said. 'My name is Alice. Besides, the only reason Dad wants to move is because he wants you back. And away from that Pierre guy.'

'I don't know what you mean,' Claire protested.

Camille scowled. 'Drop it. I know you and Dad broke up. I sure as hell don't want to leave, and I think Léna will feel the same way.'

Claire opened her mouth ready to respond, but then she closed it again. She knew her daughter better than anyone, and knew that Camille was coiled up and ready to spring into a stand-up row if that was what it would take for her to get her way. Instead, Claire shrugged and took a drink of her coffee. As their plans became firmer the task of talking her daughters round would become more pressing; they were going, she was certain of that, but for now there was no need for an argument. She saw the confusion in Camille's eyes, but Camille let it drop too. Maybe, thought Claire, she'd naively thought it a victory.

As Camille ate they heard Léna's footsteps through the ceiling above them.

'Ah,' said Camille. 'She's finally decided to show her face.' Claire could detect a hint of bile in Camille's voice. She thought the two of them might have had some kind of falling-out, and the idea distressed her. She wondered what it could have been. Things had seemed to be going so well between them.

'Mum . . .' Léna called as she came downstairs. Claire knew right away that something was badly wrong, and before she even managed to stand, Léna, dressed only in her underwear, stumbled down the final steps, falling unconscious in front of her.

Claire gasped, horrified at what she saw: a long wound running down her daughter's spine. Red, raw and looking badly infected.

32

The previous night, Adèle had got a call from Thomas to let her know things at the station were busy, that he'd be catching what sleep he could in the makeshift beds there. He didn't do it often; Adèle always told him she didn't mind, but she did.

Last night, however, not long after Thomas had called, Simon had come to the house. And for once, Adèle was grateful for Thomas's heavy workload.

When she answered the door she stood looking at Simon, still only half-believing he was real. After Léna had come to talk to her she'd realized that her own understanding had been completely wrong, that it wasn't her imagination. She brought him inside and closed the door, then put her hand on his chest, overwhelmed at his presence. 'How is this possible?' she said. 'You're here. You're really *here*.'

Simon shook his head. 'I don't know how. I promise you, I don't know.'

'Why didn't you tell me?' she said, anguished. 'I thought you were just a ghost. I thought you were in my head. How could you let me think that?'

He nodded; so, he'd at least suspected that had been what she thought. 'I was scared, Adèle. When I came here that first night, you rejected me. Then at the library, when you spoke to me and accepted me, I didn't dare say anything to break the spell. But I still hadn't understood. I hadn't known what had happened to me, or how long I'd been away. When I understood I came back again. You showed me Chloé.'

'And you still didn't tell me you were real?'

'In case I frightened you.'

She drew him close. They kissed as they'd kissed ten years ago; no awkwardness, no distance, no anger or fear. Just them.

Then thoughts of Thomas intruded, and of Chloé. She pulled away, despairing. She knew that there were no easy answers. 'We can't just pretend,' she said. 'Things have changed.'

'I know,' he said. He took her hands in his. 'It's up to you. It all has to be your decision. But whatever you decide, remember how much I love you.'

She smiled at him, tears falling, then held him tightly. 'Chloé comes first,' she said. 'Before any of us.'

'Of course,' he said.

She was filled with adoration, confusion, guilt, longing. And pride, too; that Simon was so clear that the choice was hers. He had come back a better man, she thought. 'Do you have a place to stay?'

'The Helping Hand shelter. I should probably get back there soon, or they might lock up without me.'

'Stay here,' she said. 'It's too late for you to go back tonight.'

He looked uncertain. 'What about Thomas?'

'Thomas won't be back until morning, and even then it won't be long before he goes out to work again. The attic is clean – I can make up a bed for you there.'

To her relief, he agreed to stay. She told herself that being with him would let her make up her mind about what course of action to take, probably the most important decision of her life. She had to get to know the Simon who had come back to her.

She took him up to the attic and found the camp bed and a sleeping bag. They kissed again. Only that. He was eager and wanted more, of course, but she knew her head needed to be clear if she was to take that kind of step.

In the morning, she hurried to get Chloé off to school, desperate for time with her new secret.

'I heard noises last night,' Chloé told her. 'In the attic.'

'Mice,' Adèle explained. 'It must have been mice. Don't worry. I'll go up now and check.'

'Aren't you working?'

'No, I took the day off.'

'Wedding stuff?'

The wedding. Adèle's mind stalled for a moment. Less than two weeks, and she was supposed to marry Thomas. Her decision couldn't be put off for long.

One thing at a time. The doorbell rang. 'Hurry,' Adèle said. 'Marion is waiting.'

And, like that, Chloé was off to school and Adèle's day was clear.

She made Simon some breakfast, then unlocked the attic door and took up the tray of food. 'Simon?' she called, setting the tray down.

She felt him standing behind her. His arms went to her waist, and he pressed hard against her. Her heart was pounding; his lips were on her neck, his hands touching her. Fire, all over her skin.

'No, wait,' she said, turning to talk to him, but his mouth

found hers and she kissed back, wanting him so badly, but knowing she needed this to stop.

'Simon, no,' she said. He gripped the back of her neck with his left hand, while the right found her blouse buttons and undid them. He grasped her hips, lifted her up to sit on a box, thrusting himself at her, lost.

'Stop it,' she said desperately. '*Stop it.*' He wouldn't stop. She slapped him, hard. And again. Breathless, he backed off. He was staring at her, angry. She stared back.

He saw the tray of food. 'Sorry,' he said, as if nothing had happened. He walked to the food and ripped into it as though he'd never eaten.

She dressed herself again, watching him cautiously. Deep within her was a fear she hadn't known for years.

'I've been thinking,' he said. 'We'd all be better off at the Helping Hand. For a while. At least until I find a job and we can afford our own place.'

She stared at him. 'I've not made my decision yet . . .'

'You're coming, Adèle,' he said. 'You belong with me. You know you do.'

'And what about Chloé? This is her home, Simon. She's happy here.'

'She knows he's not her dad?'

'Of course,' she said. 'I never lied to her. Thomas wouldn't have wanted that.'

'Yeah,' he said, sneering. 'He seems like a really sweet guy.'

'You have no idea,' she said, bottling her anger. She turned, headed for the stairs.

'Adèle, wait.' She stopped. 'I'm sorry,' he said. He touched her cheek, gentle now, loving.

She felt her tears fall, torn between loving him and hating him for the way he made her feel. It had always been this way, when he'd gone too far: as if he'd been the hurt one, and only she could make it better. She told herself not to give in to it, that he wasn't really sorry, but she looked into his eyes and saw.

Of course he meant it. Of course he loved her. His temper flared up now and again. But it was just a sign of his passion, of how much she meant to him.

She led him down out of the attic, and showed him Chloé's room. Showed him the pictures that Chloé spent so much of her time drawing. Then Simon led her into the bedroom she shared with Thomas. He was tender with her, gentle. She was completely lost in him, not wanting to reject him again. She was willing.

'I'm here now,' he said afterwards, cradling her in his arms. 'I won't leave again.'

He held her, and she believed him. Her fears for the future, and the decisions that were coming, were pushed to the back of her mind. They lay together, and watched each other in the afterglow.

And high up in the corner of the ceiling, through a small hole in the plaster, Thomas's camera watched too.

33

Jérôme didn't understand what was happening.

The police had already gone over his statement twice, getting more and more hostile with him as time went by and his answers remained the same.

The officers questioning him both seemed young, one particularly so. It made the distaste on their faces harder to bear somehow. The room was sparse and overly bright, hurting his eyes. He was so damn tired.

'One more time,' said the older of the two. 'Lucy's diary says you saw each other nearly every week for a year. Is this true?'

Jérôme almost felt like laughing, it was so ridiculous. How many times would he have to tell them the same thing? 'I've already told you, yes.'

'And what did you do when you saw her?'

'We talked. That's all we did, we talked. Last time I checked, that wasn't illegal.' Claire would find out, he knew – find out something, at any rate. He thought of the hostile look she'd given him as the police had taken him away. He'd assumed it was a reprimand for bringing trouble to their door and risking Camille's safety, but now he wondered if she'd heard Lucy's name before. The police had told him about Lucy being attacked, and that his name had appeared in Lucy's diary, but there was no way he would admit to what had really gone on. Absolutely no way.

The younger officer stepped in. 'You like beating up women, Monsieur Séguret?'

This was new, and the tone was much more hostile. It took Jérôme a moment to reply. 'I don't understand.'

'You heard. Answer the question.'

'I've never hit a woman,' said Jérôme. 'I've never hit *anyone.*'

'Really?' said the older officer, pulling out a sheet of paper. 'Well, it says here that a year ago you hit your daughter Léna.'

He blanched. 'What? No . . .'

'On March the twelfth you took her to the hospital with an injury they felt was "consistent with a physical assault". The girl stated that she'd fallen, but the doctors treating her noted a "high level of distress". They're obliged to inform us in that kind of situation. You know, suspected child abuse?'

Oh God, he thought. Not this, too. Not now. 'I didn't hit her,' he told them furiously. 'She fell.'

'And how did she fall? All by herself?'

Jérôme looked away, ashamed. He'd always known this would come back to haunt him.

'Exactly,' said the young officer. 'The doctors also noted that you seemed to have been drinking. Did you drive your daughter to hospital in that state, Monsieur Séguret?'

'I don't—'

The older officer came straight at him. 'And what about with Lucy Clarsen?'

He felt battered, confused. 'What are you getting at?'

'Your own statement makes you one of the last people to have seen her before she was attacked. Maybe you followed her home that night. Maybe you hit her, too. Maybe you thought she was dead and got desperate. Maybe you tried to pass it off as a random attack.'

'That's ridiculous.' The line of reasoning they were following was insane.

The young officer took his turn to throw the punches. 'You're the one who hits women. Even your own daughter. Come on. What went wrong? Lucy refused a special request? Or was she trying to get some extra money out of you – keep her quiet?'

'She's not a prostitute.'

'Really? Then what were you doing? Isn't it time you told us the truth, Monsieur Séguret?' The hostility seemed to drop suddenly. The policemen were both looking at him, expectant. 'Tell us what you really got up to with Lucy Clarsen. However crazy it sounds.'

And Jérôme finally understood. As the police had said, Lucy kept a diary. There were others, of course. Other men she'd been seeing. Jérôme had always known as much. And by now, the police had surely talked to many of them.

Some of those men must have admitted it. The police knew what Lucy really did. And they knew how difficult it was to get the men in her diary to confess.

He thought back a year, to when Lucy had come to town. He could feel his face redden thinking about how he'd first reacted to her approach. Pride. That was it. Even though he would look at himself in the mirror and see a man who'd let himself go, see the failing hairline and the puffy, doughy skin. Lucy was young. He hadn't asked but he would have put her at twenty-four. Young and pretty, and coming on to a man almost twice her age who looked even older than that.

Pride.

She'd struck up something of a conversation that night, talking a little every time she brought him a drink. Then she told him she was about to finish her shift, and maybe he'd like to talk more, upstairs?

His face must have been comical. Utter disbelief, yet egged on by that tiny piece of him that thought: _Sure, why not. I'm still young, right?_

Delusional. But she'd meant it, and even the most sceptical parts of his mind were soon proved wrong, as she stopped outside her door and kissed him briefly.

She took him in, offered him a drink, and all he could say was: 'Look. This isn't a good idea.'

She ignored him, handed him a beer, took one for herself.

'I should go,' he said.

'Please, just relax.'

She led him to the sofa, laid him back and unfastened his trousers. In moments she was on top of him, and he was inside her, the speed of it taking his breath away.

He just looked up at her, lost, wondering how the hell this could have happened, and in no time he came, but she kept thrusting, kept going and going. Then suddenly she stopped, her eyes closed, smiling.

And then.

She opened her eyes, looking towards the back wall with such intensity.

'What is it?' asked Jérôme.

'Camille is here,' she said.

It caught him completely off guard. 'What?' But the look

on Lucy's face was compelling. He believed at once, and his certainty astonished him.

Lucy gasped. 'She says she loves you. She misses you. She misses Léna, too, and her mum. What happened wasn't your fault.'

'Tell her I love her,' he said. 'Tell her we all love her. We all miss her. Tell her . . .' And he couldn't think what to say, what to tell his dead daughter.

Lucy closed her eyes again, bowed her head, let out a long breath. 'She's gone,' she said, and that had been the first time.

Every time since, it had been little different.

Every time since, he had felt like an old, desperate man. Even though Lucy never seemed to, he had always held himself in disgust.

'Monsieur Séguret?'

The older officer's voice pulled him out of his thoughts, back to the interview room. Jérôme looked up. Both officers were still waiting patiently, ready for him to tell them the details, and admit to it; to what had started in pride, and ended in disgust. Now, it only held humiliation.

'Jesus,' he said. 'Jesus Christ.'

And he told them.

34

Julie had recognized the woman who'd discovered the body. It was Nathalie Payet's cleaner, surely the source of many of the rumours her employer had taken so much pleasure in while alive.

Even after she'd fled to the safety of her apartment, Julie could easily hear the hysterical woman on the phone to the police, describing the horrific scene. It didn't take long for the police to arrive. Julie watched through the spyhole in her door as they questioned the woman in the hallway. Laure was with them, speaking with some of the other officers; she glanced over at Julie's door, then walked towards it.

Damn.

Victor was drawing pictures on the table in the living room.

'Victor,' she said, pointing to the bathroom. 'Quickly.'

Laure knocked at the door. Julie waited until Victor was out of sight and was about to open up when she realized the paper and pencils he'd been using were still visible. She hurried over and grabbed it all, shoving everything under a cushion on the sofa.

She opened the door slightly, blocking the view of the apartment with her body.

'Can I come in?' asked Laure. Julie stayed as she was, saying nothing. She sensed Laure's frustration with her rise another notch. 'You know what happened?'

'Of course.'

'Did you hear anything last night?'

'No. I was sound asleep.'

Across the hall, Julie saw the forensic officers entering the apartment. Only one question was important to her. 'Was it him?'

Laure looked at her and frowned. 'We don't know. There was no sign of forced entry, no apparent struggle. Nothing seems disturbed. The similarities are superficial, so a copycat attack is a more likely explanation. It's possible she knew her attacker. Opened the door and let them right in. But I'll place an officer on watch anyway.'

'Don't do it for my sake,' said Julie. Harsh, cold; she saw Laure wince.

'Julie . . .'

'If that's all, don't let me keep you,' she said.

Laure looked down for a second. 'Wait – I have to ask, did you know her well?'

Julie shook her head. 'Not really.'

'Did she have many visitors?'

'The woman who found the body is here from time to time. She's a cleaner, but I think Mademoiselle Payet just liked the company. Nobody else came to see her that I know of.'

The lights in the building flickered off for a few seconds, and there was a sudden sound from the bathroom, a brief whimper. *Victor*, Julie realized: panicking in the dark. 'Aren't you alone?' asked Laure.

'No,' said Julie. She smiled, hoping it looked like a gloat and that Laure would take the hint; think she'd moved on, and give her privacy.

It seemed to have worked. 'I'll . . . I'll leave you to it, then.'

Laure was turning to leave when the lights in the building went off again. Victor opened the bathroom door and ran to Julie, crying.

Julie knelt down. 'Hey,' she said, hugging him. 'What's up? What's wrong?' He gripped her tightly, trembling. 'You're safe,' she said. 'Remember?'

Laure stepped inside the doorway, looking at Victor with suspicion. 'Who's he?' she said.

Julie felt dismayed. She had no idea how she would explain it. 'This is Victor.'

'He lives here?'

Julie nodded.

'Who are his parents?'

Julie was about to lie, but Laure knew her too well. She would spot it in an instant, and right now Julie desperately needed Laure's trust. 'I don't know. Look, he was lost. It was late. He wouldn't say where he was going, so I brought him back here.'

Laure shot a look behind her at the police across the hallway and stepped further into the apartment. She pulled the door half-closed and dropped her voice to a whisper. 'Are you mad? How long has it been?'

'A few days.'

'Christ, Julie. Have you even thought about his parents?'

'No one was looking for him,' she said. 'I checked. Maybe I should have just left him in the street?' She glared defiantly at Laure.

'Why didn't you bring him in?'

'I don't trust the police,' said Julie. Another body blow for Laure to absorb.

Laure sighed but didn't reply. She looked at Julie, then at Victor, appraising the situation. Behind her someone called her name.

Laure turned. 'Yes, sir. I'm coming.'

Julie put her hand on Laure's arm. It was the first time she'd touched her in seven years. 'Please,' she said. 'Please don't take him away.'

Laure shook her head. 'I don't know, Julie,' she said. 'I just don't know.'

Laure didn't come back again until much later, when the police had finished with Nathalie Payet's apartment for the day. It didn't go well.

Julie was in the kitchen cleaning up after dinner. She'd been on edge all day, thinking again of the bag she'd considered packing in case they needed to leave in a hurry. She wished she'd done just that.

The doorbell rang. She looked at Victor. He'd been drawing again, and got up to hide. As before he'd left all his paper and pencils out on the table, but Julie went to the door first to see who it was.

Laure.

Julie let her in. The agonized look on Laure's face told Julie everything.

'I can't let you do this,' said Laure. 'I'm sorry, but I can't.'

'I knew I couldn't trust you,' said Julie. Furious, she sat on the sofa and put her head in her hands.

'It's impossible,' said Laure. 'Surely you see that? We have to contact his parents. There's no other option.'

Julie scowled at her. 'You think I'm not capable of looking after him?'

Laure sighed. 'You know that's not the point, Julie. We really have no choice. Social Services will look for his parents, and in the meantime I'll arrange for him to stay at the Helping Hand.'

Julie was too angry to reply. Then she saw what was on the table in front of her. The paper Victor had been drawing on.

'So where is he?' asked Laure.

Julie wasn't listening. Page after page had the same image, the same rough sketch. A woman on the ground, a red pool surrounding her stomach. And cats, lapping the blood. Underneath, Victor had written two words: *'Be Silent'*.

'Julie, where is he?' said Laure again; she walked to the bathroom door and opened it. 'There you are,' she said. 'Come on. Pack your things. We're going.' She looked at Julie. 'Does he *have* any things?'

'His coat,' whispered Julie. She was staring at Victor, whose eyes didn't leave hers. *I didn't tell you what I saw,* Julie thought. *So how could you know?*

And she thought of the last words she'd shouted at Nathalie Payet the day before: *Why don't you just drop dead? It'd be better for everyone.*

'Come on, Victor,' said Laure. 'We'll take care of you. Julie, I'll keep you posted.'

Julie said nothing. Laure nodded to her and took Victor, who gave Julie one final glance before the door closed.

Julie sat where she was for a moment, then tore up the drawings. As she did, she wondered what the expression on Victor's face had been when he left.

She hoped it wasn't pride.

35

Pierre had been stocking up on fuel that morning, filling another dozen jerrycans for the stores at the Helping Hand. He would feel much better once everything was in place. He was due a consignment of goods the next day. His usual supplier in Annecy had been wary of the quantities Pierre had ordered, especially of the more exotic items, but Pierre had talked him round.

That was why he was worried to see a police roadblock on the outskirts of town. If there was anything that could scare his supplier off, it was a roadblock.

They would wave Pierre through, of course – he did his best to keep his hand in with the police – but curiosity got the better of him. He pulled over and parked, spotting a policeman he recognized, one who owed him a few favours.

'Hi, Michael,' said Pierre. 'Looking for someone?'

'Hello, Monsieur Tissier. We were going to contact you about it, actually.'

'How come?' It had to be about Simon, Pierre thought. He hadn't come back to the Helping Hand the night before, and Pierre had wondered if the police had caught up with him. Not yet, it seemed, but they were certainly stepping up their efforts. When he saw Simon again, as he knew he would, he'd have to emphasize how important it was for him to stay safe.

'The man you picked up from the station, the one we

arrested from the diner? He may be implicated in another attack.'

Pierre shook his head. He knew the suggestion was non-sense, simply a way to raise the stakes. The devil's hand was at work here, he thought. 'So he hasn't reappeared?'

'No. If you hear from him, let us know at once, OK?'

Pierre smiled. 'Of course. Captain Pellerin already made that perfectly clear.'

Pierre's mobile rang. He excused himself and took the call.

It was Claire. 'I'm at the hospital,' she said. She sounded frightened. 'Léna's very sick. Can you come?'

'What happened?'

'Please, just come.'

'Is Camille at home?'

'No, Camille's here with me.'

That worried him. Why on earth wasn't she indoors? 'Where's Jérôme?'

'Jérôme's at the police station. They came this morning – they wanted to question him.'

'What about?' The idea of Jérôme having even the *capacity* to commit a crime struck Pierre as improbable. The man was simply too banal.

'I don't know,' she said, sounding frustrated. 'Look, could you try and get a message to him, and let him know where we are? He's not answering his mobile.'

'I'll have a word with the police, Claire. Don't worry. I'll be with you soon.' Pierre ended the call and walked back to the police officer he'd been talking to. 'Michael,' he said. 'Do you know Jérôme Séguret?'

'Vaguely.'

'Apparently he's at the station. Any idea why?'

'No. But leave it with me, I'll find out what I can. Least I can do for you, Pierre.'

Pierre thanked him and headed back to his car. As he got in, the road started to tremble as truck after truck went by, all tankers of some sort. A dozen in all, Pierre counted. There was a sense of intent about them that was almost military.

He could see the look of puzzlement on the faces of the police at the roadblock. He knew what was on their minds: *What on earth is this? It's so unusual.*

Unusual? Pierre thought. *Get used to it. There's much more of that just around the corner.*

He drove on to the hospital, thinking of how everything would be in place soon.

When Pierre found Léna's hospital room, Claire and Camille were the only others present. Claire went over and embraced him; Camille scowled, and when Léna saw him so did she.

'Well?' he asked.

Claire gestured to Léna's exposed back. Pierre looked at the long, reddened wound. 'What is it?' he asked. 'Does it hurt?'

'Not any more,' said Léna.

'They haven't told us much yet,' said Claire. 'They got her stabilized and gave her a painkiller, but their tests haven't come back.'

He took a closer look at the injury. It seemed infected to him. It certainly didn't look like a fresh wound. 'How long have you had this, Léna?'

'Since I came back,' said Camille. He saw her and Léna

share a look, one of mutual distrust. Claire seemed to ignore Camille's words, but Pierre felt uneasy.

He looked at Camille, then at Claire. 'It's dangerous,' he scolded. 'Having her out of the house.'

'I'm Alice,' said Camille, with a smug grin. 'Léna's cousin. Not so dangerous now?'

Pierre shot her a harsh look: she thought this was a game. 'It's still dangerous.'

'Do you think it's related, Pierre?' said Claire. 'The wound, and . . .'

Pierre realized it had been unfair of him to think Claire was just ignoring what Camille had said; she clearly thought as he did, that some connection to Camille's return was possible. It was not a thought he wished to encourage, however. 'Of course not.'

'How can you be sure?' Camille demanded.

'If it was, other people would have them too. Your mother, for a start.'

'I'm her twin sister,' said Léna. 'I'm closer to her than anyone. Maybe it's just a matter of time before Mum gets something as well.'

Camille turned to her sister, shock on her face. 'You *do* think it's my fault,' she said. Léna just glared back at Camille, while Claire looked distraught.

'Of course she doesn't,' said Claire, but Camille was already storming out of the room. Claire moved to follow, but Pierre held her back.

'Wait,' he said. 'Let me talk to her.'

Camille was outside in the corridor, leaning against the wall and staring at her feet. Pierre studied her for a moment.

Just an ordinary teenager to the passing eye. Angry and scared and bored.

But not ordinary, not at all.

'I know it's not your fault,' he assured her.

Defiant, Camille kept looking at her feet. 'How would you know? What makes you such an expert? You act like you know everything, but you don't. Not really.'

'You're right,' he said. 'I don't know everything. But I have faith in God's plan. Why bring you back, just to make your family suffer all over again? They suffered enough when they lost you the first time. You have nothing to feel guilty about.'

She looked at him sharply. 'I don't feel guilty!'

He shook his head. 'You do, Camille. You love your sister. You're worried about her. But this is not your fault, and you shouldn't think for a second that it is. You *belong* with us. You can start living your life once more.'

'Ha!' she said, looking down again. 'Tell that to Léna.'

He could see how close to tears she was. 'Deep down, Léna feels the same. You have to forgive her, Camille. Her reaction's normal. She's afraid.' He looked at her until she reluctantly brought her eyes up to meet his.

Pierre was good at his job, working with those who had gone astray in life – sometimes through wrong choices, or just having been handed a raw deal. He could see past the hardened shells of anger and defiance, see through to the real person within. Lost, confused and looking for a helping hand. One that he was happy to offer. Gazing at Camille, he wondered if earning the trust of this miraculous girl – here, now – could be one of the most important things he would ever do.

'She's afraid you won't stay,' he said. 'Once she understands – once she truly believes it – she'll be as thrilled as the rest of us.'

'And how do you know I'll be allowed to stay?'

He smiled gently at her. 'Because God is good, Camille. He has brought you back, and we will learn your purpose soon enough. And it will be glorious.'

For the briefest of moments, hope showed on her face. But then she scowled. 'Hallelujah,' she said, mocking him. She strode back into the room.

Even so, he knew she had listened. He knew that, just for an instant, she had believed what he was telling her.

Hallelujah, thought Pierre. He smiled.

36

Adèle was still in the attic with Simon when Chloé was dropped off after school that afternoon. She locked the attic door behind her and hurried down to let Chloé in. She was smiling too much, she thought – her good mood, almost manically cheerful, masked a deeper unease. She was sitting on a powder keg and grinning like an idiot.

Adèle knew she couldn't go on like this, not for long. That was why she was making the most of it. She knew there was a choice to be made. Both options called to her. Both options, for one reason or another, repelled.

Before Simon's death she had often scolded herself for letting him trample over what she wanted. She had idolized him, constantly making excuses for the way he treated her. Yet here she was, doing the same once more, and happy. She knew that in many ways Thomas was the better option for her. He was caring, trustworthy, a wonderful father to Chloé; calm and patient, two traits that had never been Simon's forte. But there was a fire in Simon, a passion; an urgent *need* about him that Thomas utterly lacked.

Adèle opened the door and Chloé walked in, schoolbag on her shoulder. 'Hi, Mum,' she said. 'How was your day?'

Adèle smiled again. Such a grown-up way to phrase things. Her daughter was getting bigger every day. She was the one thing in life that Adèle was certain of.

'Not bad,' she said. She made a conscious effort to tone down her smile.

'Did you find the mice in the attic?'

'Yes,' she said, and she felt her smile grow again. 'I sorted it all out. Do you want a snack?'

She went to the kitchen to prepare food for them all. All three of them. Whatever was going to happen, they could have one meal under the same roof.

Chloé took her schoolbag to her room, and was about to head back downstairs when she heard a thump above her. *Mice?* she thought. *Rats, more like.* She shivered.

She stood for a moment, looking up at her ceiling, listening. More sounds came. There was definitely movement up there. She frowned. A whole *nest* of rats, to make such a racket. It was loudest over by her wardrobe so she dragged her desk across the room, balanced her chair on top, and climbed up. Her mum, she knew, would have a fit if she saw her like this, perched so high up, but it meant she could hear better.

The sounds had stopped, so she waited. But suddenly it wasn't what she could hear that caught her attention. It was what she could see.

She took a closer look, then called for her mum.

When Chloé pointed out the tiny camera, Adèle felt a cold anger creeping across her, and a fear – that the man she'd been living with all these years, the man she was about to *marry*, was the kind to . . .

But he wasn't like that. She knew that was what everyone in the same position would tell themselves, but she *knew* he wasn't. Her thoughts took the next logical step, and Adèle put her hands over her mouth, shocked. She looked to the attic.

She knew what Thomas was like. Protective. *Extremely* protective.

And if there was a camera in Chloé's room . . .

She sent Chloé downstairs and ran to her own bedroom. It didn't take her long to find, now that she knew what she was looking for. And there it was. Thomas's camera, staring down at the bed where she and Simon . . . She shook her head, appalled at the thought.

Fury coming from every pore, she hunted in the garage until she found a can of spray paint and a torch, then went around the house seeking out all the cameras and spraying the lenses.

There was one in every room. Even in the bathroom, the best hidden of them all.

She went up to tell Simon and together they searched the attic; but they found no cameras up here, at least.

'Do you think he saw us?' she said. 'When we . . .'

'He can't have been watching,' said Simon, disgust on his face. 'He'd be here already, if he had. But even then, it's only a matter of time. You don't know what he might do. The moment he realizes what we've been up to . . .' His expression grew angry, and Adèle could read it: he was thinking what *he* would do, in the same position. Another difference between Simon and Thomas.

'He would never hurt us,' she said.

'How do you know?' said Simon. 'He's *sick*. Spying on his wife? On her child?'

She looked at him, and knew he was right to be angry; they both were, but there was something about Simon's reaction that made her think he was glad of it, because it left her with no choice. 'You have to go, Simon. You can't be here when Thomas comes back.'

'Why not? You can't stay with him, if he betrays you like this! Why not face it now and tell him it's over?'

'What's over?' said a small voice. Chloé. She'd disobeyed and come up to see what was going on. She took one look at Simon and turned to her mum, concern on her face. 'Is this our mouse?'

Adèle nodded. She could feel Simon's gaze burning into her, prompting her. It was the first time Chloé and her real father had been in the same room; the first time Chloé had laid eyes on him. The situation was far from ideal, but her daughter deserved to know the truth. 'This is your dad, Chloé.'

'But my dad's dead,' said the girl, confused. She gave her mum a worried look.

'He was dead,' said Adèle. 'Now he's come back.'

'Is he an angel?'

Adèle thought simplicity would be for the best. 'In a way, yes,' she said.

Chloé turned to her father and looked at him with open curiosity. 'Scary. Were you in heaven?'

Simon smiled at her. 'Yes.'

'What's it like?'

Simon looked at Adèle, unsure of how to respond, and she nodded. 'It's calm,' he said slowly. 'It's beautiful.'

'Did you see God?'

'No. He's, uh, very busy. We don't see much of Him.'

Chloé looked at her mum. 'Is he going to live with us?' There was scepticism in her voice, wariness.

'No,' said Adèle. 'He can't stay, but you'll see him again, I promise. Until then you can't tell anyone that you saw him, OK? Not even Thomas.'

'OK,' said Chloé, uncertain.

Simon gathered what little he had and got ready to go. At the door, Adèle gave him one more kiss. His eyes had the same single-minded certainty that she loved and feared at the same time.

'You should both come with me now,' he said.

Adèle shook her head. Abandoning her home – *Chloé's* home – was far too big a decision to be made in anger, but there was something else: Simon thought Thomas's spying had left her no choice but to pick her old love instead of her new, but there were *other* choices open to her. 'I want to talk to Thomas,' she said. 'I owe him that.'

Reluctant, Simon left. She watched him walk down the street until he had gone round the far corner, and then she despaired. She had wished for so long for the past to be rewritten, for Simon never to have died; for him, Chloé and herself to have lived like a normal family. And now she was being given that opportunity. *Be careful what you wish for,* she thought. In the time she had spent with him now, she had been hoping for clarity, hoping that her deepest feelings would show her what path to take.

But the moment Simon had left her sight, the thing she'd felt most strongly was relief.

37

It had been a long, long night for Thomas.

He'd called Adèle as the evening drew on, to let her know he was busy. And he was: busy watching over his town. Scouring for signs of Simon Delaître, while he also kept a close eye on his family in his own home. Making sure they were safe.

Chloé drawing in her room. Adèle watching television.

Thomas vowed not to sleep until Delaître was in custody once more.

Pascal had the entire town to search, but Thomas had limited himself to the areas he knew Adèle would have been during the day.

And at last, he found it. Delaître, arriving at the library. Delaître, leaving with Adèle, walking side by side, not touching. Poor Adèle, he thought. She couldn't be trusted, not with Simon. She had been in the man's spell for so long, and his thrall over her had almost pulled her to the grave, stronger at times than her love for Thomas, even for her own daughter.

Adèle had said nothing to Thomas about meeting with Simon, but he didn't blame her. He knew she needed protecting, from herself as much as from the interloper.

And then his heart split, wide and raw, at the sight on his screen. The live feed from the camera at the front of his house showed a man approach, and stand at the window.

Thomas saw Adèle rise. Saw her go to the door and let the man in.

He watched as Simon Delaître kissed his fiancée. He watched her kiss him back with a passion and fervour she'd never shared with him. *I see everything now*, he thought. *Everything.*

He feared the worst. Then, he had some hope: she took Delaître to the attic, and came down again too soon for anything to have happened between them.

He willed her on, willed her to make the right decisions, but he would not interfere. He had to know what she would do, when she thought nobody would find out. Surely that was the only thing worth knowing about a person?

Yet he knew there was more to his inaction. He feared that confronting Adèle with Simon there could play out in only one way: with Adèle rejecting Thomas. Leaving with the triumphant Simon. And Chloé going with her mother.

He locked his office door from the inside, and closed the blinds. He kept looking at the images of his home, as Adèle went to bed, as the lights went out. Watching, in case Delaître left his hiding place to tempt her again.

He cried as he watched; eventually exhaustion took him and he slept uneasily at his desk.

He was woken by Bruno knocking hard on the door in the cruel bright light of morning. There was no time to check on the house, though; he would have to wait until he got back and look through the recorded footage. The case that had come in was simply too serious for him not to attend personally. Another attack, fatal this time, on a woman in her own apartment. Thomas berated every officer in shouting distance about the release of their only suspect, using it as an opportunity to vent his anger even though he knew exactly where Simon Delaître was hiding.

He immediately ordered roadblocks, and it was enough to settle his nerves somewhat. At least the man would be unable to flee the town and take Thomas's family along for the ride.

Two things were clear to him now. First, that Simon had had nothing to do with either the Clarsen or Payet attacks. He'd known it instinctively before, since if he had seriously thought the man capable of that Thomas would have been back at his house within minutes. But now it was beyond doubt. Delaître had been sitting pretty in Thomas's house while the Payet attack had happened.

He went to the Payet apartment to oversee the initial investigation, all the while distracted by the thought of what Simon's intentions really were. It was late afternoon by the time he managed to extricate himself and get back to the office.

Only to be greeted with the sight of Adèle and Simon. Fucking. In Thomas's own bed, the bed he and Adèle had shared for so long.

The first thing to hit was a deep sorrow, unlike anything he'd known before. Hope left him, utterly. Hadn't he given Adèle everything she'd ever wanted, been there when she needed him, brought up her daughter as his own? And now this was the choice she'd made. Anger flooded him, but it was anger towards Simon; he still couldn't bring himself to blame Adèle. What chance did she stand, against such temptation? Against such *forces*?

Because there was something he didn't lightly admit to

himself: he was scared, both of what Simon Delaître was, and by the hold he had on Adèle.

Rage and despair built within him until he couldn't stand it. Work would have to wait. He left the station with no explanation to his team of where he was going; even he didn't really know until he pulled in outside the church.

The priest was at the far side of the nave tidying around the altar. 'Hello, Thomas,' said Father Jean-François. 'How's the groom-to-be? Not long now!'

Thomas had no time for the niceties. 'What did you talk to Adèle about?'

The priest looked at him, suddenly wary. 'Now, Thomas . . . I wouldn't be much of a priest if I shared what people say to me.'

He gripped the priest's arm. 'Was it Simon?'

Father Jean-François looked at Thomas's hand until Thomas relented and let go. 'Try not to worry, Thomas,' said the priest. 'It's only natural for Adèle to think about Simon now. But she's marrying you. I think Adèle has come to terms with what happened.'

'So she did talk to you about him.'

'Thomas, you're here. He's a ghost. She'll forget him in time.'

Thomas shook his head, frustrated. He pointed to the large cross on the wall of the church. 'When Jesus came back, was He just a ghost?'

'What do you mean?'

'He was here, wasn't He? Physically here, in flesh and blood.'

'Are you unwell, Thomas?' said the priest, concerned. 'Maybe we should sit, until you can calm down.'

Thomas had no time for this. 'Answer my question, Father,' he snapped.

Father Jean-François paused, but he still looked more concerned for Thomas than fearful. 'Some believe that,' he said. 'But the resurrection doesn't have to be read quite so literally.'

'Father, I'm not a theologian. I need to *understand*. Would a physical resurrection be permanent, or is it just a matter of time before it ends?'

'You're talking about a subtle point of theology. The question must be this – what do you believe? Faith is the important thing. The rest . . . there aren't always answers, I'm afraid.'

'I'm a police officer, Father. I deal in facts. It's my job to find the answers. So tell me, how long would resurrection last? Would it be *permanent*?'

'You're asking the wrong questions, Thomas.'

Thomas looked at Father Jean-François with disappointment, verging on disdain. 'You're giving the wrong answers.'

He left the church and drove, aimless, his police radio off. He still felt unable to go home, his mood dark and confused, not good for confrontation. Nor was he ready to face his officers at the station, feeling unable to put on a facade of strength. So he drove, watching the town through his car windscreen for a change, rather than his computer monitor. Time slid away from him; suddenly it was dusk, the sky darkening rapidly, street lights coming on for the approaching night.

He wished for Simon to appear in the road, imagined his foot hitting the accelerator. There would be irony in that, he thought, and a sour smile crept onto his face. As he drove in the gathering dark, a power cut spread across town. There had been a few of these power failures in the last week. He'd intended to contact the electricity company to find out if there was an expectation of further problems, but with everything else that was going on it had slipped his mind.

He kept driving, looking out for trouble. The streets felt more dangerous in the unlit night, as if every shadow held a nasty surprise. It was a longer outage than before, twenty-seven minutes before the power returned. When it did, he started to head back to the station, so he could use his cameras and see what Adèle was doing. Then he would have to make a proper decision on what action to take.

As he entered his office, Bruno bounded up from his desk. 'The suspect was spotted, sir,' he said. He was eager, but wary; trying to worm his way back into favour, thought Thomas, after letting the man go in the first place.

'Captured? Did you say captured?' Thomas felt the faintest stirring of hope.

'No, sir,' said Bruno. 'Spotted. A patrol saw him walking in the street. As they approached, he made a run for it. Then the power went, and he gave them the slip in the dark. We tried to get hold of you.'

Thomas felt a stab of frustration; he'd turned off his radio. Maybe, just maybe, that idea of finding Delaître in the streets himself hadn't been so crazy after all. 'Get more people out there,' he said. 'Focus on that area.' Knowing Bruno couldn't see what was on his monitor he opened his security-camera program, wanting to make sure Adèle and Chloé were OK. His face fell when he saw what was on the screen. All the cameras in his house had failed, he thought;

every image was dark. Then he noticed a corner of one image was still barely visible.

'*No*,' he said.

'Sir?'

'Nothing, Bruno. Just go. Get back to me if the suspect is brought in.'

Bruno left, and Thomas hit the desk with his fist. The cameras hadn't failed. Their view was being obscured somehow. And that meant they'd been discovered, that Adèle knew about them. He didn't relish the thought of explaining them to her.

He left the station again and drove straight home. He didn't want to call Adèle, and without the cameras he had no idea if she and Chloé were even there. If they were *safe*. As he approached, he could see that Chloé's bedroom light was on. There was movement in the room. He breathed a sigh of relief, but still checked his gun before he went to the door – Simon could have come back. Adèle was in the hallway as he entered, her face like a dark storm.

'Is he here?' asked Thomas. There was no point in trying to pretend.

'No,' she said, her voice cold. 'He left.'

She stood in the hallway, glaring at him. Irritated, Thomas walked past her.

'How long have the cameras been there?' she snarled, suddenly furious.

'So that's how you want to play it?' said Thomas. 'You think you're the only one with the right to be angry? How long have you been fucking your dead *boyfriend*, Adèle?'

'Keep your voice down,' she said, looking at the ceiling. 'Chloé.'

Thomas bowed his head, his anger deflated. Yes. Chloé. 'I installed the cameras two years ago.'

She nodded, and it was a few seconds before she spoke again. 'I'm leaving you,' she said. There was no triumph in her voice, he noted. Just certainty.

He felt all emotion drain from him, felt as cold and dead inside as the creature she claimed to love. 'You're leaving me for Simon?'

Adèle looked at him with despair, and shook her head. 'How can I trust you? You've been spying on me for two years.'

'I wasn't spying on you,' he said.

'Really?' He saw the anger grow in her. 'On Chloé, then?'

He was distraught. 'God, Adèle . . . how can you think that? I was away from home so often. I was terrified of leaving you on your own, and then sometimes you didn't hear the phone and you didn't answer it. Every time, I'd be scared that you'd done it again. I'd see you in my head, covered in blood, your wrists . . . *open*.' He felt tears start to come, thinking of how he'd felt all those times, just *imagining* Adèle like that. 'I couldn't cope with it, and I couldn't tell you how I felt. So I put the cameras in. Then when you didn't answer the phone, I could make sure you were safe. That was all. To make sure that you were OK. That you hadn't hurt yourself again.'

He could see in her eyes that she believed him. He could see her anger shrink as her thoughts settled. Then she shook her head. 'I'm still leaving, Thomas.' But she sounded far less certain than she had a moment before, he thought.

He felt a tear fall from his eye; he wiped at it hurriedly. 'For a dead man you were afraid of even when he was alive?'

She frowned at him. 'I never said that. All I said was that sometimes . . . Sometimes, I was wary of him. He never *hurt* me.'

Thomas shook his head. 'Of course he hurt you. The scars may not have been physical, Adèle, but we've both been living with them for years.'

She turned away from him, and he knew she was thinking: weighing up her options, the decision to leave him not quite made. At last, she turned back. 'If I do go with Simon, it's a chance for Chloé to know her true father,' she said, sounding desolate. 'It might be a chance for everything to be put right. Everything Simon's accident took away from me.'

Thomas closed his eyes for a moment, torn. He could let her go. Let her go, and make the worst mistake possible. Or he could fight for what they had, and tell her the truth. The secret that he and everyone else who had known had kept from her these last ten years. Their only desire had been to protect her: she'd suffered enough and didn't need to know what had *really* happened that day. But now? Now she had to be told. Had to know the truth about the man she was planning to abandon him for. For her sake, and for Chloé's.

But it would hurt, and he knew it. He opened his eyes and took her hands in his. 'It wasn't an accident,' he said. 'Simon wasn't taken from you, Adèle. He *abandoned* you.'

Adèle looked blank, unable to grasp what he meant. Then a shadow of fear crept across her face. 'What?'

'When Simon died. The priest asked us to call it an accident. But it wasn't.'

She looked at him, lost. 'What was it?' she asked. 'Thomas, *what was it?*'

He told her.

That night, he read Chloé her bedtime story. When he'd finished and returned to his and Adèle's bedroom, Adèle was still dazed, looking at herself in the mirror. Telling her the truth had seemed to shake her clear of Simon's grip, at least for now.

Thomas made a point of changing the sheets. Then he made sure to give Adèle her medication himself. Perhaps she'd stopped taking it, he thought. She'd done that before without discussing it with him, stopped it or reduced the dosage. But it was up to him, now, to take the decisions she could not. He hoped that everything he'd told her would sink in – and that she would understand.

Soon enough, Simon would be in custody again. It would be complicated. Simon was an enigma: a dead man walking through the streets of the town. No home. No family. *I'll be damned if I let him take mine*, he thought. The creature – he couldn't even think of him as a real man – was a loose end.

And Thomas didn't like loose ends.

38

When the power cut came after dusk, Pierre went to stand outside the Helping Hand. High on the valley slope, he watched the town lie in darkness, feeling the cold mountain breeze on his skin. The only buildings he could see lit were those important enough to have their own sources of power: the hospital, the police station and, further up the valley, the control room of the dam itself.

The Helping Hand was also part of that select group. This thought gave him immense satisfaction. He could hear their generator purring; they had their own source of water, too, with the borehole under the building. Everything was ready, for whatever challenges were coming.

Finally the lights came up again, spreading rapidly across the vista in front of him.

He lingered for a moment, enjoying the solitude, then heard Sandrine call his name. It was the police on the phone, asking if he could take in a nine-year-old boy while they tracked down his parents.

It was proving to be a busy night at the shelter. There was already a homeless woman staying with them, sour-faced and stubbornly silent, and as Pierre waited for the police to arrive, he had another unexpected visitor: Simon, a little out of breath, dishevelled and strangely excited.

'I wondered if I could take up your offer again,' said Simon. 'I hope I'm still welcome?'

'Absolutely,' Pierre reassured him. 'You're free to come

and go, but I knew you'd be back. Follow me. Are the police still looking for you?'

Simon grew visibly agitated. He nodded, silent.

'Then you'll have to stay out of sight. They'll be here soon with another lost sheep. Just keep your head down, and there won't be a problem.' Pierre led him through to one of the rooms at the back, somewhere quiet to wait until the coast was clear.

When the police rang again, he was half-expecting their overzealous captain to pester him about whether he'd seen Simon. Instead it was Michael, the officer he'd spoken to at the roadblock earlier.

'You asked about Jérôme Séguret,' said Michael. He was keeping his voice low, and Pierre knew that whatever was coming was confidential. 'I found out a few things, but they go no further, OK?'

'Of course,' Pierre assured him. A minor lie, he thought; telling Claire hardly counted.

'He was questioned about the attack on a barmaid from the Lake Pub, Lucy Clarsen.'

'Really?' said Pierre, shocked. 'Wasn't that why you had the roadblocks?' He'd heard more about the attack since then – the local media had played it down, but for those with an ear to the ground there were plenty of rumours that made for grim listening.

'Yes, but he's been ruled out. There were two things that cropped up as a result, though. First, he'd been visiting Lucy Clarsen regularly for quite some time. I couldn't find out the details, but he was paying her for *favours*, if you get me.'

Pierre understood at once; there were plenty of people in town eager to tell him about those they felt were of loose morals, and he'd heard about a barmaid at the Lake Pub whose virtue was for hire. The idea that Jérôme had been a customer didn't surprise him a great deal. 'And the second?'

'Something happened with his daughter Léna last year. The girl was brought to hospital with a back injury and the doctors reported it as possible parental abuse. They think he hit her. With no prior concerns it was put on file, and no further action was taken.'

'Thank you, Michael,' said Pierre. He took a long, satisfied breath. Jérôme Séguret had been an inconvenience for long enough. He considered for just a moment whether passing on the information was the right thing to do. After all, it had been Pierre who'd encouraged Claire to take her husband back for Camille's sake; that, too, had been the right thing to do, and he certainly hadn't found it easy, but now Jérôme had sealed his own fate.

It seemed only fair. He called Claire and told her everything. She sounded tired, having just got home from the hospital where she'd left Léna for the night.

'I had to tell you, Claire,' he said, sounding almost pained by the task. 'I had no choice. This kind of thing just festers if left alone. Now, you have to forgive him.'

'I don't think I can do that,' Claire said. 'I have to go. Jérôme's just got back.'

Wonderful timing, he thought. Satisfied, Pierre could hear the rage in her voice. 'I'm here for you, Claire,' he said. 'Always.'

He hung up, pleased with the way things had gone – Claire would be furious with Jérôme, and the shambles of their relationship would go down in flames. Pierre, having done all he could to help them salvage things, was blameless.

And now Simon was back, needing Pierre's help. It had been a good day, all round.

Shortly after he'd spoken to Claire, the little boy was dropped off at the Helping Hand by a female officer he recognized as the captain's second-in-command, Pierre and Sandrine both there as welcoming party. The officer seemed oddly reticent about leaving the boy with them.

'Don't worry, Laure,' he said to her, and the look she gave him made him regret being so informal. 'Inspector Valère,' he said, switching tack. 'He'll be fine.'

She stepped a little away from the boy, and lowered her voice. 'His name's Victor,' she said. 'He hasn't spoken, not to anyone. It doesn't seem to be a hearing problem, though.'

Pierre nodded, his expression suitably serious. 'Trauma, maybe,' he said. 'I'll see if I can get him to open up, but the best thing will be to make him feel safe here.' He looked Victor over. The boy was dressed in oddly outdated clothes, possibly indicating a poor home, but the coat he wore seemed new; he was gripping it tightly like a security blanket, looking around with a gaze entirely free from emotion, staying unnervingly silent.

Pierre let Sandrine show the officer out. He took Victor's hand and brought him inside the dormitory. Beds lined both sides of the room, radiators giving off some pleasing warmth. The boy certainly needed some heat – his hand was like ice.

'You can sleep in here,' he said. 'See? It's a bit like a summer camp. Pick whichever bed you want.' Pierre smiled, but the boy seemed troubled, and entirely uninterested in what he was saying. Pierre kept his smile going all the same. 'OK then, how about I choose for you? Here we are.'

SETH PATRICK

The boy sat on the edge of the bed and stared straight ahead of him. Pierre wondered if there might be deeper issues at play – autism perhaps? Still, the boy would be Social Services' problem soon enough. There was little he could do except make him feel secure.

'I'll be next door,' he said. 'Sandrine will look after you. So there's no need to be worried – just come and talk to us, OK?'

Silence.

Pierre still had that smile plastered on his face, and it was in danger of cracking. He could see the upset grow in Victor's expression and felt a sudden concern for him. He had no idea what kind of ordeal the boy had gone through. 'You're not going to cry, are you?' Pierre asked. Victor just looked past him, anxious. Pierre knelt down and took the boy's freezing hands in his. 'There's no need to be scared. You might not think it to look at me, but I was a little boy once. Just like you. And when I was scared, do you know what my grandmother would say?' The boy shook his head. 'She would say, imagine yourself somewhere else, some-where you've been happy. Imagine yourself there, and sing your favourite song. Sing it in your head.'

The boy's expression changed suddenly, and at last Pierre's smile faltered and died away.

With a mixture of recognition and fury, Victor was staring straight at him.

39

After dropping Victor off at the Helping Hand, Laure went back to the station. The boy had given her the creeps, silent the whole time but watching everything with such intensity that it put her on edge.

She was glad to pass the responsibility on. Taking him from Julie had been one of the most difficult things she'd ever done, whatever the rights and wrongs; but of course, seeing Julie at all had been hard, old wounds reopened.

Taking the boy from her had felt like a transgression Julie would probably never forgive, no matter how irrational her desire to keep him with her seemed. Before Julie had been assaulted, Laure had never given the idea of children much thought; Julie hadn't either, as far as Laure knew. But the brutality of the attack had left Julie without any chance of conceiving, and in the weeks afterwards it had become clear how devastating this was for her.

In her clumsy attempts to console and reassure, Laure had just made things worse. Julie had read everything Laure said as contempt for the very idea of them ever having children, for the idea of two women becoming parents. Then Laure had mentioned her career and Julie launched a barrage at her, calling every part of their relationship into question before shutting down. Within a few days Julie had made it known to the hospital staff that Laure was no longer welcome.

Laure had hoped that giving her time might allow things

to heal, and in the weeks and months after Julie left hospital she sent cards, hopeful and tentative, terrified that she was sending too many, fearful that she was sending too few. Julie never replied to any of them.

It had come as a shock to Laure just how quickly the most important relationship she'd ever had – and one she'd believed would go the distance – could unravel. Whether the outcome would have been different if she'd handled it better she couldn't know, but the self-recrimination that followed was long and bitter. Laure didn't need the cold look in Julie's eyes to punish her. She could manage that very well on her own.

When she got back to the station after leaving Victor at the shelter, the pathologist's report on Nathalie Payet was waiting for her. She read it over. At the scene, the pathologist's opinion had been tentative, but the post-mortem was conclusive; here it was, in black and white.

She sought out Bruno, taking the report with her. When she found him and held it up for him to see, he just nodded. 'I already heard,' he said.

She frowned. 'Christ, that got around quickly. I've only just read it.'

'Well, good news travels fast.'

Laure raised an eyebrow. Bad news travelled faster, in her experience. 'Good news for us maybe,' she said. 'Not so much for Nathalie Payet. Has there been anything on Simon Delaître?'

'Nothing since he was spotted earlier. But we have three cars searching now.'

'And Lucy Clarsen?'

Bruno raised an eyebrow. 'You haven't heard?'

She shook her head. 'Too busy on the Payet case.'

'Well, the *first* news on Lucy Clarsen is that she's still hanging on,' said Bruno. 'She might even make it.'

'They think she could pull through?' Laure was amazed. Given the injuries, even the possibility was astonishing.

'It'll be touch and go,' said Bruno. 'But yes, she might. As for the investigation, well . . . we found a diary in Clarsen's apartment. Turned out to be a client appointment book. A dozen men admitted to having sexual relations with her. Some even admitted to paying, but they all denied she was a prostitute.'

Laure was exasperated. 'How do they work that one?'

Bruno smirked. 'They say it wasn't the sex that they were paying for.'

Laure laughed. 'What, they went for a massage and got carried away?'

'No. They all say she was some sort of clairvoyant. Getting them to talk about it was like pulling teeth, but they all said the same thing. She contacted the dead.'

'Sure she did,' mocked Laure. 'And was that before or after they slept together?'

Bruno's eyes widened. 'During.'

Laure whistled, impressed. 'That's a new one.'

Leaving Bruno to his paperwork, she went back to her desk and readied herself to call Julie. When Laure had first heard about the Payet death, like everyone else she'd assumed Lucy's attacker – and almost certainly Julie's – had struck again. Most of the officers there hadn't known of the link with Julie, hadn't known that a previous victim of the attacker was living right next door to another possible victim. Laure had found it deeply concerning that the person who had been attacked was Julie's neighbour. Too big a coincidence, it would have been a significant move on the killer's part.

However, even the initial examinations at the scene had undermined this theory. There were too many disparities – in each of the three previous attacks, similar knife blades had been used, on women walking alone in isolated areas; and of course, there was the cannibalism.

None of that featured in the Payet case, and the weapon had been a pair of scissors found beside the body. Now that she'd read the pathologist's report, Laure found that the truth was even more unexpected.

And it was something Julie deserved to know, immediately. Laure took a breath and dialled her number.

'Hello,' answered Julie.

'It's me,' said Laure. She carried on speaking quickly before Julie had the chance to hang up: 'I wanted to tell you, I took Victor to the Helping Hand. He's safe there. He'll be well looked after. And I'll let you know as soon as anything happens.'

There was silence on the other end of the phone. Then Julie sighed heavily. 'Will I be able to see him?'

'Maybe,' said Laure. 'I'll try and find out. But there's something else. We found your neighbour's cause of death. It wasn't him, Julie. It wasn't the man who attacked you.'

There was another pause. 'Who was it, then?'

'She did it to herself,' said Laure. 'It looks like a suicide. I'm sorry to break it to you like this, but I just wanted to let you know.' Julie was silent. 'Are you still there?' asked Laure.

'Yeah,' said Julie. She sounded relieved.

'Will you be OK?' said Laure. 'Shall I come over? I finish soon. If you want some company, I can—'

'No,' said Julie quietly. 'Goodbye.' She hung up.

Laure stared at the phone in her hand. The offer to come over had surprised her as much as it had – presumably – surprised Julie, but Laure still cared. However much she tried to forget it.

Goodbye, she thought, and put the phone down.

40

After his interrogation, Jérôme found himself sitting in the police station for almost an hour, waiting on a vague promise of a patrol car to give him a lift home – a promise that didn't seem likely to materialize any time soon. He finally gave up and told them he would get the bus. The desk officer shrugged.

On the journey he decided to confess to Claire that he'd been seeing Lucy. He could have made up something to cover his tracks, but she would probably find out sooner or later. In a small town, he supposed there was a good chance Claire had already heard rumours about Lucy being a prostitute, and he was sure that Léna suspected.

Even confessing to seeing a prostitute, he thought, would probably be easier than the full truth. Much easier than going through the pain of the confession he'd given the police.

He walked in.

'Hello?' he called. 'Claire?'

He took off his coat and walked through to the kitchen, almost jumping when he saw Claire sitting at the table, weary eyes trained his way.

'Are you OK?' he asked, concerned. He started towards her.

The bitterness in her voice stopped him short. 'You couldn't even have called?'

'I tried earlier, as soon as they'd finished with me.

Nobody answered. What's wrong?' *Oh shit*, he thought. *She's heard about Lucy already.*

'How *could* you, Jérôme?'

He hung his head and steeled himself for what was coming. 'I'm sorry,' he said. 'I'd been seeing Lucy for a while, but it was nothing, and—'

'I don't care about the *whore*,' said Claire, almost spitting out the words. 'I already knew you were up to something like that.'

He looked at her, baffled. If the anger wasn't about Lucy then what the hell *was* it about?

'Your daughter is in hospital,' she said loud and slow, as if she thought his hearing had gone.

'Camille?' *Jesus*, he thought. If they started running tests, what would they find?

Claire shook her head. 'Didn't you even get the message? *Léna*, Jérôme. Léna's in hospital.'

'I didn't get a message,' he said, hurt that she was holding that against him. He couldn't have known. 'What's wrong with her?'

'An old injury, one that hadn't healed properly. On her back.'

His face fell suddenly, and Claire saw it in his eyes.

'How could you do it? How could you hit Léna?'

'But I didn't.' How on earth had she found out? 'I didn't hit her,' he explained. 'She fell, Claire. I mean, yes, I . . .'

She stood up. If she'd had anything heavy to hand, Jérôme was sure she'd have thrown it at him. 'Get out,' she spat. 'I want you to leave. Now.'

'Did Léna tell you this?' he said. She'd been as keen as he was to keep it quiet, but maybe so much had changed . . .

'Léna would only say that she'd fallen over in the Lake Pub. I could see there was more to it, but asking her about it just upset her.'

'So if Léna didn't tell you, who did?' he said. 'The hospital?' He saw something in her eyes just before Claire looked away, and suddenly it clicked into place. 'Pierre,' said Jérôme, thinking aloud. 'Was that who you heard this from?'

She ignored the question, and he knew he was right. 'How could you hit your *daughter*?' she said.

Pierre, Jérôme thought. Interfering with his family's lives. 'That's not what happened. The bastard wasn't even there!'

'Jérôme,' she said, teeth gritted, purposeful. 'Just look me in the eyes and answer me. Did you hurt Léna?'

Hurt her. Yes, of course he had. He'd been in the Lake Pub, and they'd told him he'd had too much. They refused to give him any more to drink, and he started to shout at them. Léna came over, half-humiliated, half-concerned, trying to persuade him to go home. And he'd pushed her away. She'd fallen over a chair and hit the ground, hard; then she'd followed her dad out, the anger overriding the pain from the gash the chair leg had opened on her back.

They'd both been horrified. He'd taken her to hospital at once; she'd only agreed to let him take her so she could get away from her friends and limit her embarrassment.

And that was all it was. *Almost* all. There was also what he'd said to her, something that had probably cut even deeper.

Léna had been wary around him ever since.

So, yes. He'd hurt her. He couldn't deny it, and any attempt to explain would make things worse.

'I want you out of here,' she said. 'It's over.'

And for the second time in their marriage, Jérôme left.

41

Léna had woken in the dark, with the touch of Frédéric's hand on her arm.

But the room was empty. She sat up, too quickly – the pain from the wound on her back flared. She swore.

Carefully, she got out of the hospital bed and went to the window. The town was in darkness, save for the headlights on the sparse traffic; a power cut, she realized. The familiar streets looked almost forlorn, lost without light.

She glanced at the door to the room and was relieved to see dim lighting in the hall. Of course, the hospital had its own emergency power; the light in her room was off to let her sleep.

She raised her arms, flexing the skin on her back, gently testing the injury. It had thrown the doctors, for a while. They'd swabbed the wound and taken samples, then claimed it was an old scar opening up again. A spontaneous keloid, they called it, but the rapid spread of it had them flummoxed.

The puzzled-looking doctor had stood beside her, all white coat and efficiency, trying to be a reassuring presence. As if they had any clue as to what was really going on. 'They can form over any kind of abrasion. Do you remember getting scraped or burned there, maybe?' the doctor had asked.

'Maybe,' she'd said. Her mum had been with her, and noted Léna's reluctance to answer. She pressed and pressed, until Léna told her the bare essence of it: she'd hurt it when she was knocked over in the Lake Pub, a year before.

Her mum pressed for more, and it all suddenly became too much. Hell, she was tired, and worried, and her back hurt, and Léna knew exactly why her mum was so eager to find something to blame.

Because the real cause was right there: Camille, hovering near the far wall like a ghost, a constant reminder of everything that was fucked up in her life at the moment.

And still her mum pushed for answers, until Léna over-reacted. She shouted at them to leave, to give her some peace and quiet. Her mum was reluctant but she eventually went, promising to be back first thing in the morning. Camille trailed out behind her, delivering one final pointed look at Léna before she left.

Meanwhile, with test results pending, the doctors had warned her of the risk of infection and ulceration. They'd given her an injection of antibiotics. Oh, and promises of some more swabs and samples to be taken in the morning. Painful ones, she presumed. They almost seemed pleased by the novelty of a mystery. *Hah*, she thought – if they loved medical conundrums they should take a look at Camille. She'd love to see what they made of *that*.

She sighed and gingerly tested her limits with the wound. It didn't hurt, as long as she kept her movements within sensible boundaries.

Then, standing in the dark, she felt Frédéric's fingertips on her arm again.

Her hands shot to her mouth. The sensation had been far too real. She had a sudden image of Frédéric, with Camille. *Surely not . . .*

Her clothes were in the cupboard on the far side of the room. She put them on over the hospital gown. The Lake Pub was maybe a thirty-minute walk. She was feeling fine. If she'd insisted, they would probably have had to discharge her anyway, she reckoned.

She crept out of her room. The dim corridors, with their emergency lighting, were almost empty; dressed, nobody would have thought her a patient. She left unchallenged. It was only when she was halfway to the pub that the power came back. As it did, a thought occurred to her: how did she even know where Frédéric and Camille were? It was like . . .

Like it used to be. Before Camille had died, back when – rare, fleeting – each could sense what the other was doing.

She reached the pub and went inside, feeling horribly weak the instant she saw them. Frédéric and Camille sitting alone, sitting close. Laughing. She saw red, suddenly, knowing the risk Camille was taking, knowing she shouldn't even be out of the *house*.

And knowing, too, that it was more than that: a deep stab of jealousy as she saw the way they had their heads together, the playful smile Camille gave him, the deliberate brush of her hand on his leg. Léna gathered herself and strode across to them.

'What's going on?' she said.

'Léna?' said Camille, guilt and anxiety washing across her face. 'Are you OK?'

Caught you, thought Léna. *Fucking caught you.* 'They discharged me, didn't they?' She turned to Frédéric and sneered at him. 'Having fun?'

Frédéric looked sheepish, but defiant. 'I invited your cousin in for a drink,' he said.

'My cousin?' said Léna, bitter. 'I don't have one.'

Frédéric's smile grew nervous. 'You don't?'

'No.'

'Come off it,' said Frédéric. 'It's obvious. You look so similar.'

Camille was getting more and more agitated. 'Stop it, Léna,' she said.

'Shut up!' hissed Léna.

'Leave her alone,' said Frédéric. 'What did she ever do to you?'

Léna took off her coat and lifted the back of her shirt. 'That.'

Frédéric stared at the wound, shocked. 'Christ! How did it get so bad?'

Léna pointed at Camille. 'Ask her.'

'Don't, Léna,' warned Camille.

But Léna felt defiant. If her sister wanted to be out in the open, if she wanted to try and steal Frédéric . . . *Let's see if he wants her when he knows the truth.* 'Tell him who you are,' said Léna. 'Or should I?' She got a blank stare from Frédéric. 'Don't you recognize her?' she whispered. 'For fuck's sake, it's Camille!'

Frédéric shook his head, angry with her. 'That's not funny, Léna.'

'Ask her, if you don't believe me.'

'I'm Alice,' said Camille, visibly furious. 'You know that. Maybe you should still be in hospital.'

Léna, exasperated, looked at Camille, then at Frédéric.

Both of them were looking at her as though she was mad. Maybe she was. That would be better than the reality.

'Fuck both of you!' yelled Léna before storming out into the darkness.

As she left the pub, she started to feel too hot. She knew she'd overdone it, that she hadn't been ready to leave hospital, but she kept on going, too angry with Camille, with Frédéric. With the whole fucking *world*.

Even as she grew weaker, she had to keep moving. Each time she paused, her thoughts roiled in her head: she thought of her sister's face, back when it was the face that they both shared, laughing and loving and without a care; she thought of standing by her sister's grave, falling apart, knowing half of her soul had been ripped out of her. And she thought of Frédéric, keeping her alive. Keeping her from going under.

Camille died, and her life turned to shit. Camille came back, and it happened again. She didn't want it in her head, any of it; she walked as fast as she could, keeping those thoughts at bay.

She reached the underpass, stumbling down the steps, barely keeping her balance. Moments later she found herself leaning against the tiles on the tunnel wall, gasping for each breath. She slid down until she was on the ground, unable to go any further.

Someone was coming. She could see a blurred shape at the far end of the tunnel. A man, hooded, walking purposefully towards her.

Scared now, she tried to stand, but it was impossible. Just before she blacked out, she saw his face, and she thought:

Thank God. Thank God that it was someone she recognized.

Toni's brother. Serge.

42

Anton breathed the early-morning air, still heavy with mist that had barely cleared. He looked out into the valley, to the shrouded banks of the lake. The water level hadn't been this low for eight years, Eric had said, since the last time the dam underwent a full maintenance cycle.

He had volunteered to walk the inspection galleries within the dam, and as he descended he found it curious how, even with the water level so low, the psychological weight of water above him felt no less than it always had. Indeed, if anything it had grown.

In the lower gallery, as he approached the far end of the tunnel, the lighting started to falter, pulsing slowly off and on. *A glitch with the power feed*, he thought, taking the torch from his belt. He switched it on, only to find that it was failing too, in perfect timing with the strips hung along the wall. He did what everyone did when faced with the impossible: he tried his best to ignore it, stopping for ten seconds or so each time the total darkness swallowed him, waiting for the light to come back. It felt as though he was playing some perverse childhood game.

Then, standing still in the dark, he heard it. Just ahead, where the tunnel finished near the western abutments. It sounded like breathing. Like an animal, scuffling around, maybe five metres away from him. Something large. He strained to hear anything more, certain it was coming closer. Closer.

Slowly the lights started to return and he could see a shape right in front of him in the gloom. He backed away in panic. The lights suddenly flickered fully on. The tunnel was empty.

He hurried out, and told Eric that there was no way he would be doing the inspection next time. 'If ever,' he said.

Eric smiled, not in humour. Sympathy. 'So you finally heard something,' he said, and refused to say any more about it. Instead he changed the subject and started to talk about his family, rambling on about this and that. Anton was glad of it, taking his mind away from the dark of the tunnels and the ragged breathing that had seemed close enough to touch.

'My grandfather once told me something about pain,' Eric said. 'People hold on to their pain, he told me. Sometimes they nourish it, the way an oyster nourishes grit to make a pearl. They take the pain and if they're lucky it becomes something positive. Something beautiful.' He swigged from the mug of coffee he was holding. 'But other times, he told me, pain was like a thorn. You try and forget about it, and years later it works its way out and leaves a hole that will never heal.'

Eric took a long breath. He stood and wandered over to the window in the control room, looking out at the lake ahead. 'And I said, "But what if it never comes out?" And he frowned and said, "Well, then it works its way in so deep, it changes what you are. Steals the good in you. Robs you of your soul." He said to me: "Eric, a body without a soul is the thing I fear most."'

He turned around to face Anton, the lake at his back. 'I was twelve years old at the time. Years later I learned that when he told me that, he'd just been diagnosed with dementia. It took him a long time to go, piece by piece. A body, without a soul.'

They sat in silence for a while, before Eric asked: 'Will you be going on any outings with our friend Dreyfus today, Anton?'

'None planned,' Anton said. The divers would come tomorrow to check the lake bed. Until then, Anton presumed Dreyfus would spend his time handling the power-station crisis. He hoped Dreyfus would have no more need of his services, and would stop filling his mind with worrying questions.

The day before, late morning, the call had come through from the power station, half a kilometre downstream of the dam. It was experiencing flooding issues and they had no idea how to deal with them, with no obvious source for the water; asking if there was a chance of leakage from the lake.

Dreyfus had taken Anton along with him.

'Just back me up,' Dreyfus said. 'Whatever I tell them, back me up.'

When they got there it was the switchyard that had been the worst affected, and the transformer arrays. The whole area was flooded and the drainage seemed to be doing nothing. As things stood Anton knew it was dangerous, that the electricity generation should ideally be shut down, but the issue wasn't raised by the power station's chief engineer. As if it wasn't even an option.

He listened in to the discussion the engineer was having with Dreyfus and he could tell at once that, for the senior staff at least, the employment situation was similar to that for the dam engineers.

Do what you're told. Don't ask questions.

Dangerous or not, the generators could keep running as long as the water didn't rise too much further. Tankers were already on their way, and would be able to pump the water out, drive it through town, and pump it back into the river downstream.

'We'll need a phased shutdown tonight,' the engineer had said. 'The maximum duration allowed.'

Dreyfus had given the engineer a long look. 'Is that really necessary?'

'We've already had outages this week. Maintenance is overdue. We're behind schedule on repairs. We need the time.'

Anton had returned to the top of the dam that night, bristling with questions. And this morning, he still had them buzzing around in his head, eager to escape. But he would keep them inside and hold on to his job. For now.

Through the control-room windows Anton looked out into the diminished lake, and wondered why Dreyfus had paled at the thought of a blackout.

In the middle of the lake, the steeple of the old village's ruined church was showing above the water. The image came to him of a thorn, working its way out.

43

Toni drove to the old house. He kept an eye on the road behind him, still wondering if the police were watching his movements. He'd heard rumours that the investigation had moved on and there were other men being interviewed about Lucy. Even so, it always paid to be careful.

He'd left Serge in the house with strict instructions to stay out of sight. If that proved impossible – since the prospect of the police showing up there unannounced couldn't be ruled out – he'd told Serge to say as little as he could.

'Who do I say I am?' Serge asked.

'When you . . . when you died,' said Toni, 'if anyone asked we would say you'd gone to Paris to find work as a mechanic. So tell them you're back to visit.'

Serge nodded, while in his head Toni thought about how few people had known Serge was there at all, even before the killings had begun. The story about Paris had been in use long before Serge's death. Long before.

He'd known from an early age that there was something *off* with Serge. It had been animals, to begin with. Serge and Toni, hunting together; Serge the loving brother looking out for Toni, teaching him the basic hunting skills he'd learned from their father. They brought home venison and rabbits, Toni proud that his brother treated him as an equal. Nothing had seemed wrong on those trips, yet Toni had known how his big brother liked to go out alone sometimes, how he would shoot to wound the animals, bring them down for the real sport he sought.

Once, Serge told him about a deer he'd shot only to discover the animal was heavily pregnant. Serge told him how he'd cut the fawn out, cleared its mouth of gore, then watched as the animal fought to live, as it stood and cried out. And then, how he'd looked *into* the mother, pulled apart the workings of life itself, peered inside and tried to understand how something could contain so much power.

'I felt blessed,' Serge said. 'To be so close to it.'

It was the first time Toni had felt the stirrings of unease at his brother's unusual fascinations. 'The mother was already dead?' he asked. 'When you cut out the fawn?'

Serge said nothing. Then Toni wondered aloud how long a fawn could be expected to live, without a mother to look after it. 'All children need their mother,' said Toni. 'To keep them safe.'

'I know that,' Serge had said, suddenly angry. 'Of course I know.'

All children need their mother, Toni thought now, as he drove to the house. But sometimes the mother wasn't strong enough. He remembered shouting at her, that terrible night. Shouting at his own mother, seven years ago: 'Why did you let him out?'

'He pleaded, Toni,' his mother said, distraught. 'He was in a prison. It was killing him. He promised me he wouldn't do anything, just walk in the forest. He promised me.'

Toni looked at her with such a lack of respect, with such contempt, that it had haunted him ever since. They had known beyond doubt after the second killing, when he'd come back to the house in a daze with a blood-caked face, but surely his mother had been suspicious even after the first, just as Toni had been. Their guilt was shared before, but now she alone had let him go. It was all on her.

He ran to his truck and drove into town. Serge had talked in the weeks he had been locked inside the house, talked of the thoughts that ran through him, the urges and the needs. He had spoken of the places he would wait, the times he knew would be best, the times that had more power. The turning of the year had been the best of all, Serge had said. When the old year dies, and the new is born.

Mother and child.

'My last,' Serge had sworn. 'Let me go. It will be the last.'

But it would never be the last, Toni knew.

He had had to work that night, but he'd promised his mother he would be home well before midnight, when he expected Serge to become more restless and harder for his mother to deal with alone. Toni was true to his word, only to find his mother had been weak. She had given in to her first-born.

As she always had, Toni thought with real bitterness.

The underpass was the second place he'd looked. If he'd gone there first, then he might have been in time to stop it. Instead, as the fireworks continued all around the town, he reached the base of the steps and saw Serge on his knees, leaning over a body.

Toni ran at him, tyre iron in his hand. As he drew close the sight made him freeze. Serge looked up, almost unrecognizable as the brother he loved, his wild eyes full of a terrible lust, his mouth and chin coated in blood. Below him the woman lay dead, her stomach pouring with blood from a dozen wounds. Serge's eyes had just enough time to focus, to recognize his brother standing over him, before Toni brought the steel down, hearing the crack of his brother's skull resonate in the tunnel, mingling with the thumps of the fireworks.

He hit him again, wanting it over. Serge lay silent but was still breathing.

As Toni bent down to lift Serge he realized that the woman was breathing too, in shallow gasps. She was unconscious, not dead after all. He stared at her for a few seconds but he knew what needed to be done.

He took her first and placed her gently in the back of the truck. Then he returned for Serge, throwing his brother in beside the woman. Seeing the severity of his head wound, he wished that Serge would stop breathing, just *stop* and end this for all of them.

He drove to the hospital. Not wanting to be seen, he left the woman in the road under a street light near the ambulance bays, hoping he wouldn't have to somehow call attention to her. He waited in the truck further on, praying. At last the bay doors rolled up; someone noticed the body and ran to it.

Toni drove.

At the house his mother emerged. 'He did it again,' he told her. For a moment she was too shocked to speak. It wouldn't last, and Toni didn't want to hear it: excuses, pleas for another chance. 'Not a word, Mum,' he warned her. 'Nothing. We've let this go on too long.'

Her tears came. She closed her eyes and bowed her head; Toni took it as a nod, as agreement.

He took a shovel and started to dig. When it was deep enough he threw Serge into the grave. His brother came round as Toni shovelled the dirt onto his face. Serge spat out the soil, dazed and horrified. 'What are you doing?' he shouted. 'Christ, Toni! Stop it!'

Toni could hear the fear in his brother's voice, but he said nothing. His mother was inside the house now, but he could see her, watching through her bedroom window.

Toni kept shovelling, remembering Serge as a boy, running through the woods together, curled up inside the house, his big brother's arms sheltering him from the cold. He remembered the stories Serge told him, of gods and wild things in the forest.

And he thought of the expression of bestial obscenity as Serge consumed a young woman's still-breathing body. Toni looked at his brother, lying in the hole he'd dug. Serge called for his mother, called again and again, but Toni knew what had to be done to a rabid animal. He brought the shovel down hard, twice, three times, sobs pouring from his body until the skull gave way and his brother, finally, was silent.

Toni's mother hadn't spoken to him again. Not really. Not beyond simple requests and instructions. They moved around each other, living separate lives in the same house, both hollowed out by the deed that had been committed. He soon came to realize, as he relived that night again and again, that what he'd taken as a nod from his mother, as her permission to do what needed to be done, had only meant she was resigned to Toni's actions. The rights and wrongs were never discussed and his mother gave up on living.

Everything Serge had done, all the pain, all the terror. All the death. Even with all that, their mother had loved him without question.

But not Toni, no. Not him. His morality had cost him that love, and the price was one he couldn't bear. Now Serge was back and Toni didn't dare hope . . .

Perhaps there was a way. A way to make amends.

As he drove up to the house, he saw Serge outside chopping wood. Only when he parked did he see that it wasn't wood he was hitting with the axe. It was a mobile phone, shattering under repeated blows.

Toni took a deep breath and walked over. 'Is it hers?' he asked.

Serge frowned. 'What?'

'Is it Lucy's phone?'

Serge wouldn't meet his eyes but he nodded.

'You should have told me you had it. If it had been switched on, it could have brought the police here.'

'I'm sorry,' said Serge.

Toni shook his head. His anger was spent, for now. He'd already railed at his brother about Lucy; raged at him all night, triggered by the self-pity Serge had shown.

'I saw her and I couldn't help it,' Serge had said. 'It's hard for me.'

Toni had become enraged. 'It doesn't matter how hard it is for you,' he said. 'You've terrorized, tortured, *killed*.' Toni talked about trust, about decency to others. He talked about how his mother loved Serge more than him, about how that made him feel. That she loved a monster, and despised a man who tried to do the right thing.

'I will change, Toni,' Serge said. 'I will change. For you. I swear it.'

Serge thanked Toni for promising to look after him, and vowed again and again to change. If only that was all it took,

Toni thought, then things would be so much simpler. Too many promises, too readily given: as many as the wind can carry, his mother used to say.

Toni knew that it was an addiction that Serge suffered from – he could only hope that this time Serge would finally be able to control it, and keep the promise he'd made.

And then, Serge had looked at his little brother, his eyes pleading. 'How did I die, Toni?' he'd said. 'I can't remember anything about it. How did it happen?'

Toni froze. Then he looked at his brother and grabbed hold of him. He hugged him tightly. 'Don't think of the past,' he said. 'There's only the future. A new life. That's all that matters.'

Serge hadn't asked about his death again.

Toni made Serge gather the pieces of the phone he'd destroyed. Then they went inside, Toni carrying a box of supplies.

'So,' said Toni. 'What have you been doing? Hunting?'

'A little,' said Serge.

'We could go together, if you want? Like old times.'

'It's getting late,' said Serge, oddly wary. 'Perhaps tomorrow.'

Toni heard a noise from elsewhere in the house.

'Is someone here?' He said it too quickly, and with suspicion in his voice. He saw the frown on Serge's face. *Trust goes both ways*, he told himself.

'No,' said Serge, nervous.

The sound came again, and Toni realized where it had come from: his mother's bedroom. He felt a moment of hope. *Please God*, he thought, *let it be her.* He took a step towards the door but Serge moved to block his way.

'What are you doing?' said Toni.

'Nothing.'

'Is it her?' he said, almost pleading. 'Has she come back?'

Serge stayed where he was, silent and uneasy. Toni considered just trying to barge past – but if it was who he hoped, she wouldn't want that. 'Is it Mum?' he asked.

Serge nodded.

For a moment Toni was overjoyed. Then he despaired, as he realized why Serge was blocking the way. 'She won't see me?'

Serge shook his head and Toni found it unbearable. His mother had come back, but only to punish him. Punish him even more than she already had. 'Mum?' he called to her, distraught. 'Please?'

Silence from the bedroom. Silence from Serge.

Toni turned and left the house, his tears flowing. He went to his truck, fearing that he would always be denied his mother's forgiveness.

Once he'd gone, Serge went to their mother's room to see if the girl he'd found had woken yet.

44

Léna fought her way back up from the deepest sleep she'd ever known. She had moments of lucidity: at one point, she knew she could hear her phone ring somewhere distant, the familiar ringtone she'd set for her mother; then the ringing stopped abruptly with the sound of something being smashed. She went under again, resurfacing to the sound of raised voices nearby.

This time she held on; clawing her way to consciousness she managed to open her eyes. She didn't know where she was. In sudden panic, she realized that the clothes she'd thrown on before leaving hospital were gone, and she was only wearing the hospital gown.

The panic made her sit up suddenly. The flare of agony from the wound on her back was enough for her to black out again, briefly. The next thing she knew she was on bare wood.

Léna opened her eyes as the man leaned over her. She was sprawled on the floor. *Serge*, she remembered. His eyes were clear blue, but she couldn't read what lay behind them – anxiety perhaps, or curiosity.

'It's OK,' said Serge, in a whisper. He helped her onto the bed. She cried out as the pain flared again; Serge helped her onto her side and covered her gently with a blanket. She lay still, and the pain settled. She noticed the musty smell in the room, and realized it was coming from the bed itself. Not used for a while, not changed for a while. The room was sparse, the walls papered in a drab green, a small table at the bedside looking like a battered antique.

'Why am I here?' she asked.

He didn't meet her gaze. 'You'd fainted, so I brought you back.'

'I should be in hospital,' she said. She felt exhausted, and was still vague about what had happened the night before. 'I left before I was ready.'

'You just looked like you needed a good sleep.' He smiled at her. There was something broken about his smile, Léna thought. 'Sleep more. I'll bring you something.'

When he left her, she remembered the confrontation with Camille, remembered stumbling out into the dark streets, leaving herself so vulnerable. *Stupid, stupid*, she thought, cursing her stubbornness.

Her exhaustion was profound; the next she knew, she was waking again, knowing she'd slept for a significant time. It was still light outside, but it felt more like afternoon than morning now.

She tested her back again, enough to convince herself that the earlier flare-up had been down to the speed she'd sat upright, tearing at healing tissue. That, and the fact that whatever drugs the hospital had given her had long worn off.

Serge must have been listening out for her to wake, and shortly afterwards he came in carrying a tray with a glass of water and a small bowl.

'Sit up,' he said, his voice gentle. 'Slowly.'

She did as he asked, wincing when she felt tender skin pull and the pain rise again.

He nodded, and produced a pill bottle from his pocket.

'Just paracetamol,' he said, handing it to her. 'It's all we have, but it'll take the edge off.'

She took two pills, and swallowed them gratefully with a swig of the water.

'Do you mind if I get a better look at your back?' said Serge.

She gave him a wary glance, but shook her head, desperate to know how the injury looked now. He went around to the other side of the bed and undid the straps on the back of the hospital gown, saying nothing. She could hear his breathing grow louder behind her.

'How is it?' said Léna, trying to keep as still as possible. 'They gave me antibiotics, it should have helped.'

'It doesn't look infected now,' he said. 'But it does look painful. It looks like a . . .' He paused. 'Like a fresh wound,' he said, his voice strangely uneven. He reached around her, holding the bowl in his hand, showing her the contents.

'What's that?' she said.

'My mother used to make this if I ever cut myself. It's a nettle poultice. It'll reduce the inflammation and seal the wound.'

She looked warily at it. Dark green slop. Disgusting. 'Nettles sting.'

'Not when you boil them. Trust me.'

Léna thought about it. If anything could help get this sorted then she might as well try it – it wasn't as if the doctors at the hospital had had the answers. 'Go on, then.'

She could hear his breathing again behind her as he spread the cold poultice on the wound. She expected it to hurt, but it didn't. Serge sounded more worried than she was; his breath grew ragged, and he kept pausing.

Shy, Léna thought. Probably uncomfortable around girls at the best of times, let alone half-naked ones. She thought she'd distract him, try to put him at his ease. 'So you're Toni's brother,' she said.

'Uh-huh,' he managed.

'Are brothers as much of a pain as sisters?'

Serge just kept on applying the poultice, without answering. After a moment he stopped. 'That's it done,' he said. He came around to the side, and grabbed a towel he'd left hanging on the doorknob, wiping the green gunk off his hands without meeting her eyes.

'Well?' she said, seeing how ill at ease the guy looked. 'I've a sister, and she's always been annoying. I say that, even though I'd do anything for her, you know?'

Serge looked at her; stared, really, as if he'd not actually noticed her before. 'I know,' he said. 'You make them promises, and no matter how hard it is you don't want to let them down. Even if they always disagree. Even if they never understand. And sometimes . . .' Serge clenched his fists. He looked torn; what she'd intended as a little small talk had turned out far more intense. She regretted saying anything. 'Sometimes you make promises you might not be able to keep.'

He was staring at her again, for long seconds. Long enough for her to feel uncomfortable; to recognize that she was alone, God knows where, with someone she knew next to nothing about. Then he sighed and looked down. 'Are you hungry?' he asked.

Léna nodded cautiously. 'A little.'

'Me too. I'll get us some food.'

45

The hospital staff had sounded almost embarrassed when they'd first rung Claire to ask if she had any idea where her daughter was. The question had struck Claire as ludicrous, as if they'd somehow misplaced Léna, or forgotten which room she was supposed to be in.

The reality dawned quickly enough.

She'd called around, without luck; Jérôme, of course, had wanted to come to the house, but she'd told him not to; that instead he should look for her in known haunts around town.

When Camille came downstairs Claire was calling the hospital back to tell them there was no sign of Léna anywhere.

'What's wrong?' asked Camille.

Claire finished her call and sighed. 'Léna sneaked out of hospital last night. Nobody knows where she is.'

'Have you tried her mobile?'

Claire raised an eyebrow, careful to keep her temper under control. 'Of course. No answer.'

Camille shrugged carelessly. 'She must be with friends then. Or Frédéric.'

Claire looked at Camille, annoyed that she was treating this so casually. 'I wish I could be so certain. She often goes places without telling anyone, but the hospital's concerned. If her condition got any worse . . .'

Camille rolled her eyes. 'She's not stupid, Mum. If she

thought she was ready to leave, I'm sure she's OK. And if she felt sick, she would call.'

Claire nodded; Camille had a point, but it didn't make her feel much better. Stubborn as Léna was, if she'd left the hospital then she must have been feeling well enough. Sneaking out behind the backs of the staff was exactly Léna's style; so, too, was switching off her phone and getting some time to herself.

All very self-centred. All very Léna.

'I know she was angry with me,' Claire said. 'About the idea of moving away. Was there anything else, Camille? Anything she might have talked to you about?'

Camille shook her head. 'The move, that sounds about right.' After a few seconds of thinking, she added: 'Do you think Léna's sleeping with Frédéric?'

Claire sighed. 'What, did she say they were fighting again?'

'No, I just . . . I just wondered.'

Only natural, Claire thought. Both of her girls had liked Frédéric. And after Camille's death, she knew he and Léna had grown close, but . . .

It had always been complicated. 'I don't know, Camille,' she said. 'We don't talk about it. We don't really talk about anything.'

When Claire rang Pierre to tell him about Léna, he soothed her fears in much the same way Camille had. *Léna's head-strong, but she's a clever girl. Try not to worry.* Claire knew that she'd been *trying* not to worry about her daughters since the day they were born. She'd always failed.

Then Pierre suggested something that took her by surprise.

She found herself a little anxious when he arrived at the door thirty minutes later in the company of a dead man.

'Claire, this is Simon,' he said. 'He's the one I mentioned. You're sure this is still OK?'

'Of course,' she said. 'It will be good for Camille to know she's not the only one.' She invited them in, trying not to show how anxious she felt. She looked at Simon. He was an attractive young man; polite, yes, and there was a vulnerability to him, but she found herself feeling uneasy. His expression was guarded and he seemed a little agitated, but there was more to her disquiet than that. Looking at him, all she could think was: *You're dead. A dead man, standing in front of me.*

It was a strange thing, she thought, to feel such reservations given that Camille was exactly the same. But then, Camille was her own daughter; Claire had no idea who this man was. It was natural for her to be uneasy.

She led them upstairs to Camille's room and knocked.

'This is Simon,' Claire explained when Camille opened the door. 'He's the man Léna met. The one who's like you.'

Claire watched her daughter's face as she laid eyes on Simon, wondering if there would be some kind of connection, some kindred recognition. There was nothing but a slight sense of awkwardness around each other. She didn't want to think too much about why that left her oddly relieved.

Simon held out his hand. Camille shook it carefully and gestured for him to come in. Claire went to follow but

Pierre put his hand on her shoulder. 'I think,' he said, 'that we should leave these two alone to talk, yes?'

Claire was reluctant to leave Camille alone in her room with a stranger, let alone a *dead* stranger, but she supposed Pierre was right. She turned to Camille. 'I expect you're hungry?' As always there was an eager nod. 'I'll make you both some food.'

Camille sat on her bed, looking at Simon with intense curiosity. 'So when did you die?' she asked.

'Ten years ago.' Simon moved across to the window, looking outside.

'I bet a lot's changed.'

He shrugged. 'Everything.'

'Do you remember what happened before you came back?'

He turned round to her, his expression distant and sad. 'No,' he said. 'I can't even remember dying.'

'That's good to know!' said Camille, smiling; then she caught herself, and wiped the smile from her face. 'Well, I mean . . . I can't remember, either. It's good to know I'm not the only one.' She fidgeted in the silence that followed. 'Do you know why we came back?'

He looked at her. Both were eager to know the answer to that one. 'I have no idea.'

'You don't say a lot,' she said. 'My sister mentioned you weren't talkative. Were you like that before you died?'

He smiled.

'Oh, come *on*,' said Camille, infuriated. 'Tell me *something*. Did you have a girlfriend? At least tell me that.'

Simon looked away and nodded.

'Not easy, is it?' said Camille. 'I had a boyfriend. They say love is stronger than death, but it's not true.' More silence; Camille tried again to engage him. 'And why am I so hungry? I mean, I'm already dead, so what would happen if I didn't eat?'

He smiled. 'If you feel as hungry as me, I don't think we'd have the willpower to find out.'

She grinned at him. 'Breakthrough! A whole sentence! So you can talk after all! I was starting to wonder why you wanted to meet me.'

He came back from the window and sat next to her. 'Actually, there is something you could help me with. If you want. A message you could deliver.'

The dead girl nodded. 'Ah,' she said. 'It's like that, is it? But I'm not allowed out of the house, and my mum's keeping a close eye on me. I think she knows I've been sneaking out.'

'I'll tell her you're sleeping. Surely you'd like to get out for a while?'

She thought for a moment and smiled. 'Tell me about it . . .' she said. 'OK, it's a deal. You cover for me, and I'll deliver your message. I guess us zombies have to stick together.'

Claire was in the middle of making sandwiches when Jérôme rang, but he had no news to give her and she had none to give him. He would continue to look; Claire would continue to wait.

He'd sounded apologetic, timid even; she could imagine his face flinch every time she spoke, the seething anger clear in every word.

She found Simon's presence in the house unnerving; she wished Pierre had stayed a little longer, but he'd insisted he had a tight schedule. What schedule, he wouldn't say, but there'd been an excited glint in his eye that intrigued her.

Just as she finished loading a tray with food Simon came down the stairs.

'I was about to bring this up to you both,' she said, making the effort to smile.

'Camille's sleeping.'

Claire was wide-eyed; she smiled with genuine relief. 'That's *wonderful*,' she said, suddenly far happier with Simon's presence, especially if that was what had allowed Camille to relax enough to get some proper rest. 'I don't think she's really slept since she came back. Did you talk?'

'Yes,' he said. 'There wasn't much we could tell each other, but it helps to know I'm not the only one. I know Camille feels the same.' Simon reached out to the sandwiches. 'May I?'

'Of course. Are you always hungry, too?'

He smiled. 'Yeah.' He took a bite.

'Pierre told me you were considering leaving town.' She was thinking on her feet, but it might be an idea to let him stay for a day or so in case he and Camille could find more to talk about. 'If you like you can stay here while you decide?'

Simon hurried to swallow. 'Thanks,' he said. 'But I don't want to impose. Only one thing makes sense to me now. To start a new life somewhere else and take my wife and daughter with me. Tonight, if I can.'

'You have a daughter?' said Claire. Simon nodded, smiling. She could see the pride in his eyes. Claire tried to smile back, but she couldn't help thinking of what being a parent had cost her. Thinking of all the loss, all the fear. The pain of it. 'It's the most wonderful thing in the world,' she said.

46

While the dead man and the dead girl had talked, across town Victor sat at a table in the fifties-styled diner with the lady who'd also been staying at the Helping Hand.

Viviane, she called herself. Viviane Costa. She'd picked a table away from the window. 'See, I told you it wasn't so far to walk here,' she said. 'But the food is better than the healthy slop they dish up at the Helping Hand. They mean well, but sometimes only junk food will do. Worth sneaking out for.' She'd told him about her husband, as they'd walked; told him how he'd not been able to deal with her coming back, thirty years after her death. She'd talked a lot as they'd made their way, filling the silence because Victor had said nothing.

When the waitress came over and handed them menus, Viviane Costa smiled at Victor. 'I recommend the Big Burger. It's filling.' She put her hand in a pocket and pulled out a fistful of change and a few notes, looking at them with a level of disdain. 'Plus, it's all I can stretch to. I had to leave my home in a bit of a hurry. I was lucky to grab anything.'

'Will I ever see my parents again?' the boy asked.

She looked at him and smiled. 'Finally, you talk to me. It's about time. I'm sure you will. They were good people.'

'You knew them?'

'A little. I remember when it happened. When your family was killed. It was a terrible thing. The grief affected the whole town.' She stopped, suddenly, and frowned, the memory seeming to trouble her. 'A terrible, shameful thing.'

'Why haven't they come back too?' said the boy.

She shook her head. 'I don't know. Maybe they have. Maybe they're looking for you right now.' She raised a hand and called the waitress over, and put in their order. 'It won't be long,' she told the boy, then laughed. 'But it'll feel like forever. Now, tell me. Pierre, at the Helping Hand. Did you know him before?'

The boy looked away, frightened.

'I saw how you looked at him,' she said. 'You don't have to be scared. No one can hurt us now.'

He looked at her, fearful yet determined. 'But can we hurt other people?'

'Oh, I don't think they need *us* for that.' She paused, leaned over the table a little, and whispered: 'Why, is there someone you want to hurt?'

Victor said nothing.

Even though Julie had lived alone for most of her adult life, her apartment had never felt as empty as it had since Victor had been taken away. She had no patients to see that day, but she knew that if she had she would have been entirely unable to concentrate on work. As it was, every few minutes she found herself coming up with excuses that would allow her entrance to the Helping Hand, just in case she could see Victor. She wondered if he thought of her, and the look that must have been on her face as he'd left. Shock, fear; the realization that Victor had been the cause of Nathalie Payet's death. She knew he'd done it to protect them both. *How* he'd done it was another question. She thought about the similarity between her neighbour's death and the vision of her attacker that Victor had saved her from – his hands holding back her own, the scissors she held ready to inflict the same kind of damage that had killed Mademoiselle Payet. What it meant about Victor, Julie didn't want to dwell on.

Even so, when the doorbell rang she desperately hoped that it was him.

It was Laure. 'Can I come in?'

'No,' said Julie, scowling. 'Has there been any luck finding his parents?'

Laure ignored the question. 'Is he here?'

'What? Is who here?'

'Victor.'

'Why would he be here?' The penny dropped. 'Christ, have you lost him?'

Laure looked defensive and a little shamefaced. 'He isn't at the Helping Hand. I called them to see how he was doing, and . . . Well, I thought he might be here.'

Julie felt anger rising. For all the talk of having taken him away for his own good, that he'd be safe at the Helping Hand, that she had no right or business keeping him in her apartment – now they'd let him disappear as easily as he'd turned up. 'You let him out *alone*?'

'I didn't let him do anything, Julie. The staff at the Helping Hand didn't notice him leave. And they don't think he was alone. He's with a woman.'

'A woman?'

'A homeless woman from the shelter. We have a good description of her.'

Julie felt almost faint at the thought. 'You left him with a *homeless woman*? You told me he'd be safe. That he'd be taken care of. He could be *anywhere*! Anything could have happened to him!'

Laure shuffled in the doorway, looking more and more uncomfortable. 'Don't worry. He can't have gone far. I'll . . . I'll find him. It's best if you stay here.'

'It's *best* if you stop telling me what to do.' Julie slammed the door shut and leaned back against it.

She thought of him out there; lost, alone. Needing her.

Needing her, the way she needed him.

'I'll call, Julie,' said Laure from the hallway. 'As soon as I hear anything, I'll call.'

Julie listened to Laure's steps as she walked away; then she slid down with her back to the door, unable to hold off the tears.

47

Thomas was tired that morning. He'd had a restless night and knew that Adèle had barely slept either, lying stiff and still beside him. Telling Adèle the night before about Simon's suicide had been painful, but necessary. He had often been tempted to let her know the truth and put an end to the way she remembered only the good about the man, never the bad. He'd thought at the time that allowing her to believe the whole thing was pure tragedy was the kindest and easiest way for her to come to terms with his death, but in the years since he'd never felt that she'd completely moved on.

Adèle's heart had not really been hers to give. It still belonged to Simon; or at least, to the version of Simon that she chose to believe in. Thomas knew she didn't understand the real man, that she had no idea what he was capable of.

Out there in town somewhere, Adèle's dead lover was waiting for her, and Thomas knew that Simon would never give her up without a fight. Whether Adèle wanted him or not. And what could Thomas do against a dead man? Lock him away for the rest of his life, however long that was? He'd do it; he'd do *anything* to make sure that Adèle and Chloé were kept safe.

The three of them ate breakfast in silence. He hated seeing Adèle suffer this way. But he could also see in her eyes the anger and disappointment she was feeling, and he knew that if Simon had come to the house right now, Adèle would have rejected him outright.

It was a school day, and Adèle was insisting on working her shift at the library, with Chloé's backing.

'It's my class's turn to visit the library today,' said Chloé. 'I only like it when Mum does it.'

Thomas was uneasy, but Adèle assured him she was fine, dismissing his worries, insisting he could trust her. Thomas hugged her to him, and knew he had to show that he had faith in her. However difficult it was.

The call from the dam came mid-morning.

He took Michael with him, driving up the steep forest roads to the dam, the shortest route. What waited for them was surely the strangest sight he'd come across in all his years on the force.

Two men introduced themselves as technicians overseeing the current maintenance works. One was older and more cagey. He gave his name as Dreyfus. The younger man looked pale, and wary to the point of fear. Anton Chabou, he called himself.

Something about their behaviour put Thomas on edge – their unease, and the way they constantly looked around themselves as if examining their surroundings for something that only they could see. When he saw what they'd called him to look at, though, he wasn't surprised at their nervousness.

The two technicians had met Thomas and Michael at the car park beside the dam control station, then had led them down the steep embankment towards the water's edge. The surface of the lake was preternaturally still, and Thomas sensed an unnatural silence as they moved closer to the dark water. No birdsong, no wind; he could barely hear the scuffle of his shoes against the rock. But it was the sight of the church spire rising from the middle of the lake that made him stop in his tracks.

'You've not seen the church before, Captain?' asked Dreyfus.

'Once, when it was last drained. That must have been nearly a decade ago. It doesn't make it any less bizarre now. Tell me, how much lower will the maintenance process take the lake? I don't remember seeing anything like as much of the spire the last time.'

The two technicians shared a look before Dreyfus answered. 'You're right, this is a more . . . *thorough* examination. But it won't fall much more.'

'The divers were here to inspect the lake floor, you said.'

'That's correct,' said Dreyfus. 'An occasional inspection is required to look for fissures or significant subsidence, much easier to do it when the water is so shallow. But then they saw this . . .'

Both officers had been distracted by the church spire; they followed the technician's gesture as he pointed to the lakeside. Where the water met the sandy incline of the bank, divers were dragging heavy corpses up onto the shore to lay among those bodies already laid out.

Dead animals.

'Jesus,' said Thomas. He thought he caught a stench on the air, the smell of cold rank water and death. 'How many?'

'Thirty-six, in all,' said Dreyfus. 'A cross-section of the forest wildlife, but mainly deer.'

'How the hell did they all get in there?' said Michael.

'All we know is that the divers found them floating in the water. Drowned.'

'But nobody had seen them enter the lake?' said Thomas. 'Nobody heard anything?'

Dreyfus shook his head and Thomas could sense a little impatience.

They reached the waterside. Divers and others were just finishing dragging the last few carcasses out, deer with their black staring eyes and jaws locked in grimaces. They had not had easy deaths, thought Thomas. 'Tell me,' he said. 'Were the animals mostly near the shore?'

'I don't know,' said Dreyfus, impatient. The man clearly wanted them out of there, presumably so the work could recommence.

Thomas walked over to where three of the divers were sitting, waiting to get back to work. He asked them the same question.

'No,' said one, glancing at the others. 'They were all in the middle of the lake. Clustered around the remains of the old village. Just floating there . . .' The diver shook his head. 'I've never seen anything like it.'

Thomas frowned.

'So, Captain,' said Dreyfus, looking at his watch. 'What's the procedure?'

'We need to have the carcasses examined, make sure there's no contamination. We'll let you know.' He started to walk away when something occurred to him. 'Oh, and Monsieur Dreyfus?'

'Yes, Captain?'

'Nobody goes back in the water until I say so, understand?'

Dreyfus glared at him for a moment, and Thomas knew he was the type who was used to having things his own way.

Not today, Thomas thought. 'Yes, Captain,' Dreyfus said at last.

It was early afternoon by the time arrangements had been made to collect the carcasses for examination. On his way to the station Thomas got a call from Adèle; she'd left the library early, taking Chloé with her. She asked him to come home.

He went straight there, to find Adèle distraught. They talked of Simon's death, and he convinced her to take a pill to help her get some sleep. Once she'd gone upstairs, Chloé came to him, upset.

'What's wrong with Mum?' she asked.

Thomas stuck to the bare truth. 'She's tired, Chloé. She didn't sleep well.'

Chloé looked at him with such pure *trust* that it made his heart ache. 'Because of the angel?'

Thomas felt his blood go cold. 'What angel?'

'Simon.'

He tried not to show his anger. He'd assumed that Adèle had kept Simon's presence from Chloé. 'You saw him?'

'He was here yesterday.'

What had she been thinking? But that was precisely the problem: she hadn't been thinking, not clearly. *Simon walks back into her life and sense walks out*, he thought. 'Did he touch you?'

'No,' said Chloé. She looked nervous, and Thomas knew she didn't want to get her mum into trouble. 'He just spoke to me. Mum said he was my real dad, come back to life. Is that true?'

Thomas looked at her, wanting to lie. But he nodded.

Chloé looked at him seriously. 'Has he hurt Mum?'

'Yes,' he said. 'And if he comes back he'll hurt her again. Mum doesn't think so, but he would. Listen, Chloé. This is very important. If he does come again, tell me right away. If I'm not here, call me. Understand?'

'OK,' said Chloé.

Thomas hugged her and felt some of his fear subside, because now he had something that was invaluable to any police officer. He had an informant.

The pathologist he'd asked to examine some of the animals called him two hours later to discuss the results. Adèle was still sleeping, and he was wary of leaving her and Chloé alone, but Chloé was his anchor now, his guarantee of their safety; Adèle would not leave her daughter, and Chloé would contact him if anything happened.

'I won't be long,' he told her, and before he left he made a call to Father Jean-François. Maybe the priest could help her understand, or at least take his share of the blame for the mess their good intentions had caused.

Thomas went straight to the hospital to see the pathologist, finding him in the harsh white examination room. The three carcasses that had been examined lay before them, cut open and partially dissected. Underneath the odour of blood and chemicals, he was sure he could smell the same stench he'd caught by the lakeside earlier – stagnant water and decay.

'This is the first time I've done an autopsy on an animal, Captain,' said the pathologist with a wry smile.

'I appreciate it, Luc. Someone could come down from

Annecy in two days, but I wanted an idea of what it might be. Because, well . . .'

'I know. They were in the town's water supply, so the important thing is to rule out poisoning.'

Thomas nodded, making a mental note to get some bottled water on his way home. 'So, can we rule it out?'

The pathologist opened up his report and showed Thomas. 'It seems so. There are no toxins in the tissue. You said they didn't know how long the animals had been in the lake?'

'Nobody saw anything.'

'Well, it looks recent. It can't have been more than twelve hours. There were no injuries, either. They weren't shot, no other signs of wounds.'

Thomas gazed at the animals; the smell of decay must be in his mind, he thought. He looked back at the pathologist. 'Then how did they die?'

'The lungs are waterlogged, Captain. They were alive when they entered the lake, which means they drowned.'

'How can that happen? Are we saying somebody intentionally drowned them?' He could remember a case from early in his career when three sixteen-year-olds had caught and drowned half a dozen cats in a garden pond. *For kicks*, one of the boys had admitted, and Thomas had found himself wanting to drown the boys in return. The thought of it still made him angry; the thought of something similar being done to wild animals, especially on such a scale, made him feel sick.

But the pathologist was shaking his head, thoughtful. 'I don't think so. There's no sign of a struggle. They were in the middle of the lake, yes?'

'Yes.'

The pathologist shrugged his shoulders. 'Then I'd suggest they panicked, went into the water, swam as far from shore as they could, then stayed there until they tired. At that point, they stood no chance.'

Thomas was horrified. 'Christ, all of them? Why the hell would they do that?'

'All I can suggest, Captain, is that they were running from something.'

'Running into the lake?'

'Don't underestimate panic. It's a dangerous thing. One animal gets it, and it's infectious. Perhaps by the time the deer realized they were in trouble, they were simply too far from shore to make it back.'

Thomas tried to think of anything in the mountains that might cause such a catastrophic response. 'But what might trigger that?'

'I'll ask around. Possibly fire, or predators. It's probably just a freak event. Nothing to worry about, I would say.'

Thomas raised an eyebrow. 'Nothing to worry about? You're saying these animals were so terrified that they would rather drown than face whatever it was that scared them?'

The pathologist smiled. 'Interesting, isn't it? We can call it suicide, if you like.'

The captain shook his head seriously. 'This isn't something to joke about, Luc,' he said, and the pathologist's smile faded.

Thomas looked at the animal carcasses in the room, at the blank dead eyes staring back. He wondered what those eyes had seen.

48

Adèle was in the library, and she felt safe. She felt safe because Chloé was there with her, along with the rest of Chloé's class, for their regular library visit.

As always, once the class had settled she asked the children if any of them had interesting news to share. One boy, Mateo, had a simple question. 'Is it true that we're running out of water?'

Adèle smiled. 'Where did you hear that?'

'I heard my dad say something about the dam.'

She nodded. 'It's an unusual time,' she said. 'But there's nothing to worry about. Have any of you been to the lake recently?' No hands went up. 'Well, maybe now's the time to go. It was in the news today that the lake is being partially drained, something that happens maybe once a decade, to allow maintenance on the dam. This is the first time since most of you were born. Do any of you know what's beneath the lake? Johan?'

'Fish?' said the boy.

'Yes, and what else? Caroline?'

'Seaweed? Beavers?'

Adèle smiled gently. 'Perhaps. Mateo?'

'Goats?'

The rest of the class burst into laughter; Adèle settled them down, but the look on Mateo's face suggested laughter had been precisely the reaction he'd been looking for. 'I don't think so. Anything else?' Most of them wouldn't know about the lake, she knew; about what was beneath its still, icy surface. Some parents tended to think it too frightening for younger ears, certainly, and the rest played it safe. But with the water level so low, the time was right to talk about it.

The past was something that shouldn't be ignored.

The thought made her pause. She took a breath before continuing. 'Do you think there might be houses?' she said, smiling as the children whispered excitedly. 'When the water level goes down, you can see a church steeple. The village church, flooded years ago when the old dam broke.'

'Are there people living under the water?' asked one girl.

Adèle shook her head, the questions coming thick and fast as the children's imaginations caught fire at the story.

'Did anyone die because of the dam?'

'Why did Simon kill himself?'

Adèle froze. 'What? Who said that?' It had been Chloé. She was sure it had been Chloé. Adèle looked at her daughter. 'Did you ask a question?'

The children watched Adèle, silenced by the intensity in her voice.

Chloé nodded, looking concerned. 'I just asked, why did the dam break?' Adèle said nothing; her face pale, the words caught in her throat. 'Mum, are you OK?'

The class started to whisper. *What's wrong with her?*

Adèle shook it off. She clapped her hands, and told the class to settle.

'You should take a pill and get some sleep,' Thomas told her at home. 'You'll feel better.'

'No, I don't think I will,' she said. It was one of those

rare occasions when she'd asked him to come home, and he had come. No emergencies. No complications. No excuses. When he came through the door he'd started to tell her something about animals being drowned in the lake, but she'd hushed him. Talking this through was more important.

'Why did you never tell me about Simon before?' she asked.

Thomas was wary. 'You know why. Because I didn't want to hurt you.'

'You didn't reckon it was important?'

'Adèle, please. Of course I did. It wasn't as if I didn't think about it. I thought about it often, but my decision was always the same. You were in pieces after his death. I was afraid you wouldn't be able to cope with the truth.'

'It might have been simpler if I'd known, Thomas.' More honest, she thought. Open. At least that.

'Is it simpler now?'

Even though he'd finally told her last night, he hadn't gone into the details. She wanted to know everything, every part of it. To read the police report. To *understand*. Why Simon had looked at life with Adèle, at life with his child, and had chosen oblivion instead.

'Do we really know he wanted to die?' she said, grasping at straws.

Thomas sighed and shook his head. 'There were several witnesses, Adèle. Please. If there had been any doubt, there would have been no need to hide things from you. You loved him. What he did was a betrayal of that. None of us wanted you to have to face such a terrible truth. Father Jean-François didn't think you would be able to cope with it. But you have to face it now.'

Adèle looked up to see Chloé on the stairs, and wondered how long the girl had been listening. She went up to her and hugged her. Then she took a pill to seek a little oblivion of her own.

Chloé was in her room, drawing, when Adèle opened the door to Father Jean-François. Chloé had told her that Thomas had gone again, having been called away for work. Adèle hadn't been sure how to feel: annoyed that he'd left or pleased that he trusted her not to do anything foolish.

She frowned when she saw the priest, and he frowned too, clearly uneasy.

'Father,' she said. 'This is . . . unexpected.' *Unwelcome* was what she meant. Still, manners were called for. She asked him in, offered him coffee, went to make it. He seemed oddly eager to delay their conversation.

'Thomas asked me to come and see you,' the priest said, as they finally sat. 'He was very worried.'

'Is it because of Simon?'

'Simon?' he said. He looked anxious, distracted. 'Yes. Thomas came to me yesterday, very confused. Talking about resurrection . . . To be honest, I think it's sheer jealousy. Today, he called me and asked me to come and see you. He sounded desperate. I'm worried about him, Adèle. He's jealous of a spirit, something that doesn't exist.'

Adèle plunged the coffee and poured. 'It's not quite as simple as that, Father. Simon is still very much with us, and Thomas wants to understand why. We both do. It's me that he's worried about. He loves me. Much more than Simon ever did, I think.'

The priest looked uncomfortable, perching on the edge of the sofa and gripping the coffee cup tightly. 'There's no use comparing them, Adèle.'

She stared at him – this fidgeting, awkward man of God, who had no idea what was really going on. 'How would you know?'

'After all the times we talked about Simon, I think I understand your feelings for him. In spite of all that you thought about the man. His moods. The rage that took him sometimes, which you always forgave.'

Adèle caught a hint of blame in the priest's eyes. She didn't like it. He had no right. 'You encouraged me to live with Simon's memory, Father. All these years, you pushed me to live with the dead. Yet you *knew* he killed himself.' He looked away, the cup in his hands shaking slightly. 'Without Thomas I'd already be dead,' she said. 'Like Simon. I thought he'd been stolen from me, and from our daughter. But all that time it wasn't theft. It was *abandonment*. How dare he come back and expect me to open my arms, and my legs –' the priest squirmed, but she didn't care – 'when he'd given up? Whatever pain he suffered, he had everything he could want. And he threw it away.'

'Adèle, the way you talk, I just don't understand. You act as if Simon . . .' He stopped; gesturing, lost for words.

'Simon came back, Father,' she said, her voice cold. 'He's alive again. As young as he was, ten years ago. As arrogant as he was.'

She saw panic rise in the priest's eyes. Panic, as if he'd already heard what she was saying a dozen times: heard it, and dismissed it as wishful thinking, as fantasy.

'I have to . . .' he said, and then he stood, looking pale and nauseous.

He ran from the house, without looking back.

The next time Adèle opened the front door it was to a young red-headed girl she thought she recognized, but she couldn't put a name to the face.

'Are you Adèle?' said the girl.

'Yes. Do I know you?'

'I have a message. Meet Simon at the bus station tonight, in time for the last coach. Travel light. That's it.' The girl turned to leave.

'Wait,' said Adèle. 'What did he tell you?'

'That you were meant to get married, and you're going to make up for lost time. He's lucky you didn't forget him.'

Adèle closed her eyes for a moment. This was it. This was the time for a final decision. She opened her eyes and shook her head. 'Tell him I'm not coming.'

'Are you sure?' said the girl. She looked surprised. 'I think he really loves you, and what he's going through isn't easy. Believe me, I know.'

Adèle saw the look in the girl's eyes and understood. 'You're the same?' she said, and then her hands came up to her mouth as she placed the girl. She looked like Léna, but much younger. It was more than that, though. Hers was the face on the T-shirt that Chloé had been given to wear for the commemoration of the coach crash, the girl whose name Chloé had to say. 'Camille. Camille Séguret.'

Camille nodded her head. 'The same. And the person I love doesn't want me. It's hard, but in the end it's your decision. Just be sure to make the right choice.'

Once the girl had left, Adèle told herself again and again: *I'm not going.*

Then she went to look up the time of the last coach.

49

Julie got the call from Laure in the afternoon. The woman who had disappeared from the Helping Hand with Victor had been spotted on CCTV, picked up and taken in for questioning.

'I'll call you when there's more news,' Laure had said, but Julie had no intention of just sitting and waiting. In the few hours since she'd found out that Victor had vanished, her mood had darkened considerably. Victor had been a lifeline – he had given her the hope that had been missing for seven years. Victor being taken from her had been bad enough; Victor in danger was unbearable, so simply waiting in her apartment wasn't something she could do. She took herself to the police station and waited there, on a hard bench in the cold waiting room, her impatience growing as time ticked by. The patronizing looks from the reception staff weren't helping her mood.

She finally caught sight of Laure, and hurried over to her.

'Hi,' said Laure. Wary, as ever. 'There was no need to come down. I said I'd call.'

'Indulge me. Well?'

'Nothing so far. She says she and the boy left together, then split up. But she's hardly reliable.'

'Why not?'

Laure raised her eyebrow. 'She says that she was born in 1943 and died thirty years ago, and that she's Michel Costa's dead wife Viviane.' Laure looked around to check the coast was clear, then gestured for Julie to follow. They reached a door with a small glass window, and Laure pointed inside.

The middle-aged woman calling herself Viviane Costa was sitting alone in a room, looking bored.

'That's her,' said Laure, catching the look of surprise on Julie's face. 'Do you know her?'

'I think so,' said Julie. With so many photographs around Monsieur Costa's house, it was a face that had gradually seeped into her memory.

'Who is she?' asked Laure.

'Do you think I can talk to her?'

Laure nodded, looking nervous. 'Be quick, though. This is completely against regulations.'

Julie went inside. The woman's face lit up when the door opened, then faded back to boredom. 'Shame,' said the woman. 'I thought you were bringing food.'

Julie pulled up a chair. 'You're really Michel Costa's wife?' she asked.

The woman looked at her and smiled thinly. 'Yes. I'm Viviane Costa. I suppose you don't believe me?'

Julie shook her head. 'No, I do. I do believe you. I was your husband's nurse. I've seen photos of you.'

'I noticed he kept those. He didn't forget me.' She smiled, and there was a hostile edge to it. 'Wasn't exactly pleased to see me when I came back, mind you.'

Julie looked at her. She hadn't changed at all from the photos. Not one bit. 'So you're . . . You're dead?'

'I'm afraid so,' said Viviane. She gave Julie a wry smile, seeming to find the whole situation amusing.

Julie took a breath. It had been in her mind, since Victor had jumped from the window. The oddness of him, his old clothes. He'd always seemed otherworldly. She'd already thought him a ghost, or a figment of her imagination – one step further wasn't too much of a push to believe. But she still needed to hear it: 'And the little boy who was with you? Him, too?'

'Yes.'

Julie thought herself a rational person; open-minded but rational. Resurrection from the dead was for those who had faith in something greater, and she had none. 'But how?'

Viviane shook her head and sighed. 'That's a very good question. You would think there has to be a reason, wouldn't you? I suppose there probably is.'

Julie waited for her to say more, but nothing came. 'When did he die?' she asked.

'Not long before I did,' said Viviane.

'And his parents? What happened to them?'

'Dead, too. All murdered.'

Julie's heart broke anew for Victor. She'd wondered what trauma he'd faced, and it was worse than she could have imagined. No wonder he hadn't spoken to anyone. He must have been terrified.

'So where is Victor now?'

'Victor?'

'I mean the little boy.'

Understanding dawned on the woman's face. 'Ah, so you're Julie? He mentioned you. Don't worry about him. He has something he wants to do. Perhaps it's why he's here – I don't know. He'll come and see you once his work is done.'

Julie nodded. 'You know that your husband . . .'

The woman smiled. 'Of course I know. I went to his funeral.'

'Why did he do that?'

'He hardly spoke to me when I came back, Julie. All those years, and he hardly said a word.' The air of smug amusement slipped from Viviane Costa, just for a moment. Underneath, the emotion was raw grief.

There was a brief knock on the door. Julie turned, to see Laure waving. *Hurry up*.

She had one more thing to ask. 'When you came back, how did you know? How did you know you were dead?'

Viviane frowned. 'Well, it didn't take long to realize.'

Julie struggled to articulate her fear – the fear that had been crouching in her mind for days, if not years, living a half-life in the shadows. 'Because sometimes . . . I wonder if I'm . . .'

Viviane broke into laughter as Julie stuttered to a halt. 'Oh, please,' she said, sounding bitter. 'I suppose you could take a leaf out of my husband's book, because there's certainly *one* way to find out.'

Julie went back home. Viviane Costa's words stayed with her, and kept sounding in her ears.

There's certainly one way to find out.

For seven years, she'd felt dead inside. The only person she'd made a connection with since then had turned out to be some kind of ghost. And now even he had left her.

As dusk fell, the air in her apartment felt stale and humid. They could do with a storm to clear things. She opened the window as wide as it would go and propped her front door open a little for some through-draught. Across the hall, the door of Nathalie Payet's empty apartment was sealed with a criss-cross of crime-scene tape. She returned to the window and looked out onto the grass below, thinking of Victor when she'd seen him down there that first night, looking up at her.

She found herself crying. He'd given her hope, and the hope had been snatched away. She sat against the window, looking down to the ground, feeling closer to Victor; she moved her legs over the frame, one at a time, until she was sitting as he'd sat, looking down to where he'd fallen. It didn't seem so far, she thought. Not so far to fall.

Not so far to find out.

'Julie?'

She looked up, dazed. It was Laure, standing in the doorway.

'I . . . the door was open,' said Laure. 'I wanted to make sure you were OK.' She looked extremely anxious, edging slowly into the room, and Julie absently wondered why.

She looked at Laure, saying nothing.

'Don't do it,' Laure pleaded. 'Don't do it.'

Suddenly, Julie understood, and realized where she was sitting: both legs hanging over the window frame. She felt cold, unable to move.

'Give me your hand,' said Laure, moving carefully towards her, reaching out.

Julie couldn't speak. She realized part of her had wanted to do it, had wanted to fall and find out the truth. Either way, maybe she wouldn't have felt so alone any more.

'Please, Julie,' said Laure. 'I love you. Please.'

Julie pulled her shaking legs inside. She couldn't look Laure in the eye. 'Well, if that's how you feel about it,' she said, dismissive.

Laure was angry. The grip she had on Julie's arm was so tight it hurt, as if she were afraid Julie might throw herself out of the window after all. 'Have you lost your mind? What the hell were you doing?'

'Don't worry,' Julie said. 'I wasn't going to do anything. I just . . . I just wanted to check something. You wouldn't understand.' It was bluster, that was all; and she could see Laure wasn't buying into it.

Laure stepped past her and shut the window. Then she held her head in her hands, stunned. 'Christ, Julie. I'm sorry about Victor. But this isn't the answer.'

'Oh, fuck *off*,' Julie shouted, suddenly furious. Laure couldn't just walk back into her life like this and expect to *know* her. 'You have the answers, do you? Are all my problems that obvious?'

Laure's expression hardened. 'Well, the next time you make a cry for help, try taking pills. You won't survive that fall.'

They glared at each other in cold silence. Laure's radio sparked to life, breaking the tension.

'Inspector,' said the voice on the radio. 'We've spotted a boy near rue Saint-Michel, matches the description.'

The hostility fell away from both their faces. Laure lifted the set. 'Thanks,' she said. 'I'm on my way.' She looked to Julie. 'That's not far from the Helping Hand. Maybe he's heading back.' Laure moved to the door; Julie grabbed her coat and hurried after her. 'What are you doing?' asked Laure.

'Coming with you,' said Julie. 'Or would you rather I stay here alone?'

50

Toni left Samuel in charge at the Lake Pub and drove home early. It felt so strange, to be going to the old house knowing Serge and his mother were both there. He left the street lights behind, driving up the forest roads. As he turned onto the rocky track that led to the family home, he knew things would be difficult – but he would make them work. With the help of his mother and brother, Serge would stay true to his word.

Toni would earn his forgiveness. Whether he could ever earn his mother's, he didn't know.

Then he rounded the last corner, and his headlights picked Serge out of the darkness: rifle in one hand, blood on his face and his shirt soaked in red.

Toni's blood froze in his veins. *No*, he thought. *Not now.*

He got out of the car and walked to where Serge stood in the headlights, slow steps taking him to hard truths.

'Where's that blood from?' he asked.

Serge shook his head. 'It's not what you think.'

Toni could hardly bear to look at him. 'Have you started again?'

'No,' said Serge. 'It was just a deer. That was all, Toni. I went hunting and killed a deer.'

'You can tell me, Serge,' said Toni. He was almost pleading. He'd only just started hoping that things could be normal again, for his mother to *talk* to him again. 'You can trust me. I won't do anything. Tell Mum, too. Tell her I won't do it again. We'll find a way through this, but I'll never do it again.'

Serge frowned, puzzled. 'Do what again, Toni?'

'I had to stop you,' said Toni, begging him to understand. 'You couldn't fight it. I see that now. But it's all in the past. I'll protect you. Both of you.'

Serge was staring at him in shock as the realization dawned. 'What? It was you?' He looked to the side as if trying to remember, then looked back at Toni, scrutinizing him. 'You killed me?' Toni's eyes went to the ground, in confession. 'You killed me,' said Serge. He swept the rifle up, pointing it at Toni's chest.

Toni looked up again, desolate. He saw the gun and wanted it over. If this was the way it had to end, so be it. 'Shoot,' he said. He stepped forward until the barrel was against his shirt. He leaned into it, challenging his brother to do it. 'Shoot! Go on. *Go on.*'

Tears filled Serge's eyes. 'Toni . . .' he said, then lowered the gun.

'Say you forgive me,' said Toni. The look in his brother's eyes was burning his soul. Betrayal. Despair. The same look that had stayed in his mother's eyes in the years before her death, the accusation there every single day. *Your fault. Your fault.* He couldn't live with that, not from both of them. 'If you forgive me, she will, too.'

Serge turned around and walked away.

'Say you forgive me!' cried Toni.

Serge walked on, out of the range of the headlights, into the dark.

51

Pierre's day had taken a turn for the worse when Sandrine came to him distressed. She'd noticed the little boy had gone missing, along with the sour-faced homeless woman. Bad that anyone could go missing, of course; worse though, for the reputation of the Helping Hand, if a child could be stolen so easily from their care.

Sandrine had been in pieces, but there was only so much reassurance he could give her. She blamed herself, blamed the frequent toilet breaks that came with early pregnancy. He packed her off home for the day. Let her husband deal with the mess.

And so Pierre was alone in the Helping Hand that evening when Victor's face appeared against the dark sky at his office window, watching him with that unnerving lack of emotion he seemed to favour. Pierre felt immediate relief, of course, that the boy was safe – reputations were fragile things, after all – but now he regretted having sent Sandrine home. He would much rather leave the boy to her. There was something about his presence that made Pierre feel deeply uncomfortable, something skirting around the edges of his conscious thoughts. Something he didn't want to examine closely.

Pierre forced a smile. All were welcome to the Helping Hand, of course, however unpleasant their company. He went to the door and unlocked it, ushering the boy inside.

'There you are,' he said. 'At last. We were starting to

worry.' He smiled at his own understatement. 'You really shouldn't have left like that. Where were you?'

'I was dead,' said the boy, calmly staring at him.

Pierre knelt slowly beside him, stunned that he'd not realized before. Dear God, all this time. All this time, it hadn't just been Simon and Camille. There had been others right under his nose, just as he'd thought there would be.

'What happened to you?' said Pierre.

'You killed me,' said the boy, stating it as simple fact. 'You killed my parents.'

Pierre stared at him. The discomfort he'd felt around Victor made a terrible sense; he'd blanked the boy's facial features from his mind, cut them from his memory. He felt weak, thankful that he was already on his knees. Even so, he had to place his hands on the floor to steady himself. 'My God,' he said. 'My God.' His mouth was dry. Judgement, at last: it had been a long time coming. 'You?' he said. 'Forgive me.' He reached out, and the boy shrank from his hand. 'No, don't be afraid. It wasn't me who killed you. He lost his mind. It all went wrong. It was supposed to be a warning, that was all, but he started . . . I was trying to protect you. Don't you remember?'

The boy's face took on an expression at last: sheer anger.

'No,' he said, glaring at Pierre. 'You *didn't* try.'

Pierre felt something, then: a gathering sense of power, all focused on the boy in front of him. Suddenly the lights in the building clicked off. The windows behind the boy over-looked the town, and Pierre saw the blackout spreading until everything was in darkness.

Victor looked to Pierre's side.

Pierre could feel it, the presence nearby. Dread filled

him. Steeling himself, he stood and turned. Then he saw. His partner in crime, the man who had lied to him, who had killed a family in cold blood . . . The man raised his gun, aimed it at Pierre's head.

'No,' said Pierre, timid again, terrified, relieved as the gun swung away slowly, pointing elsewhere. Pointing at the boy. An instant, then, while Pierre's fear held him immobile, self-preservation winning out over what was *right*. But this was it. This was the time: he was being tested.

'*No!*' Pierre shouted. He lunged at the man, grabbing for the gun. They fell, both of them together, and the gun went off. Pierre felt a searing pain in his chest, but he kept fighting, kept struggling, whatever the cost. The man wanted to kill the boy again, and it was Pierre's role – his *purpose* – to stop it happening. He had failed before, failed God and himself. *Not this time.*

The man swung his gun at Pierre's head, connecting hard enough to make him fall. Then he stood over Pierre and kicked, kicked . . . Pierre tried to recover some strength, tried to stand, but despaired. He knew the fight was lost.

Then there was torchlight shining through the windows. The front door opened, and the light swung around the room. It paused on the boy, standing quietly by the wall, staring at Pierre; then the beam came round to Pierre's terrified face.

'What did you *do* to him?' came a woman's voice. It was a police officer, the one who'd brought the boy in the first place.

Pierre could only look desperately around, trying to see where his attacker was, but the man had gone. *Vanished*, he thought. He looked at the boy, who was still watching him.

A second woman came through the door, rushed over and embraced the child. He put his arms around her and held her tightly, as though he'd never let her go. The police-woman looked from the boy to Pierre, still lying on the floor. Pierre could see the suspicion in her eyes, but couldn't tell if it was him or Victor she was most suspicious of.

The other woman just looked at him with disgust. With one arm around the boy, she shepherded him out of the door. The police officer followed, giving Pierre one last look before she went. Her eyes held many questions, but Pierre had no answers for her.

He put his hand to where he'd felt the shot hit him. There was no pain now. He pulled his hand away, clean. He lay still, trembling.

Scared of the shadows, Pierre began to pray.

52

Frédéric had been watching her all night.

Alice, he told himself. *Léna's cousin.*

She'd been the life and soul, loud and laughing, talking about her Parisian boyfriend, saying how she preferred *older* men. Flicking glances at Frédéric over and over, while he kept his distance. Whatever the bad feeling was between Léna and her cousin, he couldn't understand the way Léna had behaved the night before. She must have known how hurtful saying something like *that* was.

And he looked at the girl, and couldn't shake off the sense of foreboding.

The others all liked her. She drank like a fish and seemed none the worse for it. Then, when it came to Frédéric's turn to buy the drinks, she'd gone with him to the bar. He found himself terrified, standing beside her. What of, he wasn't sure.

'Was Léna OK after last night?' he asked her. It was the first thing he'd said to her all evening. 'Her mum called my parents this morning and wanted to know if I'd seen her.'

She pouted. 'Don't worry about Léna,' she told him.

'Why did she say what she did, Alice?'

'She's jealous,' she said. 'She knew what to say to upset you.'

He nodded. Yes, Léna always knew exactly how to upset him. 'Did you know Camille?' he asked. He couldn't look at her as he said it. He was scared of what he'd see in her eyes.

She paused. 'A little,' she said. 'Now, come on. I'll challenge you this time.'

She smiled at him. Despite his misgivings, he found himself smiling back.

One by one, she downed the vodka shots as though they were water, to squeals and cheers from those crowded around. Then it was Frédéric's turn. He'd already had too much, he knew, but he tried to keep up. One down, then the second . . . The third, though, was the last straw.

He set the shot glass down half-full, and shrugged.

'Ha!' cried Lucho. 'You lose! You have to do whatever she wants.'

'Whatever I want?' said Alice. Her smile grew sly. She walked around the table and sat on Frédéric's knee, then kissed him. Long, slow. Frédéric nearly pulled back at the chill of her lips, but his head was spinning too much to move. There were whoops of delight and catcalls from those around.

'What the hell are you playing at?' came a raging voice. Frédéric opened his eyes to see Jérôme, Léna's father. The man took Alice's arm and dragged her from her chair. She looked as furious as Jérôme did.

'Dad, stop it!' cried Alice.

Frédéric stared after them both in horror. None of the others had noticed what she'd said.

Just a slip of the tongue. It had to be.

Frédéric drank Coke for the next hour, trying to get his head straight, but he wanted to know. Wanted to know if the thoughts he was having were just crazy.

So he walked to the Ségurets' house, scared but determined. On the way, another power blackout swept through the town, but walking in the darkness suited his mood.

He didn't stop to think as he climbed the trellis at the front and knocked at the window. Alice let him inside, silent, then led him to a bedroom.

Camille's bedroom.

The only light came from candles. She sat him down on the edge of the bed and kissed him again. She was so hungry, demanding. Lost, he kissed back, letting himself push those impossible thoughts away, but they kept returning.

Tears were pouring from him. She looked at his face, concerned, wiping the tears away.

'Who are you?' he whispered.

She looked at him. There was hope in her eyes. And fear. 'You know who I am,' she said, her voice soft. 'I love you. And you love me, too. That's all that matters.'

The impossible, he thought. 'Camille?'

She nodded, once. The truth hit him hard. Shaking, he stood and backed away. Camille watched him, the pain on her face matching the pain in his heart. She held out a hand to him.

Frédéric ran.

53

Adèle sat in her house and watched the clock as the hands crept forwards, until the time of the last coach had come and gone. She'd made her choice, and she knew it was the right one; she even felt some relief at it.

When the power cut came, she and Chloé fetched candles and lit them. It felt almost ceremonial, lighting a candle for the dead, or as a prayer for hope. Here, now, what had died was her love for Simon; and her hope was for the future, with or without Thomas. Another decision to make, and make soon.

Then the patio door slid open, and Simon stepped out from behind the curtains. She'd thought he might come, but she was strong enough now, strong enough to send him away again.

He was dishevelled; puzzled and angry, he looked like a child who couldn't understand why things hadn't quite gone his way. 'Why didn't you come?' he said. 'Was it *Thomas*? Did he keep you here?'

Adèle looked at him, the passion and pain worn so openly on his face. Her heart ached, but she had to make him see. 'I'm not coming, Simon. You should leave.'

He shook his head, stubborn. 'Not without you. Not without Chloé.'

She moved to stand in front of him, looking him straight in the eyes. Willing him to understand. 'And what I want doesn't matter to you?'

'What you want? How would you know what that is, Adèle? You're under this man's spell. You can't think for yourself. You never could. I have to think for both of us.' He looked across the room to where Chloé was watching. 'For all three of us.'

'You can't stay.'

'I came for you.'

She nodded. If he wouldn't listen, she would have to ask the one question she knew would break him. 'Why did you do it, Simon? You said that I saved you. That you were happy. That you stopped thinking about suicide.'

'What are you talking about? Of course I was happy.'

'I believed you. But you finally did it, Simon. You *killed* yourself.' She saw him flinch, confused. 'It should have been the happiest day of our lives, but you killed yourself. You betrayed me. You betrayed all of us.'

'No,' he said. 'That's not . . .' He shook his head. 'Please, Adèle,' he said. 'Come with me.'

He held out his hand; she shook her head and started to back away. 'You've been dragging us to the grave,' she told him. 'Now you have to let us live. We don't *need* you. Not any more.'

There was a flare of anger in his eyes. He reached out and grabbed Adèle's arm, pulling her towards him with a firm hand, but Chloé stepped forwards. She moved between her parents, looking into her father's face with the same stubborn determination reflected on his.

'Go away,' said the girl. 'We're not coming with you. You chose to *die* instead of staying with us. It doesn't matter that you came back. You're still dead to me.'

Simon let go, his anger turning to confusion and pain. He

stared at his daughter, stared at Adèle, appalled at the rejection.

They all heard the car speeding up to the house, then the brakes screeching.

'It's Thomas,' said Chloé. 'I called him.'

Simon turned to the door he'd come through, and stepped back out into the night. Chloé took Adèle's hand and clung to it.

Outside, they heard a car door slam, heard Thomas cry out: 'Don't move! Don't move!'

They heard Simon shout, his voice full of anger and despair.

'Stop!' shouted Thomas. '*Stop!*'

Then gunfire.

Then silence.

54

At Dreyfus's request, Anton spent most of the rest of his shift on the phone.

The dive team hadn't had any time to examine the lake bed before the discovery of the animal carcasses brought everything to a standstill. They'd only been available for that day, too; as things stood, it would be another two weeks before they or any other team in the country could return to the lake.

Anton was told to try and arrange something sooner. The best he could manage was an Italian team which could come in five days, but when he tried to phone Dreyfus to let him know the man wasn't answering his calls.

It was only then, once night had fallen, that he'd realized the other engineer on shift, Claude, wasn't in the control room. Anton thought back; the last he remembered, Claude had mumbled something about a check he needed to make. At the time Anton had been on the phone, deep in argument with the leader of the departing dive team, who'd been angling for extra money – given what he described as the 'distressing circumstances' of the discovery of the animal corpses during the dive.

Claude had gone outside, and simply hadn't returned.

Puzzled, Anton stood and walked to the door of the control room, only for it to burst open. Eric stormed in, eyes wide, out of breath.

'You still here?' said Eric.

'Waiting for the night-shift guys,' said Anton.

'They're not coming.'

'What?'

'Haven't you seen?' He went outside, and Anton followed. Eric pointed to the town below, in darkness. 'The power went out an hour ago.'

Anton stared out across the town. No, he hadn't seen: the dam control room had its own generators, and the only windows looked out across the lake. If there'd been a problem, the power plant should have called him. 'Did they have another outage scheduled?'

'It's been out for over an *hour*, Anton. This is different.' Eric hurried back inside, and went to his locker. He pulled a plastic bag from his pocket and started to fill it with the locker's contents. 'Thought I'd grab things as I drove past. Everyone else probably took the south road to avoid crossing the dam.' There was a deep mechanical thump from nearby. Eric looked frightened.

'Probably just the generator,' said Anton. 'It does that sometimes. What's going on?'

Eric didn't reply. He closed the locker and turned to the door, eager to leave.

'Eric,' said Anton. 'What's this about?'

Eric leaned close, face to face and sincere. 'The power's gone. They're giving up. You should get out while you can.'

'Stay here,' said Anton. There had to be something they could do. 'Stay here for ten minutes. Let me try and find Dreyfus.'

'No.'

'Please. Ten minutes, that's all. Just watch the systems. Please.'

Reluctant as Eric was, he nodded. 'Just ten. Then I go.'

Anton drove down to the power plant. The car park was empty, save for one vehicle. As Anton ran to the entrance, Dreyfus came out of the building.

'What are you doing?' said Anton.

'It's over,' said Dreyfus. He looked shaken, even more panicked than Eric. 'The plant's flooded.'

In the darkness, Anton looked over to the switchyard; he could see glints on the surface of water that must have been over a metre deep. 'You can't just leave. You said—'

'I've done what I can. I got everyone out, and now I'm going. You should go, too. It's pointless staying.'

'There has to be something we can do.'

'It's *dead*. We tried everything. The power won't come back now. Don't you get it? This isn't something we can fight any more.'

'And what about the people in town?'

Dreyfus paused. He looked around in desperation, as if some solution might present itself. But he shook his head. 'There's nothing we can do for them.' Dreyfus hurried to his car and got inside.

'Someone has to monitor the dam, sir,' Anton shouted.

Dreyfus stared at him as though he thought he was mad. Then he drove away.

When Anton reached the dam control room again he half-expected Eric to have left, but the man was still there, sitting in front of the monitors, looking at the screens with absolute intensity.

'Did you find him?' said Eric. Anton nodded. 'And what did he say?'

'To leave.'

'He's right.' Eric stood and walked out of the door. He strode to his car, Anton following. Eric got in, then turned to meet Anton's eyes. 'If you knew what I know, you'd run from here. Do you understand? Run, and never look back.'

Anton gestured to the lake. 'There's still a mountain of water behind a dam that might be failing. We can't just abandon it.'

Eric closed his eyes, shaking his head in frustration. Then he reached across, to under the passenger seat. He pulled something out and offered it to Anton.

Anton looked at the small silver crucifix, bewildered. He took it.

'For what it's worth,' said Eric, and then he drove away, leaving Anton alone.

55

After he had run from Camille's room Frédéric wandered the dark streets, angry and scared. It was quiet, well past midnight. Was she lying to him? Was she lying, when she said she was Camille?

If the impossible had really happened, there was one way he could prove it. A plan formed in his mind. A plan he needed help to carry out.

He stood outside the town cemetery and called Lucho. Lucho had probably had as much to drink that night as Frédéric, but without the sobering-up that Frédéric had been through.

'Where?' Lucho said drowsily.

Frédéric told him again. 'You're not chicken, are you?' he said. 'And I need you to bring some things. A shovel, a torch and a crowbar.'

'What is this? Some kind of practical joke?'

'It's important,' said Frédéric. 'Just come.'

Lucho must have heard something in Frédéric's voice, though, because when he arrived twenty minutes later he didn't look as though he thought it was a joke.

They climbed over the gate, Frédéric first. Lucho was showing little sign now of being drunk; the surroundings had sobered them both, thought Frédéric. Row after row of gravestones lurked in the space beyond the torchlight.

'Tell me what we're doing here,' said Lucho as they

walked, but Frédéric said nothing until they reached the grave.

He looked at the headstone, thinking back to the funeral; to seeing her name there for the first time, carved into it. Camille Séguret. Frédéric looked at the date underneath the name, and took a deep breath. 'I've stood here so often,' he said.

'*Tell* me,' said Lucho, getting anxious. 'What are we doing here?'

Frédéric looked him in the eye. 'Alice. Last night. What Léna said. *It's Camille.*'

Lucho's eyes widened. He shook his head, but Frédéric nodded. Both looked at the grave in front of them. 'You're crazy,' said Lucho.

'So go home,' said Frédéric, but Lucho stayed where he was – scared, but unwilling to abandon his best friend.

Frédéric grabbed the shovel and took the first turn at digging.

The ground was sodden. Every lump of earth he dug out oozed the same smell, like stagnant water. But the digging was easy otherwise; it didn't take them long to reach the coffin.

Frédéric glanced up at Lucho. 'Crowbar,' he said.

Lucho passed it down and took a long step back from the grave. He looked tense, ready to turn and run.

'Hold the fucking light, Lucho,' Frédéric hissed.

Frédéric braced himself. The coffin lid didn't give up easily, but when it came it opened wide along its length. He shrank back as the same stench of stagnant water came from within.

It wasn't the smell he'd expected, not the appalling reek of decay. He stared, lost for words, knowing what he'd been wanting to see, if *want* was the right word: Camille, shrivelled and rotting in the coffin she'd been buried in four years ago.

But Camille wasn't there.

Lucho edged closer and peered down, the torchlight picking out the clear water that filled the empty coffin. They looked at each other, frozen by the sight, until shouts came from across the cemetery. They both ran.

56

Once he'd taken Camille home from the Lake Pub, Jérôme had gone back to searching for Léna. The look on Claire's face when he'd arrived with Camille, sobbing and angry with her father, had been one of accusation. *This is your fault*, the look said, even though it had been Jérôme who'd brought her back, while Claire hadn't even realized Camille had gone. She'd thought she was in her room, asleep.

He'd said nothing, though; Claire still had every right to be angry with him. Only when he got back to his search did he understand what must have gone through Claire's mind: when Jérôme appeared on the doorstep Claire would have thought, just for an instant, that it was Léna with him. Hopes raised, hopes dashed.

He went to the hospital again, just in case they'd heard anything. On the way, the dying street lamps announced another power cut. When he arrived there was no news of Léna. The staff were a little less patient with him this time, but he could forgive that. The hospital still had power, so presumably it had its own generators; even so, every now and again the lighting flickered off, returning in a cacophony of brief alarms, tired faces everywhere.

As he was leaving he saw Alcide, a young police officer who often drank in the Lake Pub. Alcide asked if there had been any sign of Léna, which was encouraging; when Jérôme had called at the station earlier, they'd handled it with such blatant indifference that he was shaking when he left.

'I'm here to see Lucy,' Alcide told him. He was holding a small bunch of flowers. 'These are to brighten her room.'

Jérôme nodded. The mention of Lucy left him sombre. 'She's still holding on?'

Alcide looked just as sombre, but he surprised Jérôme by smiling slightly. 'She's actually doing well, they say. They're amazed by how well. I heard one of them describe it as a miracle.'

'They think she'll pull through?' At least there might be good news for *somebody*, he thought.

'She might,' said Alcide, emotional. 'She really might.'

Jérôme went back to his apartment, wondering if Alcide had a crush on the girl. Must have been tough on him, hearing everything that had surely gone around the station about the company she kept, about what she did. If Jérôme had heard it himself, rather than experienced it first-hand, he didn't think he would have believed it.

Alcide was sitting in Lucy's room when she woke. It was three in the morning, deep into a blackout that was longer than he had ever known in the town. The hospital generators were struggling to keep the lights on.

He was off work the next day, and he liked to spend time with her. He liked to look at her, as well, in a way he'd never been able to while he was in the Lake Pub. It had always been enough for him to share a few brief words of conversation, even if she didn't know his name. He'd never found the courage to introduce himself, let alone to ask her out on a date. He knew the rumours about her, but he didn't care. She was perfection to him.

At first, there had been an official police presence posted outside Lucy's room, but that hadn't lasted long. Now Alcide had taken to spending whatever spare time he had near her, day or night. He slept well enough in the small chair outside the room, even if he woke cramped and disoriented. A small price, he thought, to spend time near such a woman, to make sure she was safe.

The doctors had been astonished, day by day, as the horrific wounds healed so rapidly. The only word they had to describe it was 'miracle'. Lucy should have died.

And then as he watched, she opened her eyes at last, for the first time since she'd been brought in. She looked at him, then her eyes widened in terror, and she started to scream.

The lights in the room stuttered. Alcide pressed the alarm next to Lucy's bed, and tried to soothe her, but nothing he said seemed to calm her. She looked around the room, overwhelmed with a desperate fear.

He was almost bowled out of the way by the doctors who came running, despite being overstretched and weary. Gradually she settled, and the doctors began to ask her questions, assess how she was feeling. There were half a dozen people in the room, then, but most of them were only there to do what Alcide had been doing for days: they were simply watching, grateful to witness such a thing.

'What's wrong with me?' Lucy called to them. 'Why are you all looking at me like that?'

The group of doctors glanced at each other before one of them answered: 'You were healed by a miracle,' he said, with something approaching awe.

By daybreak, Alcide had managed some sleep in the chair outside her room. When he woke, he asked if he could speak to her.

He entered to find her sitting up in bed, still in her hospital gown, looking at the vase that held the flowers he'd brought with him the night before.

'Hello,' he said, and could think of nothing to follow it with. Small talk. He was terrible at small talk, and he'd never been so acutely aware of it.

'These are beautiful,' she said, her fingers touching the petals.

'I brought you them yesterday,' he said. Beautiful as they were, he thought, none of the flowers even held a candle to her. 'How are you feeling?'

'A little better, thanks,' she said. 'When I woke I was so confused, but I still can't remember much. I didn't even know my name until they told me. The doctors say it'll improve over the next day or two. I hope they're right.' She looked at Alcide carefully. 'I feel like I know you. Were you here while I was asleep?'

'I was keeping an eye on you. My name's Alcide.' He smiled; finally, he'd managed to tell her his name.

'Thanks, Alcide,' she said.

'Lucy, I was wondering . . .' He paused. 'It may be too soon, and tell me if you think it is, but I was wondering if you remembered anything about the attack. If you saw your attacker's face, and could give a description.'

Lucy was thoughtful for a moment, then she nodded. 'I think so,' she said. 'I can't remember much about *anything*, but I remember that face.'

Alcide fetched his laptop. He'd brought it every time he

came, just in case – hopeful that this moment would come, the photofit software ready to run the instant it was required. He sat by her bed and guided her through the process, helping her assemble an image of the man who had brutally stabbed her, the man who had left her for dead.

It was the only way he could help her, Alcide knew. The only way to prove himself.

He was patient, flinching now and then if her hand should brush his as he pointed out something onscreen, but buoyed by the rare smiles she gave him. And the image built up, inexorably, until Alcide saw the recognition fill Lucy's face. He could feel a chill down his spine.

'That's him,' she said.

Alcide looked at the image on his screen and felt the full weight of justice on his side. They would have their man soon enough.

He would have nowhere to hide.

57

Claire got a call from Pierre early that morning. He asked after Léna and Claire told him that she'd still not come home. A stubborn girl, Claire said, managing to hold in the deep fear she had for her daughter. But then, she'd always had that fear. For both of them.

She told him too of Frédéric, that Camille believed he knew the truth. Pierre didn't seem fazed by the news. He said he wanted to see Claire, to talk to her in person about something very important. She thought he sounded odd, and it was only when he arrived at the house that she could see how tired he looked.

'Are you well, Pierre?' she asked, but he waved it away, almost impatiently.

'I didn't sleep much,' he said. 'I was thinking. I realized that I'd been selfish to keep the news of Camille back from the other parents. I think it's time to tell them.'

Claire nodded. Since she'd kicked Jérôme out, the prospect of moving away had vanished. She needed to share the news, and get what support she could. 'Can I ask what changed your mind?'

For a moment he looked uneasy; haunted, almost. 'I believe I was tested, Claire. To show me that I was failing, and had to try harder. To do better. There are *others*, Claire. Not just Simon and Camille.' She could see a sudden excitement in his eyes; she felt it herself, too. 'They will all need our help, so we have to have more people on our side. Do you think Simon managed to get out of town?'

'He left here before the power went off yesterday,' she said. 'I think he was headed for the bus station.'

Pierre looked disappointed. 'Very well. I think we should ask as many of the other parents as we can to come here and meet Camille. That would be enough of a shock for now. With your permission, of course.'

'And Camille's,' said Claire.

Pierre smiled and nodded. Then his expression became guarded. 'And Jérôme?'

She shook her head. 'Jérôme doesn't get to make decisions like that for us. Not any more.'

She went to fetch Camille, and the three of them talked. Camille was easily persuaded – the idea of not having to hide was welcome, and Pierre's confidence was hard to resist. Pierre set about contacting the parents, telling them only that something important had happened, something they should know about. With almost everywhere closed due to the power cut, most of those he called agreed to come. Two hours later, the small group convened in Claire's living room, everyone looking a little uneasy, a little awkward, having no idea why they'd been brought there. Outside, the day was cold and the midday sky overcast; the room was gloomy without artificial light, and there was a chill in the unheated air.

'I'm afraid I can't offer you anything hot,' Claire told them, smiling.

'Any idea when the power might come back?' one of them asked. 'Pierre, surely you've heard something by now?'

Pierre shook his head. 'The dam and power plant are both undergoing some maintenance. The recent brief power cuts weren't unexpected, apparently, but I've not heard anything encouraging about this one. Nobody seems to know when the power will be back. Of course, you can all stay at the Helping Hand if you like. We have a generator, and plenty of supplies. The dormitories are warm and we have more than enough beds.'

There were smiles and nods from around the room, but Claire thought most of them would be happier staying in their own homes until everything was resolved.

'Now,' said Pierre. 'I'm sure you realize we have something important to say. A few days ago, Claire . . .' He paused, and smiled at her. 'Claire had an experience that was extraordinary. She shared it with me, for which I'll always be grateful. Now we both want to share this news with you – because we trust you, and we need your help. What you are about to see goes beyond reason, and it will change how you view the world. I know it won't be easy, but you have to open your minds. From now on, we're all on the same journey.' The parents in the room looked suddenly wary, sharing anxious glances. Pierre turned to the stairs and called: 'Camille? It's time.'

Camille came slowly down the stairs. She was nervous, looking around the room as every mouth fell open, all eyes went wide.

Sandrine stared at the ghost she'd already seen. 'Camille?' she whispered, unable to believe it. She turned to Claire, distraught. 'But . . . but you know this is impossible.'

'It's real,' said Claire. 'If Audrey came back, you'd know her immediately.' She could sense the unease in the room;

she'd hoped the reaction would be acceptance, at least. Perhaps even celebration. Instead, everyone was looking at everyone else, their agitation visible and growing.

Pierre clearly sensed the mood too. 'Camille has come back to us,' he said, trying to sound upbeat. 'And it's our duty to make her welcome.'

Sandrine's voice was trembling now, tears pouring from her eyes. 'Does that mean . . . does that mean other children will come back?' The words drew a gasp from others. Claire watched her, knowing the pain she was feeling. The terrible pain of hope just out of reach.

'We don't know,' said Pierre. 'Perhaps there may be others, but we don't know.'

Another parent spoke. Claire recognized him as Esteban Koretzky's father, but she didn't know the man's first name. 'Does she remember what happened in the coach?'

'No,' said Camille. 'I've tried, but I don't remember.'

'And have you seen the other children?' said Monsieur Koretzky. 'Did they talk to you?'

Camille shook her head, downcast.

Sandrine had been glaring at Camille all this time. 'Why you?' she said, harsh and angry and loud. 'Why you?'

The room went silent.

Claire found herself close to tears at the way this was going. 'Sandrine,' she said, pleading with her. 'Now that Camille is here perhaps Audrey's turn will come. Like Pierre says, the fact that Camille has come back gives us all hope.'

'Easy for you to say,' said Sandrine bitterly, standing up. 'There must be a reason why she's the one who came back. Why her?' She was crying, shouting; her husband stood too, his hand on her shoulder, trying to calm her down.

Camille, distraught, turned and fled up the stairs. 'Camille!' called Claire, turning to follow her.

'Wait,' said Pierre. 'I'll go.' He went up after her.

Claire turned an accusing eye on those in the room. Nobody met her gaze. 'She's a child, and you treat her like a criminal,' she said. 'Please, she needs our help. It's not her fault.' She looked at their faces, one by one, seeing hints of Sandrine's anger in each of them, but seeing also the shame they felt at their unease.

Then she went upstairs to join Pierre, who was outside Camille's room. The door was closed.

'Go away!' yelled Camille. 'I never should have listened to you!'

Claire eased the door open and went inside. Camille was lying on her bed, so Claire sat next to her and took her hand. She waved for Pierre to come in.

'People fear what they don't understand,' said Pierre. 'Imagine how they feel.'

'What about me?' said Camille, her face wet with tears. 'Did they wonder how I feel? They're just like Léna and Frédéric. They look at me like I'm a monster.'

Pierre frowned. 'You can be so selfish.'

'What?' said Camille, shocked. Claire looked at Pierre, wary, but gave him the benefit of the doubt.

'You came back,' said Pierre. 'Do you realize how lucky you are? You're a miracle, Camille. And what do you do with it? Nothing.' She looked at him, confused. Pierre turned to Claire and sighed. 'It looks like I'm wasting my time.'

'Wait,' said Camille, contrite. 'What should I do?'

'Help those who need it,' said Pierre. 'You have the

power to ease their minds, to soothe the pain they've gone through for so long. Think of the good you could do.'

Camille considered it for a moment, then nodded. 'OK,' she said, purposeful now. 'I'll talk to them again. If they'll listen.'

58

Thomas stood in the hospital morgue looking at the still body of Simon Delaître. The air in the morgue had a chill that, he thought, wasn't just down to the temperature.

'Good of you to bring me a human this time,' said the pathologist. Thomas let that one slide. 'We can't keep him for long, though. The generator's playing up so they're planning on closing anything non-essential, which will mean transferring everyone in the morgue, and me along with them. The entire hospital may have to be evacuated, if it stays like this.'

Thomas was looking at Simon's face: pale, cold. The paperwork on this one would be interesting, he thought sourly. He half-expected the man's eyes to open. 'Is he definitely dead?'

The pathologist smiled. 'What do you think? Was it you who shot him?'

'Yes.'

'Good work. Right in the heart. Died instantly. Saves on all that messing around with paramedics.'

Thomas looked at the pathologist in silence for a few long seconds. Just to let the man know to rein it in. 'So, the evacuation,' he said. 'Does that mean you won't be doing a post-mortem today?'

'Exactly. I can do a preliminary examination, of course. But a full post-mortem will have to wait for a day or two.'

'Tell me if you find anything odd.'

The pathologist raised an eyebrow. 'Like . . .?'

'I don't know,' said Thomas, irritated. 'Just odd. Now do your job.'

By the time Thomas went home to see how Adèle and Chloé were bearing up, it was mid-morning. The outside air was just as chilly as the air in the morgue had been. He looked to the sky, wondering if the damp cold would be dispelled as the day wore on, but the heavy cloud didn't bode well. Without power, the town could have done with a sunny day to lift its spirits.

Chloé had managed to get some sleep, but Adèle looked exhausted. He only had so much sympathy for her: he hadn't slept either, and after all, this whole thing was fundamentally Adèle's fault.

Chloé ran over and gave him a hug when he came through the door, but Adèle told her to go to her room. Her voice was clipped, and Thomas couldn't read her. She clearly wanted the girl out of the way so they could talk freely, but there was every chance it could degenerate into a shouting match.

'Are you going to talk about the ghost?' asked Chloé.

'I told you to go to your room,' Adèle said.

Thomas caught Adèle's eye and shook his head. 'We should answer her questions,' he said. Adèle didn't say anything, but her expression was cold. He turned to Chloé. 'The ghost has gone,' he told her.

'Where to?' asked Chloé.

'To wherever he came from.'

She looked uncertain. 'How do you know he won't come back?'

SETH PATRICK

'Because now he knows we don't need him.' He knelt down, and hugged Chloé again. 'Officers will come and ask you questions,' he said. 'They'll ask if you knew who the ghost was. You should say no. The first time you saw him was last night in the garden. You were scared and you called me. OK?'

Chloé frowned. 'Why do I have to lie? I don't like lying.'

He looked at Adèle, and Adèle looked away. 'Because if you tell the truth, they won't believe you. They'll think you're lying. They don't believe in ghosts. So everything else is our secret. OK?'

Chloé nodded. She clearly wasn't happy about it, but Thomas knew she would hold to the story.

'Now,' said Thomas. 'Do as your mum told you. Go to your room.' He watched her go upstairs, suddenly overwhelmed by how much he loved her. How much he would do to protect her.

'Is he dead?' said Adèle. She seemed a little combative, prickly. He knew he had to be patient with her.

'He was already dead,' said Thomas. 'That wasn't Simon. Whatever it was, it wasn't him.'

'Then what was it?'

Thomas shook his head, frustrated. 'I don't know the answers. Neither did Father Jean-François, and unlike him I don't have the luxury of armchair theology. I couldn't let Simon torture you like that, Adèle.'

She said nothing for a moment. She nodded, but she was looking at him as if he'd been the cause of everything. Thomas didn't like it. 'What makes you think he's *really* dead?' she said. 'What if he comes back again?'

'If he does, I'll be here,' he said. He put his arms around

326

her, pulled her close, hugged her. He could feel the reluctance within her, the uncertainty. It would go in time, he knew. 'I'll always be here.' And if Simon did come back? There had to be ways, he thought. Ways to kill a dead man.

Once he'd dosed Adèle to help her sleep, and plied himself with strong coffee, Thomas headed back to the station. He'd done the minimum amount of paperwork necessary on the shooting, but there was still a mountain to get through. He would have to be creative, he knew, if he wanted to protect his own back. As he drove, he realized how quiet the streets were; schools and some businesses were closed, and many shops still had their shutters down. The power cut had lasted almost fifteen hours, now. Much longer, and it would become a ghost town.

'You OK, sir?' asked Michael.

'Strange times,' said Thomas. 'Any word on the power failure?' With perfect timing the lights in the building dimmed for an instant, the station generator only just managing the load.

Michael looked frustrated. 'Actually, sir, that's proving difficult.'

Thomas had assigned him to hounding the power company and making sure they were kept up to date, but this didn't sound good. 'How so?'

'The company isn't giving us much information. The last thing they told me was that the power will be back in four to ten hours.'

'Well, that's something,' said Thomas, but Michael shook his head. 'No?'

'That's exactly what they said last night, sir. Our emergency switchboard is being swamped with people asking about the power, and some other rumours that are going round.'

'Rumours?' Thomas was intrigued. 'Such as?'

'Mostly that the dam's going to burst.'

Thomas sighed. The last thing they needed was that kind of panic. It was the sort of thing he preferred to be the first to know about, but dealing with the shooting all night had left him out of the loop. 'Anything else unusual?'

Michael gave him an uneasy smile. 'There was a case last night . . .' He passed Thomas a folder. 'Here. Two boys were caught in the cemetery searching a grave.'

'Searching a grave?' Thomas opened the folder and scanned over it. He stopped dead when he saw two words: *body missing.* 'They stole a body?'

'Seems so. But they've clammed up. No explanation, and no hint of where they took it. We're waiting for a lawyer who specializes in juvenile cases.'

The two boys were still being held in the cells. He hurried downstairs and went inside alone. He didn't recognize them, so they probably weren't among the usual troublemakers. Just two young lads, he thought. Young, but they looked worn thin, fragile. He wanted to get to the bottom of what they'd been up to, and fast. Fuck the lawyers.

'Why did you do it?' he asked, being as aggressive as he knew how without getting physical. The boys both flinched when they saw what was in his eyes. 'It wasn't just desecration, was it? What were you after?' The boys looked as though they were about to shit themselves, but they only shook their heads. Thomas held up the report folder, then opened it and checked the name again. 'It was Camille Séguret's grave. Did you know her? Where's the body? When the watchman caught you, it was gone.'

'It wasn't there,' said one of them. He sounded terrified, and Thomas didn't think his questioning was the primary source of the fear.

'So where is it?'

'We never touched it,' said the other boy. 'Jesus, we're telling the truth. I was holding the torch while he opened the coffin, and all that was inside was water. It was full of water.'

Thomas looked at them and said, as gently as he could: 'Where is Camille Séguret?'

They looked at each other, then back at him, silent. Thomas could see in their eyes that they were hiding something. 'Where is she, right now?' he said. 'You know, don't you?'

The boy who'd opened the coffin nodded. 'I think she's back,' he said, his voice almost a whisper.

'Back?' said Thomas. 'Back from where?' He already knew the answer, but he still had to hear it spoken.

The boy stared at Thomas, desperate to be believed. 'Back from the dead.'

59

Claire watched as Camille spoke to the group. They all looked dazed, almost traumatized. Claire was sympathetic. She'd gone through the same kind of shock.

'It's hard to describe,' said Camille. 'First, I saw a great light that dazzled me. It felt like I was going blind. I couldn't hear anything. Gradually, I could make out figures around me.'

'The other children?' said Sandrine, her eyes wet, her expression anguished.

'Yes,' said Camille. 'But I couldn't see them very well. I just felt them there, like spirits. I remember Audrey calling to me.'

'What did she say?' asked Sandrine. She sounded almost forlorn.

Camille glanced at her mother and Claire suddenly wondered how much of this was the truth, and how much was inspired by Pierre's words. Her daughter looked so earnest, so eager to please them. It worried her that she had no idea if her daughter was lying or not, but right now the most important thing was for the group to accept her.

'She said she was safe,' said Camille.

There was a knock at the front door and the parents exchanged cautious looks. Claire went to answer it.

It was Jérôme. 'Hi,' she said, curt but neutral.

'No word from Léna?'

'No.'

He looked agitated, weighed down with frustration. 'I told the police,' he said. 'They don't care. They think she's just run off. So all I can do is look in one place, then in the next, and it's strange out there, Claire. Eerie. The streets are emptying.'

'People are staying indoors,' she said. 'It's all they can do.'

There were noises from inside. Claire felt her expression freeze, and saw the suspicion on Jérôme's face. 'Who's in there?' he said, pushing past her. He walked down the hall into the living room and looked around at the gathering, appalled. He froze when he saw Pierre. 'I might have guessed you'd be involved,' he said.

'Hello, Jérôme,' said Pierre, caught red-handed.

Jérôme turned angrily to Claire. 'What have you told them?'

'The truth,' she said, defiant. 'Jérôme, listen to me. We have to confide in those who can help, those who can understand. This is bigger than anything we can handle alone. Camille needs protecting.'

'She needs protecting from *him*,' said Jérôme, pointing at Pierre. 'He can't be trusted. He's a fraud, but you can't see it. He acts like he knows what's going to happen, but he has no more idea than the rest of us.'

Most of the group kept their eyes to the ground, letting them squabble, but Claire saw Camille's face, saw her despair at her parents fighting. 'This isn't the place to argue,' she said, but then there was another knock at the front door. Claire and Jérôme locked eyes briefly; then Claire looked to Camille, and upstairs. Camille understood and hurried up to her room. They waited until they heard her bedroom door shut before they went to see who had come.

It was the police captain, looking grimly serious. 'Can I talk to Alice?' he said. 'Your niece.'

Claire could feel the beginnings of panic and knew it was crucial that the officer didn't notice.

Jérôme had a desperate look too, but he opted to go on the attack. 'Shouldn't you be looking for our missing daughter?' he said.

The captain seemed to weigh this up. 'Exactly. We think your niece could be involved. She is your niece, isn't she?'

'Yes,' said Claire, trying to sound calm. 'But she's not here.'

'When will she be back?'

'I don't know. She has her own life.'

He looked at them both with undisguised scepticism. 'Tell your niece to come to the station with identification. Is that clear?'

Jérôme nodded. They went back inside to the hallway and shut the door, then looked at each other, relieved the officer had gone, but knowing the respite was temporary.

'We can't stay here,' said Claire. 'Whatever your feelings about Pierre, we *can't* stay here.'

And that left only one option.

Within the hour most of the group of parents had made the same decision and relocated to the Helping Hand. Some of them pretended that the power cut was the main reason, but Claire saw how they all looked at Camille. Wary, but desperate to believe. Desperate to be near. She wondered how she'd feel in their position, if it had been one of their children who'd come back and she was left questioning why Camille hadn't. She simply couldn't imagine what it was like for them.

Claire and Jérôme sat with Camille in the canteen, watching her devour the food offered by the Helping Hand staff. It was cold outside; the breeze carried a deep chill and the sun was hidden behind thick cloud. As soon as they'd come inside, the warmth that greeted them was welcomed by all. Only Jérôme had seemed cautious; coming here, having Camille in the open.

'I'll go back soon and stay at the house,' Jérôme told Camille. 'In case Léna goes back there. Your mother will sleep here, OK?'

Camille looked up, mouth full. She nodded, her attention more focused on the food than what her father was saying. She cleaned her plate. 'I'm going to see if there's more,' she said.

Always hungry, thought Claire.

As Camille passed a nearby table, the couple sitting there called to her.

'Hello, Camille,' Claire heard the man say tentatively. 'We used to see you at school. We're Esteban's parents.'

Camille paused by the table, looking a little uneasy. 'Hello, Monsieur Koretsky,' she said. 'Yes, I remember.'

'I'm sure a lot of people will ask you this, but we wondered . . .'

'Esteban is fine,' she said, smiling.

They were looking at her with a different kind of hunger, Claire thought: their appetite for news of their son was almost as insatiable as Camille's desire for food.

'Have you spoken to him?' said Monsieur Koretsky.

'Spoken? No, I wouldn't put it that way, but our souls . . . have made contact. He said he misses you. He can't wait to see you again.' The couple smiled at her, close to tears. 'Esteban is at peace,' said Camille. 'He knows you'll be together once more.'

Claire turned to her husband, smiling, but Jérôme was sullen. 'What's she doing?' he whispered, sounding worried.

'She's giving them hope,' said Claire, but Jérôme didn't seem reassured. 'Look at her, Jérôme. She hasn't seemed this happy since she came back. She's found what she needed.'

'What?'

'A sense of purpose,' she said, watching the Koretskys as Camille walked on. Both their faces had the same look of desperate grief, mixed with equally desperate hope.

'Yes,' said Jérôme. 'But whose purpose? God's or Pierre's?'

Ignoring her husband's cynicism, Claire prayed that they were the same thing.

60

When she'd got back from collecting Victor from the Helping Hand the night before, Julie had wanted to give the boy a bath. He liked the water, certainly, but he always seemed a little cold to the touch, and after a bath he felt warmer.

With the power out there was no heating and no hot water, so she'd waited, expecting it to come back overnight. But that morning there had still been no power. She'd hunted out a camping stove from the back of a cupboard, half-surprised that it was working given how long it had been since it was last used – at a summer festival she'd gone to with Laure, the year before she was attacked.

She used it to heat up some water so they could take turns to bathe.

'It's ready,' she called, looking at the pitifully shallow water. 'It's not deep, but it'll have to do.'

Victor came through and she smiled. It was good to have him back, have him safe. She hadn't asked him about the night before, about the man in the Helping Hand, but there was something she needed to know. Something she'd wanted to know since he first came to her.

'Victor?' she said. He looked at her, attentive. 'Why did you come to see me? Is it because I'm like you?'

The boy shook his head. Julie felt a sudden rush of emotion, tears welling up in her eyes. Victor stepped forward and put his arms around her, holding tight.

'It's because of the fairy,' he whispered in her ear.

Julie was taken aback, hearing his voice. It was only the third time he'd ever said anything to her. 'What fairy?'

'Mum told me that if she went away, the fairy would look after me until she came back. She said if I ever saw her, I would recognize her.'

'A fairy?' He was just looking at her, adoring, a hint of a smile on his face. 'You think it's me?' She laughed, touched by his faith in her but saddened that this was the only thing he had to cling to. 'I'm not a fairy. Fairies have nice hair, pretty dresses . . . They always smile, they have magic wands. That's not me, not by a long way.' She hugged him again. 'Now,' she said. 'You get undressed and have a wash, OK?'

She left him to it. She didn't see him remove his long-sleeved top; didn't see the state of his forearm, the dry skin patterned with darkened veins, cracked and sore in places. Victor ran the fingers of his left hand over it, looking frightened.

Late afternoon, the doorbell rang. It was Laure, in uniform. Julie let her come in, but she gave her a wary look.

'Why are you here?' asked Julie, suspicious.

'I'm not here for the boy,' said Laure.

'What is it, then?'

'We don't know how long the power will be out, so we're checking everyone's OK. People are worried. The shops have shut, and there are rumours that the power won't come back for days.'

'Days?' She glanced at the gloomy sky outside and, despite herself, shivered.

Laure nodded. 'It's almost deserted on the streets. Lots of people are planning on leaving town to stay with relatives.' She paused, before adding: 'Do you have all you need?'

'Yes, I'm fine,' said Julie. *And I certainly don't need anything from you.*

Laure's eyes barely met Julie's. 'You could always stay at my house. I have a fireplace for heating, and plenty of food.'

It took a moment for this to sink in. Then Julie laughed. 'Are you asking me to move in with you?' She hadn't meant it to sound unkind, but she saw Laure flinch a little.

'Well, I suppose.'

The offer hung out there for quiet, awkward seconds before Julie shook her head. 'We'll be fine,' she said. 'Really.' Victor was all the company she wanted now.

Early evening, the doorbell rang again. This time, after Julie had looked through the spyhole she didn't even take the security chain off the door. It was the man from the Helping Hand, and she didn't like the thought of him being around Victor.

'What do you want?' she said.

'To help you and the boy. He isn't safe here.'

'Leave us alone,' said Julie. The man had an intensity that scared her.

'Please,' he said. 'I know what he is. He's not the only one.'

Julie gripped the door handle tighter, ready to shut it if he made any kind of move. 'I don't know what you mean.'

The man looked desperate. She wondered what his connection with Victor was. 'Listen to me,' he said. 'If you stay, you're putting Victor at risk. There are others like him, and when people find out, do you think they'll just open their arms and accept him?' Julie looked to the floor, not wanting him to see that it was a fear she shared, that she knew it would be dangerous if anyone found out the truth about the boy. 'Soon people like Victor will be hunted down, and who knows what will happen to them. It's safer at the Helping Hand. We can protect him.'

The man gave her a broad, well-practised smile, but the intensity was still in his eyes. She didn't like what she saw.

'Not a chance,' she said. 'Last time you people looked after him, you lost him within a day. I think I know where he's safer, and it's not with you.' She shut the door and listened, waiting until she heard the man descend the stairs.

And she meant it: there was no chance she would let the man near Victor again, not after seeing how terrified the boy had been last night. But there were other options.

She went into the kitchen where Victor was eating a bowl of noodles. He looked up at her, full of trust. She wouldn't let him down. If that meant a few sacrifices, then so be it.

'Pack your things,' she said.

61

With the power down, Adèle and Chloé had dug out every game they could find and gone through them one at a time.

'Too childish,' Chloé would say to some of them. 'Too long,' to others.

Adèle smiled when she realized that most of the ones Chloé was rejecting were supposed to be educational. *Children aren't stupid*, she thought. They can tell when you're trying to sneak some teaching in alongside something that's supposed to be fun, as easily as broccoli in ice cream.

They played, and Adèle smiled and didn't think of Simon; or of Thomas, for that matter. All she thought of was Chloé, and laughing. But there was only so much Buckaroo you could play.

'Do you want to go out?' she asked. 'Get some fresh air?'

'No,' said Chloé. 'How about we play something else?'

'OK,' said Adèle. 'Your turn to pick.' She gestured to the pile of games, but Chloé shook her head.

'How about Truth or Dare?'

Adèle didn't like the way Chloé was looking at her. 'OK.'

'Truth. How old was I when Dad killed himself?'

Adèle nodded. The girl deserved answers, however hard it was to give them. 'You hadn't been born yet.'

'So he never saw me?'

'No.'

'Next question,' said Chloé. 'Did he want to die because of me?'

Adèle took a sharp breath. 'No.'

'Was it because of you?'

'It's complicated,' said Adèle. She wanted the game to stop, if these were the kinds of thing Chloé wanted answers to. 'You're too young to understand.'

Chloé looked upset. She jumped to her feet. 'I'll ask Thomas,' she yelled from the doorway. 'At least *he'll* tell me the truth.' Then she ran to her room, slamming the door behind her.

Adèle called out to her, then followed. She felt drained suddenly, her legs heavy. She knew just how much she'd enjoyed not thinking about Simon, but it was never going to be for long. She went into Chloé's room, where she found her crying in the corner. She knelt by her daughter and held her.

'It's natural that you want to know,' said Adèle. 'But the truth is, I have no idea why he did it.'

'Was he unhappy?' said Chloé.

Adèle sighed. 'Sometimes he was unhappy, so unhappy that nothing would stop him feeling despair. Other times, he was full of life, finding happiness even in the smallest of things. It was a kind of illness, Chloé, though he refused to accept that.'

'When he died, did he know I was going to be born?'

'Yes.'

'Do you think it was my fault?'

'I know it wasn't, Chloé. He was happy when I told him I was pregnant. Very happy.' She thought of the tears that

Simon had cried when he'd heard, and of the way she hadn't been sure, even then, how he really felt.

And she knew she could never tell Chloé the truth.

62

Toni was sitting in the empty Lake Pub when the police came.

A bottle of whisky was rapidly vanishing, but he wasn't feeling any effect. He dreaded going back to the old house now, dreaded being told again that his mother wanted nothing to do with him, that she preferred the company of a murderer to . . .

Then his thoughts tangled, as he realized that *murderer* was just what his mother thought of *him*. Støpping Serge, that was all he'd done. It wasn't murder to put a rabid dog out of its misery, was it?

Yet that was exactly the problem. Family came first, in all things.

Now Serge had made a promise to stop. Yes, he'd promised before, but this was different. It had to be. Serge was renewed. Back from whatever hell he'd been sent to. He'd got one more chance, yes? Of course he had.

Another glass of whisky. It didn't help.

The power had been out all night. He'd decided to stay closed today, but he'd had a text message from a friend in town about reports of looting. Daytime looting, for Christ's sake. No way he was going to open up if that was how things were.

He thought about his friends. None that could be described as close, but he had some all the same, not just the people he worked with day to day. He was always vaguely shocked by the fact. Since his mum had died, though, what else could he do? Talk to people. Drink with them, even. He'd moved out of the old house, into an apartment, and discovered he didn't always mind company. It seemed almost like blasphemy, now, that he'd sought any kind of comfort away from his family, but it was how he'd coped for the last three years.

By forging some kind of life for himself.

More whisky, he thought. Then there was knocking at the door. He walked over and unlocked it. It was the police, two of them.

'Are you closed?' said the first officer.

'The power's down,' Toni said. 'What else can I do? Besides, I heard about the looting.' He watched their eyes for any reaction as he spoke. They shared a look, but didn't take the bait.

'Can we come inside for a minute?'

Toni waved them through, wondering where this was going.

'So you're hitting the bottle?' said the first officer, nodding towards the bar.

Toni looked across to where he'd been sitting. One glass, half-full. And the bottle beside it? Hell, wasn't it almost empty? He hadn't thought it would look quite so damning. 'Not much else to do but worry,' he said. 'I was serious about the looting.'

The second officer nodded dismissively. 'Yeah, yeah. We've had some reports. Nothing bad.'

'Yet,' said Toni. Grim, he walked back to his glass – might as well finish the bottle now there was so little left.

'It's weird, though, Toni,' said the first officer. This was

Michael, Toni thought – not exactly a regular, but a familiar enough face in the Lake Pub. 'Everything just feels . . . pent up. Like the town's waiting for something to happen.'

The other one laughed. 'Yeah, the fucking power to come back on.'

Toni shrugged. 'I know what you mean,' he said, and took another drink. His comment had been aimed at Michael. There *was* a feeling of something about to happen. There was thunder in the air, his mother would have said.

'Anyway,' said Michael. 'Shame you're closed. We were hoping to be able to ask more than just you.'

'Ask what?'

'We have a picture of the guy who attacked your barmaid.'

Toni felt his blood freeze. Michael held up a sheet of paper. For a moment Toni was expecting a clear still from CCTV, but instead it was a photofit. 'Look familiar?' said Michael. 'Lucy managed to give us a description when she woke up.'

Toni had to stop himself staring at the officer. *Woke up?* 'They told me she . . .'

'Yeah,' said the second policeman. 'I heard the doctors had the same look on their faces. She pulled through.'

Toni found himself glad at the fact that Lucy was OK. She would be fine. Everything would be fine. Then he looked again at the picture the man was holding out to him.

It was Serge. Clear as day.

'Ever seen him in the bar?' said Michael.

'No idea,' said Toni, reminding himself to breathe. 'I have a lot of customers.'

'Put it up inside for when you get to open again,' said

Michael. 'Call me if anyone knows him. And go easy on the alcohol.'

Toni nodded, pulse racing.

It would only be a matter of time. For all the isolation he and Serge had experienced, it had never been complete. People had known Serge. That was why the story about Paris had been necessary. They'd noticed when he wasn't around.

And they would notice the picture.

He waited for the police to have safely gone. He took his keys, and knew he'd had too much to drink. That he shouldn't even consider driving.

Then he drove back up the mountain all the same.

63

In the bowels of the hospital the lights in the unattended morgue flickered and failed, then came back, the harsh white glinting sharply off the metal doors, their latches all firmly closed. There was silence. Then a slow, steady pounding began, growing in intensity. One door shook and strained with each beat until at last the latch gave. The chamber door swung wide.

Simon Delaître crawled out from the cold metal slab, shielding his eyes from the light. He turned to look at where he'd come from. Icy water slopped from the chamber like afterbirth, pooling on the floor.

Naked, he walked out of the morgue into a hallway and stumbled upon a locker room. He punched one of the locker doors, first denting it; then, with a second punch, breaking the lock open. There were clothes inside, too small for him. He moved to the next locker, then the next; on the fifth try he was satisfied with what he found, and started to dress.

In the hospital above him, Lucy Clarsen suddenly opened her eyes and smiled. Her room was empty, for once; Alcide back at work, the doctors with more pressing demands on their time. She'd been dreaming again – although *dream* wasn't exactly what it had been, more a waking vision. This time she knew the dreams had meaning. It all came back to her: everything that she'd been unable to remember since she'd first woken. Her smile grew fierce.

She got off her bed, the lights flickering and then failing again and again. She walked along the deserted corridors in her hospital gown, searching. At last she saw him, the man in borrowed clothes.

She reached him and held out her hand.

'Come with me,' she said to Simon.

As she took his hand in hers, the lights across the hospital failed completely. There were cries from corridors and rooms where no natural light reached, anguish from staff whose equipment failed them; deep in the basement there was cursing as the generators refused to restart.

The two walked calmly to the entrance and out of the hospital. And as they left, the building came to life once more.

They made their way to the Lake Pub and broke in around the back, then Lucy led the way upstairs to the room she used to live in.

'The pub's closed,' said Lucy. 'No one will find you here.' Some of her clothes were still in the room. She looked through them and dressed. 'Are you hungry?' she asked.

Simon shook his head.

'Liar,' she said, smiling.

'I've eaten enough,' he said. He sounded irritable. 'I can't stay here.'

'What will you do? Go and see Adèle?'

Simon looked at her, astonished. 'How did you know? Who are you?'

She stepped towards him. 'Your guardian angel,' she said. Then she kissed him eagerly, and he responded. She pushed him hard to the sofa, his eyes wide at the strength in her.

Each of them had as much desperate need as the other, all thoughts gone except sheer lust. Their desperation grew; she took him inside her, feral glints in their eyes. They fucked until they both came, gripping each other fiercely. Her face calmed at last, then looked pained.

'What is it?' he said.

She looked at him, distraught. 'What happened to you? Why did you want to die?'

'I didn't want to die,' he said, almost pleading.

'But I saw you do it,' she told him. '*I saw you.*'

64

Laure got home after an exhausting shift. She had news for Julie, news which she didn't really want to pass on.

It had been an insanely busy day. Bad enough that they'd been trying to speak to every resident in town, but they were short-staffed, some officers ringing in early to say that they were doing what so many of the population seemed to be considering – getting out of town until the power was sorted out.

Those with no intention of going were the old, the isolated; those without family nearby, or indeed any family at all. Some of the doors that opened to her that afternoon had revealed frightened, suspicious faces; soon enough, reports of looting had started to filter through.

Amazing how short a time it took for people to revert to that kind of behaviour, Laure thought. Cynicism was something which working on the force had a habit of nurturing, of course, but when it came to how low people could sink, and how fast, it was hard to be cynical *enough*. Civilization was only three meals away from anarchy, wasn't that the saying? And yes, desperation and hunger made for a bad situation, but the reality of it was worse. All it took was the *fear* of hunger, and everything could go to pieces in an instant.

The moment she opened the door of her house and stepped inside, the thought of looters hit her square between the eyes.

Instinct. Instinct was telling her someone else was inside. She put her hand to her gun, and took three quiet strides to her left to get a clear view of the kitchen.

Then she relaxed.

'You scared me,' she said.

'I decided to take you up on your offer,' said Julie. Beside her was Victor, tucking into a banana.

'Good,' said Laure. She was genuinely pleased to see them there. 'So you kept your keys?'

Julie nodded, and Laure thought she could see a smile in Julie's eyes. Not that Julie would have let that smile creep down and pop out on her mouth, of course, but Laure took some hope from it.

'Yeah,' said Julie. 'I don't throw anything out. With the power down, I was cooking on the stove we used in Belfort. Remember that?'

Laure nodded. She smiled, but found herself overcome and unable to reply. It wasn't just that Julie remembered that weekend, or even that she'd made the first real reference in seven years to the life they'd had together. It was that Julie's smile had actually broken through as she'd spoken.

'Come on up,' Laure managed to say, and she headed for the stairs.

Julie followed after her, leaving Victor eating in the kitchen. 'You've redecorated,' she said.

'Well, I painted. I had to do something with my time.' She threw Julie a grin to make sure she wouldn't take that as some kind of jibe. 'You can sleep in my room, if you like?'

'I'll sleep in here with Victor,' said Julie, pointing to the spare room with the sofa-bed.

'It's up to you.' The mention of Victor reminded Laure

that, with the boy still downstairs and out of earshot, now would be the time to bring up the news she had. 'Julie, something's happened.' She reached into her pocket and pulled out a folded printout. It was the photofit that Lucy Clarsen had produced of the man who'd stabbed her. 'The barmaid who was attacked pulled through. She gave us this description of the attacker. We need to know if you recognize him.'

Julie stared at the still-folded paper in Laure's hand.

'You don't have to look now,' said Laure. 'Not unless you're ready.' Julie had never produced more than the vaguest description of the man who'd attacked her, having little clear memory of his face. Laure could see the indecision in her eyes.

Julie took the paper and unfolded it with unsteady hands. She gave it the briefest of looks before handing the paper back, giving a small nod.

'You're safe here,' said Laure. She put her hand on Julie's arm. Julie stepped towards her and put her head on Laure's shoulder, and let Laure hold her. 'You're safe,' Laure said again.

65

Léna woke feeling better than she'd felt in a long time.

It wasn't just that her wound had improved, or that she'd slept well. Or that she didn't have a hangover for once, or the dry ache of too many cigarettes the night before. She felt better because she had some distance from the mess that was her family, and from Frédéric. She could pretend, for a while. Pretend that things were simple.

She got out of bed, and looked around for the clothes she'd thrown over the top of her hospital gown when she'd absconded. They were on the floor in one corner of the room, but filthy from her fall in the underpass. Worse, the hooded top she'd been wearing had a long stain from the wound on her back, dried and crusted into the fabric.

She heard the sound of axe on wood from outside. She went to the front door. Serge was out there, chopping logs for the stove. She watched him, suddenly grateful that he'd brought her here. Peace and quiet, away from the chaos.

Holding a log on the chopping block steady with his left hand, Serge brought the axe down. His aim was off, the axe glancing down the side of the log; he snatched his hand out of the way just in time.

'For fuck's sake,' he said, bending down to retrieve the log. Then he saw her, watching him from the doorway with a smile.

'Don't let me stop you,' said Léna.

'Sorry, did I wake you?'

'It's all right,' she said. The guy was awkward around her, and she found it endearing. A refreshing change from the wary distrust that Frédéric always seemed to exude. 'Can I borrow some clean clothes?'

Serge nodded, setting down his axe, gathering the logs he'd already chopped. 'I'll see what we have,' he said, coming inside. 'There's stuff in the attic, I think. I won't be long.'

She wandered through the kitchen, opening a door to a room she hadn't entered before. Around the wall were dead animals, stuffed with varying degrees of success. She smiled at an owl that had a ludicrous expression on its face. She stepped into the room, seeing the knives, the tools, the equipment. This was a hunter's lodge, she thought, kitted out for taxidermy and butchery. She wondered which brother did what.

'You shouldn't be in here,' said Serge from behind her.

Léna turned to see the unease on his face. She pointed to the stuffed animals. 'Are these yours?'

'No, my brother's.' He was holding out some clothes. 'Here,' he said.

Léna took them. 'Thanks. Whose are they, your ex's?'

'My mother's.'

'You sure she won't mind?'

Serge looked to the floor. 'She died,' he said.

Léna's turn to feel awkward. She looked through the clothes and found a simple blue cotton dress she thought would fit. She went to remove her hospital gown, and saw the way Serge was watching her, embarrassed but fascinated.

'Turn around,' she said, enjoying the guy's discomfort. When he complied she took off the gown. 'The stuff you put on my back really worked,' she said as she pulled the dress on. 'The pain's gone completely.'

'I told you.'

The dress was light and comfortable. She even thought it might look good on her. 'OK,' she said. 'You can turn around again.' As he did so he breathed in, suddenly. She couldn't help but smile. 'It suits me, doesn't it?'

'Maybe you . . .' said Serge, still staring at her. 'Maybe you should be getting home.'

'When you found me, did you find my phone? It's not with my stuff.' Serge shook his head. 'My parents don't know I'm here, do they?'

'No,' he said, then quickly added: 'I asked you when I brought you here, but you told me not to tell them.'

Léna nodded. She couldn't remember much about being found, but it sounded like the kind of thing she would say. 'Good.' Her parents. Frédéric. Camille. Let them sort things out without involving her. 'Would you mind if I stayed? Until tomorrow, at least?' Serge didn't look keen; he was almost panicky. She couldn't help but smile again. 'What, girls make you nervous?'

He turned and walked away. 'I'll get us something to eat.'

She sat at the kitchen table while he cooked up some eggs on the old wood-burning stove. The place was so rustic she was almost surprised the floor wasn't covered in straw, but there was a certain charm to it.

She tried to start a conversation. 'How come I've never seen you around?'

'I've been away.'

'Well, you're in good shape,' she said with a coy smile. 'You look after yourself?'

'Manual labour,' he said, serving up onto the plate in front of her.

She reached over and squeezed his bicep. He almost jumped out of his skin at her touch. 'OK, OK,' she said. 'Relax.'

Serge looked deeply serious. 'Toni doesn't know you're here. If he comes and sees you . . . he'll call your parents.'

'Wouldn't want that,' she said. 'I'll keep an eye out.'

'You don't like them?'

'Mum and Dad? Let's just say I could do without them for a while. They want me to be someone I'm not.'

Serge gave a solemn nod. *He understands how that feels*, she thought. He set about eating the food in front of him, taking a huge hunk of bread from the loaf on the table. They ate in silence, Serge with his uncomfortable expression, almost *furious*, avoiding looking at her. He only said one more thing during the meal, suddenly looking up, earnest. 'Can people change, Léna?' he said. 'Make a promise to change, and see it through?'

'I guess,' she said. 'As long as they want to change enough.'

'That's what I'm afraid of,' said Serge. He kept eating.

After the meal, Serge went out hunting. He would kill some rabbits, he said. Make a stew for dinner. Léna smiled at him, and Serge actually smiled back in his shy way. He was completely different from any other man she'd met. Most would have tried it on long before now, but Serge seemed almost

355

intimidated by her. She rather enjoyed the fact that he was so unbalanced and unsure around her – it was sweet.

He locked the front door. *In case Toni turns up*, he said, and it was only after he'd gone that Léna realized he'd taken the keys with him. It would've made more sense for her to keep the keys inside, she thought.

She dozed on the bed for a while, then sat up, wanting to make herself something hot to drink. She sensed movement outside and hid, just in case it was Toni, but she couldn't shake the feeling that she'd been seen. A few seconds later a knock came at the door.

'Let me in. Open up. It's Toni.'

Léna stayed still. If Toni saw her he'd make her go back, and she wasn't sure she was quite ready for that yet. A little more peace and quiet away from the undead sister and bickering parents couldn't hurt, could it?

'Open the door,' said Toni. 'Mum, please. You have to forgive me. I had to stop Serge, he was out of control. It's taken me all these years to realize I was wrong. I should have found another way. I'm sorry, Mum. I shouldn't have killed him. I shouldn't have killed Serge.'

The words rang round inside her head, the meaning slowly becoming clearer. Suddenly, Léna felt colder than she'd felt in her life.

66

'Mum,' yelled Toni again. He could feel the tears coming. He had to talk to Serge, had to warn him that the police had linked him to the attacks, that he had to stay hidden at all costs.

'What are you doing?' It was Serge's voice, behind him. Toni turned round. 'She doesn't want to see you,' sneered Serge. 'Leave us alone.' He had a brace of rabbits over one shoulder, and Toni's rifle slung over the other.

'The police are on to you,' said Toni. 'They have a description from Lucy. The picture they've put together looks *exactly* like you. You have to stay indoors while I think of something. It's only a matter of time before someone gives them your name and they come here.'

Serge opened his mouth, but said nothing. *That shut him up*, Toni thought. *He finally realizes there might be repercussions to his actions.* He was almost awed by the simple faith his brother seemed to possess in his immunity from consequence. 'Stay here,' Toni said. 'You and Mum, stay inside. Don't answer the door for anyone and you'll both be safe.' He stepped forward and took the rifle off Serge's shoulder. 'I'll protect you. I'll think of something. I'm your brother.'

Toni watched Serge go inside. He took a position in the trees overlooking the road. *I'll protect you*, he thought. *This time I'll make sure you're safe.* And then, maybe . . . Maybe he'd earn something in return.

✳

From the moment she'd heard Toni's revelations, Léna knew she had to get out of there.

I shouldn't have killed him. I shouldn't have killed Serge.

Something had been different about Serge, she'd known that. Really, she had. Something dangerous, something that had repelled and appealed at the same time.

But not that. Not *that*. Christ, she thought she'd left that kind of thing behind her in town.

Locked in the house, she took a knife from the hunting room and went to the attic. And waited. She could hear the muffled voices of Toni and his dead brother discussing things. Then at last she heard the key in the front door.

'Léna?'

She held her breath but the floorboards in the attic betrayed even the slightest shift in weight. She heard them creak and so did Serge. It wasn't long before he climbed up there to find her.

'Stay where you are,' she said, brandishing the blade in shaking hands.

'What are you doing?' said Serge. He looked disappointed; *hurt*.

'Who are you?' she said.

'Put the knife down.'

'Tell me.'

'I told you the truth. My name is Serge. I'm Toni's brother. And I won't hurt you.'

'What happened to you?' said Léna. 'Are you *dead*?'

'Calm down,' said Serge. He stepped towards her. She wanted to run at him, knife ready, but something was stopping her. 'I won't hurt you,' he said. 'I promised. You can trust me. You can *trust* me, Léna.' He stepped closer. He took the knife from her hands, dropped it behind him. He looked as though he was ready to cry. There was something so lost about him. It was an emotion she could relate to: she'd been lost ever since Camille died, and possibly more so since her return.

'I won't hurt you,' he said, but he was looking at her so strangely, as if she was entirely alien to him, as if he found the very idea of her mystifying. He put his hand on the side of her head, brushing her hair away from her ear, looking scared. 'I won't hurt you.'

He kissed her quickly – pulling back as if it was the worst thing in the world, looking almost horrified at himself. Then he kissed her again, the hunger in him demanding a response.

Léna didn't know what she was feeling. A rush of thoughts hit her. Frédéric. Camille. Her parents. But most of all, *guilt*. Guilt at what had happened, four years before, feeling Frédéric deep inside her as Camille . . .

Wanting the thoughts gone, Léna kissed back, held him, grasped for him. She was lost in it; both of them were, she knew. Two lost souls, desperate and scared.

The police came two hours later. She was in a light sleep when she heard them call out. For a moment she thought she was dreaming.

'Is anyone home? Hello?'

She felt Serge move from the floor beside her. They rose slowly, and went to the attic window. Two policemen, outside.

'Hello?' one called.

Toni slunk into view outside, rifle pointed at them.

SETH PATRICK

'What do you want?' he said. Léna watched the rifle, praying it didn't fire. The officers made a show of not reaching for their guns.

'Stay calm, Toni. We want to ask you about your brother. It's about the attack on Lucy Clarsen.'

'My brother left here years ago,' said Toni, stark aggression in his voice. 'So be on your way.'

The two officers were watching him keenly, taken aback by the confrontation. One officer held his hands out, trying to calm things down. 'Don't do this, Toni.'

The other officer reached for his weapon. Toni swung the rifle towards him and shot him in the leg; he fell to the ground, clutching at the wound, screaming. Léna jumped at the sound of the shot, but Serge was beside her, a calming hand on her shoulder.

With his hands high to show he was no threat, the uninjured policeman went to his partner's aid, helping him stand. The pair hobbled to their vehicle. They cast cautious glances back at Toni, whose gun was still trained on them.

'Get lost,' yelled Toni. 'And don't come back.'

The policemen fled. Toni sank to his knees in the grass, crying. He looked up to the attic window.

Serge pulled back out of sight. He looked at Léna. 'You have to leave,' he said. 'Please. The police will be back, and Toni mustn't see you. *Please.*'

Léna was in shock. She was staring at Serge as she let him guide her downstairs. He showed her out of a back door.

'Run,' he said, pointing. 'That track takes you down to the lake.'

So she ran. The tears came soon enough.

We want to ask you about your brother. It's about the attack on Lucy Clarsen.

I had to stop Serge, he was out of control.

She ran, losing the track. She tried to continue going downhill but kept hitting thickets that almost defeated her. She ran without a plan, and without a plan she was lost.

Dusk came and the forest darkened and changed, every step a trap.

At last the track was before her again and she followed it, the tears blurring her vision. She hoped she would reach the lake any moment, praying that she would see her parents soon, and even Frédéric. And even Camille.

The fire ahead drew her eye downhill. Someone to help her. Then she realized the fire was much larger than she'd first thought, lighting up the group that stood around it. She saw there were others further back, and still others . . . There had to be dozens of people gathered ahead of her.

She slowed, cautious, ready to shout to the people below, ask them for help. But something stopped her, some intuition she couldn't quite grasp.

She hid behind the trees and watched.

They moved slowly. Confused, strange; their clothes looking old and dishevelled. She caught a smell on the breeze under the smoke from the fire – a reek of burning flesh and hair, and with it a cold scent of rank water.

In the dusk it was growing darker with every second, but she finally understood what had stopped her from shouting to them for help.

Dozens of them, but even in the twilight she'd seen something in their eyes.

Hunger. Insatiable. All-consuming.

Feral.

One by one, the heads turned and rose, looking at her.

Léna Séguret ran for her life.

67

Claire woke at dawn from an uneasy sleep. Her first thoughts, as always, were for her daughters. Camille had slept – or at least, had lain down and closed her eyes – in the bunk beside her own.

Claire checked the phone she'd been holding in her hand while asleep. The battery was almost dead, but even then, there was no signal showing. Piece by piece, the framework of their lives was being undone, even as she'd started to hope it would all come back together. There was still nothing from Léna. The fear that something had happened to her other daughter – that it had been some kind of cruel *exchange* – was almost too much for Claire to contemplate. *One thing at a time*, she thought.

She got up and dressed. Sandrine was already preparing breakfast with Xavier, another of the Helping Hand's regular volunteers, but they declined any additional help so she went to look for Pierre.

She opened his office door. He was there at his desk, head cradled on his arms, fast asleep. She smiled and wondered if he'd been there all night.

He stirred, then sat up suddenly, gathering himself.

'Sorry,' said Claire. 'I didn't mean to wake you.'

'No,' he said. 'I've slept enough. How are you? Did you get any sleep?'

'Some,' she said. 'But I'm just so worried about Léna.'

He stood beside her and took her in his arms. It was

something that, not long ago, would have made her feel secure; Pierre her rock and support when Jérôme had been unable to provide either. Now, she just felt numb.

'I'm sure she's safe, Claire.'

He held her and gave her that smile he often did, one that he used if he appealed to the mercy of God, one she didn't quite trust. Pierre had more faith in the benevolence of the Lord than she'd ever had. 'And I'm worried about Camille, of course,' she said. 'I try and think about the future, but all I see are problems.'

He nodded. 'I want to show you something,' he said. 'Something that I hope will set your mind at rest.' He led her outside and down some concrete steps into the basement storage rooms. Inside the locked doors were shelves stacked high with supplies. He smiled at her, nodding. 'See? We're well prepared.' They walked down the long corridor, Claire admiring the sheer breadth and quantity of stores.

'That's a lot of food,' she said.

'In case we're here for a long time. Enough for a few months.'

She looked at him, astonished. 'Do you think we'll be here that long?'

'It's possible, yes.'

'Jérôme thinks we might be evacuated because of the dam. He said half the town seems to have left already.'

'We won't need to leave, I promise you.'

Claire wondered at his foresight. There was so much attention to detail – as though Pierre had been preparing for this sort of emergency for a very long time. The thought unnerved her.

He unlocked another door and led her into a smaller corridor. Within was a caged section, and when Claire saw what was inside she felt herself go cold.

An arsenal. Weapons, ammunition. Enough for a small war, she thought. She looked at Pierre, horrified, but his smile was still there, still the same. Confident and calm despite the huge cache of weaponry displayed before them, as if this were totally normal. She wondered how he'd built up what must surely be an illegal stockpile.

'I hope we won't need them,' he said, 'but we have to look after Camille. We have to protect her and the others. Because in turn, they will protect us.'

The others, Claire thought. Pierre had told her and Camille of those he knew about – Simon, the little boy and Viviane Costa. There would be more, he was certain of it, and she saw no reason to doubt him. Others would find their way to the Helping Hand soon enough.

He led her back out to the end of the main corridor, and another locked door. 'Come and see,' he said, unlocking it.

Within was a medical room, well stocked with equipment. It looked as though it was sufficient to cope with even severe casualties.

'What's going on, Pierre?' she said. It all seemed like overkill, but she knew Pierre. He didn't do anything without good reason.

'You mustn't be afraid,' he said earnestly. 'It's all happening as it was written. They are here to warn us that the end is near, Claire. That is why they've come. Harbingers of the End Times.'

'The end?'

'Yes,' he said. 'And when it comes, it will be wonderful.' And his smile told her that he believed it completely.

She went back to the dormitory to find Camille sitting up.

'Did you sleep?' asked Claire.

'No,' said Camille. 'I'm hungry, though.' She said it with some guilt.

'Let's get you something,' said Claire, upbeat. They went through to the canteen where Xavier and Sandrine were starting to serve food.

Camille loaded her plate. Claire had no appetite and took very little, just enough to stop Camille feeling too conspicuous. They sat, and after a few minutes Camille nodded towards a woman queuing for food. The woman Pierre had told them about, Viviane Costa. The others at the Helping Hand paid her little notice, seemingly unaware that she was like Camille. Pierre was clearly being careful about who should be privy to such information, Claire thought. It meant he was waiting to judge the reaction to Camille before he revealed more of those like her, and the thought worried Claire. It showed caution where she'd expected confidence.

'Can I talk to her, Mum? Just for a minute?'

Claire waited until the dead woman had sat down two tables away before nodding, unwilling to let her daughter speak to the woman unless they were close enough for her to listen. The woman gave an edge of sarcasm to everything she said. Claire had managed to speak to her the night before, alone, and she'd come away with a strong dislike for her.

Camille took her tray of food with her. 'Hi,' she said, sitting down. 'Madame Costa? I'm Camille.'

'Viviane, please,' said the woman. She gestured at both their trays. 'Enjoy the food. Before long it'll be rationed.'

'What, are you psychic?'

She shrugged. 'No, I'm a realist. It's common sense.'

'Your husband taught me at school,' said Camille. 'He was good.'

'Really? Well, he had to be good at something.'

'Did he kill himself because you came back?'

Claire winced at the question. The subject of her husband was something she'd avoided any reference to when she'd spoken to the woman.

'Yes,' said Viviane, the sarcasm rising. 'Maybe he thought I was too young for him.'

Camille was oblivious, and wasn't dropping the subject. 'But did you . . .'

'What do you want to know?' she snapped. 'Did I force him to commit suicide? You think we can do that, make people do things? Do you think I *wanted* him to die?'

'I'm sorry,' said Camille, looking down at her plate.

'He took his own life. He didn't like me being back. What more can I say?'

There was a long pause as they both ate.

Then, eventually, Camille spoke again. 'Viviane, how did you die?'

'Will you stop interrogating me?' she said, but after a moment she sighed and spoke again. 'I starved to death, if you must know. When the dam broke, we had no food for three weeks. Some people ate dead animals, they were so hungry. Animals killed in the flood, ones that were rancid, maggoty. Anything they could find.'

'That's horrible.'

'You have no idea,' she said. 'But you'll understand soon enough.'

Claire had had her fill of the woman. She stood and walked over to them. 'So why did you tell me you died in a fire?' she said.

'Did I say that?' said Viviane, all innocence.

Claire nodded. 'And you told my husband you were killed by burglars. You're just making it up, aren't you? You get a kick out of it.'

'Yes. I admit it.' The smile on the woman's face was unsettling. Cruel, gleeful. 'Just like Camille.'

'What do you mean?' said Camille, visibly anxious.

'I saw you talking to the Koretzkys.'

'I told them what they wanted to hear,' said Camille. 'It did them good.'

Viviane levelled her gaze at Camille. 'Are you sure about that?' she said. 'Why don't you look in the outhouse?'

Camille turned to her mother, fear in her eyes, then stood and ran outside. Claire went after her, glaring at Viviane, who looked back with an indifferent shrug.

The outhouse was a hundred metres away from the main building, at the edge of the area of hard standing that served as the Helping Hand's car park. Camille reached the door and was heaving it open just as Claire caught up with her. Both of them gasped in horror.

Around the walls were dozens of containers of fuel for the generator, and the same number of gas cylinders for the kitchen. And in the centre of the outhouse, hanging from the metal beams of the roof, were two people: ropes around their necks, the chairs they had used now toppled over on the floor, their dead faces red and contorted.

The Koretzkys. Eager to be with their son.

Claire recovered herself enough to put her hand over Camille's eyes and drag her away from the door. She started shouting for help, yelling Pierre's name, pulling Camille round to the side of the building. Her daughter was shrieking, terrified, and all Claire could do was hold her until she stopped.

Pierre was the first to reach them, with Xavier, Yan and Sandrine close behind. The men cut the bodies down while Sandrine stood a little way from where Claire held her trembling daughter. Claire could feel the woman's eyes trained on them.

'We have to let the police know,' said Xavier, as they came out of the outhouse and locked the door.

'No,' said Pierre. He said it with a finality that made them all look at him, wary.

'What do you mean?' said Claire.

'The police have enough to contend with,' he said, his eyes not leaving Claire's. She thought of the arsenal he'd assembled, and wondered if he'd told anyone else of his plans, or of his thoughts about the approaching end. She suspected that he hadn't. 'I've heard of looting, disorder. If they come, they'll evacuate us at a time when the town needs us most.'

'But we have to,' said Xavier, adamant. Pierre looked thoughtfully around the group. He nodded.

'If that's how everyone feels, then I understand,' he said, giving Xavier that professional smile of his. 'But let me handle it. I know the people on the force. I'll alert them. Our phones are out now, but I'll drive in later.'

Claire noticed how Sandrine was looking at Camille. A searching, suspicious glare – the accusation written clear on her face.

'What did you *tell* them?' said Sandrine.

'Leave her alone,' said Claire. She pulled Camille closer as if she could shield her daughter from the words she suspected were coming. Camille clung to her desperately.

'Camille was talking with the Koretzkys yesterday,' said Sandrine. 'I don't know what she said, but look what happened.'

'Don't be ridiculous,' said Pierre. 'Camille didn't cause this.'

Claire stared defiantly at Sandrine. 'Is that what you think?' she said. 'That she told them to commit suicide?'

'Perhaps not directly,' said Sandrine. 'But everything she said about the afterlife, it must have made them think. They couldn't stop crying.'

Camille buried her head in Claire's side, trembling.

'*Enough*,' said Pierre, with sufficient force to make Sandrine quail a little. 'There'll be no more talk like that, Sandrine. From you, or from anyone else. Everyone will be upset enough by what's happened, and we must come together to support one another. This is a difficult enough time. We need to acknowledge this tragedy, I think. Acknowledge it by celebrating their lives. A service, to help us settle down. I hope you can help me organize it?' He said this directly to

Sandrine, almost as an order. She appeared to be on the verge of tears for a moment, before nodding.

'Once you've been to the police,' said Claire.

Pierre looked at her. She could see a little uncertainty on his face, as if he didn't know whether her comment was a pointed assertion that he'd been lying, or whether it was intended to remind him to maintain the charade. In all honesty, Claire didn't know herself which she'd meant.

'Of course,' said Pierre. 'Once I've been to the police.'

68

Toni needed to rest. His lungs felt like fire. Serge had always been the fit one, Toni the hulking brute, but even Serge should have been tiring by now.

'I need to stop,' Toni gasped, and leaned against a tree. 'We've been walking for *hours*. I don't understand. We should be through the forest by now.'

Serge was looking around, pumped up, still ready to run and run. He hardly seemed out of breath, Toni thought.

After the police had driven off, Toni had been unable to think straight. Serge had come out of the house and proposed a plan: leave their mother inside, where she would be safe. The police had no interest in her, only in Serge, and now that Toni had shot a policeman, in Toni too.

Let me talk to her, Toni had pleaded, but Serge just shook his head, adamant. His mother agreed, Serge said. He and Toni would leave the house and head away from the town, through the forest. It would take them the best part of a day, but there was another road out in that direction. They'd be able to find a long-distance driver willing to take them north.

That had been the plan. In the event dusk had fallen and the moonlight they had been counting on had been lost behind cloud. Unable to be sure of their path, they'd sheltered in a thicket and waited until dawn. The cold hadn't affected Serge, but Toni had struggled.

And now, in the light, Serge had lost his way and yet still denied it.

'Is it the wrong path?' said Toni, finding his breath at last. 'We've been walking for so long, we should already be at the road. Maybe your sense of direction is off.' What worried Toni most of all was how unnerved Serge looked. Serge knew these woods like the back of his hand; if he didn't know their position, then things really were serious.

'We're going too slowly, that's all,' his brother said.

'I'm trying,' said Toni, stung by the comment. 'Go ahead and leave me if I'm slowing you down.'

Serge shook his head. 'I didn't mean . . .'

'I'm sorry,' said Toni, despairing. 'All I want now is for us all to be together like before, and it can't ever happen. Can it?'

Serge wouldn't meet his eyes.

They moved on, Toni doing his best to pick up the pace, but the terrain was difficult. Root and dip, branch and burrow all conspired. One wrong step and he would come down hard, twisting his ankle or worse, and then where would they be?

'What's that?' said Serge from ahead, and when Toni reached him he saw it. The smouldering ashes of a large fire, carelessly set, and in the ashes he could see the charred remnants of small animals. None had been prepared for cooking, he could tell – thrown on the flame fur and all, *guts* and all – yet none were whole either, part-cooked flesh gnawed and ripped. He found himself thinking of the grouse he'd seen in the house the day Serge had come home.

They said nothing more about the fire and continued for

another hour. Serge stayed close for a time, but soon enough he was well ahead again. 'I'm just scouting out the path, Toni,' he'd said. 'I'll not go too far.'

Then Serge started to swear, shouting in frustration.

Another fire, Toni thought when he reached him, wondering why Serge looked so desperate, but then he understood. It was the same fire they'd passed before.

'We're going in circles,' said Serge.

Toni felt his breath leave him. 'How is that possible?' He fell to his knees. 'How is that *possible*?'

Serge's fists clenched. He swore again. 'We have to keep going,' he said, determined.

'I can't go on,' said Toni. 'Not like this.'

'We can't stop,' said Serge, agitated, staring at the ground. Toni followed his gaze and saw one of the charred animals he'd noticed before. The way Serge was looking at it . . .

He was hungry.

'If we keep getting lost,' said Toni, 'we'll never get out of the forest.'

Serge looked at him, petulant. 'What do you suggest?'

'We go downhill from now on. Find a stream – it should take us to the lake. Then we follow the shore, away from the dam.'

Serge gave it some thought, then nodded. 'I'll see if I can find another path. Wait here until I get back.'

Toni waited. He was thirsty, and the thought of a stream made him eager to get moving. He stood, hoping Serge wouldn't be much longer. Then he heard the snap of a branch some distance away.

He looked. Someone was there, perhaps fifty metres

from him, through the trees. He couldn't see the figure clearly, but . . .

It's her, he thought. 'Mum?' he called. 'Mum?' He turned his head to look for Serge, then turned back to where the figure had been. It was gone.

69

Léna tried to scrub it all off.

She'd reached home in darkness the night before to find the house empty, her mother and Camille gone. The power in the whole *town* was out, and for a moment she wondered if they'd gone ahead with the plan to move, and left.

Left without her.

She almost wouldn't blame them if they had. Exhaustion took her as she sobbed on her bed in the darkness, alone and filled with regret.

When she'd woken at dawn, she'd found herself in borrowed clothes. She thought of Serge and of everything that had happened, and the lust that had taken her by surprise. Now she was wearing his mother's dress, a gift from him – her saviour, a man capable of who knew *what* atrocities. She just wanted to forget he even existed.

She stripped and sought the shower, scrubbing at her skin under the flow of tepid water until it was red and raw, staying there even as the water grew cold, then icy.

The same thoughts came to her again and again: the mindless hunger she and Serge had experienced for each other, the revelation of his true nature. And one question foremost: why her? *Why her?* She curled up on the shower floor, shivering and unable to move.

Then she heard a door closing downstairs. She turned off the shower, wrapped herself in a towel, and tried to stay quiet.

The only image in her mind was of the people she'd seen in the forest. When they'd turned to her, the look in their eyes had been enough for her to think that if she was caught, she wouldn't survive the encounter. She had run and not looked back, certain they were always just metres behind her. Lost, she stumbled onto a dirt track, suddenly able to put on some speed even in the dark.

Soon she was sure she wasn't being followed. She'd kept running all the same, until her lungs had felt as though they were on fire.

She wondered what the hell they were. She wondered if they'd found her, now . . .

The bathroom door handle turned. She tensed, only now thinking to look for something, *anything*, to use as a weapon.

'Léna, is that you?'

Her father.

The relief she felt was overwhelming. Suddenly she was a little child again, her father the only thing standing between her and the nightmares. She opened the door and hugged him, the tears released once more at the relief that she hadn't been left behind. 'Dad, I thought you'd abandoned me.'

He wrapped his arms around her; she felt him stroke her hair gently. 'I would never abandon you,' he said. 'You know that. *Never.*'

Jérôme drove towards the Helping Hand. He could see the stunned expression on Léna's face, driving through a town that looked so deserted in daylight. Everything seemed shut; rubbish blew across the streets.

'I'd realized the power was out,' she said, 'but I had no idea it was *this* bad.'

'It's not just the power,' said Jérôme. 'There was a rumour about the dam, and about looters roaming around. It looks like most of the people who could leave have, and the rest are cowering in their homes.'

He'd spent the night driving around the dead town looking for Léna. Then after dawn, when he'd returned to the house to grab some food, there she was. She hadn't seen the note he'd left for her on the kitchen table; the state she'd been in when he found her made him feel horribly guilty at being out when she'd come back.

He didn't reprimand her for leaving hospital – she didn't look as if she could handle it at the moment. But she was safe now. That was all that mattered. That was enough.

The power had been out for so long, communication was starting to be a problem. Landlines were down, and the mobile phone masts would all be running out of backup power soon. Although he had a weak signal on his own phone, he'd been unable to raise Claire overnight to give her the regular updates she'd asked for, or to tell her Léna was OK this morning.

He'd gone to the police station in the night in case they'd had any news, but he'd left quickly enough. They had nothing for him and every face he saw there seemed exhausted, stretched beyond breaking point. Their communications were so far unaffected, and they were swamped with calls. Stories of looting were surfacing, and it didn't look to Jérôme as though they had any capacity left to deal with serious disorder.

He'd also driven to Frédéric's house to find that his

parents didn't know where he was either. They were just as worried. Unlike Léna he wasn't prone to just disappearing without contact, but they all took some hope from the possibility that Frédéric and Léna were in the same place, safer together than they would be apart. He'd told Frédéric's parents about the group at the Helping Hand, that if need be they would be welcome there. At least it was warm.

'You didn't see Frédéric, then?' he asked Léna now. She shook her head. 'So where did you go?'

The look on her face made him pull the car over – she was overwhelmed, sobbing again. He held her, his heart breaking, wondering what she could have been through, knowing that if anyone had hurt her he wouldn't be held responsible for his actions.

At last, she pulled away. 'I'm sorry,' she said, wiping her face and trying to stifle her sobs.

He looked at her, cautious about pushing too hard. 'You want to talk about it?'

She shook her head and looked down.

'That's OK,' said Jérôme. 'You're safe now.'

But as he looked out at the desolate streets beyond the car, he wondered if any of them were safe.

When they reached the Helping Hand the tears broke out on all sides. Jérôme and Claire brought Léna into the dormitory, where Camille was reading. Camille jumped up and ran to her sister and they hugged, the happiest they'd been to see one another since Camille's return. Claire led Jérôme away, leaving the girls to themselves.

Claire was holding Jérôme's hand, he realized, and

smiling at him. It was time, he thought, to try to fix some of the damage.

'I'm sorry,' he said to her. 'My attitude to you. My hostility to Pierre. I wanted you back, I wanted to make amends. And instead I was just driving you further away.'

She squeezed his hand. 'You brought Léna home, Jérôme. You know how much that means.'

He shrugged, unwilling to take the credit. 'She found her own way home.'

'Did she say . . .?'

'Not yet. In her own time.' He hesitated. 'There's something I need to tell you, Claire. About Léna's injury.' He felt her hand slip out of his. 'I was drunk. I pushed her. She fell, and hurt her back.'

'You told me that,' she said.

'But that wasn't why she stopped talking to me, or why we never told you about it.'

Her expression became cold, tense. 'Why, then?'

'Just before I pushed her away, I said . . . I said that I wished she'd been on the coach, not Camille.' He watched her face, and saw her absorb the confession. Claire closed her eyes. He didn't want forgiveness, not that. This was all there would ever be. An explanation, bare and raw. Something said in anger, something he hadn't really meant.

But words like that could never be taken back. They had driven a wedge between him and his daughter that he didn't think would ever be repaired, not fully.

She opened her eyes again. 'There's something I need to tell you too, Jérôme,' said Claire, and she told him about the Koretzkys.

Jérôme shook his head. 'Accusing her of causing it . . .

It's obscene.' Claire nodded, but Jérôme bit his tongue. He would say no more than that, not to Claire. He wouldn't criticize the Church to her, the Church whose primary message was exactly what Camille had repeated: you would meet your loved ones again, after death. It was, he reflected, precisely why suicide was regarded as such a terrible sin. For otherwise, if anyone truly believed, why would they hesitate?

Léna lay snuggled with Camille on the dorm bed. Just being close to her sister – and that was how she thought of her, there was no doubt in her mind now – made Léna feel safer.

'Where did you go?' said Camille. Her voice was tender, the way it used to be when they spoke.

'It doesn't matter,' said Léna. 'I was angry. Part of it was seeing you and Frédéric together, laughing. Part of it was the thought that he didn't see you for who you were.'

'He knows now.'

'What made him accept it?'

'He came to my room, and we kissed. Then he looked at me. He was crying, but . . .'

Léna knew what she was about to say. For the first time since Camille had come back, she felt they were really connected again. ' . . . but he must already have known,' she said. 'Maybe since the first time he saw you. The only thing that made him deny it was that it was impossible.'

'I kissed him to hurt you,' said Camille, sitting up. 'Because you rejected me.'

'It's OK,' said Léna, sitting up too. 'I understand.'

Camille locked her gaze with her sister's. 'Léna?' she said. 'I'm frightened. I don't sleep any more, and it scares me. Maybe I'm different now. Some of the other people here look at me – not just Sandrine, there are others too – they look at me like they don't think they can trust me. And I don't know if I trust myself. Maybe I'm not safe to be around.'

Léna thought of the people she'd seen in the forest. Whoever they'd been, they were the ones who weren't safe to be around, not Camille. Her dad had mentioned looters roaming the area; that was the obvious answer, but there was another possibility in Léna's head now, something she pushed from her thoughts at once.

'You're my sister,' whispered Léna. 'And we won't let anyone say different, OK?' Then she saw something on Camille's face: a blemish. She frowned.

'What?' said her sister.

'You have something here,' said Léna, reaching out to touch it; a small patch of cracked skin on Camille's cheek. Camille put her hand up and felt it too, her eyes growing more scared as she explored the area. The fear was reflected in Léna's face.

'What is it?' said Camille. 'What does it look like?'

It looked . . .

It looked exactly the way the wound on Léna's back had looked, at first.

Like infection.

Like decay.

70

Laure woke to her alarm and started to get herself ready for work as she always did: quickly, no thinking required. Until she got some coffee in her each morning, thinking wasn't something she felt up to. Half-dressed, she went to the bathroom and brushed her teeth. On her way out she saw Julie, still curled up on the sofa-bed. The boy wasn't with her. She could hear him downstairs in the kitchen, the regular crunch of cereal being eaten. It was something she'd learned pretty quickly the night before, how much of an appetite he had.

Laure turned to go back to her bedroom and get her uniform on.

'Laure?' said Julie.

Laure stopped and looked at her, smiling. 'Good morning,' she said.

'Come here,' said Julie, hand outstretched.

Laure approached and took Julie's hand in hers. Julie pulled her in, closer, closer. Then she kissed her. Tentative, soft. Laure was cautious, but she was swamped with the desire to hold Julie, and pour kisses over every part of her.

Julie kissed harder, pulled Laure onto the bed, tugged at what little clothing she was wearing, eager. Laure felt something loosen within her, that aching desire held back for so long. She started to unbutton the shirt Julie was wearing, but a hand stopped her.

'Wait,' said Julie, anxiety in her eyes.

Laure put one finger on Julie's lips. 'Don't worry,' she said, and pulled the shirt open.

There it was. All these years, and Laure hadn't once seen the scars Julie's attacker had left behind, her stomach a patchwork of skin. She put her hand on them and looked up.

'I don't want you to see them,' Julie whispered. 'They're not what I am, do you understand? They're not what I am.'

'Then I don't see them,' said Laure and she kissed her. She was trying to hold the tears back, but they were coming all the same. So much time, she thought. So much wasted time.

Julie pulled away, her eyes locked upon something over Laure's shoulder. Laure turned. Victor was watching them. 'For Christ's sake,' she snapped, irritation at the spoiled moment getting the better of her. 'Get lost. Don't you understand privacy?'

The boy looked deflated. He turned and went back downstairs.

Laure sensed it, sensed the chill in the air. She turned to Julie, and realized she'd overstepped the mark. 'Sorry,' she said, but the damage was done. Julie sat up, pushed herself out of bed and started to get dressed, stony-faced.

Laure sighed and went to her bedroom to put on her uniform. Try as she might, she couldn't help but feel uncomfortable around the boy, after what Julie had told her about him and Viviane Costa. As she headed for the stairs, she said to Julie: 'He shouldn't stay with you. What if he's danger-ous?'

'Dangerous?' said Julie, defiant. 'He's a child.'

Laure hung her head. There was nothing she could say,

nothing that would make Julie see the truth, without making her the enemy. 'Of course he is.'

'Laure . . .' said Julie, suddenly anxious. 'Don't go. Don't go to work. Stay here with me.'

'I have to,' Laure said, hoping Julie could see the regret in her eyes. 'We're short on staff and things are critical. We've no idea if the power will come back any time soon. We need everyone.' She saw the fearful look on Julie's face. 'What's wrong?'

For a moment Julie seemed to struggle to say it, her eyes not meeting Laure's. Then: 'I think that I'm one, too.'

'One what?'

'I think that I've come back.'

'What are you talking about?'

Julie looked at her solemnly. 'After I was attacked, Laure . . . I was clinically dead. They told me that I was a miracle.'

'Julie, things like that happen more than you realize. But *them*?' She looked downstairs, meaning Victor and his ilk. 'They've been dead for years. They were buried. You're not like them. I know you're not.'

Julie was shaking her head, desolate. 'You don't understand, Laure. You have no idea. I'm not *scared* to be like them. It's the opposite. Since the attack I've felt incapable of living. I've felt like I didn't belong. What if it's because I've been dead all these years?'

By the time Laure had set off for work Julie had her emotions under control again. What had happened with Laure had taken them both by surprise and she didn't know how she felt about it. Victor had to be her first priority, though

– Laure would have to understand that, if she wanted any part in Julie's life.

She cooked some eggs for her and Victor on the camping stove she'd brought with her. Then she lit the fire in the fireplace and sat by it, glad of the heat, while Victor brought his pens and paper over and drew nearby.

She dozed for a while. Then she woke, suddenly aware that Victor had gone.

She called for him. As she approached the window she could see a trampoline in the garden of the house next door – the police captain's house, she recalled, the house where Adèle Werther now lived. There were two small figures on the trampoline, and one of them was Victor.

'Shit,' she said. She'd wanted to keep him out of sight, hidden and protected. Parading him to the outside world would invite too many questions. She put on some shoes and a warm jumper and headed outside. She stood by the waist-high split-rail fence that separated the two gardens, waving to try and get Victor's attention, but he didn't see her. She sighed and climbed over, then walked to the trampoline where Victor and a girl were bouncing.

'Hello,' she said to the girl. 'I'm Julie.'

'I'm Chloé,' said the girl, waving at her.

'Good to meet you, Chloé,' she said, and scowled at Victor before heading to the neighbour's back door and knocking.

It was Adèle who answered. 'Hello, Julie,' she said, her smile broad. She stepped out through the door. 'It's been so long.'

'Hello,' said Julie, flustered. Beyond the professional relationships she had with her patients, social interaction had become almost alien; her people skills were rusty, to say the least. 'Sorry, do you mind if he plays on the trampoline with Chloé?'

Adèle looked at the two children and smiled. 'No, of course not. Come on in, I'm making some coffee.' She went inside again.

Julie turned to the trampoline. 'Play nicely, Victor,' she said, and Victor smiled back.

Adèle sat Julie down at the table in the kitchen and went to get the coffee. As she put everything on a tray, she suddenly looked a little faint. She knocked a cup from the side: it broke on the floor and she looked at it in a daze.

'Are you OK?' said Julie.

'I just stumbled,' said Adèle. 'I think I'm a bit tired, that's all.'

'Please, sit down. Let me carry the tray over.'

Julie took the tray from Adèle and led her across to a seat, then cleaned up the broken cup.

They both sat again. Adèle looked at Julie with a sad smile. 'Weren't we less formal, once?'

'That was a while ago,' said Julie.

The conversation stalled for a moment. 'So,' said Adèle brightly. 'You're back with Laure again! I'm so glad. I've not seen much of her, in all this time. Even as neighbours.' She leaned over, conspiratorial. 'I think she works too hard.'

'It's temporary,' said Julie. Putting work first was something else that Laure would have to change, if she wanted things to progress. 'Until the power cut sorts itself out, anyway.'

Adèle nodded. 'Thomas works hard too,' she said,

frowning. Julie tried and failed to come up with a way to keep the conversation going, but thankfully Adèle spoke again. 'So who's the boy?'

'My . . . nephew. He chose a bad time to come and stay.' Julie changed the subject quickly. The less they talked about Victor, the better. 'You know, a man came to my apartment, looking for you.'

'Really?'

'He called himself Simon,' said Julie. She wondered if he'd actually paid Adèle a visit. 'At the time I didn't really think much of it, but now . . . Was it him? *Your* Simon?'

Adèle shook her head. 'Simon's dead.'

Julie could see the truth in her eyes, though. 'I know,' she said, putting her hand on Adèle's. 'But was it him? Did he find you?'

Adèle looked at her for a moment, feigning confusion. Then, with a mixture of fear and sorrow, she slowly nodded.

71

In the apartment above the Lake Pub, Simon Delaître woke.

'Hello,' said Lucy, grinning at him.

He sat up sharply, looking at her with suspicion. 'Did you drug me?' he said.

She raised an eyebrow. 'Don't be an idiot,' she said. 'And why are you angry? How long's it been since you last slept? I bet it feels like a thousand years.'

Simon kept scowling. He threw on his clothes and headed for the door.

Lucy smiled at him. 'Where are you going?' she said, pouting. 'You aren't still going after Adèle? What's the point? You can't have been that happy.'

Simon turned to her. 'Shut your fucking mouth,' he snarled, his fists balled by his side. 'You know nothing about me. You know nothing about *us*.'

Lucy shook her head. 'I think I know plenty. I mean, look at yourself. You've changed. You can feel it, right? Simon, you're dead. Face it. Come with me. I know where to go. I know what to do.'

He thought. Then he shook his head. 'I need to understand,' he said, and left.

Father Jean-François heard the door of the church open behind him. He didn't turn. He felt it in his blood, without having to see which of them it was. He'd known it was only a matter of time before one of them came.

'Hello, Father,' said the voice behind him. 'Remember me?'

Reluctant, he turned round. 'Of course, Simon,' he said.

'You're not surprised?'

'No. I was expecting that you, or someone like you, would come to see me. Just give me one minute, and I'll be with you.' He put his hand into his pocket, checking that his mobile phone was there, then went to the vestry to do what he needed to do. Before he returned, though, he sought out the bottle of brandy he always kept hidden, and took a drink. Usually it was only brought out when he delivered bad news to someone who might need it afterwards. This time, it was he who needed the lift.

Simon was sitting in a pew, waiting, a look of absolute desperation on his face.

'What brings you to me, Simon?' said the priest, avoiding the dead man's eyes.

'I died, Father. I think I came back to understand why. To understand my own death. Do you think that's possible?'

The priest nodded slowly, still not quite looking at him. 'Yes, it's possible.'

'You've known me all my life,' said Simon. 'You know my story better than I do. I need your help. I don't remember it, you see. I don't remember anything about that last day, and I need to know why I did it.'

Father Jean-François was at a loss for words. He could hardly come straight out with it, could he? 'It's difficult to say. You were a very withdrawn child.'

'When you heard about my suicide, were you surprised?'

'I was very sad,' the priest said, looking at his hands.

'But were you surprised, Father?'

'Surprised?' He shook his head. If Simon wanted to know, he had that right, surely. He made himself look up, eye to eye. 'No. It didn't come as a surprise. We had all been worried about you, for so long. I doubt anyone was surprised.'

Simon looked distraught. 'But I've changed,' he said. 'I know I have. I think I can make Adèle happy.'

Father Jean-François shook his head and felt his courage fail him. With courage, he would have told Simon that he'd heard him say exactly those words before, more than once.

And then the doors of the church opened again, and the priest stood, stepping back from Simon as the police filed inside.

'Don't move!' came the shout. 'Stay where you are.'

Father Jean-François had only enough courage left to meet Simon Delaître's angry gaze.

'Thanks,' said the dead man bitterly, and then the police were upon him.

72

Toni and Serge reached the lake quickly; too quickly for either of their liking. They found themselves at the same spot where they would have been if they'd headed straight downhill from the old house. They shared a look but didn't comment on it. Hours of walking had got them precisely nowhere, and it wasn't something Toni wanted to dwell on.

Ahead of them in the low water of the lake the steeple of the ruined church was fully exposed, and the tops of other walls were visible nearby.

'OK,' said Toni, making sure he had his bearings while he got his breath back. 'Now we head to the north-west, and hope the road there is beyond any roadblock the police might put up.' He started to walk along the shore, but Serge wasn't following. Instead, his brother was calmly taking off his shoes.

'What are you doing?' asked Toni.

Serge gestured at the lake. 'It's quicker to swim across.'

Toni looked fearfully at the cold, still water. 'Please, Serge. I can't swim all that way, not now. I'm shattered.'

'Come on. It's not that wide. We did it as kids.'

Toni shook his head, unconvinced. Yes, they'd done it as kids, but now he was overweight, out of shape and exhausted.

'Come on,' said Serge. 'Trust me.' He tied the laces of his boots to his belt at the back and stepped into the water. 'It's OK. It's not that cold. Come on.'

Toni shook his head again, but he sat and began to take off his boots. When he put a foot in the water, he yelped. 'Christ,' he said. 'Serge, it's freezing.'

'It's not freezing,' said Serge, smiling in encouragement. 'Chilly, maybe.'

Toni looked across to the other side, worried. The far shore looked impossibly distant. 'I won't make it.'

'Of course you will.'

'What about what's underneath? What if I hit something under the surface?'

'We'll avoid the old village, Toni. Look . . .' He pointed to a large rock on the other side. 'See that rock? We aim for that, and we'll avoid any trouble. OK?'

And with that, Serge waded out and started to swim. Toni had no choice but to follow, the shock of the cold taking his breath from him again, his weak strokes moving him slowly forward in the water while Serge powered on.

He could see his brother forging ahead. 'Slow down, Serge,' he yelled, having trouble keeping the water from his mouth. 'Wait for me.'

Serge stopped, treading water. 'Come on, then,' he called. 'We're almost half—' His voice cut off as he suddenly disappeared below the surface, almost as if he'd been dragged under.

'Serge!' Toni yelled, swimming urgently towards the spot where his brother had been. 'Serge!'

Toni took a breath and went under, opening his eyes and trying to see through the murky water. He dived down but he couldn't stay under for more than a few seconds before he had to resurface. He tried again and again, desperately searching, but there was simply no sign of his brother.

SETH PATRICK

It wasn't long before Toni could feel his fatigue start to overwhelm him. He knew he couldn't stay out there any longer, so he swam back to the near shore and dragged himself out. He sat, shivering, watching the water, stunned that his brother had gone.

'Forgive me, Serge,' he said, and held his head in despair.

73

Thomas sat in his office, watching the CCTV feed from the station's cells. Every now and again, the power from the hard-pressed emergency generator in the basement would flicker, sometimes enough to bring his PC down. Then, he would have to wait until it rebooted before he could watch again.

Watch Simon Delaître refuse to stay dead.

Everyone was exhausted. A third of his force had gone now, not turning up for shifts, unable to be contacted. All his remaining officers were having to pull extra hours, and he was rotating staff, sending them home for six-hour breaks. He hoped that most of those left recognized the sense of emergency and would rise to the task.

The town was still managing to get calls through to the station. It had its own cellular mast, drawing its power from the generator. And thank God, Thomas thought. The priest's call had come through, and Thomas had rustled up every officer he could spare. It was only when they'd reached the church and had their man in handcuffs that the stares began, the whispers, the wary eyes.

Here was the man their captain had killed. They'd seen the body bag. They'd seen him go to the morgue. Now he was back as though nothing had happened. *Welcome to my life*, thought Thomas grimly.

Some of those officers hadn't returned to the station, he noted. He couldn't entirely blame them, of course. If he'd been a weaker man, he thought he would have done the same. Run from it, rather than face it down. Whatever *it* was.

The last he'd heard from the mayor's office was that the power situation would be resolved within twenty-four hours.

Twenty-four hours, he thought. They could hold out for one more day before going begging for extra help from outside. As long as that hadn't just been a lie, too. He called Bruno into his office. 'Bring the prisoner up here,' he said.

'Delaître?' said Bruno.

Thomas nodded, and he could see the unease flicker across Bruno's face.

Three officers brought him up, cuffed. They sat him down.

'The three of you can go,' Thomas told them.

Bruno seemed uneasy. 'Are you sure, sir?'

Thomas looked at Delaître. The dead man was watching him with a dark smile. 'Yes,' he said. 'Leave us.'

Thomas showed Delaître some images. One was a picture of Camille Séguret, taken from the school's commemorative website. One was of the woman who had called herself Viviane Costa, something Thomas now had no doubt was true. 'Look familiar?'

Delaître said nothing.

'Are there others like you?'

Nothing.

'Why are you here? Is the power cut because of you and your *kind*?'

Delaître's smile became a sneer. 'How did you deal with

Adèle?' he said. 'It must have been hard. It can't have looked good, shooting a man who was so *inconvenient*.'

Thomas scowled at him. 'I won't let you near my family again.'

'Really? I think you'll find I'm very persistent.'

'I'll find a way,' said Thomas, teeth gritted. 'Now answer my questions. How many of you are there, and why are you here?'

But Delaître would answer nothing; he just sat there with his sneer. Frustrated, Thomas had him taken back to his cell, asking Bruno to stay for a moment.

'Nobody lets him out. Not again, not for anything. Give him a bucket to shit in. If he even shits at all.' He thought for a second. 'In fact, nobody opens the door again, you understand?'

Bruno nodded. He was untroubled by the order, Thomas noted, an order that for any other prisoner would be a breach of human rights. Bruno, it seemed, understood just as well as Thomas that Delaître wasn't exactly human. 'Yes, sir. What about meals? He keeps asking for food.'

'Nothing,' said Thomas. 'He gets *nothing*.'

He dismissed Bruno and went back to watching the prisoner on camera. There had to be some weakness – something that he could exploit. A few minutes later Delaître raised his shirt, and Thomas saw what appeared to be a wound, like a burn, covering much of his chest. Delaître prodded his own skin with a detached curiosity, seemingly unworried by a lesion that would have had any normal man rolling in pain. He pushed at the edges of the damage, peeling back a small piece which he then tore away.

As Thomas watched, Delaître held the flesh up to the light, his expression one of mild interest. And then he ate it.

I'll find a way, Thomas had told himself. Maybe now he had it. Simon Delaître would wither and waste in his cell. Adèle would never even have to be told he'd returned after the shooting. Because however long it took, the man would never leave that place again.

74

Chloé didn't know what to make of the boy. They were bouncing together on the trampoline, but he was so quiet. 'I haven't seen you at school,' she said.

'That's because I don't go,' said the boy.

'How will you learn to read?'

'I can already read,' he said.

And they kept bouncing. That was how it went until Chloé decided to confide in him – although she had a vague awareness that it was more like a boast.

'You want to know a secret?' she said. The boy nodded. 'Swear you won't tell?'

'I swear,' he said seriously.

'My dad was dead, but he came back to find me.' She expected him to call her a liar.

Instead he smiled. 'I'm dead too,' he said.

Chloé laughed. 'Stop it!' But the boy nodded. They both stopped bouncing. Chloé's laugh faded, and then her smile went too. She believed him.

'And I can show people things,' he said. It was his turn to boast.

'What things?'

'I don't know. Whatever's the biggest in their minds, I think. Even if they don't know it.'

'Show me,' she said, wary.

The boy raised his arm and pointed to the door. Chloé turned to look.

It was her mum standing in the doorway. Adèle, but from two years before. Chloé knew that somehow. Adèle, from the day Chloé and Thomas had come home, and Thomas had gone to fetch her mum, then had shouted at Chloé to get to her room, to go *now*, and stay inside, and she'd done as he'd asked. But she'd peeped once, peeped to see her mother when the ambulance had come, and she was being taken away, her nightdress covered in blood.

And now her mum stood there again in the same nightdress, blood everywhere, her wrists cut deeply open, and the life pouring onto the ground.

Chloé fainted.

Adèle was first to see her fall. She ran outside. Julie followed, to see Chloé prone on the grass by the trampoline.

Adèle knelt by her daughter, brushing the hair from her face, clearly terrified to move her. 'Sweetheart, can you hear me? Chloé?'

'What happened?' asked Julie, mainly to Victor, but the boy just stood on the trampoline, silent and solemn.

'She fell,' said Adèle. 'I saw her fall.'

Julie stepped in. 'Let me,' she said. 'I'm a nurse.'

She checked the girl for any obvious injuries before lifting her and carrying her inside, throwing one more questioning look back at Victor. She laid Chloé on the sofa, aware of Adèle behind her, watching, fretting. Julie could empathize now more than ever.

With care, she checked Chloé over more fully. Her breathing and heart rate seemed fine, and nothing appeared to be broken.

'Is she OK?' asked Adèle, shaken.

'I think so,' said Julie, feeling pretty shaken herself. 'Did you see how she fell?'

'No. I only saw it out of the corner of my eye.'

Julie nodded. She was satisfied the girl wasn't hurt. Sprains and bruises were possible, but the best thing she could do for Adèle was give her certainty. 'She may have been dizzy,' she said. 'Like you, earlier. It's probably a virus, but she doesn't seem injured. I don't think you have to worry.'

Adèle nodded. Then Chloé stirred, opening her eyes a little.

'It's OK,' Julie told her. 'Just lie still and rest.'

Chloé nodded in silence, her eyes fixed on her mother's face. The girl wore a curious expression, Julie saw – almost of accusation.

Julie turned to Adèle. 'Keep an eye on her,' she said. 'She needs peace and quiet. I'll take Victor back to Laure's. If you're worried, just come and get me, OK?'

'OK,' said Adèle, not taking her eyes off her daughter.

Julie took her leave, and marched Victor back next door.

She gripped him by the arms and crouched down to his level. 'Tell me what happened,' she said, trying to sound firm while keeping the anger from her voice. 'That's an order.'

'It wasn't my fault,' he said, clearly upset, and Julie relaxed a little. Then he added: 'I didn't mean to do it.'

She tensed again. She saw the look of genuine distress on Victor's face, and she had no defence against it. He looked so distraught she didn't think it was the right time to probe deeper, but she would have to make doubly sure to keep him inside from now on. She held him; he hugged her back tightly.

'It'll be OK,' she said.

Then she felt something through the sleeve of his shirt. Something rough, on his arm.

'What's that?' she said. He wouldn't meet her eyes. She rolled his sleeve up carefully, gasping when she saw the state of his forearm. It looked like an old wound, trying to heal but succumbing to infection. But she knew it couldn't have been there for long.

'When?' she asked. 'When did it start?'

'Yesterday,' said Victor. 'I didn't want to tell you. You might not want me near you. You might leave me.'

She drew him close again. 'Never,' she said, and held him. 'Never.'

75

When Pierre asked people to gather for the service for the Koretzkys, it took Claire a moment to spot where her daughters had gone. They were outside, enjoying the first sunshine of the day. She watched them, amazed at the way a break in the cloud could transform how you looked at things. She sent Jérôme to fetch them in, then sat a few rows from the front, keeping three seats around her for the rest of her family. The room filled quickly; after all, there wasn't much else for people to do. Claire's heart sank, though, when Viviane Costa took the seat in front of her.

'Are they your daughters?' said the woman, nodding to Léna and Camille as they entered.

'Yes,' said Claire.

'They're pretty. It's a shame.'

Claire gave her a pointed look. 'What's a shame?'

Viviane Costa smiled, a particularly sour one. 'Well,' she said. 'It won't last, will it? It never does.' She turned to face the front.

Claire said nothing, taking a long breath to stay calm. If the woman hadn't already been dead, she thought she might have cheerfully killed her herself.

Léna and Camille took the seats to Claire's right, while Jérôme sat to her left at the end of the row. There were quite a few people at the Helping Hand now. As well as the initial group of parents, more had found their way there, either through direct invitation from Pierre or by hearing about the refuge from others. The dormitories would be crowded tonight, thought Claire; the supplies would have to be used sparingly.

She shivered suddenly, realizing that she was now assuming they would be there for as long as Pierre had suggested.

'Thank you all,' said Pierre as he stood at the front and held court over the congregation. 'We're here to remember Joseph and Anna Koretzky, two cherished members of our little community. Some of you have asked why I decided to hold this service to remember them, so I feel I should explain. I'm sure you're all deeply upset by what they've done. I believe we need to express our fears, our questions, and our doubts, and to do so as soon as possible. We face an uncertain time. I have spoken to many of you already about what challenges lie ahead of us, and here, now, I think we must all hear the truth.'

Claire heard some uneasy whispers, but they soon fell away.

'First,' said Pierre, 'I would like us all to hold hands.' He smiled as bemused laughs spread across the room. 'Go ahead,' Pierre continued. He waited for them to do as he asked. 'Now, I want us all to say to the people next to us, "You can count on me." Go on.'

Claire caught the raised eyebrow on Jérôme's face. She smiled at him and shrugged. This was Pierre's way, and it served a purpose.

'You can count on me,' Jérôme said to her, and he meant it; she told him the same.

Beside her, Léna and Camille turned to each other and

said it too. It gave her a rush of hope: her two beautiful girls, back together again.

You can count on me, murmured everyone in the room.

Then Pierre talked about the Koretzkys, told of their trauma at the loss of their only son. Of their courage, and their support for the other parents involved in the tragedy. He celebrated their lives, without mentioning again the manner in which things had ended.

'I can understand your concerns, my friends,' said Pierre. 'But don't be afraid. Death is not the end. We know that. Our friends who have returned are proof of it.'

Claire glanced around the faces to see how many people were mystified by what Pierre was saying. There were some, but not many. Most knew something of what had been going on.

'The Helping Hand was chosen,' said Pierre. 'It will be their haven, as a new world arises. A new order. One that will continue as it begins – with togetherness, support and love.'

She could see Jérôme's scowl forming, and could understand it. Pierre's words held such vast implications, they were even making her a little uneasy.

In the front row, Sandrine stood up. 'Excuse me,' she said quietly. 'I need some air.' Her husband stood up beside her. She looked unsteady. Suddenly Sandrine clutched at her husband's arm and fell to the ground, crying out in pain.

People rushed to help. 'Please, give her room,' said Pierre. 'Can someone get a glass of water?'

Sandrine reached down and put her hand between her legs. When she pulled it back it was covered in blood, and

Claire saw the devastation forming on her face; grief and loss congealing there.

Miscarriage, Claire thought. *Oh God, no. It had meant so much to her. It had been everything.*

Then Pierre's words came to her, unwelcome now: *A new order. One that will continue as it begins.*

And it had begun with death.

76

Satisfied that Simon Delaître was contained, Thomas drew up the emergency rota. Communication in the town was deteriorating rapidly. It seemed that soon only their police radios would be functional; even then, the station would only be able to route the signals for as long as its generator kept working. The last he'd heard from the hospital the generators there were unlikely to hold out much longer. Treatment would be reduced to little more than triage; any emergency cases would have to be taken elsewhere, and the nearest alternative was an hour's drive away. Thomas had no intention of putting his officers at additional risk, if looters suddenly started to get violent. Having an officer shot the day before by Toni Guillard – a man he hadn't thought capable of violence who was now on the run – made him even more wary, even though the resulting leg wound hadn't proved that serious.

Overnight, they would have to patrol the town and be visible. All off-duty officers would keep their radios nearby at all times in case extra hands were required. Everyone was stretched and growing tired, so he was eager for those coming to the end of their shift to get home and sleep. He'd already made this as clear as he could, and he himself would be leaving soon.

He was shattered, of course. The night before had been a long one and he needed the rest, but he planned to come back before dawn. He wanted some time to watch over

Simon. Watch him deteriorate, he hoped. And perhaps, in a quiet moment, Thomas would pay Simon a visit. Talk to him.

Laugh at him.

Rota completed, he assembled all the officers who were still in the station and talked them through it. There was no dissent. If he'd asked them, he knew they would all have pushed themselves to the limit and worked through the night if need be, but they couldn't afford to burn everyone out. Not now.

'You OK with this, Inspector?' he said to Laure, keeping things as formal as he could. In difficult times, a reminder of rank was crucial. Informality was weakness.

Laure nodded.

'Good,' he said. 'Now, get home. Sleep well. Be back here before midnight.'

'Yes, sir. I'd like to spend a little time discussing some of the priorities with those who'll be staying, before I go.' Then, almost as an afterthought: 'If that's OK.'

He nodded. 'Of course,' he said, thankful that she'd remembered her place. 'Don't take long.'

'No, sir,' she said.

Thomas went home, on edge the moment he laid eyes on Adèle's ashen face.

'What's wrong?' he said. He saw her flinch a little and told himself to be more calm. 'What is it?'

Adèle led him through to where Chloé lay asleep on the sofa.

'What happened?' he asked. There was nothing obviously wrong.

'She was on the trampoline and fell off. She was unconscious, briefly.'

'Is she OK?'

'Julie was here. She's a nurse, she checked Chloé over.'

'Julie?'

'Julie Meyer. Laure's ex.'

He nodded, suddenly wary. 'What was she doing here?'

'She's staying next door. There's a boy staying with her,
and he came over to play with Chloé.'

A boy, Thomas thought. He'd heard something about
that, something Laure had been handling: the boy who had
gone missing with the Costa woman. 'He was there when
she fell?'

Adèle nodded.

'What did he do?' he asked, his suspicions growing.

'I don't think it was him, Thomas. I think she got dizzy,
that's all. A virus maybe.'

At that, Chloé woke.

'Are you OK, sweetheart?' said Thomas.

Chloé was looking at her mother. 'Why did you want to
die?' she said.

Adèle looked at Thomas, shaking her head, then back to
her daughter. 'What?'

'I saw you,' said Chloé. 'When I was on the trampoline.
I saw you in the nightdress, and your wrists were cut. You
wanted to die.'

Adèle looked at her daughter in horror, tears starting to
form in her eyes. Thomas turned to Adèle, certain of his
suspicions now. 'The boy you mentioned. He's next door?'
Cautious, Adèle nodded.

Thomas stood, his mind made up. He went outside,

across to Laure's house, and knocked on the front door. 'Open up,' he said. 'Julie Meyer, open up.'

No answer; no sounds from within. He knocked harder and called once more, raising his voice. Again, no answer came.

He waited, sure someone was there. After a few minutes he saw a car approach: Laure coming home. She got out, looking at her captain.

'Sir?' she said.

He nodded to the door. 'Where's he from? Your friend's little boy?' She shook her head. Thomas felt his impatience soar. 'Inspector,' he said. 'You've been keeping things from me, and it must stop. Tell me where he's from.'

Laure was reluctant, but she answered: 'We don't know.'

'I want to talk to him. Now.'

Her face stiffened. 'No, sir.'

'No?' He glared at her, appalled by the insubordination. '*No?*'

'I don't think that would be appropriate, sir. He's a child, and you seem . . . agitated.'

Her eyes went to Thomas's hand. He looked down and carefully unclenched his fist.

'Bring him to the station in the morning,' he said slowly. 'Listen to me, *Inspector*. When we go back, he comes with us. It's for your safety. Do you understand?'

She nodded. 'Sir.'

He watched her for a few seconds until he was satisfied that she really did understand, that she would follow orders. Then he returned home to make sure his family was safe.

77

Laure managed to keep herself from shaking as she opened the door. She wasn't sure how many bridges she'd just burned. Julie was sitting holding Victor close to her. They both looked terrified. The look on her face told Laure she'd heard every word.

Julie gripped Victor tighter and looked at Laure, desperate. 'Please,' she said. 'Take us away from here.'

Laure took a deep breath. She thought for a moment, but she couldn't ignore what Julie's eyes were telling her. There was no way she could allow her captain to lock the boy up – as she presumed he intended. It would destroy Julie.

'Pack some things,' she said. 'We'll wait an hour or so, until it's dark.'

'And then?'

'Then we're leaving town.' Maybe the captain would do as he'd earlier instructed her to do – sleep. Maybe.

At least their house was downhill from his. When dark was falling, they crept out and got in the car, and Laure free-wheeled down the hill as far as she could, lights off. Then she hit the lights and they drove. Laure felt good, to see the look of relief on Julie's face.

Trees flew past either side of them as they took the road towards the dam. Then Laure had a thought.

'Julie,' she said. 'My radio. See, clipped to my belt?'

'What about it?'

SETH PATRICK

'Take it off.' Julie reached across and unclipped it. 'Now throw it out of the window.'

Julie grinned. 'You'll be in trouble,' she said.

'That's OK,' said Laure. 'I was getting sick of my job anyway.'

Julie nodded. 'I think I was sick of your job too.' She wound the window down and threw the radio out. They both looked back and saw it shatter across the road, then they grinned at each other.

After crossing the dam Laure settled in for the drive. There was no other traffic around, she realized, nothing at all on the roads since they'd left home. She wanted to put as much distance between them and the town as she possibly could, even if it meant driving all night.

Soon, though, the monotony of the pines either side of the car got to her. She found herself getting drowsy. She felt the car judder, and snapped her head upright, startled and frightened – she'd almost drifted off. She wound down her window.

The blast of cold air roused Julie. 'What is it?' she asked.

'Trying to stay awake,' said Laure. As they rounded the next bend, she slammed on her brakes.

The car slid to a halt. Julie looked at her as if she was mad. 'What the hell?'

Laure didn't answer. Instead, she was staring ahead. Julie turned to see. The dam was right in front of them.

'Haven't we crossed it already?' she said.

They shared a look, and Laure drove, faster than before, feeling her pulse quicken. But again the monotony of the pines either side of the road lulled her. Again, she felt that

sudden drowsiness hit, and she looked immediately to Julie.
She could see in her eyes that Julie had felt it too.

They drove around the next bend, and there it was.

The dam.

They couldn't get away.

78

In the empty Lake Pub, Lucy Clarsen had been waiting in the dark.

She had opened the doors and propped them wide, and now she stood patiently in front of the bar. She knew this place so well, after her year spent working here. She looked around now, at the familiar tables and chairs waiting for people to come, still neatly laid out.

Not for much longer.

And now they came, at last. Drawn to her once the sun had set, as she'd known they would be. Silent, slow, they shuffled inside. Some were almost untouched by physical deterioration; others were much further gone, and she could feel their hunger most of all.

Once they were inside, they turned to her. Lucy smiled. She raised her arms slowly, welcoming them.

It was time.

79

Anton woke to find that the world had gone. All he could see was the white of thick morning mist outside. He turned to the barricade he'd thrown against the control-room door during the night: an overturned desk and a shelving unit. Not long after nightfall he'd heard someone moving outside, and the knocking had begun. Slow, repetitive. He'd called out for whoever it was to identify themselves, but there had been no response. He'd stood, listening, sensing that there was more than one person out there. The knocking had grown as others joined in.

Erecting the barricade was all he could do. Then he had moved a monitor under a desk and huddled there, watching the status of the dam's sensors with his hands over his ears, until a restless sleep had taken him.

In the centre of the control room was the alarm switch, which would manually set off the acoustic warning for the town. He wanted to trigger it. Trigger it, and drive. Let the town deal with what was happening, not him. The thought of the chaos and panic that would follow stopped him, though; he had stayed to watch for problems, not cause them.

He thought of the others: of Eric and the rest of the engineers, running from the crisis. But they had families, responsibilities that he didn't have. And the time to run had gone now – he knew it. By staying, he'd taken on a duty he would have to see through. If he'd gone when the others had, maybe he could have convinced himself that the blame fell between the gaps, and lay with nobody. Run now, and the blame would be solely on his shoulders.

He stared out of the windows into the white, hoping for the mist to clear. He had no idea what time the banging on the doors had stopped, or if those responsible had really gone. Until he was sure, he would stay where he was. He couldn't face going outside.

80

Léna and Camille lay together in the dorm bed, both sleeping.

And in their sleep they dreamed, and they understood what it was: a shared dream, but not one either of them wanted to experience.

They were Camille at first. Four years ago.

'Do I really have to go on this stupid trip?' she said.

Her father laughed, eyes to the ceiling. 'We've paid for it. It's not up for discussion.'

'But Léna's allowed to stay at home.'

'Léna's sick,' said her mum.

'Yeah, *right*. She doesn't seem that bad.'

Her mum looked at her, patience gone. 'She has a temperature. Anyway, you'll enjoy it. It'll be fun.'

'I promise you, Mum,' said Camille. 'It won't be.'

And off she went, off to school, onto the coach, her parents giving Léna the benefit of the doubt same as always.

Then they were Léna, lying in bed, feeling more than a little smug at the deception, waiting.

Waiting for Frédéric.

She'd told him to give it ten minutes once they'd gone, just in case. She heard the sound of him climbing the trellis, and reckoned he hadn't quite managed to wait the full time. Too eager. She smiled.

He knocked at her door.

'Come in,' she said, trying to sound older. Sexier.

They kissed.

They were Camille now, sitting on the coach, bored, listening to music. Wishing she was at home.

They were Léna, as Frédéric moved on top of her, and asked her: 'Are you sure you want to?'

'It's not that,' she said.

'Is it because of Camille?'

'It's not fair on her,' said Léna. 'She's sort of in love with you.'

'But I'm in love with you. *Sort of.* A bit.'

'Just a bit?' She laughed, and hit him lightly. 'You bastard!'

'A big bit.'

And they kissed again.

They were Camille, feeling uneasy for no reason she could pinpoint, watching the trees pass by on the mountain road.

They were Léna, passion raging within her, feeling Frédéric position himself.

'Léna,' he said, anxious. 'Have you ever done it?'

'No. Have you?'

He shook his head, a look of fear on his face that made her love him more. And then he was inside her, and the feeling stole her breath.

They were Camille, as a shock of sensation hit her, terrified her, and it rose and rose until she couldn't take it. She stood, gasping for air, and went to the front of the coach.

'Are you OK, Camille?' her teacher asked.

'Please let me out,' said Camille. She was close to panic now, the heat within her overwhelming. 'I have to get off.'

'You can't get off,' said the driver. 'Wait until we've passed these turns. It's too dangerous to stop here.'

'Please let me out!' she screamed, and she moved to the door, banging on the glass as her teacher tried to take her arms, as the driver shouted at her, looking at her, distracted, then saw something in the road ahead of them. Suddenly the coach veered wildly. Camille felt herself thrown hard into the door, catching a brief sight of what the driver had swerved to avoid: a small boy, the glimpse too fleeting to let her see his face, to have any more than an impression of him standing there, impassive.

The coach shuddered as it hit the safety wall at the edge of the road. At the edge of the steep drop down.

Then the coach was falling. Camille watched as the ground came to meet them.

They were Léna once more. Léna, suddenly bereft, unable to tell Frédéric what was wrong. He moved to kiss her again, and she pulled away.

Léna and Camille both woke from the dream at the same time. They sat up. All they could do was look at each other, and see the guilt and tears in their eyes.

Betrayal, they both thought. Betrayal, and more than that. *Blame*. Blame for the crash itself.

Camille was staring at Léna, stunned.

Léna held her sister. 'It's not our fault,' she said over and over. They wept together, the others in the dorm still asleep.

81

Laure woke in the car with Julie's head on her lap, and looked around. The dam was shrouded in fog, thick and impenetrable. When they'd stopped halfway across the dam last night, it had been with the intention of moving on once the light came, once their route was unmistakable. Neither of them had wanted to keep driving in the dark.

Awake, with a clear road and the sun overhead, surely whatever had happened before, whatever kink in the natural scheme had led them in circles . . . Surely that would be powerless in the day.

Not if the day was like this, she thought now. They would have to wait longer than planned.

Julie stirred.

'Morning,' said Laure. Julie smiled, and Laure looked in the back of the car. Victor was there, watching. 'How long have you been awake?' she asked him. He smiled. 'Didn't you sleep well?' He shook his head.

'He hardly ever sleeps,' said Julie.

Laure made no comment, but inside she resolved to get moving as soon as the fog had lifted at all, even if it only thinned out a little.

'Did you get some rest?' asked Laure.

'Some,' said Julie, but Laure's eyes had fixed on something in the rear-view mirror.

'What's that?' she said, half-whispering. She got out of the car, went to the back. On the rear windscreen were handprints in the condensation left by the fog. Handprints, covering the glass. Julie got out too and joined her, followed by Victor.

Laure knelt to Victor's level.

'Did someone come to the car last night?' she asked.

He nodded.

'Who was it?'

'I don't know.'

'Were there many of them?'

'Yes.'

Julie looked at her, frightened, then turned to the boy. 'Victor, this is very important,' she said. 'What did they want?'

He looked scared. 'To take me with them.'

'They told you that?'

'No,' he said. 'But I knew.'

Laure felt herself shiver. She wanted to get back into the car, out of the damp mist, but then she saw something else. A shape, only just visible, almost lost in the white. She put her hand on her gun, and took a step closer. Then the fog thinned momentarily, and she saw.

'What's he doing?' she said, and broke into a run. It was a man, standing on the edge of the dam wall, just as Michel Costa must have stood a week before. As she approached she could see him clearly, and she recognized him as Toni Guillard, the manager of the Lake Pub. The man they'd had in for questioning about Lucy Clarsen, and who for so long had been the main suspect in Julie's attack.

The man now wanted for firing on an officer the day before.

'Toni?' she called. 'Toni. Come down.' He looked

undecided about the jump, she thought. 'Please come down.'

Julie, beside her, took a step forward. 'I know him,' she said, distracted. She turned to Laure. 'I think . . . I think I know him.' Then she walked on, reaching out to him.

'Stay back here,' Laure told her, but Julie was already with him, hand outstretched. The man looked at her, dazed and shivering, then took her hand and came down.

Julie turned. She had a curious smile on her face, but the smile fell away when she saw Laure training the gun on him.

'Step away, Julie,' said Laure.

'What's wrong with you?'

'He's a wanted man. He shot an officer yesterday. Now step away.'

82

Léna woke once again to a bright room and her mother's smile. For a moment the smile confused her; then she realized Camille was asleep beside her.

'It's the first time,' said her mum. 'The first time I've seen her sleep since she came back.'

Léna just nodded. She was still processing the dream she and her sister had shared, and she knew it was something that had to stay between the two of them.

'Breakfast won't be long,' said her mum. 'And we've had some new arrivals this morning.'

'Arrivals?' said Léna. The look in her mum's eye was a little odd.

'Frédéric's here,' she said. 'With Lucho. Their parents all stayed at home, but those two came here. Apparently they'd been looking for you.' Her mum paused for a second, then added: 'You and Camille.'

Léna sat up while her mum stroked Camille's hair, with that detached smile she sometimes had. One that suggested tears just below the surface.

Camille woke. 'Mum?' she said groggily. 'Did I sleep?'

'You slept, my love.' Then her mother's smile vanished. 'What's that?'

Léna knew at once what she'd seen, but even she was shocked when she looked. The mark on Camille's face had deteriorated badly overnight.

'Is it worse?' Camille asked, her hand up to the wound,

her eyes looking terrified as she felt the edges of it – how it had grown and spread.

'What is it?' said her mother, frightened.

'It's OK, Mum,' said Léna, forcing some calm into her voice for the sake of her mum and Camille. 'I'll fix it. A little make-up, and nobody will see.' She put her hand on her mother's arm. 'Nobody will see.'

Léna took Camille to the bathroom and applied make-up to mask the wound on her face. It was so much bigger now; a dry, darkened patch of broken skin. Neither of them spoke about it, or of what it might mean. Instead, Léna told Camille about Frédéric and Lucho.

'I don't know why they came,' said Léna.

'To look after you,' said Camille. 'They're your white knights. They just want to make sure you're safe. Like Sandrine and the rest – that's all they really want, too. For you all to be safe.'

'I don't need them,' smiled Léna. 'You're not dangerous.'

Camille looked at her, serious. 'They could be right, Léna. Maybe I *am* dangerous.'

'You're not, Camille. Trust me.' And with that, Léna finished and put the make-up away. 'Wear your hair a little over it, like this.' She pulled some of Camille's hair across, and nodded, satisfied that the mark was hidden.

It was the kind of mark, she thought, that she had seen on other faces. In the dark woods, on the faces of the people by the fire who had turned to her.

Turned to her, with nothing in their eyes but hunger.

*

Jérôme was waiting for Claire and the girls when they finally came for breakfast. Claire looked uneasy, he thought. He was uneasy too. When he'd come into the canteen, he'd seen that someone had written a quotation from the Bible on the whiteboard: '*And there shall be no more death, nor sorrow. Revelations 21:4.*'

He could guess who'd put it there.

They joined the short queue and got their food, Camille generously filling her plate as always. Frédéric and his friend were sitting outside, Jérôme saw. He watched his daughters as they both looked over towards the boys while trying to appear indifferent.

'Strange to think what's happening down there,' said Jérôme, nodding through the large windows towards the town. Up the valley, the dam itself was covered in mist, which was rolling gently down to the buildings below, dissipating as it went. 'It looks so quiet, but . . .'

But. Everything had changed, of course. Pierre had taken Sandrine and Yan to the hospital the previous evening, only to return with news which Jérôme had found the most ominous of all. The hospital had been evacuated. Their generators had failed, and as a result there wasn't even an emergency presence, just a handful of doctors and nurses holding on, assisting however they could, and telling those few who came that help would be arriving soon – in the next few days, was all they had said.

Jérôme had been left with a terrible sense that those who left the town did so without looking back. He wished they'd done the same thing.

Sandrine came in for breakfast then; the four of them

watched her take a seat, eyes red, with only a cup of coffee and a glass of orange juice in front of her. Claire tilted her head towards her, eyes on Jérôme. *Should I?* she was asking.

Jérôme shook his head, to show uncertainty rather than disapproval. He would bow to Claire's judgement on something like this.

Claire made up her mind and went over. 'If I can help at all . . .' she said tentatively.

Sandrine looked up and Jérôme could immediately see how this would play out. 'I don't want your pity,' she said, bitter. 'You know what I want? I want those *monsters* out of here.' She looked over at Camille, then to where Viviane Costa was sitting.

Camille was watching Sandrine warily. 'Eat up,' Jérôme said to his daughter.

'It's not their fault,' he heard Claire say.

'Are you blind?' said Sandrine, her voice getting louder. She was drawing looks from everyone in the room now. 'This is *all* because of them. It's their fault my baby's dead. It was Camille who made the Koretzkys commit suicide. They're sucking the life from everything, can't you see it? Even the *town* is dying now.'

Pierre hurried over from the kitchen. 'Sandrine,' he said. 'Listen to me. None of us can possibly understand what you're going through, but it's not fair to blame Camille and the others.' He raised his voice a little, purposefully addressing the room. 'It's all too easy to give in to prejudice and believe that they're dangerous. But they're caught up in this, just as we are. They're not responsible for what's going on and they need our help. We must all stand together. The

Helping Hand is open to all, don't you see? That's how it's always been. That's how it should stay.'

Once they'd finished breakfast the girls went off, and Claire volunteered to help with the dishes. Jérôme bowed out. He found himself watching the town, chain-smoking through the last of his cigarettes. The last he would see for some time, he was starting to think.

He saw Pierre taking two of the other parents down the steps by the side of the Helping Hand, into some kind of basement. He waited for a minute, then followed, wanting to talk to Pierre and show that he appreciated the man supporting Camille, whatever their personal differences.

The stairs led to a concrete corridor, the door to which was ajar. Jérôme went inside and saw the extensive supplies stashed away down there, essentials that would be invaluable.

He found himself nodding, approving of the foresight Pierre had shown. He absently looked to see if the man had included cigarettes in his definition of 'essential'.

'I just wanted you to be reassured,' he heard Pierre say. Jérôme looked; there was another open door further on, and he wandered up to it to see Pierre standing with the other two parents in front of some kind of cage. Then the parents turned, coming back past Jérôme.

'Hi,' Jérôme said as he approached Pierre.

Pierre was looking at him with a familiar expression of suppressed irritation. 'What are you doing down here?' he said.

'I wanted to thank you for sticking up for Camille,' said Jérôme.

Pierre produced a magnanimous smile that Jérôme tried to ignore. 'Of course,' he said. 'Anyone who comes to the Helping Hand deserves our protection, Camille especially. We can only get through this, Jérôme, if we stick together.'

Jérôme nodded, and casually looked to his side. What he saw took his breath away. He stared at it. 'What's all that for?' His eyes moved over it all: guns, ammunition, gas masks, what seemed like *grenades*, for Christ's sake . . .

'You never know when they might be needed,' said Pierre. 'Sometimes, words aren't enough. If we need to, the Helping Hand can lock itself down. Metal shutters surround the building. There are doors down here that lead to the basement under the dorms. We can seal ourselves in, with water, food . . . and other supplies.' His hand knocked three times against the cage that held the arsenal. Then he turned, almost triumphant, but the triumph faltered when he saw the expression on Jérôme's face.

'I always thought you were out of your mind,' said Jérôme. 'Who the hell are you planning to use this lot on?'

Pierre raised an eyebrow, unimpressed. 'Think of Camille. She needs you. She needs us all.'

Jérôme suddenly felt claustrophobic. He hurried back up the stairs and took out his final cigarette. He needed it. Ahead of him, the dying town; behind him, the Helping Hand. Neither option felt encouraging.

His cigarette finished, he went into the main building and found Claire washing up. He moved close to her, whispering urgently.

'Pierre has a stash of guns,' he said. 'I think he might use them.'

'And?' said Claire calmly.

Her lack of surprise caught him off guard. 'He's a little eager for an apocalypse, don't you think?'

'So what would you do if they came for Camille? Put your hands in your pockets?'

'You knew?' he said. She nodded. 'Claire, we have to get away from here. This is madness.'

'Get away?' she said, dismissive. 'Run? That's all you ever do. You could never face up to anything. My grief, Léna's anger . . . Now you want to run again.'

He felt the strength leave him. She had every right to say that to him, every right, but now . . . 'She isn't safe here,' he said. '*None of us* are safe here.'

'She'll never be safe,' said Claire. 'Anywhere. Running is pointless.'

He looked at her, unable to respond, knowing that whatever the relationship was between his wife and Pierre, in some ways it didn't matter. He'd already lost her to the man's ideas.

He paused for a moment, then nodded. The decision was made.

They were staying. Come what may.

83

Things in town had been quieter overnight than Thomas had feared, although much of the silence was probably due to the almost total blackout of communication. People would be feeling isolated now, another reason why the patrols had to be as visible as possible.

He'd got to the station not long after five that morning, and had watched Delaître as day broke over the town. Delaître, trapped in his cell, unfed, immobile.

Thomas indulged in a moment of fantasy, seeing himself bricking up the cell, blocking out the light in triumph, hearing the final cry of anguish and defeat from the dead man.

He'd noted that Laure's car was not in her driveway as he set off for work, but she hadn't turned up at the station. It came as a disappointment, of course. By now, she would be long gone, presumably with Julie and the boy. It was a shame, he thought. She'd been a good officer. Someone so senior abandoning her post could trigger a cascade, and so Thomas quickly covered it, telling everyone that Laure was ill and would try to be in for the afternoon.

A report of overnight disturbances at the Lake Pub had come in person soon after daybreak. The owners of a nearby house had driven to the station to tell them; they were on their way out of town, and made it clear they weren't planning to come back any day soon.

Deciding it was time to get out of the station and take his

turn on the streets, Thomas took Alcide to check out the situation. He expected there would no longer be any troublemakers there by the time they reached the scene, which suited him fine.

When he radioed back to let the station know they'd arrived, he was dismayed by the level of static. He looked at Alcide.

'Atmospherics?' the young officer suggested.

'I hope so,' said Thomas. At least that way things were likely to improve, but he thought it was overly optimistic. Failing radios fitted into the pattern of attrition which the town seemed to have succumbed to.

The Lake Pub appeared to be empty, but it had taken a hell of a beating. As they approached they could see that every window was broken. Stepping with care, they entered through the open front door and surveyed the devastation within. There wasn't a piece of glass intact in the place; shattered bottles lay all over the floor. Tables and chairs weren't just overturned – some of them had been broken, legs snapped off. Light fittings had been torn from the walls and ceiling, and smashed.

'Jesus,' said Alcide, and Thomas threw him a silencing look. He'd heard a noise. He turned his head, getting a bearing on it, then pointed towards the open door to the toilets. He took out his gun and headed to the door, Alcide following a few steps back.

The noise kept going, repetitive and watery and familiar. Thomas stepped into the toilets and moved along the cubicles; one by one he pushed each door wide to find the cubicle empty. Two were left when he placed the sound.

It was like a dog lapping water.

He pushed the next door. It swung open to reveal a man on his knees, head deep in the bowl of the toilet.

Drinking.

Thomas stared in disgust. 'Don't move,' he said.

The man kept drinking for a few seconds, then stopped. His head came up slowly. Wild-eyed.

Thomas took a step back. The man's face was covered with wounds, the skin broken, dark and infected. It seemed mutilated, almost. 'Don't move,' he said again. He sensed Alcide behind him as he took a pair of handcuffs from his belt, keeping the gun levelled at the man.

'What's wrong with him?' said Alcide, but Thomas had no answer.

None he wanted to say aloud.

The man in the cubicle lurched to his feet and ran straight at them, a guttural noise coming from him like the growl of an animal. Thomas fired. The man fell, and was still.

Neither officer moved for a dozen seconds. Ears still ringing from the shot, Thomas knelt down. The man was dead.

He took the handcuffs he was holding and put them on the corpse. When he looked up again, Alcide was staring at him. Thomas could see it in his eyes, though: Alcide knew why he'd cuffed a dead man.

The station was almost empty when Bruno saw her.

As ordered, almost everyone was out patrolling, attempting to demonstrate that the town was still under control. He'd been going to check on their sole prisoner, the one nobody wanted to talk about, and as he came up the corridor she was there in front of the cell.

Smiling.

'What are you doing?' said Bruno, and as he spoke he realized who the woman was. Lucy Clarsen. Surely, he thought, she'd been evacuated with the rest of the hospital patients?

'Oh, I'm not even here,' she said, smiling still, as if she knew something, as if she was in on a joke that Bruno was about to hear.

She brushed past him, walking out. Bruno turned to check the prisoner. Delaître gave him a smile too, but it was one loaded with venom.

Then Bruno went after the woman, to tell her to leave and to stay out of restricted areas. But he couldn't see her ahead of him. He hurried along the corridor, up the stairs, out of the secure door.

Another officer was walking past.

'Did you see a woman come out of here?' asked Bruno, but he shook his head, bemused by the look on Bruno's face, and Bruno ran back down, knowing something was wrong.

He ran all the way back to find the cell empty.

Delaître had gone.

84

Adèle had felt Thomas kiss her cheek as he got up to head out to work. It had seemed ridiculously early, but she hadn't even been awake enough to check the time. She went back to sleep and when she woke again she knew it was late morning. She dressed and went to wake Chloé to ask what she wanted for breakfast.

What kind of mood her daughter would be in today, she had no idea. The night before, Chloé had veered from talking about Simon to hoping aloud that school would be shut for a few days more. The talk of Simon had left Adèle feeling exhausted, but she couldn't blame the girl for being conflicted over her father.

Adèle knocked on Chloé's door before she opened it, and was halfway through her question about breakfast when she froze.

Chloé wasn't there. Adèle could see that her shoes were missing, so she'd presumably already got dressed.

'Chloé?' she called, checking the bathroom before running downstairs. Maybe Chloé had gone out again, she thought, to see the boy staying with Julie?

But then she saw *him*, standing in the kitchen by the back door.

'Everything's fine,' said Simon. 'Don't worry.'

She could only stare. *Dead*, she thought. *You were dead*. But it hadn't stopped him before.

'What are you doing?' she said. She looked past Simon

and saw Chloé outside the patio door, frightened, a woman standing beside her. Adèle ran towards them but Simon moved into the way and put a firm hand on her shoulder to stop her. 'Who is *she*?' asked Adèle.

'That's Lucy. A friend.'

'Is she like you?' He said nothing. 'Tell her to let Chloé go.'

'Your parents need to talk,' said the woman to Chloé, leading the child into the garden out of sight.

'Let her go!' shouted Adèle, terrified now, trying to force her way past Simon. His hands held her, his fingers gripping until they hurt.

'Calm down,' said Simon, smiling. 'You know I wouldn't hurt our children.'

'But you . . .' started Adèle, before she noticed the word he'd used. 'Children?'

He put his hand on her belly. She felt herself flinch. 'You're pregnant,' he said.

She shook her head.

'Don't worry,' said Simon. 'This time it's different. I'll be with you. No matter what.'

And she could see it: no matter what she wanted, not even death would keep him away. Whatever choice she made, Simon would be there. The thought terrified her.

She stepped away from him and grabbed a knife from the kitchen block. 'Don't come near me,' she said.

'Adèle . . . Don't be stupid.' He was angry now, the smile gone, and she could see the contempt he held for her whenever she defied him. It was a familiar look.

'Simon . . .' she said, then plunged the knife deep into his gut, screaming as the blood came out around her hands, blood that somehow she hadn't been expecting.

Simon grunted and stumbled back. He looked down at the knife buried deep in his stomach, then straightened up, more determined than ever, more angry than ever.

'Adèle,' he said, sneering. The fist came out quickly, too quickly for her to move, hitting her temple, shattering the world into grey and black for a moment. She fell, hitting the floor hard with her head, then pushing herself up, up, trying to stand, dizzy, and feeling the threat of unconsciousness dragging her back down. Simon watched her and gripped the handle of the knife, tensing, then pulling it free. His eyes didn't leave her and she could see what was in them.

Punishment.

You know I wouldn't hurt our children. That left plenty of ways to hurt *her*, though.

'No!' she screamed, and ran for the cellar door, taking the key and getting inside, knowing Simon was coming, coming for her, as she could feel her consciousness fading.

She closed the door behind her, frantically trying to get the key back into the lock, her hands slick with Simon's blood.

He hit the door just as the key turned, the lock thudding home.

'Open it, Adèle!' he shouted. 'Open the fucking *door*.' He kicked at it, again, again, and Adèle fell to her knees.

With Simon's voice in her ears, and Chloé's name on her lips, darkness took her.

85

Julie stood at the edge of the dam, looking through the mist towards the town.

'I think it's clearing a little now,' she called to Laure, who was sitting in the car with the doors open. If she heard, she didn't acknowledge it. Julie knew she was angry about throwing away the police radio, even though it had been Laure's idea. A heartfelt gesture now bitterly regretted, converted into an exchange of sniping comments that had come down to two possible courses of action: take Toni to the station, or drive out of town and hand him in elsewhere. Laure wasn't willing to drive anywhere *except* town until the mist had gone, but Julie absolutely didn't want to go back. So they would wait it out on the deserted road.

Toni was sitting in silence at the kerb, handcuffed. Julie looked at him, and beside her Victor tugged at her sleeve.

'You know him,' Victor said to her, and Julie nodded. Ever since she'd seen him, she'd been trying to work out where she knew him from. Laure had said he was the manager of the Lake Pub, but she'd never been there, not even before the assault.

'How do I know him?' said Julie, thinking aloud, but Victor answered her.

'He saved you,' said the boy. Julie turned to Victor, staring. He was right. This was the man who'd taken her out of danger, taken her to the hospital.

She stepped over and knelt beside Toni. 'It was you,' she said. 'You brought me out of the underpass.'

Toni met her eyes and nodded. He looked despondent.

Julie put her arms around him. 'You saved my life. Why did you want to jump?'

'I wanted to see Serge,' said Toni, close to tears. 'I wanted to see my brother again.'

Victor tugged at her sleeve once more. Julie turned to him and he pointed along the road into the mist. He seemed agitated, but she couldn't see anything for a moment. Then they came: slowly walking along the road. She watched for a few seconds, frozen. 'Come on,' she said. 'Into the car.'

She helped Toni to stand, and the three of them got inside.

'Did you—' Laure began, but she broke off the moment she saw Julie's terrified face. Julie pointed to the road behind the car; Laure looked in the rear-view mirror and immediately started the engine. She turned to Victor. 'Were they the ones who came to the car last night?' she asked.

Victor nodded.

'Are they like you?'

He nodded again.

They drove fast, off the dam, forest either side of them; Julie realized it was towards town. 'What are you going to do?' she asked.

'I have to warn the station,' said Laure. 'We can leave Toni with them.'

'And Victor?'

Laure said nothing, eyes fixed on the road.

'Tell me,' said Julie. 'Laure!'

'He can't stay with us,' she said. 'All right? Happy?'

'What, you want to put him in prison?'

'You think we can keep him safe? We couldn't even leave town, Julie. Because *he* was with us.'

'You haven't changed at all,' Julie said, her heart sinking. 'Pull over.'

'We don't have any choice.'

Julie opened the car door. 'Pull over!'

'Christ, Julie, what are you doing?' Laure slammed on the brakes, bringing the car to a halt.

'Leaving,' said Julie angrily. She got out of the car; so did Laure, who stood blocking the passenger door beside Victor.

'Out of the way,' said Julie.

'Will you stop this? I wasn't dreaming. You saw them. You *saw* what was coming.'

'So?' said Julie. 'We don't know they mean us any harm.'

'Victor said they came to get him. You think we should just let them?'

Julie shook her head. 'Laure, all I want is for him to be safe. You saw how your captain was acting earlier.'

Laure put her hand out, and took Julie's. 'Please. If we leave Toni at the station, then we can find somewhere for Victor. OK?'

Julie looked at her, wanting to believe. Wanting to trust.

The gunshot from the car changed everything.

'Don't I know you?' said Toni to Victor, as the two women got out to argue. 'You lived in the village.'

The boy nodded.

'You're dead, aren't you?' said Toni. 'I went to your funeral, like most of the town did. I was younger than you, but I remember the photos in the paper of you and your brother.' *Brother*, Toni thought, thinking of the last time he had seen Serge, disappearing under the water; he himself flailing around, unable to help. 'My brother died as well,' he said. 'He came back like you.'

The boy looked at him with calm, cold eyes. 'You killed your brother,' he said. Toni was speechless. 'And you killed your mother, too.'

'No,' said Toni desperately. 'You don't know what—'

'It's not me,' explained the boy. 'It's all from you. It's what you think. Your mother died because you hurt her so much.'

'He was sick,' pleaded Toni. 'I had to stop him.' The boy climbed into the front seat, and opened the glove box where the officer had put her gun. He took the gun in his hands. 'What are you doing?' asked Toni.

The boy shook his head. 'I told you, it's not me. It's all from you.' He held the gun out, and another hand took it. A man's hand, in the driver's seat.

Toni smiled when he saw him. 'Serge?' His brother, with him again. Serge pointed the gun at Toni. 'What are you doing?'

'Paying you back,' said Serge, and Toni smiled, and when he did he saw there was no one in the car but himself and the boy. The gun was in his own hand, pointing into his own stomach. He looked at the boy and nodded.

'This is what you wanted,' the boy said, and Toni pulled the trigger.

86

I'm just a nurse, thought Julie. The blood was pouring from Toni's wound. Victor was in the front seat, Laure ready to drive, but Julie didn't want to move anywhere until she had some kind of plan to work to.

Think, think.

'We need to stabilize him,' she said. 'Stop the bleeding, get a paramedic out here.'

'We can get into town in fifteen minutes,' said Laure. 'I don't know if the hospital could send anyone out, even if we could contact them.'

'He'll be dead by then. I need him to lie still, I need pressure on the wounds. I can't do that on the move. Where's near?'

Laure thought, and got her bearings.

They pulled into the Helping Hand three minutes later, Julie shouting for help. A man came over. Pierre Tissier.

'Someone's been shot,' said Laure. 'We had nowhere else to go. You need to try and call for help. We need a paramedic.'

'I'm a nurse,' said Julie. 'But there's only so much I can do.'

'You did well,' said Pierre. 'Come with me.' He gestured to two others, who helped carry Toni, then he led the way down into a basement, through a corridor into a room at the end. Toni was laid on a treatment table in the middle of the room while Julie looked around uneasily at the equipment. *What the hell?*

'You'll find what you need here,' said Pierre. 'Help her,' he said to the two others. 'She'll need you.'

'But I don't know . . .' said Julie.

He looked at her, and gave her the bad news. 'The hospital was evacuated,' he said. 'You're the only one who can save him.'

Julie turned to her patient, and got to work.

87

Thomas returned to the station to the worst news possible. All the way back, their radios had become almost useless; what fragments of voice they could hear were so chopped up it was unintelligible.

He was met with a serious and shame-faced look from Bruno, who took him to the empty cell.

'How did he get out?' growled Thomas, barely above a whisper.

Bruno looked ill. 'He just wasn't there, sir. I checked the CCTV. There must have been a power glitch or something, because one moment he's sitting in the cell, the next he's not. The Clarsen woman was here, I'm sure of it, but then she vanished. And Delaître had gone as well. I . . . I don't know what happened.'

'Lucy Clarsen was here?' said Thomas. She was involved too, then? He shook his head. It didn't matter. Whatever had happened, it didn't matter. And he doubted it could have been stopped. 'How many officers are in the station?' he said.

'Ten, I think. And two patrols should be back shortly.'

'Radio them, if you can. Drive out and *find* them if you have to. Then get them to follow me. Armed response. Everything we have.'

'Where are you going, sir?'

'To get my family, before Delaître does.'

*

The door of Thomas's house was open. He ran inside, calling her name, hurrying and ignoring every rule, every procedure. There was no time.

He saw the blood in the kitchen, on the floor, and then saw the cellar door, bloody handprints across it. He froze. *If that bastard has hurt them . . .* He called again, desperation in his voice.

'Adèle!'

A noise from the cellar.

'Adèle!'

A slow dragging sound. His hand went to his gun but he refused to draw it here, inside his own house.

A key turned. The door opened and Adèle fell through the doorway, grasping at the handle to keep herself upright.

'Thomas . . .' she said, blood on her face, on her hands.

He ran to her, supported her while he checked her over for injuries. 'Are you hurt?'

She shook her head. 'The blood's not mine,' she said. 'It's Simon's.' She looked at him with terror in her eyes, terror that was contagious. 'They took her,' she said. Thomas felt his guts clench. 'They took Chloé with them.'

By the time his officers arrived, Thomas had cleaned much of the blood from her and she'd told him everything. He knew where they should look first. The man who'd offered Simon a refuge, right at the beginning.

Pierre Tissier, at the Helping Hand.

88

'Where is he?' Thomas said.

Five vehicles in the convoy. Twelve officers in all, including himself. Thomas was satisfied with the response, but now he had to find Delaître. Adèle was standing next to him; he didn't plan to let her out of his sight again.

He took a step towards Pierre Tissier, who was standing in the doorway of the Helping Hand as though it was his own personal kingdom. He repeated the question. 'Where is he?'

The Helping Hand was busy, Thomas saw. People were already rushing across, intrigued, supportive of their leader.

'If you mean Simon,' said Pierre, 'he isn't here.'

'And the others?' said Thomas. The man acted ignorant. 'You know who I mean. The other *dead.*'

'The Helping Hand is open to all,' said Pierre sanctimoniously.

Answer enough for Thomas. He moved closer, his voice furious. 'Do you have any idea of the *risk* you're taking? All these people are in your care, and you allow this kind of danger to be among you?'

Maddeningly, Pierre looked unfazed. 'If anything, we're the ones who are safe. Everyone would have left if they thought there was somewhere better, don't you think?'

Another patrol car arrived, and they all turned. It was Alcide, and he looked fearful.

'Sir,' he called, running across. 'I was at the back of the convoy. I stopped because I saw something, and—'

'Spit it out,' interrupted Thomas. 'For God's sake, tell me.'

'I saw them.'

'Them?'

'A hundred, maybe more.' He held up a pair of binoculars as explanation. 'I *saw* them, sir. Like the one in the Lake Pub.'

Thomas felt the air leave his lungs. 'All of them were like him?'

Alcide nodded.

'Where were they heading?'

'Here, sir. They were coming this way. Heading for the Helping Hand.'

89

Toni was dying. Julie could see it.

Laure had come down to offer her assistance, but Julie sent her out of the room, not wanting her here for this – an inevitable failure to save a life.

The medical room was astonishingly well stocked, but there was very little she could do. The bullet had gone right through him, leaving havoc in its wake. She'd dressed the entry and exit wounds, getting her helpers to apply pressure to minimize the blood loss, but she could see he was going into severe shock. He was just losing too much blood, and serious internal bleeding seemed a certainty.

She went through every cupboard and gave Toni a rapid drip of saline and glucose to attempt to get some fluid volume back, but everything she did, everything she tried, she knew . . .

She knew it wouldn't be enough.

Toni's breathing was rapid and he'd remained unconscious since their arrival. The man was slipping away. She left her assistants keeping pressure on the wounds as she prepared an injection of adrenaline, but it was pure desperation. She reconsidered and set it down again. Dignity was what was needed, not panic and self-deception.

She found that she couldn't speak, only shake her head and direct the two helpers to the door. The keys were still in the lock; she shut the door again behind them and locked it.

It was a time for privacy, but she didn't want Toni to be alone.

She stood, holding his hand.

Suddenly she became aware of someone standing behind her.

She turned. From the shadows stepped a hooded man. A man in tears, looking at Toni's body. It was the man who'd attacked her, seven years ago. She stared at him, thinking she was imagining it, just as she had when Victor had stopped her from stabbing herself with those scissors.

'What happened to him?' the man asked, coming to stand right with her at Toni's side.

Julie couldn't move. The terror she felt turned her insides to ice. 'You're not here,' she said.

Serge turned to her, angry. 'What the fuck happened?'

'You're in my head,' said Julie desperately. She looked at the door, the door that was still locked. But she knew the man was really there.

Then she felt Toni's hand move, leaving hers, and saw it reach out to her attacker. Reach out, and take hold of his arm. Toni's eyes had opened, and there was a smile on his face. 'Serge . . .' he said, weak and fading, and Julie looked from Toni's face to her attacker's, and it made a terrible sense.

She stepped back. Toni's life was ebbing away. His hand fell from his brother's arm as he died.

'Help him,' said Serge, pushing her towards Toni's body. 'Help him.'

'He's gone.'

'*Help* him.'

She locked eyes with the man, then moved to Toni and

started chest compressions. After a dozen she stepped back again. There was no point.

'Why have you stopped?' said Serge. 'Don't stop. Keep going.'

'He's gone,' she told him. 'He's *gone*.'

Serge pushed her aside, and started to mimic what she'd been doing, getting more and more desperate with each thrust, until Julie could take no more.

She reached out, took Serge's shoulder, and pulled hard. 'There's nothing we can do,' she said. 'It's over. It's over.'

The man sobbed, and his head fell onto Julie's shoulder. He pulled her close, arms around her, holding on as the grief trembled through him.

Julie felt the bile rising in her throat, the rage rising too. She pushed him away and went to the door, looking back at the two brothers. The man who tried to kill her, and the man who tried to save her.

Both had failed, she thought.

She wouldn't look back again. She left the medical room, taking the keys. Locking the door behind her, she went out of the corridor to the base of the stairs, locking the door there too before going up into the open air. She found the medical room key again and removed it from the keyring, then threw it as far as she could into the scrubland behind her. Then she turned to the main building, desperate to find the one person who could comfort her now.

Victor.

She saw him through the windows, looking at her with his hand on the glass. The man who ran the Helping Hand was standing at the door. He looked at her questioningly;

she shook her head and handed him the remaining keys as she passed.

She hurried inside to Victor and they held each other. Only then did she notice that the police had come; only then did she notice that something had changed up here, too.

The people around them were muted, fearful, watching the police outside.

'What's happening?' she said to Victor.

Victor looked at her, afraid. 'They're coming,' he said. 'The dead are coming for me.'

90

Thomas gave his orders.

The Helping Hand was surrounded by low fencing. He posted officers around the perimeter, and three on the roof of the building. All were armed, and had orders to shoot only on his command.

The dead were visible behind the line of trees at the bottom of the field adjoining the Helping Hand's courtyard.

Thomas watched them from the front of the main building; Pierre stood beside him.

'What are they waiting for?' asked Pierre.

Thomas looked at him. The man seemed to have nothing but hope for the encounter: a beneficent smile, a relaxed air. It was hard, Thomas thought, to imagine how someone could be any more wrong.

'Isn't it obvious?' he replied. 'They're waiting for the dark.' Around them, Thomas felt the unease grow.

Pierre must have felt it too. He turned to the others. 'Don't worry,' he said. 'They must be more afraid than we are.'

Thomas looked at the frightened expressions on the faces around him, and doubted it very much.

The unease grew as day became evening, and evening turned to night. The people inside the building were sitting, waiting, praying. He saw Laure in there, but ignored her; she had abandoned her post.

He also saw Adèle and made sure to smile at her, wanting

to give her some kind of reassurance. Whatever happened, Thomas had a single priority. Chloé. He had to get Chloé back, and safe.

Then the dead were moving again, the floodlights in the courtyard bright enough for the people inside the building to see what was coming for them. They rose as one and came to the windows, then filed out of the door to stand and watch.

Thomas looked to the men on the roof and signalled to ask if they were surrounded. The nod came back.

The dead halted again, but now their numbers were clear. More than the hundred they'd first guessed. Beyond the main gate, one of them stepped forwards into the full force of the lights.

Lucy Clarsen, Thomas saw.

He started to move towards her.

'Wait,' said Pierre. 'Let me talk to her first.'

Thomas wasn't willing to let this imbecile take charge. He kept moving, Pierre beside him. He stopped five metres away from the woman.

'Where's Chloé?' he asked.

'She's with her father,' said Lucy. She was smiling placidly.

'We were expecting you,' said Pierre. 'You're very welcome here.'

'Thanks,' she said. Her eyes were as cold as her voice. 'But we don't need welcoming.'

Thomas looked from her to Pierre, and could see that Pierre's smile suddenly had an edge of desperation to it; Lucy's had only certainty. 'What do you want?' he asked.

'There are others here who are trying to stay with you,'

she said. 'They must join us. You'll know them. Let them go.'

'And what if they don't want to go?' said Thomas.

Her smile widened. 'It only matters that *we* want them to come.'

Pierre's smile had fallen completely. 'Why?' he said. 'I don't understand. You can all stay. We'll—' Lucy shot him a dismissive glare that silenced him at once.

'If we do as you ask, you'll let Chloé go?' said Thomas.

'Of course,' said Lucy.

Pierre was shaking his head. 'But you have nothing to fear from us. I can *help* you!'

'We don't need your help,' she said, the disdain clear.

Thomas turned and walked all the way back to the watching people. He took a torch from Alcide and went through the crowd, searching.

He stopped at Viviane Costa. 'Please come with me,' he said.

She looked to the people around her, then back at him with a sneer. Her reluctance surprised him, but he steeled himself. He pointed to the gate. 'Stand there,' he said. She shrugged and moved off.

Then he walked over to Julie Meyer who was holding the boy close to her, both watching Thomas with trepidation.

'Let him go,' said Thomas.

'Don't *touch* him,' said Julie fiercely. The boy looked up at him with fear in his eyes and Thomas paused. The thought of Chloé hardened his heart, and he nodded to two nearby officers. They came over and took Julie's arms, pulling to restrain her and free the boy.

'Don't touch him!' she screamed. 'No!'

'Let him go,' said Thomas again.

'Get off me!'

Thomas saw someone move. Laure. He glared at her, and at the others. He sensed the building of resistance here, the discomfort with what had to be done, sensed it even in the faces of his own officers. It was time to make things clear. 'Listen to me,' he said to them all. 'If you think the dead aren't dangerous, then there can be nothing wrong with handing them over to their own kind. And if you think they *are* dangerous? Would you have the rest of us trapped here, with *them* among you, while their kin try and break down the doors?'

He looked to Laure to see the effect of what he'd said, and he was satisfied. She was looking away, tears in her eyes. She agreed with him, however hard it was.

'Now,' said Thomas to Julie. 'Let him go.'

Julie looked around desperately, but there was no support in the faces surrounding her. Nobody to help. The officers moved towards her again. 'Don't,' she said, holding her hands up. 'I'll go with him.'

Thomas nodded. If that was what she wanted, then who was he to stand in her way? 'If you like.'

It was too much for Laure. She stepped forward to Julie. 'What are you doing?'

'I told you,' said Julie sadly. 'I can't leave him.'

Thomas nodded to the officers to escort Julie and the boy.

'Wait,' said Laure. 'I love you, Julie. Stay with me. Please. I beg you.'

Julie embraced her, and kissed Laure's cheek. 'If things had been different, Laure,' she said. 'But it wasn't to be. He needs me, and I can't let him go alone. They won't hurt me, I know they won't.'

The two women parted, Laure watching in tears as Julie and the boy were led away.

Thomas raised his eyes again. There was one more.

He looked for the Séguret family. The eyes of the other people had already turned to them, betraying their location at the back. The father stood barring the way.

'Move aside,' said Thomas.

'Not a chance.'

Three officers moved in and took hold, wrestling Jérôme to the ground as he struggled, overwhelmed. All he could do was watch as others stepped towards Camille.

'No!' shouted Léna, lashing out at them, trying to get between them and her sister. An officer took hold of Léna's arm and dragged her away. 'Let me go!' she shouted. 'Let me go! Let me go with her!'

Camille and her mother stood there alone, arms around each other, holding on desperately, both in tears.

'Do something!' Claire cried at the bystanders. Pierre, who had come back from the gate, was simply standing there watching powerlessly. 'For God's sake, do something!' Even Frédéric just stood where he was, distraught but frozen.

'There's nothing to do,' said a voice. It was Sandrine. She spoke without triumph, only exhaustion. 'She's one of them. If she stays, we'll pay for it.'

Claire hung her head. 'I'll go with her,' she said, meeting Jérôme's eyes as he and Léna were strong-armed into the building. She took Camille's hand.

'Take everyone inside,' said Thomas. He locked eyes

with Pierre, who looked bereft: things hadn't remotely gone the way he'd expected. *You've finally understood,* Thomas thought.

Once indoors, Jérôme and Léna ran to the window. Léna started banging on the glass, crying out to her sister and mother as her father held her. Claire and Camille looked back at them.

91

Thomas made the group halt a little way from the gate before he opened it. He walked up to Lucy. 'Where is she?' he said. 'Where's Chloé?'

Lucy turned. Into the light stepped Simon, Chloé holding his hand, terrified. The sight of her, unharmed yet vulnerable, made Thomas's throat tighten. He nodded to her and saw the hope in her frightened eyes.

Simon looked at Thomas with a malicious smile, then bent down and whispered into Chloé's ear. He let her go.

Chloé ran to Thomas; he knelt and held his arms out to her, then picked her up as she clung to him, trembling.

'I have you,' he told her, holding the tears back. 'You're safe now.' Glaring at Simon, he gripped Chloé tightly to him. Then he gestured for the others to come.

Viviane Costa passed him with only a look, a shake of the head: *Shame on you.* Thomas felt it, but holding Chloé he knew there were more important things than principles.

Claire Séguret and her daughter Camille came next, hand in hand. They didn't even look at Thomas. He was glad. He didn't think he would have been able to meet their eyes, a mother and daughter he was sacrificing for the sake of his own family.

Finally, Julie Meyer and the boy.

'Come on, Victor,' said Julie. She was trying to put on a smile.

The boy tugged at her sleeve. She knelt, and he looked at

her with adoration. 'Louis,' said the boy. 'My real name is Louis.' Julie hugged him hard. They took each other by the hand and walked out past the reach of the lights, towards the waiting dead.

Thomas turned to walk away.

'There's one more,' said Lucy Clarsen. 'One more who must be made to come.'

He turned back. 'Who?'

'Adèle.'

Thomas stared. 'What do you mean? Adèle's not like you.'

'She has to come with us,' said Lucy. Beside her stood Simon, the smile on his face terrible to see, vindictive and triumphant. 'If she doesn't, we'll take her.'

Thomas looked at them both for a few seconds. Nothing would make him hand over the woman he loved to these creatures. He turned and started to walk back to the building. 'Close the gate,' he told the officers. *For what good it will do*, he thought.

Adèle was at the doorway of the Helping Hand. She wanted to run to her daughter, but the officer at the door shook his head. She waited, and let Chloé run to her.

She held her daughter, unable to speak, hugging her with overwhelming relief. She looked up at Thomas, smiling through tears.

'Get inside,' Thomas told her.

She nodded, but then realized that Thomas was staying where he was; that there was something wrong.

'What is it?' she asked. 'Aren't they going to leave?'

Thomas stepped closer and hugged her. 'Don't worry,' he said. 'We'll keep them away.'

'I love you,' she told him. She led Chloé inside the building, not taking her eyes off Thomas. She still didn't know if she would stay with him, even after all this, but she knew the most important difference now between him and Simon. There was real fear in Thomas's eyes, but a determination to see things through. Everything Simon had ever done, it had ultimately been for himself. This kind of selfless act would always be beyond him.

Thomas ordered the remaining few civilians to get inside the building, and his officers to remain outside. As the last people filed in, Laure approached him.

'You abandoned your position, Laure,' said Thomas.

'Not this time, sir,' she said.

He looked at her for a moment, then nodded. 'Welcome back, Inspector.' With all the civilians inside, he closed the door and gathered his officers together.

'We can't know what they'll do,' he said, looking down to where the dead stood. 'But these people only have us to defend them. Are you all with me?'

'*Sir*,' said his officers.

He sent Bruno and Michael to check that all the weapons had been removed from the convoy vehicles, and once everything had been distributed every officer had a sidearm and either a shotgun or rifle.

Alcide was looking at his pistol as if it was a spider preparing to bite him. 'Will these stop them?' he said, terror plain on his face.

'It stopped the man in the Lake Pub,' said Thomas. 'It'll

stop them long enough. They have to know that.' He looked to the front door. Adèle and Chloé were there, looking at him. He smiled at them, seeing the fear in their eyes. They needed someone in there with them. 'Alcide,' he said. 'Laure. You two stay indoors. Keep everyone calm.'

Alcide went to the door and opened it, waiting for Laure; she stood where she was.

'If it's all the same, sir,' she said. 'I'll stay out here.'

Thomas nodded and turned to Alcide. 'Pierre Tissier has the keys. Take them, and lock the doors. Then close the shutters. Don't let anyone inside. Understood?'

'Yes, sir,' said Alcide nervously. He went inside. After a few moments, all around the building the metal shutters started to slowly rumble down into place.

'Everyone else take positions,' said Thomas. He locked eyes with Adèle as the shutters descended. The moment he lost eye contact, he felt a terrible foreboding.

Laure caught his attention and nodded towards the gate, where the dead had been holding their line. Not any more. Now, slowly, they were making their way towards the Helping Hand building.

'They're coming,' said Laure.

Once the shutters had fully closed, Adèle looked at Chloé and brushed the hair from her eyes. 'It's OK, my love,' she said. 'We're safe in here.'

Chloé leaned over and whispered in Adèle's ear. 'They want to come and get you,' she said. 'They want your baby.'

Adèle felt the blood drain from her.

They could hear some of the officers take their place on

the roof above them. Two minutes passed. There were shouts, short orders barked by Thomas. Gunfire began.

Above them, they heard a loud thump, as if something had hit the roof hard. Suddenly all the gunfire was cut short, replaced by total silence.

Everyone in the room strained to listen, moving closer to the windows, trying to hear what was going on out there.

The lights in the Helping Hand went out. There was a cry of anguish from everyone. Torches came on, a patchwork of light on the walls and windows.

They all stood, tensing; another minute passed before the first impact on the shutters, the sound of a hand hitting metal. Regular and slow at first, the strength and number of impacts grew inexorably. People huddled together, faces pale and frightened.

From the middle of the room, Pierre looked to the shuttered windows. 'I don't understand,' he wailed, despairing. 'This wasn't how it was meant to be.'

Chloé was trembling. 'Close your eyes, my love,' Adèle told the girl. She covered Chloé's ears with her own hands to block out the cacophony. Unable to do the same for herself she was forced to listen, as the noise became overwhelming.

As the dead showed their anger.

92

Anton stood in the lower gallery of the dam.

The mist had finally cleared before dark fell. He'd still been weighing up his options when the first of the gallery sensor arrays had gone quiet. Within minutes, much of the lower gallery was effectively unmonitored. It had been known to happen before, just a breaker at the central junction, but if it wasn't resolved soon there was a chance that the automatic systems would trigger the acoustic warning themselves, as they were designed to do if enough of the monitoring capability failed. Panic and terror in the town, all for the want of a simple switch.

Easy to fix. Quick to deal with.

He'd come this far. He just had to go down there.

Just this, he promised himself. Just this, and the next time he left the control room would be to get the hell out and drive.

When he reached the lower gallery, the lighting strips were dimming repeatedly. Regularly, he thought. Rhythmically.

Sure enough, the breaker had tripped. He flipped it back and waited a few seconds in case it immediately tripped again. While he waited, he cast his bright torch beam along the gallery.

He saw something, and ran further along to make sure of what he was seeing.

Water was dripping from the ceiling. Not much, just a

steady drip, forming a small circular dark patch above him. He wiped it away. The drip stopped and he tried to work out where it had been coming from. There was no sign of a crack, the concrete seemingly sound. He waited for the drip to reappear, but nothing came. He wiped at the damp with his hand, confused. Then he saw it again, four metres further up. Another circular patch, dripping incessantly. He walked to it, and the moment he reached the drip it stopped. Anton looked further along the gallery, and there it was another four metres on, where he was certain it had been dry seconds before.

Nothing about this suggested any kind of structural failure. The water just seemed to be passing right through the fabric of the dam itself.

He closed his eyes for a moment, feeling his pulse quicken, trying to make sense of what he was seeing. Then he followed it, the path being set out for him, followed it as the drips ahead of him appeared, with a steadily increasing rate to match his own pace. And each time, the flow of water ceased as he reached it.

Leave, he thought. *Run.*

But he had to see where he was being led.

The beam of his torch picked out the end of the gallery, where there had always been a rough cap of concrete terminating the tunnel. Now, all he could see was a dark hole. By the time he reached it the flow of water from the ceiling was a steady stream, falling to the ground at his feet.

And in front of him, where the concrete tunnel should have ended, the walls instead continued, becoming rock, opening out into a deep dark cave extending into the side of the valley.

He walked on, taking care on the uneven floor. The only light was the beam of his torch. He put his hand on the bare rock, finding it curiously warm.

Sounds came from the darkness ahead. The same animal noises he'd heard the last time he'd come down here. Slowly, he raised his light. Twenty metres ahead stood a figure. Human, filthy; head bowed, face covered by its hands. Clothed only in dirt.

The hands fell to its sides. The head came up. Seeing its face, Anton retreated, crying out; retreated from the cave until his hand touched concrete again.

He turned, ready to run without looking back. He felt air on his face, a breeze; he heard mournful sirens start to sound far above him. The automated systems had set off the acoustic warnings, taking over the one action he'd stayed to perform.

Then Anton saw the dark wall of water rushing towards him. Icy and vengeful, as he'd always imagined it would be.

93

The assault on the Helping Hand stopped as suddenly as it had begun.

As the terrible noise grew, Alcide kept a watchful eye on those people close to panic, stepping in to reassure, telling them that the building was secure; that those outside couldn't breach their defences.

He didn't believe it, of course. The moment he'd heard the gunfire from his colleagues suddenly silenced, without a single cry for help, he had known the forces outside were powerful beyond reason. The crescendo of fist against metal grew to a peak, and Alcide thought it was only a matter of time before the dead would be upon them.

And then it stopped.

It had lasted less than an hour, but it had felt like years. He looked around the faces of the people there, pale and scared, as the warning sirens at the dam began to howl.

The sirens stopped just before dawn, and Alcide insisted on waiting until daylight before he would consider looking outside. The thin lines of sunlight coming between the joins in the shutters were comforting, he thought, yet oddly made the building feel more claustrophobic.

He sought out Pierre Tissier. 'Is there a way to see what's out there before we open the shutters?' asked Alcide.

Pierre seemed like an empty shell, moving in a stupor. He shook his head.

'A way for me to get out alone, then?'

Pierre thought, then nodded, talking slowly. 'There's a doorway in the basement,' he said. 'It leads to another locked door, then to the outside stairs at the side of the building. I could let you out and lock the basement door behind you.'

The bundle of keys Alcide had taken the night before were clipped to his belt. He took them off and handed them to Pierre, who hunted for the key that would unlock the outer door. Pierre worked it off the keyring and handed it to Alcide.

They went down to the dark basement, torches in hand. Pierre unlocked the inner door and opened it. Alcide stepped out into the corridor, clenching the key as Pierre locked the door behind him.

His mouth was dry. He played the beam of the torch along to the end of the corridor and saw there was a doorway gaping wide, darkness beyond. The door had been forced open, the jamb splintered. He pocketed the key, took his pistol from its holster, and approached slowly.

'Hello?' he called. He thought back to the man in the Lake Pub rushing the captain, and tensed. He moved through the doorway, noting just how powerful the blows must have been to force the door.

Force it from *within*, he realized.

Inside was some kind of medical room. He'd heard that an injured man had arrived at the Helping Hand shortly before the police had come; he'd also heard that the man hadn't made it. This must be where he'd been brought. Bloody cotton swabs and towels lay on a padded treatment table, which itself was covered in blood, but there was nobody in the room. The man's corpse wasn't here, either.

With gun and torch raised, Alcide left the room and headed for the other end of the corridor. The key was in his pocket, but the suspicions he'd had since seeing the broken medical room door were confirmed as he approached the exit.

Although the exit door was closed, he could see that the lock had been forced here, too. With no need for the key Alcide pushed the door open, wincing as the daylight hit his dark-adapted eyes.

Carefully, he went up the steps. When he reached the top he could only stare at what he saw in the distance, stare in horror, but he had a task to get on with. He tore his eyes away from the town and slowly circled the building.

There was no sign, no sign of anything. His colleagues had gone; the dead horde was nowhere to be seen. There were no guns lying on the ground, and no blood. The metal shutters showed small dents in places, but other than that there was no clue that anything had even happened here, in the dark of the night.

When he was certain there was no threat, Alcide returned to the basement door. Pierre let him back in, and Alcide raised the shutters. Questions came, especially from the captain's fiancée, but he had little to tell them. *No trace. No trace at all.*

He unlocked the door and led the way outside. All he could do was stare again at the sight before him in the valley. Alcide looked to his right, and in the distance he could see the dam. *Impossible*, he thought. Despite the sirens that had sounded, it was intact.

One by one the others joined him. One by one they all stared.

At the drowned buildings.

The drowned buildings, in the flooded town below.